Joanna Nadin

2 books in 1

double trouble

Another simple

OXFORD
UNIVERSITY PRESS

OXFORD
UNIVERSITY PRESS

Great Clarendon Street, Oxford OX2 6DP

Oxford University Press is a department of the University of Oxford.
It furthers the University's objective of excellence in research, scholarship,
and education by publishing worldwide in

Oxford New York

Auckland Cape Town Dar es Salaam Hong Kong Karachi
Kuala Lumpur Madrid Melbourne Mexico City Nairobi
New Delhi Shanghai Taipei Toronto

With offices in

Argentina Austria Brazil Chile Czech Republic France Greece
Guatemala Hungary Italy Japan Poland Portugal Singapore
South Korea Switzerland Thailand Turkey Ukraine Vietnam

Oxford is a registered trade mark of Oxford University Press
in the UK and in certain other countries

'The Meaning of Life' first published 2008
'My (Not So) Simple Life' first published 2009

First published in this edition 2010

British Library Cataloguing in Publication Data

Data available

ISBN: 978-0-19-278992-1

1 3 5 7 9 10 8 6 4 2

Printed in Great Britain by CPI Cox and Wyman, Reading, Berkshire

Paper used in the production of this book is a natural, recyclable product made
from wood grown in sustainable forests. The manufacturing process conforms
to the environmental regulations of the country of origin

Contents

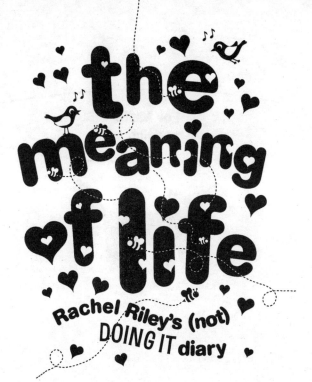

the meaning of life

Rachel Riley's (not) DOING IT diary

january

NIT COMB →

VITA-MINS

ALKA SELTZER

Monday 1
New Year's Day

10 a.m.
It is official. I am going out with Year Twelve sex god and part-time meat mincer Justin Statham. It is after our New Year's Eve midnight snog in Scarlet's wardrobe. I am utterly jubilant because I have spent two years trying to be his girlfriend and he is finally totally in love with me. And, most importantly, he is the ONE, despite him having small nipples (which is why Sophie Microwave Muffins Jacobs will not go out with him any more, she prefers Mr Vaughan's supersize ones, which would be fine except he is our French teacher and his nipples, fat or otherwise, should be out of bounds). For a minute, due to wardrobe blackout situation, I thought I might be snogging Jack. And was sort of hoping it was. But that was obviously just a mental lapse as Jack is Scarlet's brother. And we have far too much in common, i.e. our radical political convictions and love of tragic literature and Waitrose hummus etc. Whereas Justin and I have nothing in common and so it will be love across a divide, like Prince Harry and Chelsy Davy. Or Lembit Opik and the Cheeky Girl. We will argue about all sorts of things. If I went out with Jack we would end up on the sofa watching *Casualty* and eating HobNobs every Saturday like Mum and Dad. Although I do not think Mum and Dad will be doing any hobnobbing any time soon. They

5

are still not speaking after last night's hoo-ha with Mum's ex-driving instructor Mike Wandering Hands Majors and Tuesday's ex-alcoholic mum Edie who is seemingly in love with Dad. She is mental. He is called Colin and wears vests. Which is why he and Mum (Janet, also vest-wearing) are ideally suited. Anyway, cannot go out with Jack as he is not talking to me now after he opened wardrobe door to find Justin with his tongue in my mouth and his hand hovering dangerously close to my bra strap. Scarlet is not too happy either. It is because Justin is not a goth, wears Gap, and mops up meat blood on a Saturday, and she is a strict vegetarian. That is why she is going out with John Major High head-goth Trevor Pledger, who has rats and a floor-length leather coat. Although that might not last now she is giving up her hardline bat tendencies and going more EMO, so that she can wear skinny jeans. At least second-best friend Sad Ed understands me. It is because he is in a total love-across-the-divide relationship with Tuesday, i.e. her dad is gay and American and her mum is a drunkard, whereas his parents are in the Aled Jones Fan Club. Also Tuesday has tattoos and Sad Ed just has a birthmark shaped like Gary Lineker's head. It is on his left buttock. I have seen it.

10.30 a.m.
Why hasn't Justin rung? We have not seen each other for almost eight hours. Will check mobile phone again in case

it is on silent by mistake and have missed crucial message of love.

10.35 a.m.
Did miss message but was not from Justin, was from Scarlet saying when is someone coming to fetch Dad as Edna (the non-Filipina, Labour-friendly cleaner) wants to hoover up canapé crumbs and he is sprawled inconveniently on the Habitat rug. Will tell Mum.

10.45 a.m.
Mum is refusing to get Dad. James has gone instead with the dog. I feel sorry for Dad. James is more menacing than Mum when it comes to being thin-lipped and pedantic, which is impressive for a nine year old. I would go but am far too busy worrying about love life. Where, oh where, is Justin? Will check phone again. He might have called while was downstairs.

11.00 a.m.
No messages.

11.30 a.m.
No messages.

12 noon
Still no messages. Dad is home, but has been sent to Coventry (i.e. the bedroom). Mum says he is not allowed

out until he has thought about what he did last night and apologized. Dad says he cannot remember what he did last night due to uncharacteristic excessive intake of Suzy's life-threatening punch. Mum says that is the point. Mum is in no position to lecture Dad. She got a lift home with Mike Wandering Hands due to her uncharacteristic excessive intake (i.e. two glasses) of sherry. James says he is thinking of calling Childline.

1 p.m.
No messages. Dad is still in the bedroom. Have taken him a cheese and pickle sandwich and some Alka Seltzer. James says he should say sorry for everything, including the time he tried to hoover up spilt tea and broke the Dyson, and offer to descale the iron every month as penance. He is unusually well-versed in the ways of women (or Mum, at least) for a nine year old.

2 p.m.
Dad has apologized using James's method. He and Mum are now on the sofa looking at the John Lewis sale catalogue. But there is still an air of frostiness lingering over the pictures of polycotton duvet sets. I predict the Mum, Dad, Edie, Mr Wandering Hands love square is not over yet.

3 p.m.
No messages. Maybe it is all over and Justin was just using

me in a bid to win back Sophie Microwave Muffins Jacobs from the clutches of possible pervert-in-school Mr Big Nipples Vaughan. I am just a pawn in his giant game of love chess. Oh God, will have to spend another entire year being single or snogging underage rat boy Kyle O'Grady.

5 p.m.
It is not over! Justin has called. He was not trying to win Sophie back. He was asleep. It is because he is in Sixth Form and it is compulsory to lie in a black-painted bedroom until at least 3 p.m. at weekends and school holidays, preferably listening to gloomy music and reading Jack Kerouac. Although Justin only reads *What Guitar* and graphic novels (aka comics), which is why we are totally across a divide, as I am currently reading *Nineteen Eighty-Four*. It is excellent and all about Room 101 and Big Brother, which is odd as I did not think George Orwell got Channel 4. Anyway. I am totally in love. We are meeting tomorrow at his mock-Tudor mansion on Debden Road. I do not want him coming round here yet. Mum will ban him for sure. He has long hair and has done 'It' (allegedly). Oh God. What if he wants me to do 'It'? Know nothing about sex. Except dubious facts gleaned from *a*) PE teacher Miss Beadle (overweight, facial hair, bulgy eyes like Joey in *Friends* or rabbits with myxomatosis) and her plastic penis model and *b*) Thin Kylie and her unnecessary details about Mark Lambert and his very real and active penis. Am going to

have to get help from Scarlet's mum and dad Suzy (TV sex counsellor) and Bob (abortionist) fast. Or at least by sixteenth birthday.

<u>New Year Resolutions:</u>
1. Prove that Justin is the ONE by having excellent relationship on every level—brain as well as pant-covered parts.
2. Do not, under any circumstances, let brain or pant-covered parts start thinking about Jack.
3. Do 'It'. And in earth-shattering, meaningful manner. Not on a giant bag of potatoes round the back of the Co-op, like Fat Kylie. Because, as Sad Ed says, sex is not just sweaty thrusting, but is actual, in fact, MEANING OF LIFE.
4. Rekindle Mum and Dad's romance. Do not want to end up in care. It may be utterly tragic and could possibly write best-selling memoir about inevitable mental torture but they might send me somewhere in Harlow, which is at least an hour from Justin by public transport (people in care do not have convenient Passat-driving dads to ferry them to Barratt homes).
5. Get Saturday job so can buy vintage outfits suitable for girlfriend of rock god. And not in Woolworth's or will end up putting on two stone in pick-and-mix like Anita Nolan.
6. Take dog to training classes. Am sick of it devouring possessions and lounging hairily around on sofa

10

when it should be eating Pal and sitting neatly in kennel à la *Dog Borstal*.

Yes, that is definite recipe for year of utter LOVE. Hurrah.

10 p.m.
Have just remembered other essential resolution:
7. Pass GCSEs. Or will end up sweeping up hair with the Kylies at Curl Up and Dye. Or, worse, Mum will disown me and send me to live with inbred Cornish relatives and will have to eat Fray Bentos pies and say 'that it be' a lot.

Tuesday 2
9 a.m.
Hurrah. Am going round Justin's this afternoon for breakfast (his, not mine, have already consumed essential brain and heart stimulating Shreddies). Have just six hours to plan wardrobe and hair, and revise essential snogging tips. Have texted for reinforcements i.e. Scarlet and Sad Ed.

10 a.m.
Scarlet has texted back to say she will be over at one for lunch and summit meeting and can Mum not try to conceal ham in her quiche again. Sad Ed has not texted back. Maybe he is getting in practice at lying in bed for hours for Sixth Form next year. Or more probably he is fiddling with

Tuesday under the covers. His mum is totally gullible. She thinks they are having a *Famous Five*-style sleepover when in fact they are doing very non-Enid Blyton things.

11 a.m.
James's frogs have escaped again. He is very excited as it means they have worked out how to act as one giant frog force to push up the lid of the aquarium. He thinks they may be magic frogs, like the Ninja Turtles. He has renamed them in honour. Mum is not so excited. She says they are going back to Petworld as soon as they are located.

11.15 a.m.
Mum has found Donatello. He was in the toilet (again), making a break for freedom (or trying to get back to sewer headquarters, according to James).

11.30 a.m.
Michaelangelo located in kitchen in half drunk cup of tea. Mum is livid—she says he could have given Marjory next door a heart attack if he had stuck his head out of the PG Tips during their tea and chat session (i.e. moaning about the Britchers' woeful lack of interest in their front garden, and whether or not the BBC should look to a remake of *To The Manor Born* to boost its ratings.)

2 p.m.
Oh God. There has been a terrible accident. Scarlet has

trod on a frog, possibly Leonardo. He is clearly not magic. He is just very squashy and dead. She says it was like stamping on slightly crunchy jelly. Am going to definitely wear slippers from now on. A bit of him got stuck between her toes. We flushed rest down toilet. Will tell James he must have made it back to sewer HQ (not a total lie). He will be devastated if he knows he is a victim of our haste to find hair mousse. Scarlet is lying down on my bed with the curtains drawn. She says it is the most traumatic thing to happen to her since Gordon and Tony (cats, not Labour party supremos) ate her gerbils. She says she cannot possibly dispense snogging or wardrobe advice under such circumstances. Have only got one hour to go before I have to meet Justin. Am going to go for a very innocent and covered-up look in the hope he will delay any sexual interest until I have managed to glean advice from Scarlet. Will wear one-armed fluffy jumper (it's a look, sort of) and denim mini, with Oxfam fleece-lined boots. (Which are almost like Sienna Miller-style Uggs, except for the Clarks label inside. So will not be taking them off, obviously.) Hair is successfully less Leo Sayer, due to use of entire can of mousse.

3 p.m.
Raphaelo still missing. Plus Mum has demanded to know provenance of frog-like stain on stair carpet. I said it is an utter mystery but probably something to do with the dog. (I know this is unfair, but the dog is an easy target. He is

13

nearly always the cause of any hoo-ha so one more incident won't affect his record.) James is demanding that we take the dog to the vet's for an autopsy to find the missing frogs. I said I could not get involved in the discussion as I had to go out, and that Scarlet was meditating upstairs and not to disturb her. James demanded to know where I was going and what time I would be back. I said it was a band rehearsal (not a complete lie, he might do some guitar-playing to woo me) and I would be back by *Eggheads*. (James's favourite TV quiz. He has written in twice offering to take them on single-handedly but the BBC have been strangely quiet in their response.)

3.05 p.m.
Oh God. Cannot believe have used word 'woo'. Sexual education cannot come fast enough. Or maybe it makes me like Elizabeth Bennet. Yes. That is it. I am repressed rural beauty who will be awakened magnificently by cosmopolitan and sexually experienced (two times, allegedly) Mr Darcy, i.e. Justin Statham. Hurrah.

6 p.m.
Was not totally *Pride and Prejudice*-style awakening thing. We watched his Led Zeppelin DVDs for three hours. Admittedly it was in his bedroom (not black, actually pale blue with racing car border), and we did do some excellent snogging when they played the *Top of the Pops* theme tune (no groping due to vastness of jumper and inability to find

14

entry point). But it is early days. I predict he will be flinging me manfully against his Angus Young posters by the end of the week.

Scarlet was still meditating when I got back. She asked how it was and what he had touched. I said it was seminal and that he had touched only my heart. She will not understand our love. It is too poetic.

James is still two frogs down. The dog definitely got one after all so I feel no guilt. On the plus side, Mum has agreed to let Michaelangelo and Donatello stay, on the grounds that they no longer have the power to lift the lid up. James is happy. He thinks they will devise a new and Ninja-like way of escaping, so they can fulfil their destiny of fighting Shredder.

Wednesday 3

Am going to fulfil New Year Resolution number 5 and get a Saturday job. Will present myself at shops in Saffron Walden and offer my services. Am going to forsake vintage clothing for a day and wear more business-like outfit, i.e. school uniform, and target Waitrose, as they pay more than minimum wage and also you get a discount in John Lewis, which will please Mum, and free past-their-sell-by cakes, which will please James. Sad Ed is coming with me. He is also looking for work to fund his Mars bar and condom requirements. I do not think he will get a job. He is notoriously lazy and dishevelled. Mum is not entirely

backing my job search. She says it could cost me my GCSEs. I said the only cost involved was the increasing one of vintage clothing due to Oxfam getting wise to trend-setting celebrities and raising the price of their Sixties rail to £20, and if she wanted to up my pocket money then she could do so. She said no. Then James took the opportunity to ask if he could get a job as the frogs were costing a lot in meat (they are strictly non-vegetarian). Mum said he could earn himself 50p by cleaning the dog's teeth. He accepted; it is her highest offer yet. He has been ripped off though. The dog has bad breath.

5 p.m.
Have found job. It is not at Waitrose. They only had one vacancy and it was herding trolleys so they gave it to Sad Ed. I said that was sexist but they said it was more weightist, as he had the hefty upper arm requirement. Yes, and slightly distant expression. My job is at lentil-smelling health food outlet Nuts In May, run by hunchback Mr Goldstein and his ailment-ridden assistant Rosamund. I am going to be stacking carob bars and tofu. On the plus side, they have a pro-vintage clothing policy (Rosamund wears only hessian skirts and hemp blouses) and the shop is opposite Goddard's Butcher's, so I will be able to catch a glimpse of Justin hacking chops through the Linda McCartney display. They are paying me £2.70 an hour. Which is barely legal. But is better than Mum.

Justin says we can meet for lunch (and a snog) at one in the Mocha. Hurrah.

Thursday 4

Went round Justin's for more Led Zeppelin watching and snogging. His mum was doing Jade Goody's Body Challenge in the living room in a mauve leotard and footwarmers. She is frighteningly fit. Justin says she is determined to keep the body of a twenty year old for as long as possible. I asked him how old she was. She is forty-three. Maybe that is what Mum needs to win Dad back. I will suggest it.

3 p.m.

Suggested that Mum joins the gym. She says she is not wasting £35 a month to writhe around on the carpet in someone's else's sweat to 'bangy-bangy' music. Nor will she take up swimming as the pool has a notoriously high urine content. But she is considering calming yoga at the Bernard Evans Youth Centre. It is a step in the right direction, i.e. down the path of love.

Friday 5

10 a.m.

Am not seeing Justin today. I have told him it is essential that I spend quality time with friends (according to

Cosmopolitan), and make it clear to them that they are of equal priority. Especially in case he chucks me and I will totally need them then (did not say that bit to him, obviously). Am going to invite them for general hanging out in bedroom and moaning about school starting on Monday.

11 a.m.
Scarlet has gone to the London Dungeon with Trevor on a goth pilgrimage and Sad Ed is grounded because Mrs Thomas has discovered the X-rated nature of the *Famous Five* sleepovers. She came in with a midnight feast of scones (at 8 p.m.) and caught them doing some 'exploring', and not on Kirrin Island. Am going round Justin's after all. It is not my fault if friends do not want to be prioritized.

5 p.m.
Did forty-three minutes of snogging and read four *Batman* comics. Tried to initiate conversation on *Pride and Prejudice* but Justin got all excited about Keira Knightley and made me watch *Pirates of the Caribbean* instead. Johnny Depp needs some voice coaching lessons. He was barely understandable. Mrs Statham was doing *Davina Power of Three* today. She has an entire wall devoted to celebrity fitness videos including *Dancercise* with someone out of *EastEnders* and *Pole Dancing with the Dingles*. I asked her who was best. She said Kylie's

Hotpants Workout, if you could get round the gold lamé shorts. Asked if I could borrow it for Mum. She said yes but she needs it back by a week Monday so she can 'pump up her glutes' for her dirty weekend at Champneys with Mr Statham.

7 p.m.
Mum refusing to do *Hotpants* workout. She has booked herself in for over-forties yoga at the Bernard Evans Youth Centre tomorrow.

9 p.m.
Oh God. Have just witnessed horrific sight. James is attempting to firm his buttocks with Kylie. Except he has the sound turned down and Classic FM on instead. Mum is doing crap yoga practice at the same time. It is like a scene from a Stanley Kubrick film. Thank God they are fully clothed or I might well need counselling. Also thank God Dad is round at Clive's looking at the new cornicing. He would be ruling dirty weekends out of his diary for good. Ugh. Just did shudder at thought of Mum and Dad doing 'It'. Maybe they don't any more. Maybe they just read Jeffrey Archer books in bed and argue about the dog. I don't know which is worse.

11 p.m.
Can hear Kylie *Hotpants Workout* music downstairs. Oh

God. Think Dad may be watching it for non-fitness reasons. Will investigate.

11.15 p.m.
Was not Dad. Was Grandpa Riley, who had let himself in to 'borrow' (i.e. steal) a pint of milk for Baby Jesus, as the so-called 24-hour garage shuts at ten. Told him to go home before Mum caught him ogling bottoms. He did as he was told. He is frightened of Mum at the best of times.

Saturday 6
7 a.m.
First day in world of work. Am very excited. I have to be in at half past eight to restock the lentil bins. Am going to fortify myself with a bacon sandwich. It will be the last meat I get to smell for a whole day. Unless you count the odour of raw pig oozing from Goddard's.

6 p.m.
Am utterly exhausted after day of lugging sacks of muesli around (with help from neither Mr Goldstein (hunchback) nor Rosamund (eczema on fingers)). Plus had to listen to Rosamund talk about her various ailments for eight hours. As well as eczema, she has hot flushes, cold feet, tennis elbow, and ringing in her ears. And hairy legs (she did not mention that one, it is just an observation). She is on twenty-seven vitamin supplements, beating Mum. Did not

get to meet Justin at Mocha at one either. The sausage machine was on the blink and he was struggling to hand stuff four kilos of pork meat into a sheep's stomach thingy. Went to watch Sad Ed heave trolleys around in a brown overall instead. He was under the supervision of former Criminal and Retard Gary Fletcher who has been moved from the pet food aisle after getting caught eating Bonio. Sad Ed says he is finding his work less than stimulating. I said all prospective suicidal musicians have to do dead-end jobs, it is a rite of passage. That seemed to cheer him up and he went to collect a fleet of trolleys from the top of the multi-storey while Gary smoked a Bensons behind a Volvo and I ate a prawn sandwich. Got paid £18.90. But minus the prawn sandwich, and the giant chocolate cookie, and the copy of *Vogue* (essential for looking vintage and mature), now have just over £10, which will not even buy me a kaftan sleeve in Oxfam. I may well write to Tony Blair to demand a minimum wage for Saturday girls.

Got home to find Baby Jesus watching *Lovejoy* repeats with Dad and James. Grandpa and Treena are going on belated honeymoon to the Canaries and forgot to book him a ticket (so they claim), and Dad has agreed to look after him for the fortnight. Mum is still out at yoga and knows nothing of this arrangement. I predict she will be less than thrilled.

6 p.m.
Mum is back but is not at all calmed by her yogic experience. She and Dad have had a heated debate and

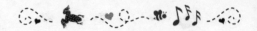

he is now driving Baby Jesus to the airport at top speed in the hope that the flight has been delayed/cancelled. Mum has instructed him to pay whatever the airline demands for a ticket. She has also cancelled all future yoga classes. She says she is not wasting £5 a week to listen to Barbara Marsh chant and make bee noises.

7 p.m.
Flight not delayed. Mum is cursing British Airways. She is angry they have chosen this one day not to have a baggage handling crisis or terrorist threats. James pointed out the positive side though—she has two weeks to instil her strict regime on Baby Jesus. He will be off the crisps and cartoons and on to health-giving rice cakes and jolly phonics in days.

. . . .

Sunday 7
7 a.m.
Jesus is up and demanding television (by clinging to it lovingly and saying 'mmm'). Mum is refusing to switch it on. She has put him on the floor with a selection of Ladybird books and some educational Duplo. I do not think he will be brainwashed this easily. He is used to the perpetual sound of Jeremy Kyle.

7.15 a.m.
The television is on. Jesus managed to destroy all the books

and feed several pieces of Duplo to the dog. (I do not envy him having to poo it out. The pieces are enormous and pointy.) Mum is making him watch CBeebies though, instead of his preferred ITV and shopping channels.

7.20 a.m.
Jesus has changed the TV to ITV2. He is obviously highly trained in the use of remote controls.

7.25 a.m.
TV back on CBeebies.

7.30 a.m.
TV on ITV2

7.35 a.m.
TV back on CBeebies and remote control hidden under sofa.

7.40 a.m.
Remote control missing. Dog shouted at and banished to shed, as usual.

7.45 a.m.
TV back on shouting inbred channel.

7.50 a.m.
Thorough search of Jesus has revealed remote control

stashed in Babygro. Dog released from shed and allowed to listen to his favourite CD (Bonnie Tyler's greatest hits) as way of apology. Mum says Jesus may have gone too far down the road of criminality to be rescued. I said Supernanny didn't give up this easily, in the hope this would bait her into further action, but she just sighed wearily and shut herself in the kitchen with *The Archers* and some Fruit 'n' Fibre.

4 p.m.
Went round Sad Ed's to escape clutches of Jesus. He is worse than the dog at stealing or eating valuables. So far, he has managed to post one of Dad's credit cards down a crack in the skirting board, broken a porcelain deer (James's and vile) and eaten four liquorice pipes (Dad's and also vile). Only the dog is happy. It appears positively angelic in comparison and is enjoying a relatively shout-free day. Ed has spent his wages (£21.50, i.e. more than me, but then he does have to wear unflattering brown and talk to Gary Fletcher) on a Joy Division CD, a copy of Sartre's *Nausea* and packet of condoms (pineapple flavour). I said he should think about saving for the future, but he said there is no point as he is still planning an untimely death. Mrs Thomas made us keep the bedroom door open. I do not know why. There is no way I want to explore Sad Ed's nether regions.

School starts tomorrow. Hurrah. I will be able to see Justin every day and we can snog outside the Sixth Form

common room, which will buy me loads of kudos with the lower school—they are easily impressed. Although it will be the first time I have seen Jack since the wardrobe incident. According to Scarlet he is immersing himself in his drums. I expect he will have forgiven me and Justin. He will not let his thwarted love threaten the musical genius of Certain Death.

8 p.m.
Not that Jack loves me.

9 p.m.
And, even if he did, it is not true love as he is utterly not my ONE and am going to stop writing now in case brain or pant-covered parts start wandering.

. . . .

Monday 8
Back to school.
Mr Wilmott gave us a talk in assembly about how it is a crucial year for all of us and it is time we knuckled down etc., etc. He is right. I am absolutely going to knuckle down. Although it is hard to concentrate in French when Justin is playing football outside in his shorts. He is doing eight resits and AS level PE. He says it is a cinch. All you have to do to pass is know the off-side rule and run around the sheep field in less than fifteen minutes.

Saw Jack outside the mobile science labs. He nodded and

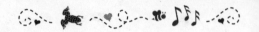

said 'All right, Riley?' I said I was totally fine and asked after Marie-Claire (his annoying Pantene-haired French model girlfriend whom he was snogging prior to the wardrobe incident). He said it was over, and that he is concentrating on his career, as A Levels are only eighteen months away and he needs at least five As so he can go to Cambridge and become Foreign Secretary and win the Mercury Music Prize. I said that I too was concentrating on my work. He said, 'Yeah, right, which subject, French KISSING?' He is being very childish. That is the sort of humour I expect from Mark Lambert or any of the O'Gradys. Not from someone who has read Proust and actually understood it.

Also Jack and Justin were not hanging out together at lunch. Jack got Bombay mix out of the nut-dispensing machine and Justin went to Mr Patel's for Wotsits.

5 p.m.
Jesus has broken the washing machine. He climbed inside so that he could poke Rice Krispies through all the little holes.

. . . .

Tuesday 9
James has a black eye. Mum is furious and says he cannot play with Mad Harry any more. But James said it is not Mad Harry or Stephen 'Maggot' Mason, who eats mud. There is a new gang leader at St Regina's Primary. It is Keanu, the youngest and deadliest O'Grady boy. He has

taken over the playground and is now ranked first toughest in the infants.

. . . .

Wednesday 10

James is refusing to go to school in case Keanu duffs him up again. Asked him how old Keanu was. He is five. But he has a weight advantage and menacing earrings. Mum says he is going to school, Keanu or no Keanu, as she is struggling to cope with the dog and Jesus as it is, and doesn't want James lurking about as well. This is not like her. She is usually itching to have a go at an O'Grady. Jesus is obviously taking up the entire anti-anti-social behaviour bit of her brain.

4 p.m.

There has been a crisis in the world of rock. Certain Death have split up! Jack told Justin this morning. He claims it is because of artistic differences but I fear it is all over me. I am like Layla in that song and they are Eric Clapton and that one out of the Beatles that died and isn't John Lennon. Justin says he is not worried. He predicts Jack will be begging him to come back by the end of the week as no one else in Saffron Walden can play more than four chords or has access to a Transit van.

Also James has another Keanu-inflicted injury. It is a Peperami inserted up his nose. Mum has relented and is going in tomorrow to talk to Reverend Begley. It is not so

27

much the violence, more because James said the Peperami smelt nice and she doesn't want him falling into the clutches of junk food.

. . . .

Thursday 11

Asked Scarlet about Certain Death during Rural Studies (drawing pictures of chickens). Scarlet says Jack is branching out in a new direction, music-wise. Asked her if he was branching out love-wise. She said he is definitely off women now that Marie-Claire has chucked him because he told her she was not the ONE. I asked Scarlet if she knew who the ONE was. She says it is his drum kit—all top musicians are married to their music first and their women second, that is why they are such inconsiderate lovers. She got that from Suzy who once did it with one of Status Quo's roadies. Lesson abandoned early due to Mark Lambert letting live chicken models out onto C Corridor and whole class having to round them up before they infiltrated the ventilation shafts like last year.

Mum is livid. Reverend Begley is refusing to do anything about the Keanu situation. He says he is going to let it run its course, i.e. wait for someone else to duff Keanu up and take over again. It is because he is scared of Mrs O'Grady. Mum says it is like *Lord of the Flies* in the playground at St Regina's.

. . . .

Friday 12

Hurrah. Got detention for snogging Justin in the upper school boys' toilets when should have been in library pretending to read maths text book (as if). Am totally rebellious and my reputation as lover of ace guitarist will be all round school by Monday and will get canteen privileges and the respect of all Year Seven EMOs.

4 p.m.

Saw Jack on way home after detention. He was talking to Justin's ex Sophie Jacobs (of big nipple perversion) outside Mr Patel's. They were obviously telling jokes because they laughed hysterically as I walked past. I did not say hello. I am above their puerile humour.

James is suspiciously injury free. Asked him about it when Mum was changing Jesus's nappy (it is best to stay outside a three-room radius due to shrieking and flying faeces). Apparently he and Mad Harry have bowed to demands and are now acting as minders to Keanu. He says it is the only way to survive the cut-throat world of a Church of England primary school.

Saturday 13

Work. Mum and James came in to buy mung bean seeds for her cultivator and Nuts In May patented oat and raisin bars for Jesus, to wean him off KitKats. She has no chance; I have tasted one and they are like

29

chewy gravel. Rosamund has developed a new ailment—it is head lice. Offered to run to Boots to get her some louse-eliminating chemicals but she says she prefers the natural method of tea tree oil and a nit comb. Spent rest of day avoiding her (two foot long) plaits.

Met Justin for lunch on the bench in the market square (broken pork pies, courtesy of Mr Goddard—at least it saves my minuscule wages). He is getting restless, music-wise. He says he is giving Jack until Monday to beg him to come back to Certain Death and then he will have to consider Plan B. Asked him what Plan B was. He said he hadn't planned it yet.

6 p.m.
Mum has asked if I am 'courting'. Marjory spotted me on the bench while she was buying a sink plunger in Gayhomes (not homosexualist shop, but crap hardware one). Plus the toilet snogging rumour had reached her via school secretary Mrs Leech (bad hair; too much face powder; biscuit habit) who told her cousin Enid who told Mrs Carter from number 47 who told Mum in the queue at Barclays. Denied everything. It is essential teenage behaviour to conceal love life from parents. Plus Mum will try to talk to me about 'urges' if she finds out I am snogging a rock god, which will be potentially hideous.

Sunday 14

Justin has rung. He is in shock. Jack has got a new band. They are called the Jack Stone Five, which is ironic, apparently, as there are only four of them, and they have got a gig next month at the Air Training Corps hut (youth group for the criminally weapons-obsessed). Asked Justin how they are managing without his transport options but apparently they have got Matthew Quinn on bass, whose dad has a fish delivery van. Justin says he is going to form a better band. Am going round his to think up names after lunch.

7 p.m.

Band still unnamed. My suggestions of Ambient Monkey and Cats Don't Wear Pants utterly rejected. Also it has no members except Justin. I have offered to do vocals but Justin said he was going to put an advert in *NME*. I suggested the A Corridor noticeboard might be better. We are going to reconvene after school on Wednesday in the mobile music room with potential members. Sad Ed says he is definitely auditioning. Although, if he gets in, which will be a miracle, frankly, given his fat fingers, it may only split the Jack v. Justin camp further with Scarlet on one side of the artistic divide and me, Sad Ed, and Tuesday on the other.

Monday 15

Oh my God. Tuesday is IN the Jack Stone Five. She is lead

31

vocals and tambourine. She is totally overexcited and is planning her stage outfits already. She is going for a Blondie meets Bat for Lashes look (i.e. slutty fortune teller). Sad Ed says they will not let it affect their love life. They are going to be utterly grown-up and keep business separate from pleasure. Plus he says it may heal the divide between John Major High and the Quaker school that Tuesday is forced to go to and we will be able to mingle freely instead of hurling Mojos at each other across the High Street.

8 p.m.
Sad Ed rang. Tuesday is not speaking to him because he said she sounds more like a Sugababe than Courtney Love. He has suggested Justin gets Tuesday's Quaker friend Daisy Truelove Jones on vocals to annoy her. Plus Daisy's dad runs BJ Video (aka Blow Job Video) and can get us free DVDs.

. . . .

Tuesday 16

The Certain Death split is causing havoc at the Alternative Music Club lunch table. Die-hard Certain Death fans (several Year Eights and Stan Barrett who once saw Paul Weller in John Lewis) are refusing to let any of the Jack Stone Five or their minions sit with them. So they have commandeered the table by the fire extinguishers (formerly Goth Corner). And now the goths are up in arms as they are bored with Goth Corner Mark II (next to

32

woefully empty trophy cabinet) and want to move back to their old table. Luckily Mrs Brain got annoyed with all the rearranging and threatened everyone with her doughnut tongs (disused due to Jamie Oliver enforcement of fruit eating).

Also Jesus has released the frogs. Mum says she only took her eye off him for a second. James gave her a withering look and said, 'That second could be the difference between life and death. You should know better.' Mum said she was distracted by the dog trying to dig a hole in the stair carpet. Jesus is now in quarantine (in his cot) while the house is forensically swept for Michaelangelo and Donatello.

6.30 p.m.
Frogs located in cot. Jesus had been hoarding them in his nappy. Mum says the wetness may have been their lifeline. James has washed them with Carex though. He is not taking any cross-infection chances.

Wednesday 17
8 a.m.
Hurrah. It is our inaugural band meeting tonight. Note use of 'our'. I am sure to get starring role, as Justin's girlfriend. Maybe I will be the next Lily Allen and will not have to pass GCSEs after all, but will affect a cockney accent and learn how to drink five pints of cider without

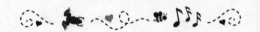

vomiting. Sad Ed and several Alternative Music Table
members are coming. Scarlet is refusing unless he can
give her assurances that they will include Marilyn
Manson as one of their influences. Justin says he cannot
give her that peace of mind. Our first point of business is
the name. I have an excellent new suggestion—The
Banned. It is utterly clever. Plus all excellent bands have
a 'the' in the title. Like The Editors. And The Strokes. And
The Libertines.

8.15 a.m.
But not The Wurzels. Obviously.

8.17 a.m.
Or Editors apparently.

6 p.m.
The band is not called The Banned. It is 'Don't Let the
Pigeon Drive the Bus'. It is Stan Barrett's idea and is
named after his favourite book. Also am not lead vocals.
Or even in band, exactly. Justin says he does not want
anyone thinking we are ripping off the Jack Stone Five
with a girl as the front man. He is going to do vocals and
lead guitar. Stan Barrett is on bass, Dean 'the dwarf'
Denley is on drums, and Sad Ed is on second guitar, on the
proviso that he only plays when he actually knows the
chords. I am going to do promotion and management.
Which Justin says is better than being in band. He is right.
I will be like leprechaunish impresario Louis Walsh and

the fat one who got sacked by the Spice Girls, and will make millions from my ability to spot raw talent.

Why is head itching?

7 p.m.
Oh God. Have got head lice. Mum caught me scratching during *Look East* and did a forensic check. It is Rosamund's fault. They must have leapt across the Well Woman shelf while we were rearranging overpriced organic sanitary towels. Mum has banished me to the bathroom with several bottles of chemicals (she has no concern for the environment, her only goal is to be pest-free). But cannot get nit comb through gigantic hairdo so now have millions of dead lice clinging to hair. It is like killing fields of Baghdad. Or wherever they were. Am considering shaven look. Although Justin will chuck me for sure. Oh God. What if I have given them to Justin during one of our snogging sessions. They may have wandered carelessly across onto his rock star hairdo. The shame.

8 p.m.
Dead nits are out. Mum did it. Am in agony. She is ruthless with her comb technique. Will check Justin surreptitiously tomorrow.

. . . .

Thursday 18
Tried to check Justin's hair during band meeting at lunch (crucial decision—do we want the O in 'Don't' to be

35

shaped like a skull or is that just naff. Conclusion—naff, it is going to be the pigeon's eye instead) but he was wearing a hat (de rigueur in Sixth Form for aspiring Kurt Cobain types). Am going to resort to Plan B (unlike Justin, I actually have one) and blame any potential scratching on Oona Rickets. She is notoriously unclean. Anyway, have far more pressing things than nits to worry about. Justin's mum and dad are going on their dirty weekend to Champneys on Saturday (his and hers massages, colonic irrigation, and romantic carrot stick dinners) and he has asked me to stay over, which is boy speak for 'do It'. Have to think of excuse not to go. Am still hopelessly unschooled in what goes where and when, plus am not legal and may get exposed by *Daily Mail* or something. Will think up Plan A, and Plan B as matter of emergency.

. . . .

Friday 19

8 a.m.
I think the lice menace may have spread. I caught James scratching over his toast and Marmite. Did not mention it to Mum as do not want to be punished as source of outbreak.

4 p.m.
James has been sent home from school with lice. He is not ashamed. Apparently Keanu has had them twenty-five

times and also has semi-permanent ringworm.

4.15 p.m.
Dad has been sent home early with lice. In stark contrast to James's devil-may-care attitude, he is entirely ashamed. Mr Wainwright, his boss, saw one walking around his collar in a meeting about the coffee machine. Mum has ordered everyone to form an orderly queue at the bathroom door. She is doing Jesus and the dog as well, as precautionary measures.

. . . .

Saturday 20
Work. Another seven hours with Rosamund and her parasites beckons. Also am supposed to be going round Justin's tonight for sex and still have no Plan A or Plan B to get out of it other than feigning death or claiming to be religious. Will text Scarlet, she has a year's worth of experience of fending off Trevor's sexual advances. They were planning on doing 'It' at the winter solstice but at the last minute she told him her biorhythms were all wrong and they would have to defer until Hallowe'en.

1 p.m.
Mr Goldstein has turned my mobile phone off. It is at Rosamund's request in case the radiation gives her cancer. Am going to see Sad Ed on trolleys instead in the hope he has some words of wisdom. Will tell Justin I am

37

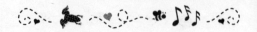

out on Nuts In May business and he will have to eat his reject pork pies on his own today.

1.30 p.m.
Sad Ed too busy inventing time travel with Gary Fletcher. He is going to get the sack soon if he is not careful. So now have six and a half hours to think of way to retain virginity. Obviously could just say no, as recommended by PE teacher and 'sexpert' Miss Beadle, but do not want to get reputation as prude or lezzer.

6 p.m.
Hurrah! Am not going to have to have sex after all. It is because Mum has incontrovertible evidence of me and Justin snogging behind the Passat (digital photos by Marjory. She should set up her own detective agency— neither of us heard any rustling in the privet) and has banned me from going over there except under strict adult supervision. I have never been so happy at her medieval regime. Phoned Justin to tell him. He is less thrilled. Not even when I told him we were totally like Romeo and Juliet. I said we could meet in secret at dawn on Barry Island (car park on Common where O'Gradys go to rev up their Datsuns) but he said he would be asleep and would see me at school on Monday. He is just annoyed at having to suppress his urges. I think it is all utterly tragic and romantic. Will watch *Casualty* with excellent air of thwarted teenage sexuality. i.e. sulking

and huffing a lot. Will also drop 'you've forgotten what it's like' into conversation somewhere. Although suspect Mum never knew what it is like. The only time she is overcome with passion is when she has a bottle of Cillit Bang in her hand.

. . . .

Sunday 21

11 a.m.
Grandpa and Treena get back this afternoon. You can tell Mum is happy because she has let James set up a frog assault course in the bath. He is training them for their potential death match with Shredder. They have to scale down the flannels, drop onto his plastic submarine, sail to the plughole and finish by jumping over an arrangement of Head and Shoulders bottles. There is no way they are going to complete it.

11.30 a.m.
I take it back. The frogs have completed their challenge and are being rewarded by bits of off-cut organic lamb (i.e. Sunday lunch). Mum does not know about that part. She is restricting them to second-rate mince but James says a high quality diet is crucial to their world domination powers.

2 p.m.
Jesus has been repatriated to Harvey Road. Grandpa and

39

Treena picked him up after lunch. Although it turns out they have been home for three days but could not be bothered to get him. Mum does not care. Those three days were crucial in her battle to save Jesus from sin.

6 p.m.
Grandpa has rung to say Jesus has refused to eat his chocolate Ready Brek and is uncharacteristically watching *Songs of Praise*. Apparently Treena is in complete panic. She can only do toast or heat up things in the microwave, and Aled Jones brings her out in a rash. Mum, on the other hand, is jubilant. Her track record of raising compliant children is back to 100 per cent.

. . . .

Monday 22

Met Justin for lunch (aka snogging on the sheep field, now that toilets are out of bounds due to possibility of surprise raids by Miss Beadle). He is still sulking about his wasted empty-house opportunity. Asked him whether he had spent the night in torture on his bed. He said, *au contraire*, he had gone round to Tim Newbold's instead to watch *Spiderman 2*. Am now in panic. Tim is the brother of Pippa Newbold, who is best friend of Sophie Microwave Muffins Jacobs, who is ex-girlfriend of Justin. What if she was there? What if she is over her fat nipple perversion and wants him back? Oh God, he is bound to want her, she is a 34C now (official measurement), which

40

is several sizes bigger than me. Am going to have to improve size of bust if I want to keep Justin. I know he should love me for my intellectual superiority etc., but I fear hefty breasts may trump my freakish ability to recite Kipling.

Also, there has been a nit outbreak at John Major High. The entire upper school was scratching in non-denominational assembly this morning. Asked Mrs Leech casually if she had identified the source yet. She says it is bound to be an O'Grady, or possibly Nigel Moore who once had potato blight. I agreed. Although it was not potato blight. It was impetigo.

* *

Tuesday 23

My life is one perpetual cycle of potentially life-altering decisions. This week it is A-level choices. Have not even started revising for GCSEs yet and we are having to start worrying about the next barrage of exams. It is utterly unfair. May well write to Education Secretary Alan 'I've got an iPod' Johnson to complain about this culture of constant testing. James has already had three sets of SATs and he is not even ten. Although he says he actually enjoys them and that the only people who dread exams are the weak and the stupid. He got that theory from Mum. We are allowed to take three each plus an AS. Except for Emily Reeve (peanut allergy, knee-length socks (and not an ironic Japanese way),

41

vast doll collection) and the maths club geeks who are taking five each and several AS levels. It is because Mr Wilmott thinks it will compensate for the rest of the school who will get Ds and Es if they even bother to show up.

Am going to do English and Drama (so can be either Gwyneth Paltrow or Sylvia Plath, or both, possibly, in a remake of *Sylvia*!), French (we get to go on an exchange, potentially in Paris, world centre of tragic and literary things in general), and AS Philosophy (so can avoid repeat of Year Nine Karl Marx/Marx Brothers mix-up). Sad Ed wanted to do English, Drama, Music, and Art. I said he may be restricting himself career-wise, given his as yet unproven talents in the creative areas (his portrait of Scarlet looked like the one with the pointy ears out of *Lord of the Rings*). He said he is not unproven, just unappreciated. But has swapped English for AS Philosophy none the less. Scarlet is doing English, Politics, Economics, and Philosophy. She is aiming to be the next Ruth Kelly, but with better hair and a normal voice. Justin is not picking any, he is pinning all his post-resit hopes on Rock Foundation at Braintree FE College.

. . . .

Wednesday 24

Had band rehearsal after school, i.e. watching Sad Ed strum vaguely along to the White Stripes while Justin shouted chord changes at him. At least Dean 'the dwarf'

Denley can play the drums, although he has to sit on three cushions and even then you cannot see him over the cymbals.

Justin asked Sad Ed for inside info on the Jack Stone Five's set. He says Tuesday is still not speaking to him about business matters following his questioning of her on-stage presence. Although she is still letting him fiddle with her business areas. They are doing it at Mr Wilmott's house now, as he is notoriously ineffectual when it comes to disciplining teenagers.

· ·

Thursday 25

Oh my God. Someone at John Major High is with child, according to Mark Lambert (he did not say 'with child', he said 'up the duff'). He overheard security-unconscious Mrs Leech on the phone to the council while he was waiting to be punished for jamming Dean 'the dwarf' Denley in a toilet (again). Ali Hassan and the maths club geeks are opening a book on who the perpetrators are. All fingers point to Fat Kylie and Mr Whippy. She is well known for eschewing contraception, due to her Catholic beliefs, and he is well-known for his inability to keep his 'magic cone' to himself.

· ·

Friday 26

Bollywood beauty Shilpa Shetty has won *Big Brother*. It

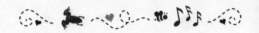

is a victory for non-racists everywhere. Grandpa Clegg has rung to complain (Mum, not Channel 4). He says he is not being racist (he is) but it is because that one out of Steps should have won. News of Ian 'H' Watson's gayness has clearly not made it across the border into Cornwall or Grandpa would be campaigning to have him banned from TV for good.

. . . .

Saturday 27

Oh God. The Dad as potential sex-beast situation has reared its ugly head again. Worse, it happened in lentil-smelling Nuts In May in full view of hunchbacked Mr Goldstein and ailment-riddled Rosamund. Dad and Mum had come in to allegedly buy James some Sesame Snaps (in reality, check up on my career as health food outlet assistant) when Edie suddenly appeared from behind the protein supplements looking like an ageing Amy Winehouse with all manner of excessive eyeliner, tattoos, and come hithering. (Tuesday actually had to tell Edie to cover herself up, something I am unlikely ever to be forced to do with Mum, she thinks knee length skirts are skimpy). Dad pretended to be far more interested in the eco-friendly deodorant but Mum dragged him out of the shop immediately and into Goddard's on the pretext of buying chops (also a lie; in fact to assess suitability of Justin as suitor) without paying for

James's health-giving snack. The 36p was docked from my pitiful pay packet. It is lucky Mr Goldstein is so tolerant. (It is his Jewish background. And the hump.) Also he is desperate as there were no other applicants for my job apart from Fat Kylie, who is unemployable. It is also lucky Justin was out the back of Goddard's swilling meat mess down the drain. He is yet to experience Mum's Paxman-like cross-examination technique, and will need special training in how to deflect trick questions.

Why is Edie so interested in Dad? Maybe it is because he is her first love and she has never got over him. Maybe he is her ONE. Oh God. Am so going to be child of broken home, which will utterly ruin my GCSE prospects. On the plus side, Tuesday will be my stepsister and I will get instant access to her wardrobe. It is a fine line.

Texted Justin to see if he wanted to meet in secret after work but he texted back to say he was working on some new material with the band. Offered to come and watch but he said no. He is definitely going off me. Went home immediately to do bust increasing exercises, as demonstrated by Thin Kylie during French oral, and she is a C cup. Measured bust. Still 32A. Maybe it is like Mr Muscle sink unblocker and works overnight. Will just do a few more and go to bed.

Sunday 28

8 a.m.

Bust still minuscule size. Maybe just need to do more.

10 a.m.

Chest in agony after two hours of continual muscular squeezing. And still only 32A. Plus Mum burst into bedroom to demand what suspicious groaning was. (She has been given the fear by Mrs Thomas.) But her search of potential Justin-concealing places (in bed, under bed, in wardrobe, in shoeboxes (he is not contortionist, as have pointed out, but she is clearly not taking any chances)) proved fruitless so she has gone back to supervising James and Mad Harry who are making toffee apples. I only hope they are intended for consumption and not for use as weaponry by Keanu's playground gang.

Monday 29

Fat Kylie is not pregnant. She got off hockey with period pain this morning. Miss Beadle said menstruation is a normal bodily function, not an excuse to read *Heat* magazine in the changing rooms, but Fat Kylie said, 'Three Tampax an hour ain't normal, miss, and what if it, like, gushes?' Miss Beadle was clearly panicked by Fat Kylie's potential gushing and said she could be referee instead (result 0–0, and teams reduced to two a side with everyone else thrown off for 'shitness'). Suspicions now rest with

Primark Donna, trainee chavette and little sister of Leanne Jones, notorious free giver of sexual favours. The Maths Club are going to interview her at the first opportunity.

. . . .

Tuesday 30

James has been given a gang nickname by Keanu—it is 'Brains'. Asked what Mad Harry's was. He said, 'It is Mad Harry, duh.' (He is getting decidedly brattish since his new-found acquaintance with an O'Grady, even if it is in the name of self-preservation.) Why have I never had a nickname? Actually I know why; it is because Mum has forbidden me ever to acquire one. Even shortening of names is strictly out of bounds. Am going to invent one. Will drop it into conversation until people have forgotten I was ever called Rachel. Will be like 'Minnie' Driver, real name Amelia.

8 p.m.
Have shortlisted nicknames, with aid of 'Brains' Riley:
- Books (as am literary goddess)
- Hack (potential journalistic career, though possibly also makes me sound like machete murderer)
- Ray (cool and slightly androgenous, à la Andie in *Pretty in Pink*)
- R'n'R (James's favourite due to similarity to pasty-faced rap genius Eminem though makes me sound backward with all the 'arring')

Think will go for Ray. Will start usage tomorrow.

. . . .

Wednesday 31

It is my and Justin's one-month anniversary, which is positively long-term by John Major High standards. We are meeting after school for a celebratory snog. Also have got him a card. And signed it from Ray! Scarlet asked if he had told me he loved me yet. I said not exactly, but almost. She said how exactly. I said he said he loved the way my hair sproinged back no matter how hard you squished it down. She said that is not the same thing at all. Sad Ed says he is probably waiting until he has 'tested all the goods'. I said that our love was above matters of the flesh. It is more spiritual. Except that I am not sure that is entirely the case. He has shown no interest in my suggestion of reading Rossetti poems to each other on the banks of (admittedly shopping-trolley-clogged) Slade river. But maybe playing X-Box is a modern meeting of minds. Yes, that is it. Totally.

5 p.m.
Had excellent snog with Justin down Battleditch Lane (aka dogshit alley). Gave him my card. He said, 'You've spelt your name wrong, Riley.' I am not disheartened. Nicknames take weeks to embed. Like investigative journalists.

february

Thursday 1

It is Glastonbury registration day. Me, Sad Ed, Tuesday and Justin are all going to put ourselves on the list. Scarlet and Jack do not have to stoop to such measures. It is because Suzy knows the Eavis man with the Amish hairdo and gets free tickets and a pass to the VIP toilet area every year. Sad Ed has taken photos of us all with his mobile phone for uploading. His camera is rubbish though. Despite fourteen attempts I still look like a man. Justin does not mind. He says I have the look of someone called Robert Plant about me. Have signed up under my new name Ray Riley. Having a street nickname will totally increase my chance of getting in. Although it is all hypothetical as there is no way Mum will let me go. She thinks I will end up 'smoking ecstasy and juggling'. They are equally evil in her eyes.

Friday 2

My excellent nickname is still not catching on. I texted Scarlet saying 'Meet me in toilets, X Ray' and she went to Mr Wilmott to tell him my phone had been hijacked by sex pest Raymond Jackson (aka X-Ray) in Year Eleven who once asked Scarlet to lick his toes. She did not. They are hobbit-like and possibly fungal.

Saturday 3

8 a.m.

Why, oh why, did I get a Saturday job? It is utter torture having to get up at half seven to sell vitamins and mung beans to badly dressed people (i.e. hippies, lesbians, and hypochondriacs) when I could be at home in bed reading life-changing literature, or at least on the sofa watching Dick and Dom with the dog. Have begged Dad to call in sick for me but he said he did not get where he is today (Financial Adviser to Wainwright and Hogg Office Supplies) by wheedling his way out of his Saturday job. Asked what his Saturday job was—he said he cleaned Grandpa Riley's car for 50p. Anyway, that is not the reason, it is in case Mum finds out. He is driving me there to make sure I do not detour to Scarlet's on the way.

6 p.m.

Work utterly unfulfilling. Monotony punctuated only by getting to snog Justin round the back of the meat bins. Although the smell and bloodstains are a bit offputting. Am consoling myself with thought that all artistic types have to suffer menial jobs and poverty-line pay packets, whilst writing their masterpieces by candlelight. When I am famous they will put a blue plaque on the peeling plaster at Nuts In May saying 'Rachel Riley once toiled here'.

Sunday 4

Granny Clegg rang to check none of us died in the night. It is because her gyppy hip is playing up and she says it is a portent of doom. The last time she got the gripes, three of Hester's chickens keeled over in the night. Mum said we are all very much alive, although the dog is living on borrowed time, as usual. Mum said Granny should get her hip looked at if it is that gyppy, she might get a nice new metal one on the NHS. Granny Clegg said she'd rather have a Disprin. It is because she doesn't like going to the doctors since Dr Trelawney (male, English, ancient, doles drugs out like Smarties) retired and got replaced by Dr Kimber (female, Australian, youthful, prescribes drugs only in proven cases of infection, and only after 'putting up with it for a week' has failed to see an improvement).

Went round Justin's for band practice this afternoon. Gave Sad Ed managerial advice, i.e. to hang guitar lower on strap as it is very high up and makes him look like evangelical music teacher Mr Beston instead of cool one out of Kaiser Chiefs. Also to practise playing as he is still struggling with G and even Mark Lambert can play that. (As evidenced by performance at Mrs Duddy's Annual Criminals and Retards 'We've Got Talent' show. No longer annual due to lack of any discernible talent and abundance of fighting.) Sad Ed said he cannot help it if his arms are disproportionately short and his fingers slightly oversized. Then he demanded that managers (i.e. me) should be banned from rehearsals and stick to what

they are supposed to be doing, i.e. booking gigs and getting record deals. I said it was imperative to 'understand their sound' if I was going to secure top listing at Bernard Evans Youth Centre, let alone get them on Arctic Monkeys' MySpace page. Luckily Justin agreed. Plus he said it is useful to have someone to fetch orange squash and crisps, and to wipe sweat off his brow during guitar solos (he did not say that bit, I just like doing it).

Monday 5

Ali Hassan asked to see my stomach in Citizenship. I threatened to report him to Ms Hopwood-White for perving but he says he is just conducting checks for signs of weight gain. It is for the Maths Club school pregnancy gambling ring. Showed him stomach. He made notes. Demanded to see notes. Demanded to know why I was listed in the possibles category. He said there is definite swelling. I said it is not pregnancy, obviously, it is illicit can of Diet Coke, purchased as love gift by Justin from Mr Patel, and that if swelling is the only criteria then Sad Ed must be a contender. He said there are three categories. The others are first break vomiting and buying tuna surprise off Mrs Brain (only pregnant person could crave this) and they are being cross-referenced at the Maths and Science Club joint AGM on Friday (aka freaks and geeks convention). Noted that Scarlet was on the first break vomiting list. It is not pregnancy, it is because Suzy

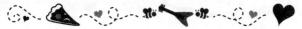

is away filming her TV sex show and Edna is in charge of breakfast.

. . . .

Tuesday 6

James got sent home from school early. It is because he and Mad Harry have been refereeing Keanu's new lunchtime Fight Club. He was in his bedroom with the dog when I got home, eating a penitent's tea of crackers and an apple (the dog is being punished for chewing the stairs). I asked him what went on at Fight Club. He said, 'The first rule of Fight Club is that you do not talk about Fight Club.' Mum is right. He is being brainwashed by an O'Grady. I have suggested we call in reinforcements, i.e. his ex-best friend Mumtaz. She would be an excellent calming influence with her Eastern religion and jingly music. Mum is not so sure. She is going to consult Dad on boarding schools. She says St Regina's is in danger of going the way of St Maxentius (closed due to overhigh O'Grady count) and it might be better to get out before it is too late.

. . . .

Wednesday 7

Dad is refusing to send James to boarding school. He says it is a hotbed of future fascists and perverts (he cited Boris Johnson as an example, though I am not sure in which category). Plus we cannot afford it due to the continual

dog-related damage and Mum's appalling clutch control (Fiesta bills already through roof). James is disappointed. He was hoping to be packed off to Eton each term with a tuck box full of home-made jam and Liquorice Allsorts. No chance. Mum would fill it with fluoride tablets and anti-bacterial wipes. It is a relief. Not only would it be reputation ruining in the uber-left-wing Sixth Form to have a relation at boarding school, it would mean Mum's focus was entirely on me, and I rely heavily on James and his frog chaos to divert attention from my minor spillages and misdemeanours.

* * *

Thursday 8

Suffolk is riddled with bird flu, according to the BBC. Mum is in a panic in case any of our sparrows have been crossing the border. She says it is all Bernard Matthews's fault and is divine (or Jamie Oliver) retribution for his Turkey Twizzlers. (She thinks Jamie Oliver is a saint, despite his speech impediment and overuse of cockney phrases.) On the plus side, she is easing her ban on continental imports, as France has now been officially declared disease-free. We are back on the Bonne Maman jam and Normandy butter.

Grandpa Riley rang. Jesus said his first word today. It is 'skip'. Mum got excited as it was one of the key words on the flash cards she was terrorizing him with during the honeymoon, but it turns out it was a demand for one of

Treena's prawn cocktail crisps. Grandpa is jubilant none the less. He says Baby Jesus is a genius and he is going to get him tested for Mensa. James says they will not let him in. He is just annoyed because he was refused entry last year on grounds of not being boffiny enough. Which is frightening as James can recite all the books of the Bible, and the periodic table, off by heart, in song.

. . . .

Friday 9

Last day of school.

The John Major High pregnancy scandal has been solved, and not by cardigan-wearing (and not in a this-season way) 'mathletes' either, but by Dean 'the dwarf' Denley. Mrs Leech and Mr Wilmott were discussing it over custard creams at first break, and had not noticed 'The Dwarf' (as he is now known) standing at the desk waiting to hand in a note (to get off PE on the grounds that he is persistently picked last and has been used as a ball on several occasions). Astonishingly, it is not Primark Donna. It is Emily Reeve! Wearer of knee-length socks and owner of vast doll collection! She is three months gone, i.e. due in crucial GCSE season. This is what happens when your parents do not let you go to sex education with Miss Beadle and her plastic penis, or you do not have access to Thin Kylie and her stack of *Cosmopolitans*.

Scarlet says she has thrown her entire future away for

five minutes of fumbling. She is right. Emily will be knee-deep in nappies and vomit while the rest of us are enjoying the high life of Sixth Form. (Also possibly vomit, as Sad Ed pointed out, but not nappies. I hope.) Mr Wilmott is especially outraged. It is because her potential absence will bring down his grade point average and we will be beaten yet again in the league tables by Burger King Sports Academy (formerly the Harold Wilson Modern). The Maths Club are happy though. They have made excellent profits (£37.50, including several stakes from members of staff) and have opened another book on who the father is. It is a good question. I might befriend her and she will confide in me and I can win big. Or refuse to tell and put others off the scent to protect our friendship. She is excellently tragic and Julie Burchill-esque after all. Oooh, I could write a novel about it.

8 p.m.
Just had worrying thought. If Emily Reeve, who wears cagoules and days of the week pants, is doing 'It', then the pressure is piling on me, especially as I wear vintage and own black pants (present from Scarlet and hidden from Mum in Postman Pat moneybox). Although, to be fair, Justin has made no sexual demands on me yet. Maybe he is a New Man and is respecting my body etc. Hurrah.

9 p.m.
Or maybe he does not want to do 'It' with me because I

am utterly non-sexual. Oh God. Am absolutely going to devote entire half term to bust expansion.

. . . .

Saturday 10

Grandpa Riley and Treena visited me at work today with Baby Jesus. Mr Goldstein offered Jesus a 'treat' of dried figs but Jesus just said 'Skip, Skip' repeatedly until Treena fished a bag of them out of the pushchair. Mr Goldstein looked visibly disappointed. I do not blame Jesus though. The figs are vile and look like shrivelled poo. Treena bought Ginseng and Royal Jelly, i.e. sex stimulating products. I am amazed they need any. They are always at it. Unless it is because they are trying for another baby. I hope not. As Mum pointed out, by the time Jesus is ten, Grandpa Riley will probably be dribbling or dead.

. . . .

Sunday 11

4 p.m.

Band practice called off on account of the drum section (i.e. The Dwarf) being inconveniently at his Aunty Sheila's for lunch and second guitar (i.e. Sad Ed) being inconveniently at Tuesday's for snogging. Am considering sacking them. I bet Snow Patrol do not have to put up with these sorts of poor excuses. On the plus side, me and Justin got to 'hang' i.e. he played his guitar while I nodded appreciatively at intervals.

I wonder what I would be doing if me and Jack were together instead. Maybe sitting in an arty café sipping red wine and discussing Hegelian Dialectic (as advertised in Head of Philosophy (and hairy librarian) Mr Knox's pro-AS-level flyer). Or buying vintage overcoats together. Oh God. Stop thinking about Jack. He is utterly out of bounds. Plus there are no arty cafés in Saffron Walden; the Mocha just has fruit machines and a velvet Elvis.

4.15 p.m.
And am with love of life i.e. Justin. So do not care about discussing philosophy with random boy.

4.30 p.m.
Oooh. Velvet Elvis would be a good name for a band. It is much catchier than the Pigeon thing.

. . . .

Monday 12
Half term
10 a.m.
Bust increasing endeavours start today (still 32A at last official measure-in at Scarlet's, compared to her 32Bs). Have done twenty minutes of crunching and stretching and am now moving on to googling herbal remedies on James's computer. (Christmas laptop still being 'fixed' by Malcolm 'the geek' at Dad's office.)

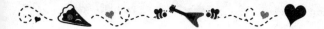

11 a.m.
Am pinning hopes on obtaining product called 'Wonderup' instead. It is from Japan and has seven kinds of herbs in it. Ooh, I wonder if Mr Goldstein has it. Maybe he will give it to me at a discount. After all, what is point of working in health product shop if you do not make best use of health boosting (or breast boosting) products.

2 p.m.
Mr Goldstein does not stock Wonderup or Grobust or any other natural breast-enlarging supplements. (It is a wonder he is in business at all really, he does not seem willing to move with the times.) And have no credit card to buy things with over interwebnet so am back to daily exercises.

. . . .

Tuesday 13
James and Mad Harry have offered to 'mesmerize' my bust into growing. (They checked the search history on Internet Explorer and discovered my plight.) Asked what this involved. Mad Harry said he would need to assess the 'size of the problem' first. Declined. Do not want to flash breasts at low-rent Paul McKennas. Especially as one is my brother.

Anyway, am not depressed. Because it is Valentine's Day tomorrow and I do not have to worry about whether or not I will get a card this year as am totally guaranteed one as have lovely boyfriend.

. . . .

Wednesday 14

Valentine's Day

10 a.m.

No card. It is obviously delayed in Britain's notoriously haphazard postal system. Or else is being delivered by hand later at our romantic dinner (i.e. Luigi's Pizza). But, controversially, one has arrived for Dad and it is not from Mum (hers was on the table with his Shreddies this morning, plus she would not buy anything with a pink pearlized envelope, or squirt it with Poison). Mum is beside herself with potential love rivalry. James has suggested steaming it open with the kettle. But I said this broke all sorts of trust issues and she should respect Dad's right to privacy.

10.15 a.m.

Mum is steaming open the card with the kettle. God, hope it is not from Edie but from random stalker, or actually for James by mistake (not completely out of the question, as he has eight this year, a new record. It is due to his high ranking as a gang member.)

10.30 a.m.

Card is from Edie (she signed it 'your Weirdy Edie' followed by seven kisses). Mum is threatening to go round to Mr Wilmott's and have it out with her (do not rate Edie's chances—she is in a weakened state due to alcohol withdrawal and Mum is nutritionally tip-top,

thanks to fruit muesli and granary toast.) Have called Dad to warn him. He is coming home immediately. Which means there is a definite crisis looming. He did not even take time off when Mum had gastroenteritis and James had to cook his tea (I was banned from cooking at time due to my inability to follow recipes or keep ingredients off floor).

12 noon
Dad is back and has gone straight into the talks suite (i.e. the dining room). James is positioned at door with an upturned glass (Mum would ban *Blue Peter* if she knew that was where he had learned this trick).

12.05 p.m.
Dad has called Mum a 'meddler' for opening his post.

12.10 p.m.
Mum has accused Dad of being a philanderer for receiving said post.

12.15 p.m.
Dad is out and is demanding to see evidence of said philandering post.

12.30 p.m.
Evidence not located. Dad accuses Mum of fabricating evidence.

12.45 p.m.
Dog is sick (pink pearlized, scent of Poison) outside back door. Mum points to sick and says, 'Read that and weep, Colin Riley.'

1 p.m.
Colin Riley declines to read sick but declares he has no interest in Edie, that she is clutching at straws following their brief liaison in 1982 and that, as everyone knows, high school love affairs are meaningless and fizzle out after a few years unless you are blessed with the imagination of a newt (or Clive and Marjory) and it is university ones that go the distance (he met Mum at accountancy college). Mum agrees, following statistical evidence produced by James and his trusty companion, Google. (Justin and I will be the exception to this rule, obviously.)

1.15 p.m.
Peace is restored and Dad returns to work with cottage cheese sandwich, prepared by loving wife. Sick is cleaned up and flushed away, along with evidence of Edie's undying passion for Sex Beast Riley.

Thank God crisis is over. Am going to have to raise the issue with Tuesday though. Will tell her she needs to rein in her mother's urges, or she will be possibly responsible for putting me into care and thus ruining my chances of passing my GCSEs and being generally brilliant.

5 p.m.

Am meeting Justin in an hour at our assignation point (i.e. Barry Island for pre-meal snogging). Am going to wear floaty scarf (as seen on Sienna Miller at V festival, although this is one of Mum's 1970s M&S cast-offs, not genuine Pucci). Scarf looks very vintage plus will disguise lack of activity in breast area. (James's idea. He got it out of Trinny and Susannah.) Think tonight may be the night, i.e. when Justin declares his love for me. Scarlet says Trevor 'pledged his troth' on Friday 13th—a special goth day (the Stones do not celebrate Valentine's Day, due to it being overcommercial and possibly made up by chocolate manufacturers). Mum says I must be home by ten or she will come and collect me herself in the Fiesta. Will be home by 9.30. Do not want Mum ruining mood of love with her current anti-romance stance, or her usual carping on about the lack of food hygiene on the help yourself salad bar or the rogue apostrophes on the menu.

9.30 p.m.

Am back from romantic dinner i.e. ham and pineapple pizza and all-you-can-eat ice cream factory. Result—no declaration of love but some excellent across table snogging. Asked him about card. He said I was right, it is trapped in the woeful Royal Mail. (I may well write to mad-eyebrowed Trade Secretary Alistair Darling to complain—he is thwarting love lives up and down the country. Especially as it is bound to be literary and tragic

with seventeenth century paintings of lovestruck beauty on it. Unlike Edie's whimsical puppies effort.) Then floaty scarf thing caught fire on the Valentine's candles and Justin threw glass of 7Up at me to quash flames i.e. save my life. Am definitely in love. Stomach feels all gurgly with excitement. Justin is the ONE after all. Hurrah.

2 a.m.
Have been sick. It is nerves from love-fuelled dinner.

2.30 a.m.
Oh. And again.

3.00 a.m.
More sick. Maybe it is not nerves, but Hawaiian pizza. Or Mr Whippy style chemical ice cream.

3.30 a.m.
Sick definitely fault of Luigi. Have just got text from Justin cancelling our romantic lunch (baguettes from Pie Shop Pearce) as he is locked in his Tudor-style toilet on Debden Road also being sick.

. . . .

Thursday 15
4 p.m.
Still feeling ill. Mum has called Uttlesford Environmental Health (i.e. Mrs O'Nion aka Mrs Onion) to demand

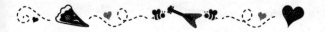

Luigi's Pizza is shut down immediately on grounds of salmonella and false advertising (Luigi is actually called Dave and is from Sible Hedingham, not Napoli). Mrs O'Nion says she needs proof, i.e. a vomit sample. Mum is now hovering with a bucket in the hope I produce some more.

Justin is too weak to visit. He has lost half a stone in six hours. Sad Ed was not too weak to visit (he could do with getting food poisoning—may suggest it as a diet tip). He had brought a Get Well Mix CD of 'soothing' New Wave Indie pop. Had to ask him to turn it off after a while as the twangy guitars and tuneless lyrics were causing new waves of nausea. Told him about the Edie crisis. He says he will mention it to Tuesday but that Edie is on a knife edge at the moment and rejection could send her straight back into the arms of Jack Daniels and Johnny Walker. I said I did not care who else she snogged as long as it is not vest-wearing Colin Riley.

Friday 16

Am still weak from pizza poisoning. Mum is not best pleased though as have failed to produce more vomit for her forensic sample. I said she should be relieved I am on the mend. She said on the contrary, what would make her happy is shutting down Luigi's rat-infested kitchens. Have called Scarlet to cancel planned shopping pilgrimage

to Cambridge with Suzy for Converse footwear and Topshop skinny jeans. She is going to take Trevor instead as he wants to buy some black nail varnish from the big Boots. Have texted Justin but he says he is still sipping Lucozade in a darkened room and does not want to walk the fifteen minutes from his Tudor-style mansion to no-apparent-style Summerdale Road in case he collapses. I texted back to say it was very rock star to collapse on a pavement. He said yes but from alcohol poisoning, not crap pizza.

4 p.m.
Got text from Jack—HP U BETTER. NEED ANYTHING? MAGAZINES? GRAPES? WIPES? Texted back saying thanks but that I had full supply of fruit and mopping up equipment and that I needed nothing.

Oooh. Although maybe a magazine would be nice. Maybe should text back and ask him to come over. Oh he has texted back already.

4.10 p.m.
It says SUIT YOURSELF RILEY. He is so moody. Maybe he has boy PMT. Rosamund says it is entirely possibly due to excess oestrogen in the water supply (pill-taking people weeing). She only drinks bottled Evian and fresh rainwater. Or else it is nerves because of inaugural Jack Stone Five gig tomorrow.

Saturday 17

8 a.m.

Ugh. Work. Was going to phone in sick (almost genuine) but Mum says there is no way I am going out tonight to get sweaty with a load of rampaging teenagers if I am too ill to price up Fruesli bars first. Plus she is refusing to pay £3.50 for the ticket so I need to earn my entrance fee. James is backing her strong work ethic. He has amassed £4.00 this week by washing the Fiesta, spring cleaning the frog tank, cutting the dog's toenails, and learning the Latin names for garden birds. I said I didn't get paid to be clever and maybe I should get money for passing my GCSEs. Mum said my reward would be the joy of knowing I have worked hard to improve my career chances. I said I'd rather have £10 an exam. Then James demanded £10 for every spelling test he passes and at that point Mum told us to stop the money madness and eat our Shreddies.

Am taking gig outfit to work so I can get changed at Justin's. All the members of 'Pigeon' (as it is now known because we are all bored with the full length version) are meeting there so we can go in as one and show our solidarity. Except for Sad Ed who is on late trolley duty and will have to walk to the ATC hut in his brown overall. Justin is very excited. He thinks he will be like Nigel Tuffnell in Spinal Tap and that Jack will see him in the audience and be overwhelmed with regret and call him on stage for a Certain Death reunion. I said he should not

care about his old band and that Pigeon is the future of music in North Essex. He said The Death will always be Number One in his eyes.

12 midnight

Justin did not get called on stage for a reunion. Even more depressingly, the Jack Stone Five are excellent. Tuesday is totally Lily Allenish and did songs about the cars at Barry Island and drinking coffee at the new Starbucks (formerly the White Horse, spiritual home of Treena). Although I think their version of 'LDN' ('WLDN') was pushing it a bit. I can think of a million reasons why I would want to be anywhere else than Saffron Walden, sun in the sky or not. Worse, Jack looked really good on drums and smiled at me loads. Unlike Justin who leant moodily against the wall with a Fanta and refused to talk to anyone.

Walked home with Sad Ed and Tuesday as Justin said he was too down to snog. Tuesday was on a complete high. She says she is single-handedly breaking down the barriers of apartheid that separate the Quakers and John Major High with the power of her voice, and likened herself to Nelson Mandela. I said I was not sure he would look so favourably on the comparison but Tuesday said I was just jealous because I am behind the scenes and she is in the limelight. It is the story of my life.

On the plus side, Tuesday said she has told Edie not to send Dad any more love letters. Edie said she would try,

70

but that he is like an addiction and she may not be strong enough to fight it. I said she had better be or she would have Mum to deal with, which will be worse than going cold turkey from the Smirnoff.

. . . .

Sunday 18

Justin is fully revived and I have the lovebite to prove it (concealed with floaty scarf before Mum sends me to borstal)! He says he is not taking the Jack Stone Five's success lying down and we are going to come back bigger and better. He has instructed me to book the ATC Hut for Friday 2nd March. Rehearsals start in earnest after school on Wednesday. Hurrah. It is because he went home and watched *The Doors* starring the crap Batman and realized he IS Jim Morrison. I said Sad Ed claims HE is Jim Morrison too but Justin says he has the wrong hair and that Sad Ed is actually Ray Manzarek (as played by the menacing dentist out of *Desperate Housewives*). Anyway, he is banishing Sad Ed's crap guitar and is making him learn the synthesizer immediately. He is going round later with his Bontempi organ. He says he will upgrade it for a Yamaha when we have sold out our first tour. He may be waiting a long time.

7 p.m.

Went round Sad Ed's to see how he was taking the news of his new role but could hear 'Chopsticks' being played badly out of bedroom window on the Bontempi so

decided to leave him to his music. Plus have school tomorrow and need to mentally prepare for tough GCSE teaching schedule.

. . . .

Monday 19

Did not have tough GCSE teaching schedule. Instead got sent home with a fake baby. It is for Citizenship and we are supposed to work out when it needs feeding and nappy changing and not dropping on its head etc. We have all got one, except Emily Reeve who will have a real one to not drop on its head in six months' time. Plus Ms Hopwood-White said it is pointless as the idea is to terrify us into not getting pregnant and it would be like shutting the stable door after the horse has bolted. I have called mine Desdemona (after tragic Shakespearean heroine). She is resting peacefully on the sofa. Will obviously make an excellent mother, once have conquered literary world.

Also tried to befriend Emily Reeve in attempt to gain her confidence so she can confess who the father is etc., but she asked me to go away as I was eating trail mix (replacing Maltesers in Mr Wilmott's new-style vending machine) and the peanut particles could kill her and her unborn child. She is so ungrateful. If I were in her position I would be taking up all offers of friendship I could get.

5 p.m.

Have fed Desdemona and changed nappy (i.e. pressed

appropriate buttons on control panel). She has not cried once. Hurrah. Am obviously a natural at this. I bet things are not so peaceful in the Sad Ed household. He will have killed his for sure already with his fat fingers.

8 p.m.
Desdemona is crying incessantly. Which is very annoying as am trying to watch television but Mum has banished me from the room as she can't hear Bill Oddy above the wailing. Will feed her again.

9 p.m.
And again.

10 p.m.
And again. How can she still be hungry? She is worse than the dog.

2 a.m.
Aagh. Desdemona still crying. Have fed her and changed her but she will not shut up. Have locked her in shed. Ms Hopwood-White will never know.

. . . .

Tuesday 20
Shrove Tuesday (i.e. Pancake Day)
Ms Hopwood White says I have killed Desdemona with neglect. I said she was malfunctioning and overdemanding

73

food. Ms Hopwood-White said, *au contraire*, I had overfed her and given her chronic colic. Did not tell her about shed. She has reset her and says I can have another go. In stark contrast the Kylies have highly contented fake babies (Dolshay and Jordan-Jade). It is because they have the unfair advantage of getting to practise on all the many mini O'Gradys.

4 p.m.
Mum is not allowing Desdemona back into the house. Apparently Marjory came over at breakfast convinced that murderous urban foxes were digging a lair in the shed last night. Anyway it does not matter. I have had a genius idea. Am going to get Treena to look after Desdemona. She has to get up for Jesus anyway so one more baby will be no bother at all.

6 p.m.
Desdemona dead again (fatal blow to head). Treena killed her within an hour. This does not bode well for Jesus's future. Have reset her and brought her home. Will just have to try harder not to overfeed this time. Mum says one bout of colic and she is a goner.

10 p.m.
Desdemona fed and changed. All is quiet. Have definitely got hang of it all.

Wednesday 21

Ash Wednesday

7 a.m.

Have had excellent peaceful night and Desdemona slept all the way through, which is more than I can say for the dog who was making a racket in the living room at 4 a.m. Maybe I will become a child-rearing genius like that Gina Ford person. I will patent my method and make a fortune.

7.15 a.m.

Oh God. Dog has killed Desdemona. She is not just dead, but viciously hacked in several pieces. And one arm is missing, presumed eaten. Am going to fail Citizenship. And possibly be banned from ever having children (by Mum, not school, she has far more jurisdiction in these matters). Maybe will leave remains at home and say she is doing so well would like to keep her until end of week. Yes, will do that. And in meantime can purchase talking Tiny Tears as replacement.

6 p.m.

Ms Hopwood-White agreed that I can keep Desdemona until Friday. She says she is glad I am taking the challenge so seriously and I am an inspiration to the rest of the class (bulk of babies dead, including Scarlet's fake son Frankenstein who got killed when she tried to give him a gothic baptism in a bath of blood (red food colouring)).

75

Only survivor is Jordan-Jade. Fat Kylie is now thinking of becoming a nursery nurse.

Band practice was very exciting. The new sound is a definite improvement. Justin is sexier than ever in his ripped shirt and beads. And Sad Ed has learned 'Baa Baa Black Sheep' and the theme tune to *EastEnders* in the space of three days. He says he will have 'Light My Fire' off by heart by the gig. Also we have a new name. We are The Back Doors in homage to the mighty Jim.

10 p.m.
Oops. Have to book gig. Will do so after school tomorrow.

Thursday 22
Hurrah. Valentine's Day card has arrived. Admittedly it is eight days late and is novelty rude one with unrepeatable joke inside, as opposed to previously imagined portrait of star-crossed lovers. But is a card none the less and further proof of Justin's undying love for me. Plus, it escaped Mum's rigorous taste checks (it would have failed for sure due to inclusion of word pussy, possibly not in a cat context). She is not having a sudden progressive streak. She is preoccupied due to her and Dad having a Bupa medical check today. Dad looks nervous. He thinks they may find out he is riddled with life-threatening conditions. In contrast Mum is not scared. She welcomes exams of any kind and says she will pass with flying colours.

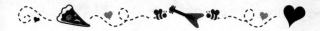

Scarlet is outraged though. She says private healthcare is the province of the 'chattering classes' (which is rich as Suzy excels at chattering), is anti-Labour and a blow to left-wing radicalism everywhere. She says it is creating a two-tier health service where the rich can pay to have their cholesterol-clogged arteries swooshed out or whatever it is they do and the poor have to wait on trolleys in their own wee. I said Dad got it free at work and that she was being un-Labour by highlighting trolleys, waiting lists, and dirty hospitals. She went white. She has never been accused of being un-Labour before and had to immediately reconnect with her left-wing roots by reading *Das Capital* under the table in maths.

5 p.m.
Mum and Dad are back from their Bupa check and, in a shock move, have both been given stern cholesterol warnings. Mum is livid. She is blaming Granny Clegg for feeding her Fray Bentos and beef dripping in her formative years. Dad on the other hand is jubilant that he is not alone in his battle against the bulge. But his happiness was short-lived because Mum imposed an immediate embargo on all dairy products and has driven to Waitrose on an emergency skimmed soya milk and Benecol mission.

Friday 23
Had skimmed soya milk on my Shreddies at breakfast. It

is vile and tastes of liquid cardboard. Threw it away and tried Marmite and Benecol on toast. Also unsatisfactory. Worse, Mum wants to invite Justin for tea after work on Saturday. He is going to chuck me for sure if she makes him eat her new cholesterol-free fayre.

And have failed to purchase talking Tiny Tears to replace Desdemona so James has glued the original back with some Copydex. Am worried Ms Hopwood-White might spot teeth marks and constant tinny whirring noise. Also doll is still one arm down. It is lodged somewhere inside dog's vast intestinal system, along with the Duplo and two AA batteries.

4 p.m.

Ms Hopwood-White says she has never seen such an abused child and if this was a real situation I would be on my way to prison. I said if it was real, I would not have left Desdemona in the fridge for the night (soundproofed), from whence the dog snatched her while it was looking for cold ham. She said I should hope not, and gave me a bill for £100 to replace the baby. That is a lot of money for a doll. Treena would sell Jesus for that sort of money.

Also, asked Justin to 'meet the parents'. He says is there any way of not coming. I said not really, or he was risking a permanent ban. He is worried my dad will be like Robert de Niro and menace him with his overprotective ways. It is not Dad he should be worried about. He will just nod at appropriate moments and go

78

back to watching golf. It is Mum who will be using CIA-like tactics to catch him out.

5 p.m.
Mum says the Desdemona bill is the last straw. She is ringing Grandpa tomorrow to collect the dog. I said she was condemning it to a life of misery on Harvey Road, and it may get chewed to death by Fat Kylie's poodle Tupac or forced to take part in an illegal dog baiting ring, but Mum said it should have thought of that before. James said she had a heart of stone but then she threatened to exile Michaelangelo and Donatello as well so he went upstairs to do anti-Shredder training with the frogs.

. . . .

Saturday 24
Am very nervous about Meet the Parents-style high tea. Have begged Mum to supply éclairs and Duchy chocolate things but she says she cannot trust Dad to stay away from cholesterol-laden goods and is going to bake a no-fat courgette cake, as detailed in *Good Housekeeping*. James is helping her. He is in charge of weights and measures, as he is meticulous in these areas. But maybe it will not be disastrous. Maybe he will think they are slightly bohemian and new-wave and will love me even more.

7 p.m.
Meet the Parents tea was disastrous. Courgette cake was

like eating moist savoury flannels. 'Entertainment' was supplied by James who decided to seize the moment to sing the books of the Bible song. Plus Mum wore support tights which are decidedly unbohemian. Worse, Justin cracked after only ten minutes of Paxmanesque grilling and confessed to once passively inhaling the smoke from a joint at which point Mum's lips went so thin they disappeared and I could tell she was planning to rework her anti-drugs lecture. It is lucky he did not confess that said joint actually belonged to Suzy or I would be banned from Scarlet's for ever more. In the end Dad offered to give him a lift home. I think he was glad to escape the fraught fat-free atmosphere as well.

On the plus side, the dog has gone. So I can abandon Resolution 6 to train it. The house is now a hair-free and pest-free zone. Although the frogs are still vile. And they are showing no signs of being magic Ninja frogs either. They just float aimlessly around their tank eating mince.

Sunday 25

Went to band practice. Justin still slightly dazed from yesterday's interrogation. I said he will get used to it. He said, 'Yeah, maybe.' Not sure what that means. The Back Doors sounded quite good though. God, still have not booked gig. Am crap manager. Will do it in morning behind bike sheds (i.e. smokers' and illegal mobile phoners' corner).

Monday 26

Oh my God. Scarlet says she is thinking of chucking Trevor. Apparently he is not happy about her move towards EMO (as predicted by me, Rachel Riley) and is questioning her commitment to the dark side. It is the new skinny jeans and the non-regulation Converse (i.e. they are pink as opposed to goth-approved black). Scarlet says he is trying to control her identity, which is the first sign of domestic abuse. I said Trevor didn't look much like a wife beater but she says it is the quiet ones you have to watch out for. And the weedy bat-like ones apparently. She is going to give it a week to see if his attitude improves. Am in shock. It is like Angelina threatening to chuck Brad. If Brad wore white make-up and a floor-length leather coat.

Tuesday 27

Mum has just reminded us it is Dad's birthday tomorrow. Have to get card and present after school. Will get Justin to come with me. He will know what men like. James has already purchased his gift. It is a giant staple gun.

5 p.m.

Have bought Dad the *Best of Countdown* on DVD. Justin says all old men like Carol Vorderman, it is genetic. It is true. She is Dad's favourite intellectual TV presenter.

Wednesday 28

Dad's birthday

Gave Dad his *Countdown* DVD. He and James were both delighted (James is not interested in Carol, it is Des Lynam he likes). Mum failed to make 'oh what a nice idea' comments which accompanied opening of giant stapler though. She is obviously still reeling from the Edie/Sex Beast thing and worried intellectual Carol may fan the flames of desire with her short leather skirts and conundrum-solving skills.

Also school has gone naked *Harry Potter* mad. Even Ms Hopwood-White is drooling over the photos of Daniel Radcliffe's pubic bone. I do not see what the fuss is about. He looks the same as before except without the glasses and cloak i.e. he is a naked nerd, instead of a speccy nerd.

5 p.m.

Dad's stapler has been quarantined. James has stapled all his socks to the wall. He says it is modern art but Mum does not agree.

march

BALACLAVA

MENTIL

Thursday 1

St David's Day (Wales)

Had final band practice before tomorrow's debut gig and had awful realization that have utterly failed to book venue. Asked Justin if he thought maybe we should delay a bit, given our fledgling new sound, but he said it is too late, the posters are up in the common room and he has already sold seven tickets. Am too ashamed to admit truth to Justin so am just going to turn up and hope for the best. It is bound to be unlocked as the Brownies will have been in there for toadstool jumping etc. after school.

. . . .

Friday 2

6 p.m.

Thank God. Brownies were still in there doing semaphore when we arrived. Roadies (i.e. me and three Year Sevens who are trying to gain access to the Alternative Music Club table) have set up equipment and sound check is now under way. It is very exciting as the hordes will be arriving in less than two hours.

7.30 p.m.

No sign of hordes as yet. So far audience is Justin's mum and dad, Stan's mum and dad, the surprisingly tall Dwarf family, the roadies and Tuesday (Sad Ed's parents do not believe in music unless it is Welsh and religious i.e. Aled Jones). Am sure it will be busy by the time The Back

85

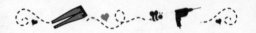

Doors take the stage, i.e. in thirty minutes, and the gig will be legendary, like the Beatles at the Cavern Club, or Blind Mice at Hadstock Village Hall.

10 p.m.
The gig was legendary, but not in a good way. The only hordes to arrive were the ATC who had been out practising machete skills on the fields behind the recycling centre (aka the dump) and were expecting a talk on semi-automatic weaponry. Tried to broker peaceful deal whereby they could look at pictures of guns in the car park while the gig finished but forgot that ATC membership includes Mark Lambert, Mr Whippy, and several O'Gradys. Plus at crucial moment, Justin cued the band in for their version of 'People are Strange', which the ATC took as deliberate provocation and seized their chance to attack. Scarlet showed up with Jack and Trevor just as Dean the Dwarf got hurled into the disabled toilet. Jack just said 'Great gig, Riley,' and walked out again. On the plus side, Scarlet got caught in the crossfire and Trevor nursed her tenderly under his giant bat cloak so he is in her good books for the moment. I, on the other hand, have been sacked. Justin says it is a purely business decision and is nothing to do with our personal relationship. But that is what Jennifer Garner said to Vaughn when she wrote him out of *Alias* and then two weeks later she chucked him for cheese king Ben Affleck. It is a bad sign. Plus breasts still barely discernible. I have no chance.

Saturday 3

Work. Justin seemed distinctly distracted during our lunchtime meat bin snogging. I asked if he had found a new band manager yet and he said he had someone in mind. Oh God. What if it is Sophie Microwave Muffins? Her dad can get free cake mix and logo T-shirts after all. What can I offer? Health-giving snacks and James's fabric paints. There is no contest. I have to do something excellent and Simon Cowell-like to win back his trust or risk losing him to an older woman. With 34C breasts.

Sunday 4

A strange man keeps walking past the house. He is wearing a balaclava, several tattoos, and a distinctly menacing look. James has catalogued him in Mum's ASBO notebook (Mum was otherwise engaged with Jesus and her flashcards—we are baby- and pet-sitting while Grandpa and Treena enjoy some quality time together, i.e. having sex and watching Sky). I pointed out that you couldn't ASBO someone for walking but James said he has done it twenty-seven times, which constitutes persistent lurking and/or potential obsessive compulsive disorder. Tried to get the dog to go out and scare him away but he was too busy watching Noel Edmonds.

Monday 5

The menacing man was back again after school. He sat on

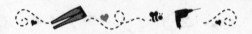

Thin Kylie's wall pretending to read *Vogue*. Maybe he is a gay burglar casing us for weaknesses in our security arrangements. He will be sorely disappointed. Mum has fitted two different kinds of window lock and has a sawn off hoe by the back door for bludgeoning miscreants. Plus Marjory has eyes like a hawk. She once spotted Sad Ed performing an illegal wheelie two roads away.

· ·

Tuesday 6

No menacing burglar today. It is highly disappointing. I was quite enjoying having a potential madman lurking about. It makes a change from watching Terry and Cherie picking fag ends up from the lawn in their woefully revealing dressing gowns.

School utterly boring. Except for Rural Studies and that was only because we got to round up goats. It was not for GCSE, it was because Mark Lambert and Davey MacDonald had sneaked them out at lunch for an illegal goat race and the goats, unsurprisingly, had not stuck to the track but had veered off towards the gates and their ultimate freedom.

· ·

Wednesday 7

Hurrah, menacing man back this afternoon. Reading *New Woman* this time. He is surprisingly eclectic in his reading tastes for a burglar.

Also, Mum has found evidence of illicit chocolate

eating on Dad's work clothes. She says there is Twix caramel congealed in his jacket pocket. Dad is denying it but Mum says there is no mistaking its claggy consistency. She is threatening to perform random swoops at Wainwright and Hogg.

. . . .

Thursday 8

I have found my Golden Ticket back to music impresarioness (not entirely sure that is a word but cannot think of right one), and, more importantly, to Justin's heart. The *Walden Chronicle* has declared a Battle of the Bands! It says:

> Are you the next Antarctic Monkeys?

(Answer—possibly, although this band is clearly made up duc to ace reporter Glen Davies's utter lack of musical knowledge.)

> Does your drummer have more rhythm than Phil Collins?

(Answer—no, but he is marginally less freaky looking despite being a dwarf.)

> Then the Walden Chronicle needs you! WHERE?—Lord Butler Leisure Centre, Jockey Wilson Suite

(i.e. not Wembley but a step up from the ATC hut.)

> WHEN—Saturday 28 April.
> Be there or be square!

Best of all, one of the judges is newspaper editor (and wife of owner) Deirdre Roberts, my former work experience supervisor. So I have connections to the judges and may be able to sway their vital decision. Hurrah! Obviously I will not use underhand methods to purchase success (as have no means of doing so even if wanted to, am still paying off £100 doll bill with Nuts In May wages) but will merely point out the Back Doors' potential for world domination. Now just have to persuade Justin to enter, persuade him to take me back as manager, and persuade Deirdre to meet for musical discussions.

. . . .

Friday 9

9 a.m.
Tackled Justin about the Battle of the Bands and my imminent reinstatement as manager outside Mr Patel's before school. He said he is not entering 'amateur hour' because the competition is likely to be a bunch of ten year olds on recorders (possibly true—James is at this very moment trying to persuade Reverend Begley to let him form a chime bar duo with Mad Harry).

10.20 a.m.

The Back Doors are in the Battle of the Bands after all. It is because the Jack Stone Five have already posted their entry form and £5 fee to Deirdre. Justin says there is no way he is letting that bandwagon-jumping Brit Pop pretty boy steal his thunder. He says rock will rule, and the Back Doors will conquer Saffron Walden, and then, who knows? Sad Ed said Harlow. But I think it was meant to be rhetorical because Justin rolled his eyes and went off to practise catching peanuts in his mouth (he is second best in the lower sixth, after Whitey Wilson (albino, but with unfair advantage of oversize mouth)).

Also, he says he will be making a management announcement at band practice tomorrow. This does not bode well. What if it is Sophie Microwave Muffins? She might forbid him to have a girlfriend in case it interferes with his music. And then he will be at her total mercy.

. . . .

Saturday 10

Could not concentrate on my work (i.e. sweeping up rogue lentils) due to Sophie Microwave Muffins management turmoil. Had to abandon lunch in favour of emergency mission to the Waitrose trolley park to discuss crisis with Sad Ed. He said I am worrying about nothing. There is no way Justin would let Sophie manage the band as she has no understanding of rock, i.e. she went to see Girls Aloud on tour. He said the manager

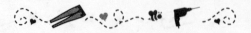

will be someone who has cavernous musical knowledge and an appreciation of the technical side of band management. Which is totally me! I am excellent at plugging in amps.

. . . .

Sunday 11

The new manager is not Sophie. Or me. It is Sad Ed! He is a total traitor and has been pestering Justin for weeks apparently. I demanded an immediate vote. But Justin said I should not put myself through the inevitable humiliation. I said I was not afraid of the opinion of the people i.e. the band. So we had a vote. I lost by two to one. (Only The Dwarf stood by me in my hour of need.) I pointed out Sad Ed's poor track record on organizing large-scale events (his tenth birthday party had an attendance of three—me, him, and Scarlet) but Justin said it is just better to keep these things in the band. I said it was jobs for the boys but Justin said there are plenty of jobs for the girls, like chief groupie. Asked what this involved. Basically I have to snog Justin. Which I do already. But if he is busy, he can pass me on to another band member. I said this was utterly anti-feminist but he said *au contraire*, it is utterly liberating and Kate Mossish. So said yes. Hope do not have to snog The Dwarf though. He will have to stand on a box. Or I would have to kneel. Which is just weird.

. . . .

Monday 12

Commonwealth Day

Asked Scarlet if she wanted to be second groupie for the Back Doors. She said she would rather chew tinfoil than prostitute herself to a bunch of semi-talented schoolboys, especially as one of them is Sad Ed. I said it was utterly not prostitution but very Kate Mossish. But she said Kate Moss does not let other members of Babyshambles grope her when Pete Doherty is busy in a drug-induced stupor. Anyway, she has a better idea. We are going to form a girl band and beat the boys at their own game! Admittedly, there are only two of us, and we can play no instruments at all other than the recorder, but, even so, it is an excellent plan. Scarlet says we will be like Janis Joplin and Joni Mitchell. I agreed, even though have no idea who these people are. She is bound to be right—she has the advantage of Suzy's vast musical (and sexual) knowledge. Scarlet is going to learn the guitar in record time and I am going to be chief lyricist i.e. write some songs, as I am potentially excellent poet type. We already have a name—it is Velvet Elvis. Am glad I did not waste it on Justin now! Cannot wait to tell him about our band. Now we are totally like Kurt and Courtney as we are both musical geniuses.

5 p.m.

Justin not quite as embracing of my musical career as had hoped. In fact, he begged me not to go on stage and sing.

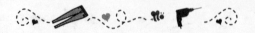

He says he is just worried I will not be able to handle the cut-throat world that is the music business. But it is probably fear that I will outshine him musically. Anyway, have resigned as first groupie and said we must keep our snogging on a strictly non-business arrangement.

6 p.m.
But what if he gives job to someone else, i.e. Miss Nipples Pervert Jacobs? Will ring him immediately and demand reinstatement.

6.15 p.m.
Am groupie and girl band member. That way I am not closing off any options, should one career falter.

. . . .

Tuesday 13
Treena rang. Jesus has taken his first steps. Treena has been luring him using a trail of Cheetos. Asked if he could walk on water (as a joke) but Treena obviously has not read the Bible, as she said she didn't know and would try immediately. Oh God. Hope she is not going to get him to stride across the Slade. He will drown in the trolley-infested waters, or get bitten by a rat.

5 p.m.
Jesus cannot walk on water. He sank to bottom of bath, injuring Grandpa Riley who was submerged in Radox at

time. Both are now being revived with hot towels and Wagon Wheels.

* *

Wednesday 14

James has offered to be in the band. It is because Reverend Begley has refused him and Mad Harry permission to form a chime bar duo. (I do not blame him. The chime bars would never be the same again.) I have also said no, on the grounds that he is a boy and we are strictly a girl band. Plus he can only play crap instruments (i.e. chime bars and triangle).

* *

Thursday 15

Wrote a song during rural studies. (Was supposed to be learning about yoghurt-making but when will I need that skill? That is what Waitrose is for.) It is called 'Bad Bat Boy and the Skinny Jeans' and is all about Trevor and Scarlet and their relationship issues. It is essential to take inspiration from real life. Although have not used actual names so Trevor will never know it is about him.

I have two verses and a chorus so far:

Bad Bat Boy and the Skinny Jeans
Your eyes are red, (contact lenses—not blood),
Your clothes are black,

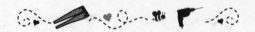

You've got a pair of wings, (this is true—they are
black net ones, made by his mum)
You wear a floor-length leather coat,
And twenty-seven rings.

But you don't love my skinny jeans,
Yeah, you don't love my skinny jeans,
Yeah, you don't love my skinny jeans,
So you just don't love me.

Your hair is long with purple streaks,
You have a cage of rats,
But secretly you really wish,
That it was legal to keep bats.

Chorus etc.

Scarlet says it is excellent. She is going to write some
music in Citizenship then we are going to jam at hers on
Saturday.

. . . .

Friday 16

James's pedantry has reached new levels. He has written
to Mr Patel to complain about the bubble gum machine
outside, which claims its contents 'taste like your
favourite fruit'. Apparently Keanu got some and it did not
taste like his favourite fruit at all (i.e. banana). James has

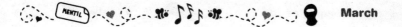

taken on his cause. I admire the way he is fighting with his intellect, rather than his fists. Maybe he will inspire Keanu to give up his life of violence.

. . . .

Saturday 17
St Patrick's Day

Hurrah. Am going over to Scarlet's after work for band practice. Told Justin during lunch (past sell-by sausage rolls). He said he hoped I was not going to put my music career before my love life. I said on the contrary I would stop by for a snog after *Casualty*.

9 p.m.

Band practice was promising. Scarlet is better at guitar than Sad Ed already. Suzy says she has inherited her talents from her. (She did the background clapping and swaying in a David Bowie video once.) Jack came to watch us do 'Bad Bat Boy and the Skinny Jeans' (it is our only song so we did it eleven times). He said, 'Not bad, Riley. Maybe we could work on one for the Jack Stone Five.' I said no chance, it would be like Gary Barlow writing a song for Westlife. He said, 'Whatever', and went back to his blackened room to philosophize. Or possibly read *Nuts* magazine. (Justin's current favourite. He says it is not the semi-naked women he likes, it is the book reviews. Which is possibly true. Loads of famous writer types have been published in *Playboy* after all.)

97

Went round Justin's after *Casualty* for prearranged snog. He asked how it had gone. I said excellently and that even Jack was impressed. Then Justin got all annoyed and said he had to go and practise moody rock looks in the mirror. He is obviously still funny about Jack after the wardrobe snog confusion. He has nothing to fear. I do not love Jack. Although it is quite nice that he is jealous. It is because I am utterly vintage and lovely.

10 p.m.
Or maybe it is Jack that he is sad about. Maybe it is like *Brokeback Mountain* and actually he wishes it was like before when they hung out together and played guitar and did man things. Ooh. And I am like the glamorous rodeo girl i.e. American beauty Anne Hathaway.

10.15 p.m.
Or maybe I am dowdy one with too many babies who gets all shouty and marries the grocer.

10.30 p.m.
Think am getting carried away with gay boyfriend thing. There is no way Justin is homosexual. He does not like *Will and Grace* for a start.

. . . .

Sunday 18
Mothering Sunday (i.e. Mother's Day)

98

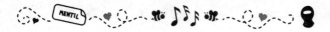

8 a.m.
James and I are up and are going to make Mum breakfast in bed. We are doing scrambled eggs and bacon.

8.30 a.m.
Breakfast in bed cancelled due to Mum refusing to stay in bed during breakfast making. Apparently the fear of egg spillage (and potential cholesterol ingestion) was giving her hives and so Dad sent her down to put her mind at rest. Made relatively risk-free Marmite on toast instead.

10 a.m.
Menacing man is back. He is watching Dad wash the car from behind *Grazia*. Mum has called 999 but Tracey Hughes's mum who answers the phones got quite annoyed with her and said she could be prosecuted for wasting police time. So she said, 'Why, what are they doing that is so important, walking the Alsatians round Waitrose car park?' Obviously this is exactly what they were doing, as she quickly agreed to send a patrol car round to investigate. Mum said it had better be sharpish in case the menacing man is armed, or bipolar, or both, and attacks. She has made Dad come back in as a safety precaution.

11 a.m.
No sign of patrol car. Menacing man still looking at pictures of Kerry Katona's cellulite.

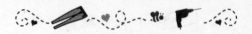
12 noon
No patrol car.

1 p.m.
Menacing man finishes *Grazia* and moves on. Possibly to purchase *Heat*.

3 p.m.
Patrol car arrives. Mum goes out to read riot act to PC Doone. He apologizes but they had a last-minute call out to a brawl in Tesco's condiments aisle. It is bound to be an O'Grady. Or possibly several. Mum said it will be on his head when the menacing man goes bonkers with a Colt 45 (Mum only knows guns from Westerns due to Grandpa Clegg's John Wayne fascination) and showers shoppers with bullets. Then I distinctly heard PC Doone mutter that Mum is a paranoid fantasist (possibly true), but luckily, the frogs chose that moment to get stuck in a soggy Smarties tube (James was trying to acclimatize them to the sewer) and Mum had to go upstairs to release them (liquid soap and a good poke with a toothbrush).

. . . .

Monday 19

Granny Clegg rang to report that her hip of doom had been right all along. According to Maureen Penrice in Spar, Denzil, as in Denzil's Crazy Car Warehouse in Camborne, choked to death on a sherbet lemon at the

weekend. Mum pointed out the several-week gap between the hip pains and ensuing death but Granny Clegg says the fateful sherbet lemons were purchased from Redruth Woolies pick 'n' mix the very day her hip had started playing up. Then Mum got annoyed with the whole magic hip thing and told her she should call up the Home Office as her hip could play a vital role in murder prevention. But now she is in a panic as Granny Clegg does not understand sarcasm and is bound to actually do it.

Tuesday 20

Granny Clegg has rung again. Apparently Devon and Cornwall Constabulary are strangely uninterested in her potential crime-solving hip. She says they are mad and that her hip could be their very own Miss Marple. She is thinking of offering its services to the Russians instead, just to spite them. (The Cleggs think we are still locked in cold war conflict with the Communists. They also think the iron curtain is an actual iron curtain. Dad asked them where it was once. Grandpa Clegg said somewhere in Poland.)

Wednesday 21

The hip of doom is hurting again. Granny Clegg has phoned the police but they have told her to call Dr

Kimber or rub it with Deep Heat. Mum is with the police but Granny says we will all be sorry when one of us keels over or is shot by terrorists. Mum said she is willing to take her chances.

. . . .

Thursday 22

Mum has rung Granny Clegg to see how the hip of doom is this morning and if it has foretold any more deaths in the night. Granny Clegg says it is much better but that she is still investigating yesterday's premonition (i.e. popping over to see Maureen in the Spar every half hour to check gossip on local illnesses and deaths).

. . . .

Friday 23

It is James's birthday tomorrow. He says it is his coming of age. It is not. He will be ten, which is admittedly double figures, but is not sixteen, which is what I will be in less than five months' time. Hurrah! Have bought James a label maker from WHSmith. He is not having a proper party after last year's near-death experience at the Lord Butler Leisure Centre. He is having three friends to tea i.e. Mad Harry, Maggot, and Keanu. Mum is not happy about Keanu but James insists. It is because he will get demoted gang-wise if Keanu is not permitted entry. Mum is going to hide all the valuables in her combination lock suitcase.

. . . .

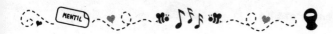

Saturday 24

James says it is his best birthday present haul yet. As well as the label maker, he got a book about frogs (Mum and Dad), a packet of frog mince (the dog), a talking Nicola out of Girls Aloud (Grandpa and Treena), and a power drill (Granny and Grandpa Clegg—it cost £5.99 from Trago Mills. They had left the label on as usual.) Mum says he is only allowed to use the drill, and talking Nicola, under adult supervision. She means herself. Dad is not classed as an adult in her book.

5.30 p.m.

Got home from hard day at work to find Mum scraping misspelt labels off all the furniture and James banished to his bedroom. Apparently Keanu took control of the label machine and has labelled everything in the house, including the dog. But he cannot spell and so it says 'GOD' on its forehead. Which could not be further from the truth. Also the table says 'TAYBEL', the bathroom says 'TOYLIT' and Dad has one on his back that says 'MENTIL'.

Thank God I am going round Justin's tomorrow. He and Sad Ed are lucky to be only children. They have never known what it is to suffer the horror of sibling rivalry. Or sibling idiocy.

Sunday 25

Summer Time begins (i.e. clocks go annoyingly forward)

Went round to Justin's at three as arranged but he was still in bed due to non-changing of clocks in Statham household. I am definitely going to write to Tony Blair to complain. It is utterly inconvenient, as well as playing havoc with the video, which recorded half an episode of *Vicar of Dibley* instead of Amy Winehouse live in concert last night. Did some groupie work at band practice, i.e. snogged Justin heavily after triumphant guitar solo.

Also, it turns out Justin is not an only child. He has a twenty-one-year-old stepsister called Kelly who is a runner at GMTV. She gets to make tea for breakfast beauty Kate Garraway. It is the height of glamour. Am going to get to know her at first opportunity so she can get me a job one day. I am practically family so she cannot refuse me.

* * *

Monday 26

There is a suspicious pile of dog poo on our drive. It is definitely not the dog as he is over a mile away pooing happily on the Whiteshot Estate. Mum has cleared it up using industrial rubber gloves and James's Bob the Builder spade (now quarantined). She is thinking of reviving her anti-dog-poo campaign in the *Walden Chronicle*. I hope not. It did not do my reputation at school any good amongst the dog-owning mafia. She says she has her suspicions anyway. They lie with Fiddy, Thin

Kylie's annoying yapping thing, also former lover of dog, and mother to his equally mental offspring Bruce (now resident at Granny Clegg's).

5 p.m.
I hope it is dog poo and not possibly menacing man poo. He was back again after school today, reading *Elle Decoration*. Although maybe he is just admiring our double glazing and creosote fence.

Tuesday 27

There is more dog poo this morning. Mum took it straight over to Thin Kylie's on the smelly Bob spade. But Cherie is denying everything. She says it is too big to be one of Fiddy's, hers are more like chipolatas and our suspicious poo is like a saveloy. Which is true. Mum is going to ring the council later to demand an anti-dog-poo sign.

4 p.m.
The council say they cannot put up an anti-dog-poo sign as their pooing dog stencil is broken. She asked what other animals they had. They said cows or turkeys (there is a turkey farm on the Haverhill road and the turkeys are notoriously cunning at escaping and wandering aimlessly around the B1057). Mum hung up. She does not want a pooing farm animal picture up outside the house. She

says it may confuse the perpetrator into thinking domestic dog poo is acceptable.

. . . .

Wednesday 28

Poo on drive again. Although this time it was wrapped in a peach-scented nappy bag. Mum now thinks it might be the milkman. She says he has been waging a vendetta against us since her dairy-free stance. She has already accused him of overjangling his bottles at 6 a.m. She is going to intercept him tomorrow morning.

. . . .

Thursday 29

Mum was up at five to intercept the milkman but was thwarted by total absence of poo. She tackled him anyway but he says he is more of a cat person. Then he tried to get her to sign up for yoghurts so she came back in before he could befuddle her with his marketing pitch. He has no chance, no one has ever befuddled her before, not even the Kleeneze man, and he once got Marjory to buy a gross of 'Christmas'-scented plug-in air fresheners. (He was also the recipient of one of James's pedant letters on the grounds that Christmas has no official smell.)

. . . .

Friday 30

Last day of school. It is also the last day that Emily Reeve

106

has to wear school uniform. It is because her bump cannot fit under the regulation kilt any more so Mr Wilmott has given her permission to wear concealing smocks etc. She has still not confessed to me who the father is. I have tried to reach out across the nylon carpet to offer my hand of friendship but she will not shake it. It is her loss. I would be an excellent confidante. I am utterly good at keeping secrets. I lasted three days when Scarlet told me she fancied the Incredible Hulk (green version, not Bruce thingy) before I told Sad Ed.

Also, the poo is back. Mum says it is the final straw. She is going to stay up all night to catch the culprit in the act. I said she would never manage it but she says she has stocked up on Nescafé and has the new Alan Titchmarsh novel to plough through.

Saturday 31

Oh my God. The dog is the phantom poo menace after all! Mum caught Grandpa letting him do it behind the Passat at midnight. She hauled him inside for interrogation (Grandpa, not the dog. The dog does not respond to questioning of any sort.) and he caved under pressure and admitted it was him all along. He said he was just taking the dog for a long walk and it always seemed to get the urge when it got to our house. So Mum demanded to know why he was going on long walks late at night and Grandpa confessed it is to avoid Treena and her sexual

demands (That is what the ginseng was for after all!) He says he is too old to cope with her nightly pawings and he fears his heart might give way. Mum said what about Wednesday night (the mysterious no-poo night). He said *Dirty Dancing* was on ITV2 so Treena was glued to Patrick Swayze and he could rest in bed in peace. Mum is outraged. She has told him that the dog is to poo on its own doorstep from now on or she will be forced to take sanctions. (I wonder what these would be?) Then Grandpa got all teary and said he was seventy-five tomorrow and it was near the end for him and all he seemed to get was shouted at by women these days. So Mum felt sorry for him and made him a cup of Bovril and gave the dog a custard cream. But not that sorry because she refused to let him sleep on the sofa and sent him back to sex-crazed Treena at 2 a.m.

Bought something called Goat Weed off Mr Goldstein at work. Rosamund says it is an ancient libido-restoring herb. Am going to give it to Grandpa at his birthday party tomorrow, along with Suzy's phone number.

Sunday 1
Palm Sunday
8 a.m.
Am up and going to Scarlet's imminently. It is because Glastonbury tickets go on sale at 9 a.m. and we need to be poised with the interwebnet and Suzy's credit card (she has agreed to fund me and Sad Ed and we are going to pay her back on a twenty-five-year interest-free loan plan). Am utterly excited. Although getting a ticket is a minor hurdle compared to actually persuading Mum to let me go. Justin is going to do his at home. He does not need Suzy's funding. His dad owns a chain of bathroom shops.

11 a.m.
Oh my God! Have got a ticket for Glastonbury! Hurrah. Hurrah. Am totally vintage and Sienna-like. Will get to wear patterned wellies and trilby hat whilst drinking hot cider and listening to Shirley Bassey (in ironic manner of course). Scarlet says it is a total rite of passage and I am now in a very exclusive club. Along with 125,000 other chosen few. Which sadly does not include Sad Ed. He has been turned down! Suzy says it is not personal, it is a lottery. She is wrong. It is bound to be because he is not edgy-looking enough. Also, he applied under his real name of Edward Arthur Thomas, whilst I am Ray Riley! Scarlet and I are planning our wardrobe already. We are going to share a tent. She will be in one compartment

111

with Trevor and me and Justin will be in the storage bit. She says their sex noises will not keep us awake as they will be drowned out by repetitive drumming, druid chanting, and drug-induced vomiting on the tent pegs. It sounds excellent. But will not tell Mum yet. Need to formulate excellent plan and wear her down gently.

2 p.m.
Justin has not got a ticket for Glastonbury. He says he does not care as it is overcommercial and frequented only by wannabes, liggers, and Radio One DJs. Hurrah. It sounds excellent. Although it is sad that he is not coming, obviously.

4 p.m.
Grandpa and Treena came over with Jesus and the dog for celebratory diamond jubilee birthday party lunch. Grandpa Riley delighted with Suzy's phone number. Not so delighted with goat weed. He says there is no way he is consuming urine again. Asked him why he had drunk urine in first place. He said it was during World War Two when he was marooned in a Navy frigate off the coast of Africa. Mum reminded him yet again that he was only seven when World War Two started and that the Navy had turned him down for entry three times on height, eyesight, and intelligence grounds. So he said it must have been on holiday then. His memory is definitely going. Mum says it is just selective, like his hearing i.e.

112

he pretends to be deaf when it suits him, which is often i.e. whenever anyone tells him to do something he doesn't want to do, like stop eating all the Twiglets, or take the dog for a walk. But Grandpa says it is a sure sign he is on his way out. He is not. He is just fishing for compliments.

Monday 2

Hurrah, it is the holidays. Although they will sadly not be spent in usual manner i.e. watching *Friends* repeats on sofa with dog and James, as am now full-time employee of Nuts In May. Mr Goldstein phoned at eight this morning. Rosamund has decided to go on an emergency yogic retreat to restore her chakra and he cannot cope alone due to high shelves and hunchback. Anyway, it is excellent as will practically be able to pay Suzy back her Glastonbury money by the end of the week.

6 p.m.

Hurrah. Have been promoted to till in absence of Rosamund. It is excellent fun. Although actually quite tricky as till is vicious and has trapped fingers several times. Have acquired new-found admiration for Waitrose cashiers. Which is very left-wing and pro-working class. May even join union.

Tuesday 3

6 p.m.

Till down £13.73. Mr Goldstein has docked it out of my wages. Also have plasters on two fingers due to till injury. May ask to go back to stocking muesli.

Also, Dad has had a funny phone call at work. Someone called Mr Jones rang on pretext of querying a paperclip invoice and then just breathed heavily into receiver. This happened three times. Dad says he is probably just someone from Walton and Walton, as they are all 'hilarious' practical jokers. Mum says he should report them immediately as practical jokes are a menace and can easily get out of hand. This is after the time Grandpa Riley taught James to stretch clingfilm over the toilet seat and dog got entangled and stopped breathing for several seconds—it was trying to drink out of toilet bowl.

. . . .

Wednesday 4

6 p.m.

Am sick of full-time work. Do not know how anyone copes with it. It is will-sapping, and finger-maiming stuff. Have bruises where hand actually got trapped in the pound coin drawer and Mr Goldstein had to free me with a stick of coltsfoot rock. No wonder Rosamund needs to restore her chakra. The only consolation is that Justin is on full-time mincing duty too so I get to watch his muscly arms ramming bits of cow into the grinder all day. It is a

114

thing of beauty.

Also, Dad has had another four heavy breathing phone calls. He has taken tomorrow off in a bid to throw the perpetrator off-track.

. . . .

Thursday 5

Asked Mr Goldstein where exactly in India Rosamund had gone to. He said she is not in India, she is in a barn in Steeple Bumpstead with a man called Guru Derek.

Also, telephone menace has tracked Dad down at Summerdale Road. There has been a funny phone call at home. James answered in his fake Dad voice (freakishly accurate) and then just got an earful of panting. I said it might be the dog as it has been known to knock phone off hook at Grandpa's and then lick it madly but James says the dog has never said 'You're mine, Colin Riley. You're mine.'

Mum has called the police. She says terrorists are tracking Dad's every movement and are obviously ready to pounce and that they should have listened when she warned them about the *Grazia*-reading hooligan on Thin Kylie's wall. They are sending an officer round to interview Dad after *The Bill* (it is compulsory training for the police).

10 p.m.

Police say evidence suggests it is not terrorists, but just run-of-mill pervert, as they cannot trace any link

between law-abiding non-Muslim Colin Riley and any potential Al Qaeda splinter cells operating in the area. Mum said she wasn't aware there were any Al Qaeda operatives in Saffron Walden. But PC Doone said we are all (he does not mean we, he means Muslims) guilty until proven innocent. I said wasn't it supposed to be the other way round, but he said I have been watching too much *Morse* and modern policing is all about suspecting everyone. I countered by saying he had been watching too much *Midsomer Murders* but he says he cannot abide John Nettles and he is more of a *Murphy's Law* man. Then Mum made him leave as the TV detective conversation was threatening to get out of hand and was not helping at all in the hunt for Dad's stalker. PC Doone said we should be looking closer to home because it is always the person you least expect. Dad is now watching Mum's every move. Mum is watching James. And James is watching the frogs.

. . . .

Friday 6

Good Friday

Hurrah, no work. Mr Goldstein has shut up shop for the day due to everyone being too busy panic-buying hot-cross buns and giant Toblerones to stock up on sunflower seeds

House is a hotbed of who is stalking Dad controversy though. Even Clive next door is under suspicion. Mum made him breathe into the phone when he came round to borrow the long-handled secateurs. Dad and James have ruled him out though as his panting wasn't deep and throaty enough.

11 a.m.
Oh my God. The menacing man is back. James and I are watching him through the binoculars. He is reading *Tatler* at the moment. But he could flip any minute and firebomb us. Mum has called the police again but they are permanently engaged. (It is due to Easter revving at Barry Island. The sugar and e-numbers send the O'Gradys into joy-riding frenzies.)

11.15 a.m.
Menacing man now fiddling with mobile phone. Maybe he is sending for reinforcements. Oh God. We are all doomed.

11.20 a.m.
Oooh. Our phone is ringing. Hope it is Justin. I will need to say goodbye if I am going to be murdered by fundamentalists any minute.

11.25 a.m.
Mum picked up. It was not Justin. Or three-minute bomb warning. It was heavy breathing phone menace. Mum says it is too much of a coincidence that menacing man is on phone at same time. She is going out. Have warned

her that he may be suicide bomber with explosives strapped to his chest. But Mum says suicide bombers do not wear Marks & Spencer macs. Dad is watching from behind the curtain.

11.30 a.m.
It is worse than Mum (and Dad) feared! Menacing man and phone pervert is not Al Qaeda minion or even man, but is Edie Weeks, née Wilmott! She has been dressing up in Mr Wilmott's clothes and lurking about in hope of catching a glimpse of Sex Beast Riley. (Although why Mr Wilmott has a balaclava is entirely suspicious. May report him to police as potential Al Qaeda operative. Would make excellent detective. Maybe they will ask me to join force and I will be youngest ever DCI!) Anyway, after Mum whipped the balaclava off, Scooby-Doo style, Edie confessed all, in her throaty, Rothman-ruined voice. She says she has never got over Dad and her life will be meaningless if she cannot have him. Mum said it is tough luck as he is very much not on the market any more. Then Edie broke down and wept all over the John Lewis rug and Mum had to call Mr Wilmott to take her away.

Dad did not come out from behind the curtain until Edie had been safely removed from the crime scene. It is not because he is scared of Edie, it is because he is scared of Mum. He has had a temporary reprieve anyway because Mum has taken James and has driven off in Fiesta. Oh God. Just had awful thought. What if she has

118

walked out on us? She has taken her favourite child (i.e. James) with her and run away to Granny Clegg's and left me and Dad to fend for ourselves. He will have burned house to ground by Monday in chip pan fire and I will be in care and will never see Justin again. Oh God, the image of the Fiesta disappearing round Loompits Way is the last I will ever see of her. Must burn it onto brain so I do not forget her.

2 p.m.
Mum and James back. They had not run away to Cornwall but to Premier Travel to get brochures for emergency break. Mum says it is the only way to wean Edie off Dad. I said flying to the Bahamas would be an excellent place for us all to recover from the trauma and could I bring Justin but Mum says *a*) she has already ruled out all long-haul destinations due to James's persistent travel sickness issues and *b*) no I cannot. So then I begged to be left at home revising but she says I cannot be trusted to spend a week with my head in books and not mooning about over that 'long-haired layabout' (she does not consider 'rock musician' a valid career choice).

Ooh, I wonder where we will be going though. Maybe behind (now drawn back) iron curtain to visit war-ravaged villages. Or possibly to a souk in Morocco. It will be like that film *Hideous Kinky* and we will abandon our Western ways and frolic in kaftans and smoke hookah pipes.

Saturday 7

We are not going to souk. We are going to a French gîte in somewhere called St Abattage. Mum says it will be excellent for my GCSE revision and has lifted her embargo on continental travel especially. I have instructions to tell Mr Goldstein that I will not be available to sift lentils next Saturday. I also have instructions to say my goodbyes to Justin tonight as we are leaving for the ferry at five in the morning and I need to pack sensibly. Am not too depressed as it is utterly romantic and Jane Austenish to be kept apart by scheming parents. Also Johnny Depp lives in France. He is utterly tragic and edgy and we would be excellent friends, despite the twenty-five-year age gap. Oooh. Maybe he lives in St Abattage to keep away from glare of media. I can befriend him and we can discuss existential cinema in French whilst sipping Bordeaux and eating offensive cheese.

10 p.m.

Am home after very intense pre-separation snogging session during which I lost all control and let Justin put his hand inside jumper (but not inside Brownie T-shirt— am not total slut, yet). Have told him I will write to him every day but he said to call instead as the letters will take weeks if they get here at all. I said I only had £2.10 of minutes left but he has lent me his £50 Christmas present minutes voucher in case of emergency. I can pay him back from my Nuts In May wages. Once I have paid off doll and Suzy.

10.15 p.m.
Oops. Have not packed. Will just throw some things in a case in the morning. I expect that is what Sienna does. Hurrah. By ten tomorrow will be sipping café au lait with Johnny Depp in picturesque St Abattage.

Sunday 8
Easter Day
10 a.m.
Am not in picturesque St Abbatage but stuck in ferry queue at Dover. There is a strike on the French side of the Channel. Dad says it is probably over the filling in their over-subsidized baguette lunches. Will call Scarlet to find out. She has inside information on all matters left wing. Mum is seething. She has entire holiday planned on a very strict itinerary and this is messing with all her food and toilet-stop timings. Have eaten entire Easter egg haul already (pitifully low this year due to Granny Clegg's hip of doom preventing her stalking the aisles of Trago Mills for cut price chocolate).

11 a.m.
Strike is not over baguette fillings. It is over the colour of their uniform. Also have had lengthy chat with Scarlet

about possible new lyrics. She says 'Bad Bat Boy' is excellent but we need fresh material. Will start as soon as we settle into our inspiring French country retreat.

12 noon
Colour of uniform obviously agreed on as we are now on board ferry.

12.15 p.m.
Ferry departs British waters.

12.20 p.m.
Mum has panic attack due to sudden realization that frogs have been left home alone and may cause all manner of hoo-ha when they make inevitable bid for freedom. (Note that she is not concerned that they may die of mince-starvation.) She instructs Steward Barry 'Hi, How Can I Help You' (freakishly small hands, severe dandruff, definitely gay) to inform captain of *Spirit of Adventure* of impending frog-related catastrophe and demand that he turn boat around immediately and return to English waters.

12.30 p.m.
Barry 'Hi, How Can I Help You' informs Mum it is not like *Miami Vice* and captain cannot just swing boat around in middle of Channel, and anyway it is not a boat it is a ferry. Mum commandeers Dad's phone to make emergency phone call to Marjory to get her to break in

and confiscate frogs. James is staying strangely silent throughout. Maybe he is in shock due to possible demise of Ninja frogs.

12.45 p.m.
Marjory reports back that she cannot break through Mum's excessive security arrangements but that Clive went up a ladder to observe any signs of frog escape in James's bedroom and says lid is on but he cannot see frogs in tank at all. Mum says they may have gone already and covered up their tracks by replacing lid, and to call police if she hears any strange noises. James still silent.

12.50 p.m.
James says he is feeling possibly travel sick and goes to toilets.

1.15 p.m.
James still not back from seasickness episode. Mum says we are perilously close to French shores and she does not want him getting left on board like on the Safari Boat at Longleat. Dad despatched with box of wet wipes to investigate and possibly mop up.

1.20 p.m.
James discovered locked in disabled toilet. Not with head in loo but giving Donatello and Michaelangelo a swim in sink. He had smuggled them on board inside his Ninja Turtles lunchbox and they were getting dehydrated. Mum

said we must hand them in to the authorities at once but Dad said we could get arrested for importing livestock into a restricted zone and the best plan is to conceal them in the Passat.

1.30 p.m. GMT (aka 2.30 CET i.e. French time)
Passat departs *Spirit of Adventure* with passengers safely strapped in seats and illegal immigrants (i.e. frogs) safely hidden in glove compartment with soggy wet wipes for survival. Mum gets stack of French maps out but Dad says we will not be needing them and sets trusty SatNav to continental mode. SatNav estimates arrival time in St Abattage as 7.45 i.e. just in time for steak frites in local rustic bistro. Mum adjusts itinerary, cutting out three toilet stops and one meal. Entire car synchronizes watches, taking account of having 'time travelled' an hour ahead.

1.45 p.m.
Passat stops at Carrefour to purchase emergency mince as frogs are getting restless and croaking noisily inside their plastic prison.

5 p.m.
SatNav estimates distance left as 130 miles.

5.30 p.m.
SatNav estimates distance left as 150 miles. Mum

demands a change from male voice to female as the man SatNav is obviously not so hot at map reading. Dad tries to explain the technical points of satellite navigation but Mum makes lips go thin and he switches to female mode.

5.45 p.m.
Female SatNav claims we are at our destination. Passat stops and Dad investigates. We are in middle of motorway. SatNav returned to more authoritative male mode.

6 p.m.
SatNav man claims we are in Latvia. Dad hits SatNav. SatNav man goes ominously silent. Mum retrieves stack of French maps from boot of car. We are not in Latvia. We have detoured to somewhere called Marly le Roi, i.e. several hundred miles from St Abattage. Mum re-estimates arrival time at 10 p.m. precisely.

6.15 p.m.
James banned from saying, 'Are we nearly there yet?' (In fact a reinforcement of an earlier ban, as it was initially imposed five years ago after particularly traumatic Easter queues on the A303 to Cornwall.)

8 p.m.
Passat stops for dinner on verge. Not steak frites but in fact Marmite sandwiches and satsumas. Or mince, in case of frogs.

8.10 p.m.
Mum packs everyone back into car in accordance with her rigid itinerary.

10 p.m.
Passat arrives at gîte. Mum claims victory over SatNav, and Dad, as he is responsible for transport (she is responsible for accommodation and activities).

10.10 p.m.
Dad claims victory over Mum as electricity in gîte not working.

10.15 p.m.
Mum claims victory over Dad as torch is missing from car emergency toolkit.

10.20 p.m.
James claims victory over everyone as he has packed his Tweenies torch (in lunchbox with frogs, in case they got scared of dark).

10.30 p.m.
Riley family clean teeth by torchlight and retire to rooms. Frogs retire to temporary shelter arrangement in what is presumed to be kitchen, though is hard to tell in dark. Am too tired to unpack. Will do it in morning. Will just phone Justin quickly though to say goodnight.

11.30 p.m.

Just put phone down. It is excellent that there is clear phone reception in the middle of nowhere. The French are obviously uber-efficient at communication matters. Unlike the Cornish who have patchy coverage at best, and none at all in Granny Clegg's house. It is a shame Justin is stuck in Saffron Walden though and not here in France enjoying ancient stone gîte in rural idyll, where the only sound is the murmur of wildlife.

Monday 9

Easter Monday (Bank Holiday UK and Rep. Ire.)
5 a.m.
Wildlife murmur escalated to shrieking sound. It is inconsiderate French chicken heralding dawn outside room.

5.15 a.m.
Chicken is not outside room but is busy heralding inside room. It must have sneaked in when we arrived. Or maybe it lives here. Mum has given it a hefty thwack with her sheepskin slipper and it has disappeared downstairs somewhere. Although now it has set frogs into croaking frenzy. Wish was back in Saffron Walden listening to drone of minibikes and distant M11 traffic. Am going back to sleep.

8 a.m.
Hurrah. Have had excellent extra beauty sleep and am now up and ready to investigate historic St Abattage. Will get dressed after breakfast of croissants and hot chocolate.

9 a.m.
No croissants. Nearest baker is ten miles away and Dad is refusing to drive due to his hands being welded in steering wheel position following yesterday's epic journey. And Mum is refusing to take us as she can only drive Fiestas and only on the right (in both senses of the word) side of the road. Also no hot chocolate due to continuing electricity issue (gîte still in semi-darkness). Ate Marmite on stale Waitrose wholemeal and drank warm Evian. Frogs ate mince. Dad now in damp-smelling cellar looking for fusebox with Tweenies torch. Also, why did I not pack properly in Anthea Turner manner? Have managed to bring bridesmaid's dress with me. Why did I think that would be useful? It is not even wearable at a wedding any more due to compost stains. Also, did not pack books so am destitute, literature-wise. Mum says she will lend me a Maeve Binchy or Rosamund Pilcher. I said no thanks as will perish intellectually. She said well it's that or James's *Young Bond*. Have borrowed the Maeve Binchy. Will start reading once have explored history-steeped medieval St Abattage.

10 a.m.
Have investigated St Abattage with James. It is not

history-steeped medieval village at all but French equivalent of Cornish backwater St Slaughter, complete with straw-chewing inmates. There are no magic Chocolat shops, à la Juliette Binoche, and absolutely no Johnny Depp. There is a café full of old men smoking Gitanes, a car mechanic called Monsieur Voiture, and a French Spar run by a woman with one eyebrow. Thank God I have contact with outside world. Am going to phone Justin immediately.

11 a.m.
Am off phone. Dad has discovered electricity. Not in Thomas Edison way but has located fusebox behind pile of damp mattresses. Lights are on and revealing catalogue of substandard accommodation issues as follows:

1. Gîte is not *Elle Decoration*-style rural retreat but breeze-block stable conversion in Granny Clegg Decoration style, i.e. swirly carpet, pictures of dogs in hats playing snooker, and excess formica.
2. Shelves do not contain vast collection of GCSE-improving French literature, as imagined by me. In fact contain china shepherdess display and brass clock (not working).
3. Bathroom is infested by grotesque insect life. Is like episode of David Attenborough every time you need the loo, causing several wee-on-wall accidents in case of James. Frogs have been installed in sink to

prey on them. But this means cleaning teeth in bath as frogs do not like minty spit.

4. There is a chicken living in the cellar (it has access via a gigantic hole in the wall). Dad discovered it when it pecked him on the head during the hunt for electricity. He is going to block the hole later once the chicken has gone out.

5. Electricity supply is entirely random i.e. lights go on and off for no apparent reason. James is enjoying it and says it is like being at a disco but Mum is concerned strobe effect may cause fits.

These have been catalogued and are now running against Mum in unofficial 'who organizes best holiday?' competition. Mum is countering by organizing lunch trip to authentic village café. She will not be beaten. Hurrah. Will be sipping Pinot Noir shortly in continental manner (it is compulsory for children to drink wine in France).

5 p.m.
Lunch at authentic village café (the ambitiously-named Café de Paradis) was suspicious soup consumed in fog of Gitanes fumes. Also did not get to drink wine. Got warm Evian. Mum says she learnt her lesson after Thin Kylie's birthday party when I did purple Pernod sick several times. Dad says it is another point to him but Mum has trumped him with the revelation that the village has a

bistro and we are booked in for a steak frites supper (or *le croque monsieur* in her case as she does not trust French to have eliminated mad cow disease). Hurrah. I expect it will be actually Michelin-starred restaurant that people drive hundreds of miles to just to sample their peasant cuisine.

8 p.m.
Was not Michelin-starred restaurant. Was not even bistro. Was Café de Paradis but with candles stuck in old Ricard bottles and extra Gitanes fog. Ate more suspicious soup under gaze of hostile locals. Mum and Dad are going to Carrefour tomorrow to stock up on tinned goods. Am now retiring to bed early due to utter lack of entertainment/literary stimulation/electricity. But not before have just had quick chat with Justin.

10.30 p.m.
Phone has gone dead. Think may have used up all minutes. Will just borrow Dad's in future. He will not mind. It is all paid for by Wainwright and Hogg anyway.

Tuesday 10
10 a.m.
Woken at five again by chicken in cellar. It has obviously fought its way back in through Dad's inadequate defences. (Point to Mum.) Plus chicken is a bad influence on the

131

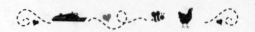

frogs. They are chorusing constantly now. James says it is a sure sign they are building up for their death match with Shredder. Reminded James that Shredder is a cartoon. He said, 'That's what they want you to think.' He has gone to Carrefour with Mum and Dad. He wants to be sure they purchase essential items like Shreddies. Am going on mind-expanding trip to museum when they get back. Hope it is better than Cornish Museum of Mines. That is just a dark passageway and some ancient pasty remnants.

5 p.m.
Museum not better than Museum of Mines. It was Museum of Footwear (seriously). Exhibition consisted of Neanderthal socks, a piece of leather allegedly from one of Napoleon's war boots, and some trainers (not even Nikes), to represent Modern Man. It was all *complètement ordure* (note excellent use of French). Only James seemed happy. It is because they had an 'interactive display' where you could measure your own feet. I said he could do that at Debarrs for nothing but he said it is not the same as the numbers there are not in French. He is a *grand imbècile*.

8 p.m.
Have eaten tea (Bird's Eye fishfingers and peas). Lights currently out so cannot possibly do any revision. On plus side, darkness makes it easy to borrow Dad's phone. Will just call Justin to say goodnight and obtain Saffron Walden gossip.

10 p.m.

Nothing is happening in Saffron Walden as usual. Unless you count Mr Patel's controversial new neon shop sign. Asked Justin what he was doing to while away hours until I return. He says he is playing our song on his guitar (i.e. 'I Bet You Look Good on the Dance Floor' by Arctic Monkeys, not that one by The Darkness as they were clearly one-hit wonders and cannot have has-beens as theme tune) and wandering aimlessy around the Waitrose snack aisle. He is definitely in love, no matter what Scarlet says.

Wednesday 11

5 a.m.

How does chicken know what time it is? It is accurate to the second.

10 a.m.

Mum has pointed out that have been here three days and I have not communicated properly with any locals i.e. am going to fail my GCSE. I pointed out that I had asked one-eyebrowed woman in Spar for *'le chocolat, s'il vous plait'* earlier. But Mum says that is not A* grade material. She says I am in charge of all communication with foreigners today. This does not bode well. We are going to Café de Paradis again for lunch later. Mum says it will be fine if we sit outside to avoid fumes.

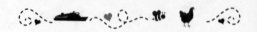

2 p.m.
Lunch not entirely successful due to less than A*
conversational French from Rachel Riley. Think have
possibly eaten horse. Also Dad got apple pie in gravy due
to slight confusion between pommes and pommes de terre.
We are off to vineyard now. At least will not have to talk
too much there. Will just nod at interesting grapes. Have
asked Mum if can at least gargle and spit wine out in
authentic manner. She says as long as she can see visible
spitting.

5 p.m.
James has been sick down side of Passat. Mum was so
busy checking that I was spitting she forgot to monitor
James. He had swallowed several glasses of vin rouge
before Dad noticed he was behaving erratically (i.e. not
asking a million questions and taking notes). (Mum is
claiming victory as she says sick incident occurred during
transport phase of visit.) I on other hand spat in
professional manner and also used several excellent
French words like *'superbe'*, *'magnifique'*, and *'zut alors'*.
Am totally going to get A*.

8 p.m.
James asleep in darkened room with bucket and Cillit
Bang (brought from home in case of just such an
emergency) next to bed in readiness.

Thursday 12

5.05 a.m.

Chicken gone off boil. It is five minutes late this morning. But making up for inaccuracy by issuing single, earshattering scream. Am going to reinforce damp mattress defences later when have recovered from shock.

10 a.m.

James is still actually green. He says he has learnt his lesson and will be staying away from the demon drink for the rest of his life. He has declined a visit to Europe's largest sausage factory and has taken to his sick bed again with a glass of Evian and a dry cracker. Have also declined invitation on grounds that I can watch Justin do it for free every Saturday. Instead have purchased *Le Monde* from monobrow Spar woman and am going to immerse myself in current affairs, French-style. Chicken is safely locked out (hole reinforced with fertilizer sack) and Dad has left phone in case of emergency. I am to call *les police* in cases of the following: fire, flood, possible perverts, or attack from hostile forces.

10.15 a.m.

Le Monde is not as easy as I thought. Have just read article that seems to imply Nicolas Sarkozy eats cats. Or maybe it is true. The French are renowned for embracing exotic foodstuffs.

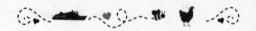

10.30 a.m.
Oops. Just remembered am supposed to be doing band practice with Scarlet tonight. Will just call her quickly to remind her am in France. It is emergency after all.

11 a.m.
Ooh. And Sad Ed to find out how Edie is dealing with utter rejection by Sex Beast Riley.

11.01 a.m.
Must stop calling him that. He is not Sex Beast. He is Dad.

12.15 p.m.
Edie is back in rehab. Apparently Mr Wilmott found her slumped across the polished pine kitchen table with the entire contents of his drinks cabinet inside her (half a bottle of brandy and a litre of Advocaat). It is so unfair. Mum would never do that. I may well raise a formal complaint as it is completely holding me back, literary-wise, having such normal parents. Their normality could be the reason for me failing English GCSE. Ooops. And French GCSE. Had better return to *Le Monde*.

12.30 p.m.
Am bit peckish. Will just eat stimulating French lunch (aka Marmite sandwich).

1.30 p.m.
Ooh—just remembered, Scarlet said we need new

136

material for Battle of Bands. Will write about inspiring experiences in France. That is almost as good as conjugating verbs. Will be like Jim Morrison writing 'Spanish Caravan'. Will call it 'French Gîte'. Possibly.

2 p.m.
Breeze-block gîte not entirely inspiring source for song. Also, chicken is watching me through window menacingly. May go for inspiring walk in village.

4 p.m.
Oh God. Something terrible has happened. The chicken has killed Donatello and Michaelangelo and eaten the evidence! (Frogs are missing and chicken is parading around bathroom with menacing look and bloodstained feathers.) It is also now refusing me entry to the bathroom. James will be devastated. Oh God. Where is James?

4.15 p.m.
James missing. Am calling police immediately. Think chicken may have killed and eaten him too. Is not chicken at all but one of those evil bird creatures out of *Harry Potter*. Have barricaded it in bathroom in case it comes after me next.

4.20 p.m.
Have rung police and informed them of emergency i.e. *Le poulet diabolique avez mangez mon frère et deux grenouilles.* Think they are coming soon.

4.30 p.m.

Oh, hope police hurry up. Chicken is throwing itself at door. It is like horror movie. A claw will get through the polished pine any second and then its beady eye will appear with my terrified face reflected in it. (Ooh, would make excellent horror writer. Maybe could be like female Stephen King and make millions from gruesome bestsellers but be snubbed by Booker judges for being populist. That is, if I survive the chicken attack.)

5 p.m.

Thank God. Can hear voices outside. Will throw myself at their mercy and let them take out the chicken with heavy artillery.

6 p.m.

Was not police. Was Mum and Dad with James. Chicken had not eaten him after all. Instead he had woken up and, to his delight, found house empty and gone to village to buy lightbulbs, string, and paint. He was hoping to fulfil his lifelong ambition i.e. being left Home Alone, and battling burglars with ingenious gadgets. Told them not to enter house due to scene of utter carnage. Then it was like a slow motion bit in a film because James cried out, 'Donatello, Michaelangelo,' and dropped the lightbulbs and paint in his rush to save his Ninja frogs. Chicken seized its chance to escape and flew over his head and out of front door, taking remains of frogs

138

with him. James is now being revived from shock with French chocolate milk (suspiciously named Cacolac). And I, on other hand, am shut in room without even Maeve Binchy for comfort as punishment for woeful inability to babysit. On plus side still have Dad's phone in pocket. Will just call Justin and tell him about my near-death experience.

8 p.m.
Justin says I am lucky to be alive and that he could not go on if I had been eaten by a giant chicken. (Exaggerated exact size of chicken a bit for effect.) I asked if he would have committed suicide à la Romeo. He said no, he meant he would not bother washing his hair for a week. Which is almost the same and totally romantic. Ooh. May write song about it all.

9 p.m.
Mum has just been in. The police have agreed to let me off the false emergency phone call. Mum made them do it as she said she would report them for failing to respond to an emergency, false or otherwise, in sufficient time. ('Conversational French for the Over-40s' is obviously more useful than I imagined.) Also they have given her permission to use any force necessary to despatch the chicken. Have apologized for demise of frogs. She said I am forgiven. Think she is secretly relieved as she will not have to smuggle them back across the border now.

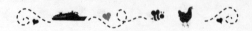

9.15 p.m.
James has just been in. He is revived by Cacolac and has a new mission. He thinks the chicken might actually be a Ninja now, because it has absorbed the powers of the frogs. He is going to catch it and tame it and bring it back to Saffron Walden to fight Shredder.

9.30 p.m.
Have written song. It is called 'Death Chicken'.

Death Chicken

Your eyes are full of menace
My heart is full of dread
You stalk me in my dreams at night
And peck me in the head
Death chicken (bloodcurdling squawk sound)
Death chicken

That is it. There was an excellent second verse about that film *The Birds* but could not think of anything to rhyme with Tippi Hedren.

Will just phone Scarlet and read her the lyrics.

11 p.m.
Scarlet says new song is very goth horror and could well secure our victory in Battle of Bands. She says she loves that it is allegorical about George Bush. I agreed. Though have no idea what she means. Maybe I am so good it just happened subliminally. Also she says she has utterly incredible news. But that it is too

140

huge to relate details over phone. It is bound to be about her and Trevor. Maybe they have broken up after all.

Am very tired after traumatic day. Thank God chicken has fled. Will be able to lie in in peace.

. . . .

Friday 13
5 a.m.
Chicken is back (Friday the 13th style) and is louder than ever. As is Mum. She shouted, 'Colin, do something useful for once in your life.' Followed by Dad's unmistakable grumbling and heavy plod downstairs.

5.10 a.m.
Chicken silent. Dad has obviously chased it away. Thank God. Although James will be disappointed at the disappearance of the new Ninja chicken.

9 a.m.
It is last day today so am going to Spar to purchase presents for Scarlet, Sad Ed, and Justin. Mum says I must be back by 12 as she is cooking celebratory French lunch.

12 noon
Present shopping not entirely successful due to woeful lack of tourist fayre in French Spar. Have got Cacolac for Sad Ed, Gitanes lighter for Scarlet (for incense sticks), and a Johnny Hallyday (no idea) bag for Justin. Will say it is ironic.

141

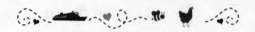

3 p.m.
Lunch was delicious and traditional French coq au vin.
So got to drink wine. Sort of. Am glad am not still in
vegetarian stance. The French are very unaccommodating
when it comes to non-meat eaters, i.e. it is practically illegal.

5 p.m.
Have just had thought. Do not remember Mum bringing
chicken back from Carrefour. And one-eyebrowed
woman definitely does not stock poultry. Oh God. Think
we may have eaten the death chicken. Which means we
have also eaten Ninja frogs. Gross. Am going to confront
Mum immediately.

5.30 p.m.
It is true. Mum has confessed everything. She is
unrepentant and says chicken is chicken and the frogs
just add to the flavour. She will be sorry when I have told
James of our cannibalism. He will be devastated.

6 p.m.
James not devastated. In fact is delighted as he now
thinks not only has he avenged the deaths of the frogs,
but he will have absorbed their powers. He is now
checking himself for visible signs of Ninjahood. Also,
apparently Dad killing menacing chicken with bare hands
has inflamed Mum's passion as they have gone on
romantic walk. Will exploit peace by calling Justin to

remind him to meet me at the unhygienic phone box at 9 tomorrow night (in accordance with return itinerary, SatNav issues pending).

Saturday 14

11 a.m.

Ooops. Have just woken up. As has everyone else in house. We are now two hours late according to our return itinerary. Mum is blaming Dad for killing the trusty, if annoying, chicken alarm clock. But Dad says he is used to relying on her waterworks waking him up when she goes for a wee and is blaming her uncharacteristically capacious bladder. Mum has responded by axing two wee stops and all food stops from the return journey. We will have to eat sandwiches on the move. A reckless act, in my opinion, as crumbs in the car are one of Mum's banned items.

2 p.m.

Mum is making everyone hang out of window to eat sandwiches, risking near death from overtaking traffic, in James's case. Dad is being handfed by Mum with a Tupperware lid held under his chin to prevent spillage. According to Mum's maps we are 208 miles away from Calais and ferry is due to leave in three hours. James says we have no chance of making it unless Mum lifts her ban on exceeding 60 miles an hour. He says 70mph is the bare minimum required. Mum has compromised on 65.

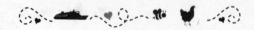

4 p.m.
There are still 82 miles to go and only 60 minutes to do it in. But Mum is asleep so Dad is taking the daring move of driving at 90 miles an hour. He is very excited and thinks he is Jeremy Clarkson. He will not be so fuelled with testosterone when we hit the back of a Renault Megane and Mum bans him from driving ever again. Or, worse, makes him drive the Fiesta.

4.55 p.m.
Mum has just woken up but Passat is already safely on board the *Spirit of Adventure* and is, amazingly, dent and speeding ticket-free. She is thinking of writing to the RAC to inform them their map distances are all out. James (also asleep for most of journey) told her it is not distance but is because his Ninja powers allowed us to subvert the space-time continuum.

6 p.m.
Ferry still very much in French waters due to leaky hold. Barry (still gay with freakishly small hands and severe dandruff but now with ill-advised ash blond dye job) is handing out complimentary mints and sick bags while someone plugs hole. Oh God, am going to miss Justin at our pre-arranged snog. Ooh. Or maybe ferry will hit an iceberg in stormy ocean and will be like *Titanic* with me as Kate Winslet and we will fight with the people on Deck B (scabby deck) for spaces in the lifeboats. Hurrah.

8.45 p.m. CET (aka 7.45 p.m. GMT i.e. Saffron Walden time)
Ferry has docked in Dover with no *Titanic*-style incident.
Have told Dad he has just over an hour to drive the 120
miles to Saffron Walden (i.e. 96mph according to Ninja
Riley). He says he does not know what I am thinking of,
as he would never break the speed limit. James says he
will use his Ninja powers again.

9 p.m.
Ninja powers not in evidence. Justin is waiting for me in
a stinky phonebox outside the library whilst we are very
much on the M25. Have begged Dad to lend me his
mobile but he says it is for emergencies only and my love
life does not in any way constitute one, according
Wainwright and Hogg rules. Will not mention other
'emergencies' in France. He will never know. Bill
probably gets paid by direct debit anyway.

10.30 p.m.
Am home. Will just call Justin to apologize for missed
rendezvous (see, am still speaking French, it is like
second nature now and am totally fluent). Will only be
five minutes as Mum has strict rule on phone usage. Will
not tell her I am calling his mobile. That is utterly
banned.

11.30 p.m.
Hurrah. Justin is not at all cross that I did not turn up at

the phonebox. He says Darryl Stamp set fire to the rubbish bins and it was 'mad'. Said I thought he would be above minor pyrotechnics what with him being artistic type etc., but he said there is nothing more interesting than watching chavs burn stuff. Maybe he is just in touch with his working-class roots (Mrs Statham is from Leytonstone, which is very *EastEnders*). That must be it. He is like Paul McCartney. Except without the jowls and maroon hair. Ooh. Wonder if I have time to find out Scarlet's amazing news? Will just call. Maybe she and Trevor have not broken up but have done 'It'!

12.15 a.m.
It is sex news. But not about Scarlet. It is about Jack. He is going out with Sophie Microwave Muffins! They got off with each other round at Melanie Shave's 'get the troops out' ironic tarts and vicars party. She says Justin doesn't know yet. I said why would he care? She said, 'Don't get minty with me, why do you care?' I said I am far from minty, I am just pointing out a fact. She said France has obviously made me continental and sulky and she will call me tomorrow when I am back to being English. She is right. I am tired from all the deep and meaningful French discussions. That and the killer chicken. That is why I am cross. Will sleep it off and be refreshed in morning and happy for Jack and his new love.

Sunday 15

Am not refreshed at all but have woken up in state of utter gloom. It is because of Jack and Sophie Microwave Muffins. They are utterly wrong for each other. It is like Jeremy Paxman going out with the blonde one in Girls Aloud. Unlike me and Justin, which is love across a divide, which is totally different.

3 p.m.

Justin knows about Jack and Sophie Microwave Muffins. Scarlet just rang to tell me that Jack says Justin saw them walk past his house holding hands and gave them a definite dirty look. I said he must be mistaken as Justin does not get up until at least half three, but she says E4's schedule overhaul is causing havoc with Sixth Form lie-ins and that wake-up call is now midday. I said the dirty look was probably just tiredness then. She said, 'Get real.'

I am real. Unlike Sophie Microwave Muffins who is several shades lighter than Barry 'Hi, How Can I Help You' on the L'Oréal scale. Anyway. I do not care about Jack. I will be reunited with the ONE, i.e. Justin, in two hours and will do excellent snogging and may even let him touch my décolletage, now that I have been to France, which is renowned for being sexually liberated.

8 p.m.

Justin is in funny mood. He did not even do any French kissing let alone try to grope my décolletage. I said is this

147

about Jack and Sophie Microwave Muffins and he said only because she and Jack are totally wrong for each other. Which at first I thought was a bad sign but on reflection it is actually good, because it is exactly what I thought. So we even think alike, we are so totally suited to each other, which proves even more that he is the ONE. In fact, am so inspired am going to write a song about it.

10 p.m.
Have written song. It is called 'Is She Really Going Out With Him?' and is sort of to the tune of 'Sk8ter Boy'. (Which have also stolen some themes from. Only is not stealing, according to Scarlet, is postmodernism.)

Is She Really Going Out With Him?
He watches news, BBC 2,
Documentaries on Africa,
He plays the drums, writes his own songs,
Based on books by Salinger.

She reads Heat, *thinks kittens are sweet,*
Thinks Newsnight's *for geeks and flakes,*
Hates politics, says MPs make her sick,
Thinks all parties come with cakes.

Am still working on a chorus but think it has definite MySpace potential.

Monday 16

School is awash with Jack and Sophie Microwave Muffins excitement. Even Mrs Leech is banging on about it. She says it is like when political brain JFK married society beauty Jackie Onassis. I said it was more like his illicit liaison with glamorous but stupid Marilyn Monroe but Mrs Leech was too busy restocking her medical kit (i.e. emptying gypsy creams into a tin) to hear me.

The Maths Club have already opened a book on them being named head boy and head girl in June. It is pathetic. They have only been going out for five minutes, unlike me and Justin who are celebrating three and a half months of snogging. Although there appears to be a current lull in proceedings. He turned down my offer to snog on the sheep field at first break in favour of lurking at the fruit and nut machine. Scarlet says he is hoping to overhear Jack and Sophie gossip but she is wrong. He is just upping his nut consumption for health reasons, he told me. And I have seen the KP packets to prove it.

Also, Sad Ed is depressed. (I mean, really depressed, as opposed to his usual state of perpetual gloom.) It is because Edie is threatening to move back to America to get over her rejection by Dad, which means Tuesday will have to go with her, which means he will be utterly single again and will have to work on his upper arm flab. We have called an emergency meeting at Scarlet's on Friday night. Suzy is going to chair.

149

Tuesday 17

Justin is revived by all the nuts. He says there is only one way to counter the Jack and Sophie Microwave Muffins phenomenon that is threatening our position as official edgiest and hottest couple, and that is to be even edgier and hotter.

12 noon

Plans to regain status as school couple *de jour* slightly thwarted. Justin threw me recklessy against the fruit and nut machine at lunch time but the force made the machine dispense raisins all over the parquet and Mr Wilmott had to call the caretaker Lou to clean up. Justin said it was our chemistry but Lou said it was because my 'arse had jammed a knob the wrong way'. It would have been better if we had just lounged provocatively on the saggy sofa in the Sixth Form common room like Jack and Sophie Microwave Muffins. Except that not only has she got bigger breasts she is also sixteen i.e. legally allowed in the common room. Unlike me, who is only permitted to lounge on the sheep field which is damp and poo-ridden, as well as being infested by snogging Criminals and Retards.

Wednesday 18

Showed Scarlet lyrics for 'Is She Really Going Out With Him?' at band practice. Scarlet said, 'Is it about Jack and Sophie?' I said no it is totally made up about fictional characters. Like 'Bad Bat Boy and the Skinny Jeans'. She said that is about Trevor. I said *au contraire*, it is about universal issues of love and fashion. She did not look convinced but has agreed to include it in our set. She has no choice. The competition is less than a fortnight away and we only have two songs. ('Death Chicken' has been axed on the grounds that it might incite violence against animals, only has one verse, and Scarlet cannot change from G to A minor that quickly.)

Cannot tell her song is about Jack. She will not understand our complicated relationship.

5 p.m.
I do not understand our complicated relationship.

6 p.m.
Not that we have a relationship.

Thursday 19
Granny Clegg's Easter eggs have finally arrived. They are squished irreparably. Mum told Granny Clegg she will complain to Royal Mail but Granny Clegg says they were like that when she bought them off Maureen for 50p. James says he does not mind eating broken chocolate pieces but Mum says the mess from the shards will be incalculable and she will melt them down for alternative use. If it is anything like when she melted

down slivers of old soap to make new giant soap during an economy drive, the results are to be avoided at all costs.

. . . .

Friday 20

Went round Scarlet's for emergency Edie summit. Justin was annoyed as it meant we could not snog in the bus shelter but I said this was a matter of life or death (not quite true but Sad Ed is threatening to stop speaking to me unless I find a way to keep Tuesday in the country—he is blaming me for Dad's unwillingness to cheat on Mum with Edie). I invited Justin to help us formulate a plan but he said he had better things to do than hang around with a twat. (He means Jack, who, I pointed out, was more likely to be in the bus shelter snogging Sophie Microwave Muffins but this seemed to make him more sulky.)

Anyway, Suzy had come up with a genius plan. It is to find someone else in Saffron Walden to go out with Edie so that she forgets about Dad completely. Suzy has compiled a list of potential suitors using her in-depth knowledge of all things sexual and relationshippy. There are three so far:

- PC Doone (Suzy says he has the potential to keep her on the straight and narrow and also she has it on good authority that he has a big willy);

152

- Mr Vaughan (no evidence of big willy, but definite supersize nipples);
- Barry the Blade (single, has also been in mental institution so they have something in common, and possibly desperate).

She also had Mr Wilmott on there, on the grounds he is perpetually single and in dire need of womanly comfort, until Sad Ed reminded her he was Edie's brother. Suzy has relisted him under possibles. She does not let taboo, or the law, stand in the way of love. She is going to matchmake by inviting them round to dinner. They will come for sure. She is a TV sex guru and Saffron Walden's biggest celebrity. (Marlon has moved back to Emmerdale and the least-famous McGann has been downgraded to not-at-all famous as people now think he just looks a bit like one of them and may be a lookylikey masquerader after all.)

Jack was not at the bus shelter. He was in his room. Could hear the unmistakable idiotic high-pitched laugh of Sophie Microwave Muffins piercing the kitchen ceiling every few minutes.

Saturday 21

There is no escape from Jack and Ms Muffins. I could clearly see them through the raisin display lurking in Goddard's this morning while Sophie bought a steak slice. It is obvious she does not appreciate Jack's vegetarian tendencies. If I

was going out with him I would only bring him to Nuts In May, which is completely meat free (James checked, in case he could write one of his pedant letters).

Also Rosamund is back at work. Apparently Guru Derek has performed miracles and not just with her chakra, but also on her eczema, tinnitus, tennis elbow, and persistent headlice. She says she has been reborn and has instructed us to call her Moonchild from now on. She is trying to persuade Mr Goldstein to let Derek touch his hunchback with his healing hands. Mr Goldstein says no one touches his hunch, not even Mrs Goldstein. So she asked if I had need of any miracles. I said yes but unless Guru Derek could shrivel 34C breasts then not to bother him. She said mine looked more like As than Cs to her so I sighed and went to restack the prunes.

. . . .

Sunday 22

6 p.m.

Grandpa and the dog are back. They have been thrown out by Treena over their mismatched libidos (Grandpa's, not the dog's). Apparently the last straw came when Grandpa said he would rather watch Michael Aspel than massage Treena's buttocks with cooking oil. I do not blame him. It is punishment, not pleasure, to go near Treena's buttocks, especially with a bottle of Mazola.

Mum said at least he has not got custody of Jesus, but Grandpa says, *au contraire*, Treena is being very generous and has given him full visiting rights. Jesus will be coming to stay every weekend as well as several nights a week, i.e. whenever Treena goes to the Queen Elizabeth. Mum pointed out that, as Jesus is in nursery every day, this means Treena does not actually do much looking after Jesus at all. But Grandpa says it is hard being a single mum and he is determined to do his bit during this trial separation. Mum said it had better be a trial one not an actual one.

Only James is delighted. He has a Ninja companion once again, i.e. the dog. He is going to train it to sniff out criminals and attack them with silent but deadly moves. He has no chance. The dog is a constant source of noise pollution. Also, it has no ability to spot criminals. It is always trying to lick Fat Kylie. It is the Snickers residue.

8 p.m.
Oooh. Have just had an excellent thought. Maybe Grandpa could go out with Edie. He is a Riley, after all, which could satisfy her obsession. And I would get wardrobe access without going into care. Plus I bet she is not as sexually demanding as Treena. All that vodka will have killed off her nerve endings.

Monday 23
St George's Day (England)
Grandpa Clegg rang to moan about St George's Day. It is not because he thinks it has been overtaken by flag-

waving jingoists and possible racists like the Britchers (this is a good thing in his eyes), it is because he wants the government to officially recognize St Piran's Day (i.e. the moronic patron saint of tin-miners, who sailed to Cornwall on a stone). He says he is thinking of signing up to fight the campaign for Cornish independence and that he is prepared to spill blood for his beliefs. Mum then pointed out that it is not an actual battle with swords like at the Civil War re-enactment at Bodmin four years ago. At which news Grandpa was apparently disappointed. Mum says she is not worried anyway. He is notoriously fickle when it comes to political campaigning, like the time he went shopping for pants instead of marching against the hunting ban.

Tuesday 24

Have told Scarlet to tell Suzy to add Grandpa to Edie's list of single men. She says the first hot date is already scheduled for Thursday next week (vegetarian moussaka with PC Doone), but she will see if he can be squeezed in later in the month.

Also, Mum and Dad have been given the cholesterol all-clear by Bupa. I said it was a relief that the soya milk regime is finally over. But Mum said on the contrary, it is very much in place in order to maintain their clog-free arteries. Dad is having none of it though. I saw him eat

eleven chocolate digestives while Mum popped over to Marjory's to borrow an Oxo cube.

* *

Wednesday 25

The BBC (who never lie, in Mum's book) have reported that soya milk may cause cancer and sex change issues due to high oestrogen content. We are back on non-transgender semi-skimmed and Lurpak. The milkman is jubilant. He has signed Mum up for seven semi-skimmed, a six-pack of yoghurts, and two crème fraiches. Although Mum is thinking of giving James a glass of vile soya a week. She claims he has been far less aggressive since the changeover. I said it was more to do with the fact that Keanu has been off school with alleged meningitis for several weeks. Apparently Mrs O'Grady and Dr Braithwaite (huge hands, lazy eye, bottle of whisky in desk drawer) are not as quick to spot purple Crayola as Mum.

Have got band practice after school. Tonight we are devoting several hours of rehearsal to choosing our outfits. It is a key decision. Look at Kate Nash who used to wear ice wash denim and gold chains and was crap, and then she put on a vintage dress and became totally brilliant and famous.

* *

Thursday 26

Two days to go. Justin and I have agreed to forsake

snogging for the sake of artistic endeavour. It was Scarlet's idea—she and Trevor are also abstaining for the rest of the week. She says it is like boxers not being allowed to do it before a big fight. It might detract from our performance.

Saw Jack at Scarlet's after school. I said shouldn't he be rehearsing, instead of watching the Kerrang channel. He said, on the contrary, Kerrang is entirely educational, band-wise, and anyway, the Jack Stone Five were booked in for practice in the Jockey Wilson suite at 8 p.m. in order to check the acoustics and maximize their chances of clinching the title. I accused him of cheating but he said it is not cheating it is just cleverness. It is cheating. Justin agrees. He is sneaking the Back Doors in after over-50 aerobics tomorrow so they are not at a disadvantage. I asked Scarlet if we should go but she says our lyrics and composition will shine through like a beacon in the night and anyway, no one sounds that good in a room with sticky carpet and portraits of fat darts players on the walls.

Friday 27

School has gone Battle of the Bands mad. It is after the *Walden Chronicle* announced that one of the prizes is a support slot on a mystery tour this summer. The corridors of John Major High are now awash with rumours of who the headline act are. Fat Kylie claims it is 50 Cent as Mr Whippy heard it off 'ace' reporter Glen Davies when he was buying a Feast on the common last week. The goths are going for Spear of Destiny, whose drummer once drove through Saffron Walden, while the Alternative Music Table are crossing their fingers for a reformed Led Zeppelin. Personally I hope it is Lily Allen as then we could bond over our disaffected youths and swap clothes. Not that she would want to wear my science experiment jeans and too-small Brownies T-shirt (my agreed stage outfit, due to lack of anything else suitable at all).

9 p.m.
Am home from final band practice. Scarlet has blessed her guitar and my voice with a vial of goth blood (fake vegetarian from Toys 'R' Us) and says our fate is now in the hands of supreme beings (she does not believe in God, only in Dracula). It is a shame the supreme beings include Hugo Thorndyke, evil Tory MP for Saffron Walden and environs. There is no way he is going to vote for Scarlet. Her parents are Labour councillors and sex workers. (Not in the prostitute sense though. Although Suzy would probably do quite well at that too.) Texted Justin to wish him luck. He says he does not need luck. He has the spirit of Jim Morrison in his fingers. He has also instructed me to be waiting backstage after the gig for resumption of full groupie duties. Am not sure I want Jim Morrison's fingers anywhere though. It is a bit weird.

Am not texting Jack. He will be too busy with his idiotic groupie. Hopefully it will sap all his artistic energy and he will be rubbish on stage tomorrow.

10 p.m.
Just got text from Jack. GD LUCK, RILEY. X. Have not texted back. It is probably a joke and Sophie is laughing at me this very minute. Thank goodness I am not hung up on him any more but am with love of my life. Otherwise I might have spent hours pondering the significance of that X.

11 p.m.
But what if Sophie wasn't there and the X is actually a kiss and he actually cares whether I win or not?

11.15 p.m.
Which is question I do not need to know the answer to. As only care about Xs from Justin.

Saturday 28

8 a.m.
Hurrah. It is Battle of the Bands day. By this time tomorrow me and Scarlet could be lying on the floor of the Hawley Arms in Camden (essential hangout for drunken and drug-crazed celebrities) with half of Babyshambles. Excellent. I cannot wait. Have not told Mum this news yet. She will worry too much about my GCSEs and not having anything to fall back on. In fact have not even told her am in Battle of Bands. Am claiming I am going round Scarlet's for a science revision

party. She thinks we are going to play name that annelid. If I win it will be like that bit in *Dirty Dancing* and Justin can say, 'No one puts Rachel in a corner,' and I will stun them with my musical skills. Although she will probably not even notice I am gone anyway as Jesus has arrived for his custody visit. Treena dropped him off at half seven with a Teletubby, a bag of nappies, and a six pack of Wotsits. I checked for any wistfulness in her expression as she handed him over to Grandpa but she just said, 'Watch him, Ern. He's eaten a shitload of grapes.'

Am taking my stage outfit to work and will get changed in the lentil storeroom. Do not know how I am going to get through eight hours of Mr Goldstein and Rosamund though. At least Justin gets to take his adrenalin out on chuck steak.

Wish me luck, dear diary. My next entry could be as Britain's next biggest export, after the Beckhams and tractors.

. . . .

Sunday 29
10 a.m.
Head hurts. Not sure why. Will investigate in mirror.

Have huge bruise on side of head and what looks like chewing gum stuck in hair. But no idea how it got there. In fact cannot remember Battle of the Bands at all. Oh God. Am like Edward Norton in *Fight Club*. Maybe I have an insane alter ego that looks like Brad Pitt. Or possibly

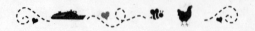

Angelina Jolie, in my case. That would be excellent. Will call Scarlet to see if I was behaving oddly last night.

10.15 a.m.
Am not like the one in *Fight Club*. Apparently it is due to Sophie Jacobs knocking me out with Scarlet's guitar after our rendition of 'Is She Really Going Out With Him?' Asked Scarlet for summary of events at the Jockey Wilson Suite. They are as follows:

8 p.m.
Back Doors give seminal performance, marred only by Sad Ed insisting on wearing dark glasses and not being able to see a lot of his keyboard.

8.15 p.m.
Jack Stone Five also give excellent performance. Fans go wild for Tuesday singing 'WLDN', as do judges, who are thinking of adopting it as theme tune to encourage more tourism.

8.30 p.m.
Velvet Elvis walk on stage.

8.34 p.m.
Trevor Pledger exits Jockey Wilson Suite in swish of voluminous goth cape, having taken offence at 'Bad Bat Boy and the Skinny Jeans'.

8.38 p.m.

Rachel Riley falls off stage after being thwacked with a Fender by Sophie Jacobs. Jack and Justin swarm stage to end potential bitch fight but end up wrestling on carpet tiles in actual battle of bands. Rachel carried to medical area (roller skate store) and handed to expert St John's Ambulance volunteer Roland McCafferty (high waist jeans (and not in a Stella McCartney way), centre parting, snorkel jacket).

8.45 p.m.

Velvet Elvis, the Back Doors, and Jack Stone Five all disbarred from Battle of Bands for bringing competition into disrepute.

9 p.m.

Roland declares Rachel is concussed, not brain-damaged, and needs to go home to rest. Scarlet suggests Roland take her there in St John's ambulance. Roland points out that St John does not actually own ambulance and that he got a lift to the Lord Butler on the back of his brother's racer.

9.15 p.m.

Rachel ferried back to Summerdale Road by Bob in sick-smelling Volvo who informs Mum I have passed out due to excess revision. Amazingly, she believes him. Thank God Scarlet's parents are born liars and drug-takers.

10 p.m.

The Hermit Crabs, who Tippex their teeth and sing Beach Boys covers, win Battle of the Bands. Their prize is not as support to Lily Allen. Or 50 Cent. It is a tour of the Great Yarmouth area with cheeky cockney duo Chas 'n' Dave.

Oh God. Just had thought. What if Justin read too much into the lyrics. What if he has chucked me but I have blocked out the memory?

2 p.m.

Justin has rung. Obviously he did not read anything into lyrics. Possibly did not even understand lyrics at all. Thank God he is not intellectual marvel. I said it was totally cool that he rushed to my rescue against evil Sophie Jacobs and he is obviously utterly modest because then he went all quiet. I love him even more. Asked if he was coming to see me later but he said he is grounded over the fight with Jack for a week. He is my hero. I do not care that Velvet Elvis did not win the Battle of the Bands. My prize is greater—it is true love.

9 p.m.

Jack has just been round. Which was totally weird. He said he had come to check I was OK after the fight. I said I was fine, no thanks to his insane girlfriend. He said, 'Well, thanks for writing a song about me. I didn't know you cared.' I said I don't and anyway it wasn't

about you it was about important themes of
compatibility and politics. He said I am in denial. And I
made an excellent joke about denial being a river in
Egypt and I definitely saw him smile but then he said
it's a shame it was me not your boyfriend who carried
you to the medical room. Which is weird. As Justin
didn't tell me that. So I said maybe he was in shock and
too traumatized to carry me. But Jack said he was too
busy talking to Sophie in the badminton changing
rooms. I said that was a total lie so Jack said, 'Where is
he now then?' I pointed out that he is grounded,
thanks to his fight with Jack. But Jack said, 'Whatever,
that's why I saw him hanging around Pleasant Valley
earlier.' Which is where Sophie lives. Then I didn't
know what to say so I didn't say anything. And Jack
came and sat next to me on the M&S duvet and said
'Are you OK, Riley?' And I still didn't say anything so
he held my hand. Then we just sat there for five
minutes until 'Back to Black' got stuck on my CD player
and I had to get up to stop Amy Winehouse saying
'rehab, rehab, rehab' repeatedly. Then Jack got up too.
He said, 'Do me a favour. Don't tell Sophie I was here.'
I said, 'As if. We don't even speak the same language.'
(Which is totally a line from *Breakfast Club* but sounded
excellent here.) Then he went.

And now am totally confused. Why didn't Justin take
me to the medical room when I could have been dead for
all he knew? And why was he lurking near Sophie's if he

is grounded? And why does Jack care anyway? Oh God, it is worse than GCSEs as there aren't even multiple choice answers. Am racked with indecision.

10 p.m.
Am unracked. Have had brilliant thought. It was not Justin on Pleasant Valley but was malodorous lesbian Oona Rickets. She has similar hair and men's shoes and was probably trying to sway Sophie to the 'other side'. Yes, that is it. It doesn't explain the rest of it, i.e. the lack of concern at my impending death, but at least it proves he is not a liar. Am glad Battle of the Bands is over. It has brought nothing but conflict to Saffron Walden.

. . . .

Monday 30
School is still obsessed with Battle of the Bands. Apparently rumours have reached such epic proportions that most of Year Seven thought I was languishing in intensive care in Addenbrookes with a plectrum lodged in my brain. Ms Hopwood-White had started a collection to pay for my wheelchair. On plus side, Justin and I are back as John Major High celebrity couple and no one is speaking to Sophie. Asked Scarlet how these ridiculous rumours start. She said Sad Ed.

Scarlet and Trevor are still not talking though. It has thrown Goth Corner Mark II into chaos. The boy goths are all backing Trevor for his hardline anti-EMO stance,

166

but the girl goths, who see the attraction in colours other than black and purple, are behind Scarlet. Mrs Brain had to separate them at lunchtime with an overcooked Foccacia. She has designated a Goth Corner Mark III for Trevor and his bat friends next to the povvy table (aka Free School Dinners table). Scarlet is delighted as it is infinitely inferior to Goth Corner Mark II.

Have not mentioned my previous doubts to Justin. It is because, according to *Cosmopolitan*, love is all about trust. And sex. But mostly trust. And if I do not trust him totally we are doomed anyway so might as well not say anything. It is total Catch 22.

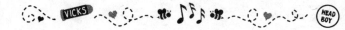

Tuesday 1

Saw Jack on the way to school. He said, 'You still with Justin?' I said, 'You still with Sophie?' He said, 'Just.' I said, 'That's good.' He said, 'Yeah.' For someone who wants to be a politician he is not very good with words.

. . . .

Wednesday 2

Velvet Elvis have officially broken up. Me and Scarlet have decided to concentrate on our GCSEs for a bit before conquering the music scene. Scarlet made the announcement in the canteen at lunch. Goth Corner Mark II and the Alternative Music Club table Mark I are in mourning. Unlike Goth Corner Mark III (i.e. Trevor's table) which is having a goth celebration of chewy fang sweets and blood (Ribena) to mark the occasion. Have told Justin I will be able to devote myself utterly to groupie duties from now on.

6 p.m.

Oh God, have just had awful thought. The *Walden Chronicle* comes out tomorrow. What if there are gruesome paparazzi shots of my injuries? Mum still doesn't know I was even at the Jockey Wilson suite. She has been spot-testing me on the periodic table all week. Have only got three out of ten. Unlike James who got 100 per cent. And in song. He says I am

looking at a D grade if I am lucky, and I had better pull my socks up.

. . . .

Thursday 3

Sad Ed is on tenterhooks. It is because Edie has her first desperate housewife-style matchmaking date tonight with PC Doone. If all goes well Edie will be 'feeling the force' by eleven o'clock and will utterly not have to leave Saffron Walden and break up Tuesday and Sad Ed's love-across-a-divide relationship.

4 p.m.

Thank God. The notoriously ineffectual and reactionary *Walden Chronicle* has completely covered up the Battle of the Bands scandal. Instead the cover features a photo of the Hermit Crabs superimposed next to Chas 'n' Dave under the headline 'Cockney Duo Catch Crabs'. Scarlet is outraged. She says it is like *Pravda*. I said, hardly. It is more like Primark. She said, '*Pravda*, not Prada, you heathen. It is an evil Russian propaganda newspaper. Like the *Daily Mail*. Which you would know if you had at all revised history.' Am definitely going to revise tonight. There was a blurry crowd shot of the Jockey Wilson suite inside, in which you can just see my science experiment jeans sprawled across the floor. But no one will be able to identify me from that.

172

4.15 p.m.

Mum has just demanded proof that I was revising at Scarlet's on Saturday night. She has been studying the *Walden Chronicle* with her magnifying glass gadget and says she is 99 per cent sure those are my chemically enhanced jeans under the pool table. Have texted Scarlet. Suzy is always happy to lie.

4.30 p.m.

Suzy has just called Mum to check I enjoyed myself at the science revisionathon. She says she personally kept a very strict eye on us and that we did not even turn the telly on once. I think she may have pushed it a bit. Mum will never believe that.

4.45 p.m.

Mum has called Suzy back to say her version of events on Saturday is flawed as there is a woman in the top left of the photo on page 27 who looks exactly like Suzy i.e. heaving bosoms and not much clothing. Suzy immediately launched evasive tactics by pretending to have a bad line then hanging up. Mum has now grounded me for a week and banned me from any so-called revision parties at Scarlet's for ever on the grounds that Suzy cannot be trusted. I said she did not have incontrovertible proof that it was me or Suzy in the picture. She said she is happy to carry out forensic checks on my clothing for evidence of cider and passive smoking. I declined. She can

sniff out teenage debauchery at twenty paces. I will accept my punishment gracefully and use the time to better myself. Also as Justin is grounded it does not matter. We can just talk to each other on our phones. It will be like phone sex. Except about Jim Morrison and guitar strings, rather than sex. Obviously.

Friday 4

Sad Ed is depressed again. Edie and PC Doone did not hit it off over vegetarian moussaka. Instead Edie binge-ate Nigella's whisky and marmalade pudding in a bid to get drunk and escape PC Doone going on about his truncheon (his actual one, not the outsized one Suzy hoped he was referring to, which it turns out is not outsized—Suzy 'accidentally' walked in on him in the bathroom). So Tuesday is facing repatriation once again and Sad Ed is facing a lifetime of abstinence. I said what does it matter if he is dying soon anyway. But he said that is not the point. He wants to enjoy as many vices as possible during his few moments left. I asked what other vices he was enjoying, given Mrs Thomas's strict regime? He said gambling and drink. He means the lottery and the half a pint of shandy Suzy bought him at the gig.

Saturday 5

Nuts In May has been thrown into turmoil by some

devastating news. Moonchild, i.e. ailment-ridden Rosamund, is leaving. She is moving in with Guru Derek at his chakra-healing compound in Steeple Bumpstead. Mr Goldstein is particularly hunched. It is the worry of finding a replacement. There are not many people who can stomach the smell of patchouli and liquorice root six days a week.

Scarlet is coming over later, as I am not allowed out into the free world. We are going to actually revise this time. She is bringing a DVD of Simon Scharma. She says it covers the entire history syllabus.

10 p.m.
Have not actually watched DVD but have absorbed information from the blurb on the cover. It is because we had important business to attend to, i.e. the Trevor situation. Scarlet is undecided as to whether or not to go back out with him. He has agreed to be seen with her in her skinny jeans but has drawn the line at retro ruffle skirts and Dita Von Teese lipstick. She says she is not sure whether this is a bad thing i.e. it is masculine oppression denying her the right to self-expression etc. Or a good thing, i.e. that his devotion to the dark side is unwavering i.e. he is not an infidel (what would that be—a fidel?). We did not come to a conclusion because at that point the dog fell down the stairs and the screams woke up Jesus. James was trying to teach it to fly. It is part of his Ninja training. It is not working.

Texted Justin to see how he is coping at our separation. No answer as yet. He is probably too miserable to reply.

. . . .

Sunday 6

There has been another shocking revelation in Saffron Walden. Treena was spotted coming out of the Queen Elizabeth last night with none other than her ex-husband Des. There is photographic evidence, as taken by Marjory, on her way home from Jenga Club. She and Mum should definitely go into the private investigation business, they would make a fortune. Grandpa is devastated. So is Mum. She was hoping to have ousted him and the dog by next week. Also, she is cross because it means Baby Jesus will be having contact with someone with a criminal record and a tattoo (both high up her banned list).

Still no reply from last night's text to Justin. Will text again in case he has committed suicide due to separation.

5 p.m.
No answer. Will try again in morning. If has committed suicide will not be able to do anything about it anyway.

9 p.m.
Am being remarkably calm considering Justin has possibly killed himself. Maybe I am one of those people

176

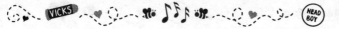

who is excellent in a crisis and does not panic. I could be a hostage negotiator. Or the queen.

. . . .

Monday 7

May Day (Bank Holiday UK and Rep. Ire.)
9 a.m.
Still no word from Justin. Have called Scarlet to tell her of possible Justin suicide. She says give it until midday and then inform police of death.

11 a.m.
No word still. Have called Sad Ed for more advice. He says I should be thankful that Justin will be at peace with himself now. Also he is annoyed at Justin stealing his untimely death thunder. He is thinking of bringing the timetable forward.

11.45 a.m.
Cannot take it any more. Have called police and told them that rock legend Justin Statham has taken his own life in the attic of his mock tudor mansion. They asked if I had seen the body? I said not technically. They said how technically? I said it was just a hunch. They said they do not work on hunches. I said the woman out of *Murder She Wrote* did and she got it right 100 per cent of the time. They have agreed to send someone round. They do not want to be outdone by an eighty-year-old woman in comfortable footwear.

2 p.m.

Justin has just rung to complain about the police disturbing his bank holiday lie-in. Apparently he got woken by an Alsatian licking his hair. It turns out he has not committed suicide. He has repetitive strain injury from an all-weekend X-Box marathon and his text thumb is only just recovering. He said I sounded very calm considering he was potentially dead. I said on the contrary I had been on the verge of flinging myself into the Slade in a suicide pact (not true but it sounds good). He said 'You could have just rung.' This is true. Why did I not think of that? Anyway it is excellent that he is alive. I will value him all the more now.

. . . .

Tuesday 8

Mr Vaughan has reminded us that we are supposed to be performing our drama GCSE pieces next week in preparation for the external examiner next month. He said he hoped that they are all well on the way to curtain up readiness. Did not inform him that have yet to actually choose monologue. Though it is not hard to decide. Obviously will do tragic heroine i.e. Juliet, as I am practically her i.e. my family and Justin's are from different sides of the tracks (i.e. Debden Road) and we practically committed suicide in a tragic pact at the weekend. Sad Ed has already picked his. He is doing Othello. Though I think he may be asking the examiner

178

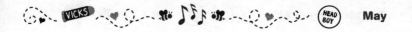
to suspend their disbelief a little too far. He is neither dynamic nor black.

. . . .

Wednesday 9

Grandpa's moping has reached new heights. He says he is too old for all this hoo-ha, that Treena has already rejected him because of his shrivelled thingy, and Mum will throw him out next like past-its-sell-by cheese and then no woman will have him. It is having a bad effect on the dog as well. It is lounging around in a most un-Ninjalike fashion, eating toffee and sighing every so often. Am going to call Suzy immediately and get Grandpa moved to the top of Edie's prospective lover list.

5 p.m.
Suzy says she is going to check with Edie to see if she has an upper age limit.

7 p.m.
Suzy says Edie will push sixty-five tops. I lied and said Grandpa was sixty-four.

7.15 p.m.
The hot date is confirmed. Grandpa is having dinner with Edie at Suzy's on Friday. Grandpa is now in a panic. He says there is no way he can pass for under seventy due to his white hair and droopy man-breasts. I said there was

nothing I can do about man-breasts (gross) but that he should purchase some Grecian 2000 tomorrow and revive a natural, youthful look. He has agreed. Am excellent matchmaker. Like Barbra Streisand in *Hello, Dolly*, but without hideous perm, big nose, and vast dresses.

. . . .

Thursday 10

Grandpa has purchased Grecian 2000. But is not natural light brown shade. Is black. I said he was supposed to be returning to his natural colour. He said I didn't specify whose natural colour. So I asked whose he was going for. He said Robert de Niro in *Taxi Driver*. He is thinking of doing the dog as well. He said it might cheer it up.

7 p.m.

Grandpa does not look like Robert de Niro. He looks like an ageing pervert. So does the dog. It is embarrassing. Grandpa is delighted though and is strutting round the house saying, 'You talking to me?' a lot. Mum is livid as all the beige M&S towels have indelible purple streaks on them. It is because the dog caught sight of itself in the mirror during the dye process and had a panic attack.

. . . .

Friday 11

Am in trouble. Dad got his mobile phone bill from

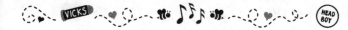

Wainwright and Hogg today. It turns out it is not paid automatically by Direct Debit and his personal calls are not all free. He owes them £378. I said maybe his phone had been intercepted by French rat boys. But Mum dialled one of the suspicious numbers and got Justin who said, 'All right, Riley?' Mum said she was Mrs Riley to him and was not all right at all, and hung up. The bill has been added to the money I still owe her for the Desdemona hoo-ha. According to my calculations will still be paying debt off at Christmas unless I get a substantial pay rise from Mr Goldstein. Am definitely going to write to Tony Blair to complain about poverty pay. And mobile phone tariffs. How are teenagers supposed to cope with the escalating cost of living? It is no wonder so many of us turn to glue or *The X Factor*.

6 p.m.

Grandpa is dressed for his date. He is wearing a brown suit, last seen in 1960, and a pair of trainers that he got off Ducatti Mick for £10. He says he got the idea for his look off *Doctor Who*. I said yes but *Doctor Who* is utterly gorgeous David Tennant, not seventy-five-year-old with black wig look and man-breasts. Even James is against it all. He says Grandpa is making a fool of himself. Plus he is annoyed as the hair dye is ruining the dog's training. Every time it walks past a window it goes bonkers and flings itself at the strange reflection. Mum has demanded

181

to know where Grandpa is going dressed like an Eastern European. He said he has a date with destiny. Thank God he did not say Edie. She would have banned him from leaving the house for sure.

11 p.m.
Grandpa is back. Apparently the *Doctor Who* look worked as he and Edie are meeting on Sunday for a second date. Asked how far he had gone on the first date. He said to the second door on the right. Have no idea what it means.

. . . .

Saturday 12
Have got a broken finger due to being on Nuts In May till duty all day today. It is because Mr Goldstein was in the stockroom conducting interviews for Moonchild's old job. I suggested he should be looking for someone young and dynamic to bring Nuts In May into the twenty-first century. He said he was quite happy in the current century (i.e. the nineteenth in his case) and to get back on the shop floor as lentils do not sell themselves. He is wasting an opportunity. If he got rid of the Beanfeast display he could add a computer and be a health food internet café so that people could Google their many symptoms and drink nettle tea before purchasing homeopathic so-called cures. I should be on *The Apprentice*. I am definite thrusting entrepreneurial type.

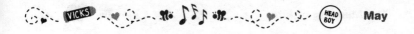

Unlike the candidate list which consisted of:

- Mrs Noakes from WHSmith (no chin; bad perm; calls trousers 'slacks') who is only thinking of changing job because it gives her more chance to observe potential drug-users and deviants (hippy types and teenagers buying Buzz Gum).
- Mrs Goldstein (Unlikely to get job as Mr Goldstein says she is too meddling. Dad would sympathize here. Mum once applied to Wainwright and Hogg and Dad intercepted the form and burnt it. Mum still thinks she was turned down on the grounds that she was overqualified.)
- Mrs Thomas (i.e. Sad Ed's mum. She says she needs to start saving for Sad Ed's college education. Did not tell her he is hoping to be dead before graduation.)

Mr Goldstein is giving the job to Mrs Thomas. He said she is exactly the right sort of person Nuts In May needs i.e. old and averse to change. Except that she can't do Saturdays due to her many Aled Jones Fan Club fixtures so now Mr Goldstein needs a new Saturday girl. Have suggested Scarlet. Then we can use potentially wasted hours working to discuss ongoing Trevor crisis.

Met Justin behind meat bins as usual for snogging/lunch. I said it is excellent that tonight is my last night of being grounded i.e. watching *Casualty* with Mum and Dad when I could be usefully watching it at Justin's. He said, 'Mmm.' His mouth was full of scotch egg at the

time so I expect he meant, 'I cannot wait to spend
Saturday night in your loving arms again.' It is a known
fact that absence makes the heart grow fonder. He must
be bursting with love for me by now.

. . . .

Sunday 13

Am devoting the day to perfecting my performance as
Juliet. Justin is coming over later to be the audience and
am aiming to stun him into flinging me on the Lenor-
scented duvet and snogging me within an inch of my life.
Although am under strict instructions to leave bedroom
door open at all times for anti-sex spot checks.

Grandpa is devoting the day to his performance as
Robert de Niro/*Doctor Who* with Edie as his audience.
They are taking Jesus and the dog out for a romantic walk
on the common. I said it might be better to leave Jesus
and/or the dog at home if he was hoping for romance but
he says he wants Edie to see him warts and all (he is not
being entirely metaphorical, he actually has warts). Also
he needs them as cover for Mum. She will be suspicious
if he goes out unaccompanied. He is making a mistake.
Edie absolutely should not be seeing Grandpa's warts at
this stage of their relationship. She will dump him within
minutes. Although at least he will not have Mum or
James checking that he is not touching proscribed zones
every five minutes.

184

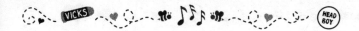

5 p.m.
Romantic walk not quite as planned. Apparently things began to unravel when they bumped into Treena and Des at the swings. Grandpa took his whole timelord/gangster thing too seriously and launched himself at Des in a frenzied attack. Des is now in Addenbrookes with a bleeding ear. It is not from Grandpa. Or the dog, who refused to follow the command to 'kill' as it was too busy spinning on the roundabout. It is from Treena. Apparently she and Edie share similar tastes in crap hair dye and 1960s nylon suits as she got all wistful about Grandpa's youthful look and took a swing at Des with her handbag.

Grandpa and Treena have gone for immediate summit talks at the Queen Elizabeth. Edie brought the dog and Baby Jesus home.

Also am excellent Juliet. Justin definitely impressed. Did not exactly fling himself at me with abandon, but said it was very 'emotional'. It is the special crying effect— thanks to Vicks inhaler rubbed under eyes. Tried to summon up depressing memories in method acting style but nothing tragic has happened to me yet so have had to resort to artificial means.

Monday 14
Grandpa has gone back to the bosom of his family. Treena says that Des was a just a sex thing and Grandpa is her ONE. Yes and Grandpa is not on probation which helps.

The dog is still here though. Treena says it is a condition of their reconciliation. I am amazed she didn't try to leave Jesus as well.

5 p.m.
Oooh. Maybe Edie will get together with Des. He could be her bit of rough. He has excellent credentials including GBH and attempted armed robbery. Will call Suzy immediately and suggest it.

5.15 p.m.
Edie says she will try Des but that she is hoping to get Mr Vaughan in next as she thinks he may be the one due to his former (and possibly current) drug habit.

. . . .

Tuesday 15
Had horrid shock at breakfast. Have dentist appointment with sadistic Mrs Wong at eleven. Mum says it is nil by mouth until then. I begged for some nerve-fortifying Marmite on toast but Mum says she does not want Mrs Wong complaining about crumbs in my molars. On plus side I will miss French i.e. two hours of Mark Lambert trying to pronounce '*l'hôpital*'.

4 p.m.
Oh God. Have horrifying news. Mrs Wong says I have to wear a brace. Am going to look like Danny Stanton in

Year Eight aka Jaws. Justin will not want to snog me in case he gets lacerated on the metal bits. And will have bits of lettuce stuck in them all the time. Am going to be social pariah and virgin for rest of life. Or at least for six months. Though Mum has agreed to delay fitting until after GCSEs to lessen my trauma. She is worried it may cause a speech impediment and interfere with my French oral.

Also saw Emily Reeve in waiting room looking fat and nervous. It is because all your teeth fall out when you are pregnant. At least that's what Granny Clegg claims is the cause of several of her missing teeth.

5 p.m.
Mum says it was not pregnancy that made Granny Clegg's teeth drop out. It was drinking tins of condensed milk.

Wednesday 16

Mr Vaughan said my Juliet was promising. If a little overwrought. He says a bit less crying would help. It is because I overdid the Vicks Vapour Rub in my enthusiasm. Was still crying in rural studies. Cowpat Cheesmond had to send me to Mrs Leech with suspected 'girls' trouble'. She gave me a tissue and a bourbon biscuit and said, 'They are all bastards.' I just nodded through my tears.

Also Mr Vaughan is refusing to go out with Edie. It is the age difference. (He is not so fussy when it is the other way around.) So is Barry the Blade. He says it is

not the age but that he is in love with white-flare-wearing wee-smelling Mrs Simpson. Although she is in love with dead gay singer Freddie Mercury. She claims his spirit lives in her airing cupboard and is dictating a novel to her. She is planning to sell it and make millions, once Freddie has finished. Suzy asked Barry what the story is about. It is about a dead singer who lives in an airing cupboard.

Sad Ed says he is doomed to singledom. I said if his relationship was as rock solid as mine and Justin's then he has nothing to fear. He said 'Oh, great.'

Thursday 17
8.30 a.m.
Oh God. Think may have been dumped. Fat Kylie has just texted me to ask if I want Mr Whippy to duff Justin up. She says he will happily 'stick his ice cream scoop where the sun don't shine'. What is going on? Am going to text Scarlet.

8.35 a.m.
Scarlet says Jack says that Sophie heard he was going to dump me but was waiting until after my exams in case Mum blamed him for me failing. (He is right. She would do.) Oh God. It is utterly tragic. I am single and he doesn't even have the heart to tell me himself. It is totally like *Pretty in Pink* where Blane is too embarrassed to admit he

188

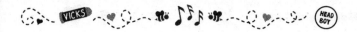
does not want to take Andy to the prom because she is poor and wears second-hand clothes and her dad is jobless and wears vests (not under things, like Dad, but as actual clothes).

9 a.m.

Am not dumped. It is just a vicious rumour started by security-unconscious Mrs Leech due to the Vick's Vapour Rub incident. Justin says he would not chuck me just before my GCSEs. That would be cruel and heartless. He is so thoughtful. I am lucky to have him.

Sad Ed is happy too. He and Tuesday have come up with a new plan to keep Edie in Saffron Walden. They have signed her up for driving lessons in a bid to give her something to aim for in life. And to stop Tuesday having to rely on Mr Wilmott and his car of shame (i.e. the Vauxhall Cavalier) turning up to collect her.

Friday 18

Treena has rung to invite me to her thirtieth birthday party tomorrow. Asked her who was going. She said her cousin Donna (who is 'totally mental') and some of the old ladies from the Twilight Years Day Centre (the continent and mobile ones). Asked if I could bring anyone. She said yes but it is girls only so that they can watch *Dirty Dancing* and leer at Patrick Swayze without having to turn over for *Match of the Day* (or *Hollyoaks Late*

Night in Grandpa's case). Am going to take Scarlet. She is all for female caucus things. She says it is an essential demonstration of sisterhood. It is more likely to be a demonstration of tequila drinking in Treena and Donna's case. Have told Justin that I am 'out with the girls'. He did not seem too disappointed. It is because he totally trusts me and is secure in us having our own interests and time apart. (I learnt that off Suzy. I also learnt some horrible facts about penises, which I cannot even bear to write down.)

. . . .

Saturday 19

Am sick of being on till. Now have bleeding knuckles which is not good look for party. Luckily Suzy came into shop (to purchase incense sticks to cover up a burning cat-hair smell—Edna has singed Gordon with a Rothman's) and told her to remind Scarlet to offer herself up for work immediately before I actually lose a limb. Also reminded her to tell Scarlet to meet me at 19 Harvey Road at 8 o'clock precisely as do not want to be left alone with Treena and her girl gang for too long. Jesus is round ours already. He is riding the dog up and down the stairs. So is Grandpa. (Round our house, I mean, not riding the dog. That would be impossible, not to mention probably illegal.) They have had a lucky escape. I fear Treena's all-girl thirtieth will descend into anarchy and shrieking before Patrick has even taken his shirt off. Or maybe turning thirty will mark a new

190

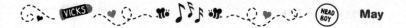
and thoughtful period in Treena's life. Now that she is middle-aged and a mother and wife.

. . . .

Sunday 20

Oh God. Have seen Mark Lambert's dad's willy (aka Mr Hosepipe's hosepipe). Think that is definitely illegal. It is because Donna hired him to be the fireman strippergram. Though at least have not touched it. Which is more than I can say for Elsie Stain (eighty-nine, four foot seven, false teeth which clack and fall out when she gets overexcited, which is a lot).

Party was as predicted i.e. anarchy and shrieking. It is because Treena invited the neighbours, i.e. Fat Kylie, who ignored the girls only rule and brought with her not just Thin Kylie and some female O'Gradys (Mrs and Paris-Marie) but also all the male ones too (Stacey, Dane, Finbarr, and Kyle plus two others I have never seen before, both called Liam). At least she left Keanu and Whitney at home. She did not bother with a babysitter. The walls are paper-thin and you can hear the screams even over Jennifer Warnes at full volume. Drank only Red Bull so as to avoid another O'Grady snogging fiasco. Scarlet should have followed my restrained example. She drank four cans of Carlsberg and ended up snogging one of the Liams (not sure which, they both have the same look of Celtic menace). It is lucky I was sober and also strengthened by excess caffeine intake as managed to prise

them apart and drag her to safety (i.e. Summerdale Road) before anything else happened. She is still asleep on floor in my Millets sleeping bag. Have followed Mum's example and put bucket and Cillit Bang next to her head in case of vomit. She looks peaceful. It will be sad to have to wake her and impart the news that I am no longer alone in my shame and that she too has swapped saliva with an O'Grady.

11 a.m.
Scarlet still snoring. Am actually quite jealous as only got two hours sleep due to excess Red Bull. Ended up manically solving quadratic equations until five in morning.

12 noon
Scarlet still asleep.

1 p.m.
Have woken Scarlet up as do not want to miss Sunday lunch or *Ugly Betty*. Told her terrible news and asked if she would be ending it with Trevor forthwith. She says on the contrary, it has only confirmed her true love for Trevor. She feels renewed in their relationship, and in her goth vows, and is going round there now to offer herself up to his goth mercy (after she has showered all traces of O'Grady off herself, obviously).

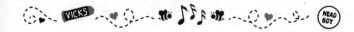

Monday 21

Scarlet and Trevor are officially back together. Goth Corner Mark II is a haven of peace and bat toys once again. Scarlet says they are going to allow each other their freedom to wear whatever clothes they want. (Except Tommy Hilfiger. Even I would draw the line there.) She also said this time they are going to be utterly honest with each other and tell each other everything. Asked if she had confessed about the O'Grady liaison. She said no.

Tuesday 22

Mum and Dad are sulking again. It is because Dad is annoyed as it took him two hours to get home from work this evening due to a car crash. Mum is not annoyed that he is late. She is annoyed because the crash involved a Ford Fiesta wedged across one of the myriad mini-roundabouts. Dad is blaming Fiestas for a persistent steering fault. Mum has countered by quoting Passat crash statistics. James is now acting as official statistician to both sides and is googling evidence as I write.

8 p.m.

It gets worse. Sad Ed has rung. The crash was no ordinary Fiesta. It was one of Mike 'Wandering Hands' Majors's driving school fleet. And at the wheel was none other than Edie. The news has not gone down well with Mum. She says Edie is sabotaging Dad from afar by stopping him

getting home in time for his liver and onions. Not only that but she is putting a pillar of the community (i.e. Mike Wandering Hands) at risk of death from her inability to follow rules of any kind. Dad says the crash was probably due to Mike's wandering hands wandering too close to Edie. They are now watching *Top Gear* in strained silence. James has taken the dog upstairs. He says all the hoo-ha is not good for its Ninja sensitivities. Am inclined to agree. Although the dog is still not showing any potential as a superhero. This morning it fell in the toilet.

. . . .

Wednesday 23

Saffron Walden is awash with rumours about Edie and Mike. Mum is livid. She says it will all be over by next week once he realizes she is a law-breaker. (Binge drinking is illegal in Mum's book. Which is an actual book. It is the one she uses to write down ASBO behaviour in.) I said she should be happy his wandering hands are occupied as it kills several birds with one stone. Mum says it is not Mike's hands she is worried about. It is his devotion to upholding the Highway Code. She thinks he will go all lax under Edie's malign influence.

. . . .

Thursday 24

Sad Ed has confirmed Mike and Edie rumours. Apparently

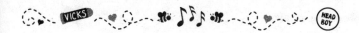

the near-death experience of wedging a Fiesta into a traffic bollard has brought them closer together, literally and metaphorically. Vest-wearing Colin Riley is off the hook and Tuesday can remain a British citizen and girlfriend of Sad Ed, until his untimely death, that is. He is very pleased. Not only will he get regular sex until that event but he will have someone to weep hysterically and fling themselves on his grave at his funeral. In addition to Mrs Thomas.

Friday 25

12 noon

Hurrah. It is the last day of lessons for Year Eleven. I am another giant step closer to non-uniform wearing, black coffee drinking, uber-left-wing Sixth Form, with just the minor hurdle of an entire month of GCSEs to cross. Mr Wilmott herded everyone into the canteen for his annual motivational assembly, success rate negligible, since we are still languishing below the Burger King Sports Academy in the league tables. But this year he has an added incentive. Clearly Tuesday has been influencing him with her American ways because he has announced that there will be a 'prom' for Years Eleven to Thirteen. Am overwhelmed with potential *Pretty in Pink* excitement. Think will use occasion to abandon myself to Justin i.e. do 'It'. Although he has not pushed point for a while. If at all. I know will not be technically sixteen but will mark the end of my childhood, i.e. GCSEs, and

anyway it is practically compulsory to have done 'It' to be allowed entry into common room.

Mr Wilmott also announced elections for head boy and girl. All current Lower Sixth are eligible. Justin says no one in their right mind would want to be head boy as it means having to wear a crap badge (made by Mrs Leech and her Fisher Price badge making machine). Plus the only actual powers you get are patrolling the Criminals and Retards and telling them to stop breaking things. The campaigns will begin immediately after GCSEs end. Mr Wilmott says it is so we can give our full attention to the various manifestos and not just make rash judgements on looks (or smells in the case of Oona Rickets who is bound to stand). He is wasting his time. It will all come down to 'shagability'. The Maths Club have proved it with several correlation charts.

3 p.m.

Justin has put his name on the list for head boy. It is not because he has had a change of heart over the crap badge or minimal powers, it is because Jack and Sophie have signed up and he refuses to be beaten by Jack, even at things he does not want. I pointed out that he is leaving Sixth Form after retakes, but he says he has put in for emergency A level choices (PE, Music, and Drama). I said he must not give up his musical career for me, even though it is utterly romantic and almost like taking a bullet! He said he is not. It is because Braintree's

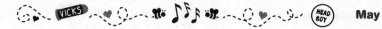

Rock Foundation is under threat from a 'Mickey Mouse course' crackdown.

* *

Saturday 26

Oh my God. Mr Goldstein has employed a new Saturday girl. Except it is not a girl. It is Jack. I demanded an employee conference immediately but Mr Goldstein said Jack was the only applicant and there was nothing to discuss, besides which he had gyppy hump and not to bother him. So I texted Scarlet to ask why she was not here and her treacherous brother was. But she was obviously too busy rediscovering Trevor's gothic bits as she did not reply.

It is utterly unfair. Especially as Mr Goldstein has let Jack have lunch at one and moved my lunch break to twelve, so Justin and I will have to forsake our meat bin snog. Maybe Jack is doing it on purpose to annoy me and Justin. He is definitely up to something. Am also worried he may be trying to oust me as top dog in Mr Goldstein's eyes. He has a vegetarian progressive sex guru mother who has a cabinet full of homeopathic cures. Whereas my mother is more acquainted with sausages and Tixylix.

9 p.m.

Told Justin about Jack situation after work. He said I should use it to our advantage, i.e. to wheedle potential

campaign-shattering information out of him. I said that would be totally underhand and evil. He said exactly.

. . . .

Sunday 27
Whit Sunday (Pentecost)
Granny Clegg has rung. The hip of doom is gyppy again. She says it is so painful it may be foretelling a whole mass of potential deaths. But Mum says she has had enough hip of doom hoo-ha and has ordered Granny to make an appointment with the doctor. Granny has agreed but says she will still be keeping an eye on the news for serial killers, mass salmonella poisonings, and train crashes.

. . . .

Monday 28
Spring Holiday (UK)
9 a.m.
Think will start revision today. Although Suzy says it is essential to have relaxing 'you' time during this traumatic period. So maybe will watch a bit of T4 and have brain-stimulating Shreddies first.

12 noon
Am utterly relaxed after *Friends* marathon. Will get down to history revision now. Although am bit hungry again. Will just eat vitamin-filled apple. And watch *Popworld*.

198

12.55 p.m.
Now will start.

1 p.m.
Oh. Lunchtime. Tuna sandwiches. Had better eat it as it is full of omega 3 which is essential exam-passing food.

2.30 p.m.
Am now tip-top brainwise. Oooh. Text from Sad Ed. His CD player is on blink and he cannot play 'The Best of Leonard Cohen' (a misnomer, it is all horrible) which means he cannot revise at home. He is coming over to hijack mine.

2.45 p.m.
Cannot revise with sound of mournful moaning in ear. (Leonard Cohen, not Sad Ed. Although he is quite annoying too as he keeps trying to sing along.) Will fetch digestives to shut him up and revise when Ed has gone.

6 p.m.
After tea obviously.

7 p.m.
Hmm. It is quite late and do not want to tax brain into having meltdown. Think will watch television and start tomorrow.

Tuesday 29

8.30 a.m.

Am totally ready for revision. Will just eat Shreddies and then will get down to it. James is uncharacteristically absent from the Shreddie table. He has taken a giant roll of paper, his set of 100 washable felt pens (actually 99 and not washable, according to Mum, and now subject of pedant letter and potential lawsuit) and some stickers to his bedroom. It is obviously Ninja-related. He is probably drawing up a blueprint of the sewer for the dog to learn. He is wasting his time. The dog gets lost in the kitchen with the lights out.

9 a.m.

Maybe just need one episode of *The OC* to prepare mentally.

9.01 a.m.

The OC rudely interrupted by James with a patented, colour-coded, reward-based revision schedule. He says he cannot let me fritter my future away on cheap American import television (this is rich coming from someone who worships at the shrine of the Turtles) and is taking over as chief adviser during this essential period. Have pleaded with Mum to rescue me but she says she is backing him all the way. He is like her mini-me.

James says it is rigorous, but, on the plus side, it is easy to follow. It is divided into hourly timeslots from 7 a.m. to 6 p.m., with half an hour for lunch and ten minute breaks

for digestives at eleven and three. Each subject has a different colour and I get a sticker for every hour successfully completed. He will also be conducting tests at the end of each day and, if I win, I get a *Lord of the Rings* figurine. He says it is a tried and tested carrot and stick method, with the stickers and action figures being the metaphorical carrots. Asked what the stick was. He said spending the rest of my life as one of the great uneducated of our family i.e. down a tin mine like Grandpa Clegg. Have agreed. Do not want to be in same mental bracket as pasty-waving moron.

7 p.m.
Am exhausted. But have won two orcs (history and science). Only narrowly missed Gollum. (Rural studies—chickens do not have a nine-month gestation period. They lay eggs. Complained that it was a trick question but James said it is like *Millionaire* and there are no trick questions, just stupid answers.)

Wednesday 30
7 p.m.
Have completed second day of Riley-patented exam method. Am totally going to beat Scarlet, who is following Suzy's 'exams aren't everything' mantra. She is doing two hours a day interspersed with yoga, hummus, and snogging bat boy. I on other hand am too focused to snog

Justin and have texted him to stay away during this crucial period. He does not care. He is hanging out at the Mocha trying to win over the key waster vote. Pointed out that he was supposed to be revising too but he says he did it all on Sunday.

- -

Thursday 31

7 p.m.

Got a hobbit (French) and Legolas (English) today. Although James handed them over with a tear in his eye. It is not delight in my achievements. It is because Konnie Huq is leaving *Blue Peter*. He says it is the end of an era. It is the end of him and Grandpa Riley ogling children's television.

Also Granny Clegg rang. Apparently (and predictably) Dr Kimber does not believe in the hip of doom. She says it is a hip of arthritis and needs replacing. Granny Clegg is now on the waiting list for a new, non-death-predicting one. Grandpa Clegg has told her not to worry, it will be years before the op and she has plenty of time to solve crime until then. Told Scarlet. She says he is a typical unreconstructed *Daily Mail*-reading Thatcherite and that, on the contrary, thanks to Labour's heavy investment in the NHS and controversial targets, Granny Clegg will be having a new hip inserted within weeks. Although she may get MRSA and die before she actually gets to use it.

Friday 1

Am definite genius. Have completed all but two slots in James's chart (one due to dog-related bathroom fracas, and the other an overlong lunchbreak as it was Mum's goulash which is notoriously chewy) and passed 75 per cent of James's 'tough but fair' exam quizzes. Am now only missing Aragorn and that Liv Tyler one from *Lord of Rings* figurine collection. Though obviously will be giving them back to James as am *a*) not loser and *b*) he has made clear they are only on temporary incentivizing loan.

Saturday 2

No revision today due to actual work. Mum says I should give up for the duration of the exams but I said the maths needed to add up lentil bills and operate the till of death would be excellent revision. Also have worked out am still around £576 in debt due to death of Desdemona, Glastonbury ticket, Dad's phone bill, and having to repay Justin his £50 mobile minutes so cannot afford to give up. Was sweeping up muesli bits when Justin texted me to remind me to use my time at work to glean head boy information out of Jack. Decided to go for open, journalistic approach (as am excellent at it, as proven by brief career at *Walden Chronicle*) so asked him why he was standing for position. He says it is all good practice for when he is an anti-war foreign secretary. Also he says he has a groundbreaking manifesto for a vastly improved

Sixth Form, including a new sofa and a condom machine. Which I must admit does sound good. But had to be loyal so said he had no chance of winning now that Justin was in the running. Jack said no one will vote for Justin as he is utterly transparent and is only doing it to impress Sophie. I said didn't he mean me. He said, 'Yeah, right.' He was obviously slightly high from the overpowering smell of hemp oil. Or else he has Sophie Microwave Muffins on the brain. Anyway he is wrong. Everyone will vote for Justin. He is a living legend. And has lovely arms.

9 p.m.
Justin not impressed with information. (Although he says he may 'borrow' some of the manifesto ideas. Especially the new sofa, as one of the springs pierced his left-weave Gap jeans last week.) He says he wants dirt. Like sex secrets or skeletons in the cupboard. I said I did not think Jack had any skeletons in his cupboard. He said all politicians do so I asked him what his was. He said his mum once made him wear his sister's pants to school when she forgot to wash his. He is right. That sort of information could cost him the campaign if it was ever made public.

- -

Sunday 3
Am having total GCSE panic. Is less than twenty-four hours until I potentially seal my fate as literary genius

or pie-serving shopgirl. Mum is not helping by pointing out that she got nine O levels all at Grades A and B. James asked Dad how many he got. He said not as many. James said how many. He said six. None at Grade A. And two of them were woodwork and metalwork. But that is not the point because exams were harder in those days and today his results would translate into at least eleven A*s. James agreed and said that modern GCSEs are not worth the paper they are written on. So I said might as well not bother but then Mum intervened with her well-practised 'exams are the meaning of life' speech. (Which is sort of like the 'I have a dream' speech but with fewer references to black people. And more spoon-thrusting.) I said I thought sex was the meaning of life as without it we would all be dead. Mum said on the contrary exams are what separates the wheat from the chaff and in fact there ought to be an exam before anyone has sex, which in her opinion, neither I nor James, nor any of the O'Gradys would ever pass. Then James said we were both wrong and that in fact the meaning of life is '42'. So Mum sent us both to our rooms for questioning her version of events. She is like a creationist in her academic zeal.

Anyway she is wrong. Sex is the meaning of life. And once have finished GCSEs, will concentrate on passing next test i.e. doing 'It'.

Monday 4
D-Day

8 a.m.
Am totally ready for first GCSE i.e. maths. Have eaten special breakfast of boiled omega 3 eggs and Shredded Wheat with omega 3 milk (purchased by Mum in panic exam-passing bid).

8.15 a.m.
Scarlet has texted to make sure I have packed my lucky mascot. She is taking a mini Marilyn Manson and Sad Ed has got a toy rabbit called Frobisher. Oh God. Do not have lucky toy since dog ate Larry the lamb. Will have to borrow one off James.

8.18 a.m.
Am taking talking Nicola from Girls Aloud. It is the only one he is willing to part with except for a high fee, which I cannot afford due to scale of debt crisis. It will be good anyway. It is ironic and also can use it in science for anatomy questions. Have texted Justin special good luck message.

8.19 a.m.
Got special message back from Justin. 'TA, RILEY'. He is obviously too overwrought at thought of failing English for second time to send me good luck back. Will not

208

worry about it. Will remember that in six weeks will be united with him in sexual ecstasy. Possibly.

3 p.m.
Exam delayed by an hour due to lucky mascot issues. Mr Wilmott says calculators and revision folders do not qualify. Nor do live pets. This is because Davey MacDonald brought in his hamster Beckham which escaped and was last seen heading for Mrs Brain's canteen. It is obviously as mental as Davey MacDonald as no one goes there voluntarily. Mr Wilmott also questioned the talking Nicola. He is worried it may have been reprogrammed with exam answers. Offered to let him press her breasts to hear it in action. He did. It said, 'I'm just a love machine.'

Think have done OK though. Questions remarkably untaxing e.g. 'Five people like watching the *News*. Twelve people like watching *Police Chase*. How many more people like *Police Chase* than the *News*?' Even Mark Lambert cannot get that wrong. It is seven. Obviously. James is right. GCSEs are not worth the paper they are written on.

3.05 p.m.
Oh God. What if it was a trick question? Cannot think about it. It is too late. Have to get back to James's new exam time schedule (still colour-coded with stickers but without *Lord of Rings* figurines as he has run out of them since dog bit Aragorn's head off during *Antiques Roadshow* last night).

Tuesday 5
Have got English Lit. today. Which am not worried about as am practically literary marvel anyway.

3 p.m.
A cinch. Had to write about a weak character in *Of Mice and Men*. It is obviously the old man called Candy as he is ancient and shrivelled.

3.05 p.m.
Unless it was metaphorical. In which case the answer could have been giant retard Lennie. Anyway it does not matter as there are no right or wrong answers in English. Only opinions.

3.10 p.m.
Unless you are Fat Kylie and put down Smike who is not even in *Of Mice and Men*. That is not an opinion, that is just mentalism. At least is science tomorrow. There is no opinion there, just fact.

Wednesday 6
Although if do not know facts then opinion would be easier. What, for God's sake, is immobilized lactase? Is English again tomorrow. Thank God.

Thursday 7
English Language rescheduled to Friday due to Retard-related incident in exam hall.

. . . .

Friday 8
School shut due to lack of electricity. According to Mrs Leech, there is rodent damage in one of the fuse boxes. All fingers point to Beckham the lucky hamster. English rescheduled to Monday, along with French and maths.

Scarlet has threatened to go on strike against the giant exam marathon but Mr Wilmott says if he leaves it any longer then criminal elements (he means O'Gradys and Mark Lambert) will get hold of the exam papers from the Burger King Sports Academy and cheating will be rife. Scarlet pointed out that this could raise his grade point average several marks and he did waiver for several seconds but has erred on the side of the law. Also, he underestimates the O'Gradys. They can get exam papers in one hour, via a web of loose-moralled motorcycle couriers operating in the Bishop's Stortford area, as testified to by Thin Kylie who sat science in isolation an hour late on Wednesday due to an alleged brain tumour. So-called school nurse Mrs Leech checked her over for symptoms using a stethoscope from the Drama wardrobe department and a biology textbook. Thank God she is not an actual nurse. She diagnosed her with rickets but said she could get treatment after the exam.

211

Am actually looking forward to work tomorrow. It will be welcome relief from general hothouse atmosphere. Also, saw Sophie lurking around Justin outside Mr Patel's. Am going to let him touch breast tomorrow night. It will lure him away from Sophie, even if it is a minuscule A cup. Not sure which one though. Maybe the right one as it is discernibly bigger, by at least three millimetres according to Scarlet.

Saturday 9

Breast touching did not go according to plan. Justin was concentrating on trying to make his hair look exactly like Jim Morrison's on the cover of eponymously titled album 'The Doors' so said I felt constricted and asked if he minded if I took my top off. But, and this was the cunning part, I was not wearing anything underneath except my bra. But somehow I got wound up in a sleeve and fell backwards and knocked a glass of Vimto over his turntable. So instead of groping my breast, he just said, 'Jesus, Riley. That's bloody vintage Zepp.' I pointed out there was also some dripping on the cream shagpile and said he should use Stain Devils but not the one for red wine, the one for ink. It is one of Mum's tried and tested tips.

Sunday 10

Granny Clegg rang. The hip of doom has gone ominously

silent. She thinks it could be something to do with Armageddon. She says Maureen at the Spar says her hairdresser says the world is going to end on Tuesday. Or possibly Friday. Mum said, thank God. It is because James has flooded the bathroom. He was trying to recreate a sewer-like atmosphere for the dog. Mum said he could have just taken him for a walk in the shopping-trolley-clogged Slade.

Monday 11

8.15 a.m.
Have had double omega 3 eggs in preparation for marathon exam day of maths, French, and English Lang. Am fully revised and nothing can go wrong.

8.20 a.m.
Where is talking Nicola? Oh God. Am utterly going to fail if cannot locate lucky mascot.

8.30 a.m.
Nicola is missing, presumed in dog. It is feigning innocence but every so often there are faint snatches of a scouse accent from its general direction. James has offered giant Des Lynam cutout or naked Will Young as a replacement. Neither look particularly lucky. Am going to depend on brain power instead. Lucky mascots are not actually lucky. It is all in the mind.

3 p.m.

Why, oh why, did dog eat talking Nicola? It is all his fault I could not concentrate in any exams. It is because Nicola has a calming presence and I can stare into her empty plastic eyes and the answers come springing to my mind. Today just had to stare at back of Fat Kylie's head which is utterly uninspiring and not at all calming due to gel to hair ratio.

* * *

Tuesday 12

Hurrah. Am totally going to pass English though. Had to write about a typical day in my household to show aliens what life in England is like. Was very informative including details of the various ongoing bans in force in the house (Ribena, ITV, E4, overusing the word 'like') although used artistic licence when describing James or they will think I am making him up. No one is that pedantic or weird in real life. The dog came off well too. I skirted around him eating ginger Nicola and said it was a model of Tony Blair. It makes me sound more politically aware and the dog possibly anti-war. Is drama tomorrow. Am going to get into the Juliet mood now and stay in character until tomorrow. It is not hard as have utterly Capulet-like restrictive parents. May get Justin to shout up at window later in a lovestruck manner.

8 p.m.
Justin is refusing to pledge undying love for me down the side of the garage. He is worried Mum will take umbrage and throw something at him. He is right to be scared. She is always flinging stuff at cats. And Thin Kylie.

Wednesday 13
Mum says I am taking the in-character thing too far. It is because I refused omega eggs and demanded more Juliet-like gruel. Got Ready Brek in end. With golden syrup. Even Juliet would have had syrup on gruel. Stomach feels a bit funny now though. It is nerves at exam. Or maybe have become Juliet and it is love for Romeo!

10 a.m.
Think it is not love but possible overeating of Ready Brek. Am doubled over in pain. But will soldier on like professional.

3 p.m.
Mr Vaughan says my Juliet was fascinating, especially the decision to play her as a hunchback. He says it was excellent planning to work with Mr Goldstein as research and will be lobbying the examiner to give me extra marks for this dedication to the art. Hurrah.

Thursday 14

Yet more science. Which is hard and pointless. Who cares what the valency of boron is? At least is French tomorrow. That is easy and useful.

. . . .

Friday 15

I take it back. French was utterly impossible and did not involve the words *'superbe'* or *'zut alors'* at all. Do not know why we learn the language anyway. No one speaks it except the French, who are economically irrelevant, and Celine Dion. We should be learning Japanese so that we can all run IT conglomerates. And purchase ironic knee-length socks on our travels. May well write to Alan 'I've got an iPod' Johnson to complain about this backward-looking languages policy.

. . . .

Saturday 16

Hurrah. Glastonbury tickets have arrived. Jack gave me mine at work. It is marked 'sex—male'. And claims I am thirty-five. It is an understandable mistake. After all have used excellent nickname Ray. Plus do actually look bit like boy. Told Jack I still hadn't managed to persuade Mum to let me go. Or even mention it to her in fact. He said I could tell her we are all going to visit Granny Stone in Jersey for healthy post-GCSE recovery featuring

216

bicycle riding and horses. He says he will happily lie for me, as Mum will not believe Suzy. Was so pleased forgot to dig for head boy battle dirt. Will make something up to Justin later.

9 p.m.

Mum has agreed to let me go to Jersey on the proviso that I do not go near the indigenous criminal fraternity. She is *Bergerac*-obsessed and thinks all the millionaires are diamond-smuggling lotharios or drug dealers. It is lucky she has never met Granny Stone. According to Scarlet she smokes marijuana. I said it is practically legal if it is for arthritis purposes. She said it is not. It is for getting high purposes.

Sunday 17

Father's Day

Revision interrupted for day due to arrival of Jesus and Grandpa for multi-generational Father's Day celebration. Mum pointed out that they had not been invited but Grandpa said Treena was sick of them getting under her feet. Mum said why, is she doing the hoovering for once? Grandpa said no. It is one of Mrs O'Grady's get fit videos. Treena is wasting her time if Mrs O'Grady is anything to go by. She is gargantuan. On plus side they acted as a distraction from fact that I had utterly forgotten Father's Day. Dad said not to worry as passing my GCSEs will be a

present in itself. Wish had got him golf balls now. He is going to be doubly cross if I fail.

. . . .

Monday 18

Oh my God. Have just had geography exam. Did not even remember I was doing geography and omitted it entirely from revision schedule. It is lucky I sat exam at all and is only down to Scarlet texting me to ask me where I was and what was the capital of Bulgaria. Will do better than Emily Reeve anyway. She had to go to the toilet ten times in two hours. (According to Mark Lambert it is because the baby is sitting right on her bladder. Asked him how he knows. He says Mrs Duddy has been teaching them about babies, 'which are, like, the meaning of life'. Did not get into repeat of sex versus exams versus 42 argument. And admire Mrs Duddy for teaching the Retards and Crminals something they will actually need to know, as opposed to raffia owls and *Olga da Polga*.) Fat Kylie also went to the loo several times. She is not pregnant. She had got a packet of Jaffa cakes stashed on top of the cistern.

Have got history tomorrow. Will do cold war questions as am excellent on that e.g. *Pravda* is not a fashion brand, is an evil Russian *Daily Mail*-type paper. And iron curtain is not in Poland.

. . . .

Tuesday 19

But should probably have found out what *perestroika* and *glasnost* were. Oh well. It is too late now. Only rural studies to go and no one has ever failed that.

5 p.m.

Except Stacey O'Grady. And that was only because he was in custody for kidnapping a police Alsatian on the day of the exam. (The police should be the ones in trouble. The Alsatian put up no resistance and broke several codes by accepting sweets from strangers and getting into their car.)

. . . .

Wednesday 20

Do not remember ducks being on syllabus. Or maybe we were all watching Mark Lambert do the Macarena at the time instead of concentrating on the interactive whiteboard.

Anyway it will be declared null and void because Emily Reeve went into labour in the middle of the exam. Fat Kylie shrieked, 'Sir, Emily's pissed herself, sir.' Mark Lambert, with his newly discovered obstetrician skills, said, 'No she ain't, you fat retard, her waters have broke, innit.' And he ushered her to Mrs Leech for bourbons and a sanitary towel. Everyone is on tenterhooks now waiting for news. Mark, Emily's self-appointed midwife, has gone in the ambulance and is going to text with news. He is

hoping it is a boy so it can be named in his honour. The rest of us have decamped to the Common with several bottles of cider to celebrate the end of exams.

4 p.m.
Text from Mark. Emily is five centimetres dilated. What is dilated? Thought only eyeballs got dilated on drugs. Maybe it is the gas and air. Though five centimetre-wide eyeballs would be a bit excessive and mental looking.

5 p.m.
Text from Mark. He has seen Emily's hoo-ha. And it is hairier than Thin Kylie's.

5.30 p.m.
Text from Mark saying this will be his last text as phone is being confiscated by fat mardy woman. He means Mrs Reeve.

11 p.m.
Emily Reeve has got a baby girl. Mark says she is named after him. Have texted to say cannot have girl called Mark.

11.40 p.m.
He says baby is called Lola Lambert Reeve and is totally ginger. He has sent a photo of him holding her. She looks kind of content. Even in the perilous grip of a criminal.

Thin Kylie is excited. She thinks he will get broody now and 'knock her up' so she can have one too.

11.45 p.m.
The Maths Club have narrowed the field for potential father down to Danny 'Duracell' Carrick in Year Eleven, 'Ginger' Rogers in Year Nine, and Mr Whippy, who has orangey stubble.

11.50 p.m.
Maths Club have ruled Mr Whippy out of running after Fat Kylie threatened to sit on them. She says there is no way Mr Whippy would stick his 99 in anyone that 'minging'.

Scarlet says it is very deep and meaningful (though is not 'meaning of life' per se, that is still sex) that a new life was born into Year Eleven just as we were all finishing our GCSEs and symbolically ending our childhoods etc. Except for people doing GCSE needlework who have got a tapestry practical to go next week.

12.15 a.m.
Oh, and people doing AS PE who have got a keepy-uppy test on Tuesday i.e. Justin, which is why he says he did not want to come out and celebrate in case it jeopardized his technique. (He is so dedicated.) Anyway, can sleep peacefully now, imbued with knowledge that have nothing to worry about any more.

1 a.m.
Oh God. Am going to Glastonbury tomorrow and have not even begun to plan wardrobe.

. . . .

Thursday 21

Mum and Dad have given me a present for finishing my GCSEs. It is a digital camera. Mum says I can use it in Jersey to record my post-exam health-giving holiday. Presents from Mum are never straightforward. It is like when she finally got me a mobile phone so that she could check where I was at all times. This is just a further test to catch me out lying. Will just take photos of us looking rosy-cheeked against grassy backdrop. Glastonbury is bound to have loads of those. Have packed essential camping clothing i.e. miniskirt, flip flops, lacy vest thingy, gigantic fluffy one-armed jumper, and sheepskin boot things (in case of inclement weather). Am ignoring Scarlet's warnings to bring waterproof clothing. There is no way I am wearing a cagoule, not even in a hurricane. I will just look like Mum. Plus my wellies are not uber-trendy pink Hunters. They are red Woolworth's ones. Will just shelter in dance tent or something instead. Bob is picking me up in the sick-smelling Volvo at eleven, to give us plenty of time to find a good camping spot and pitch tents before dark. Hurrah, am so excited. It is first foray into alternative drug culture. By this time tomorrow will be holding Pete Doherty's heroin for him while he waits in the queue for the Portaloo.

222

12 noon

Am here. But only just. Queue to get near Worthy Farm was stretching back to the Taunton turn-off. Had to sit for five hours on the M5 wedged in Jack's armpit. Then had panic attack about not being allowed in due to ticket claiming I am a thirty-five-year-old man called Ray. Suzy offered to swap as she has no fear about lying to authority, but decided I am more convincing as middle-aged man than busty sex guru. Either security is lax or I really do look like Robert Plant as the white rasta in the fluorescent vest who was checking tickets waved me through with a nod of his blond dreadlocks. Probably he is on drugs already. It is compulsory to take several while you are here. I am aiming for cider and herbal tea.

Anyway, am still too close to Jack's armpit for comfort now due to Tony and Gordon (cats, not leaders of free world) having sprayed his one-man dome (they are not spayed, Suzy says it is an affront to their masculinity) and the smell being unbearable. We are now having to share the storage pod in Scarlet's tent. Jack refused to bed down with Bob and Suzy in case they got tantric urges in the night. Have made a barrier from food supplies (crisps, biscuits, chocolate brioche rolls) down the middle in case he gets tantric urges and forgets I am not Sophie. Though one look at my 32As will remind him otherwise. Also it is raining and sheepskin boots are already soggy. Am hoping they will dry inside tent but humidity is currently

at eighty per cent due to four sweaty teenagers in airtight nylon. Though on plus side am not cold. Am going now as Jack has told me to turn off Tweenies torch and stop rustling. It is not me. It is the Doritos.

. . . .

Friday 22
8 a.m.
Have had no sleep due to constant crap samba drumming from two tents down and constant crap rain drumming on roof. Also the temperature dropped to Arctic conditions in the night and there is actual frost on the sheepskin boots.

9 a.m.
Trevor and Scarlet have gone out for day already in their waterproof gothwear. (Black wellies and poncho capes, which they claim are like bat outfits. They are not, they are like ponchos, which went out of fashion two years ago after Catherine Zeta Jones started wearing them.) They asked if I wanted to join them on their journey of discovery (they are going to the Lost Vagueness field with Bob and Suzy, which is for hardcore mentalists and ageing hippies only). Declined due to footwear issues. Will try to heat boots up on calor gas stove to thaw them out.

10 a.m.
Have scorched hole in sheepskin boots. Jack says it only

adds to their interesting look. He is just trying to make me feel better. They look crap. Am going to wear flip flops.

12 noon
Have lost flip-flops in boggy patch on way to toilet queue. Am going to have to purchase wellies from Millets stall. Jack says he will piggyback me there to save me getting even muddier. Have accepted. Am desperate.

3 p.m.
Have purchased green wellies at extortionate price of £25 plus cagoule for £30. (Have accepted will have to look like Mum as all clothes now soggy. But will wear it with miniskirt as opposed to M&S elasticated waist beige linen.) Jack has lent me the money. Am so far in debt now, another £55 will not matter. He is being very nice. He carried me through the muddy hordes and only dropped me twice. Once when he tripped over a two year old in a tiger print leotard and once when we saw Richard Hammond in the toilet queue. Have texted Scarlet to see if she is coming back to the tent before Amy Winehouse but she says she is busy having her crystals read and may have to miss it. Jack says he will go with me. I pointed out he can't stand Amy Winehouse due to her freakishly big hair and small arms. He says he is warming to her retro soul standard sound. Nodded as have no idea what he meant.

5 p.m.
Amy Winehouse is a total genius. Although Jack is right about her hair and arms. She looks like a troll on a lollipop. Plus could not understand word she said due to her being drunk. But all creative types have to battle with demons. Look at Les Dennis. We are going to play I-spy in tent until Kasabian as it is too wet to go out and the queue for food poisoning noodles is right around the circus field.

8 p.m.
Have played 'I-spy', 'animal, vegetable, or mineral' and 'who'd you rather' (e.g. Mr Wilmott or Barry the Blade—answer Mr Wilmott, on hygiene grounds) for four hours and eaten entire supply of Doritos and Yoyos. Jack suggested we borrow Suzy's VIP pass and watch Peaches Geldof fall out of her Winnebago but is still raining and tent is warm again from hot Dorito breath. We are going to open a bottle of Strongbow instead and play more games.

1 a.m.
Have had very weird moment. It is not my fault. It is Jack's. Or possibly the man who invented Strongbow. Anyway, we didn't even go to Kasabian because it was too far and anyway we can hear them from inside the tent which is almost the same as being there only without 125,000 people stamping on your feet or spilling warm

beer on your head. But Jack said he was bored with 'parlour games' and suggested we played Truth or Dare. Which is usually fun because he used to dare me to jump off the shed roof or watch Eamonn Holmes for ten minutes without getting itchy and screaming. Only this time was kind of different. Jack picked Truth so I asked him why he was going out with Sophie. He said, 'Because she has 34C breasts.' Then my face must have gone funny because he said, 'Joke, Riley. I don't know why. Because she was there. And she's not complicated.'

Then he asked me why I was going out with Justin. And I thought about it. Because there must be a hundred reasons. Like his good hair. And that he can play 'Stairway to Heaven' on guitar. But none of them sounded enough. Then I remembered the stuff about trust. So I said, 'Because he tells me everything.' And then I told him about Kelly's pants to prove the point. Jack said, 'You're wrong, you know.' I said, 'No. He told me. It was in Year Ten.' Jack said, 'Not about that.' So I said, 'Fine, your turn.'

Then he looked at me for what felt like a really long time, but I know for a fact was only a few seconds because I was actually counting in my head for some reason, and then he said 'Dare'. And then, and I don't know why, because *a*) I am going out with Justin and *b*) it is a total Truth or Dare cliché, I dared him to kiss me. But for some reason at that moment it didn't sound bad, or like a cliché. It sounded like a good idea. And he must have thought so

too, because he did. And it was like that moment in *Bugsy Malone* again when I tried to think about Aunty Joyless but I still felt funny inside. And I realized that it never feels like that with Justin. Not once. But then my phone rang and it was Scarlet to say that she and Trevor were sleeping in a tepee with some Aztecs and a man called Horse so I could move pod if I wanted. But, even though the moment was gone, I didn't want to move. And nor did Jack. So we are now lying next to each other listening to someone playing Kaiser Chiefs really badly on a banjo. But the Doritos barrier is gone because we ate it. And I am not sure what is going to happen next. And I am not sure what I want to happen next.

1.05 a.m.
Jack just told me to stop writing because he is trying to sleep and my elbow is digging him in the ribs every time I finish a line. Which is an answer I guess.

. . . .

Saturday 23
11 a.m.
Things are back to normal with Jack i.e. we are not speaking again. Woke up with my head on Jack's arm. Said, 'Sorry.' He said, 'It doesn't hurt.' I said, 'I didn't mean that. I meant last night.' So he said, 'I'm sorry too.' Then I said, 'It didn't mean anything.' Because that is what you are supposed to say—I have seen it in a million

films and then he says, 'But it did to me,' etc., etc. But Jack obviously has not seen these films because he said, 'Too right.' So I said, 'Totally. Because I am in love with Justin.' So then Jack said, 'Has he called you?' So I said, 'No. But it is because there is no signal between here and Saffron Walden. Or else he is busy on his head boy campaign.' Jack just said, 'Whatever you want to believe.'

And then before I could say anything witty Scarlet and Trevor arrived back from the Aztec tepee. She said the man called Horse sang Dolly Parton songs all night and they have had no sleep so they have bought herbal sleeping pills off a man with a helmet shaped like an eel and are going to bed for the day. Which they did.

Then Jack said, 'Scarlet is mental. Those tablets could be anything.'

So for some reason I said, 'I think I might take one, actually, as I have had not very much sleep (which is true, due to wondering what Jack would do in the night: answer nothing, as he can clearly sleep through several drunk Brummies playing bongos on a saucepan and singing 'Every day I love you less and less') and I want to feel refreshed for the sublime Lily Allen later.'

Jack said, 'Don't, Riley. You don't have to prove anything to me.'

I said, 'I'm not doing it for you. I'm doing it for me.' And then I swallowed it with some warm Tizer. But it is obviously a fake as do not feel any differ—

. . . .

Sunday 24

9 p.m.

Oh God. Have somehow lost entire day. Thought had woken up at five after several hours of refreshing sleep in time for Lily Allen and the Killers but actually have been asleep for thirty-two hours and need to wee really badly. There is no sign of Trevor and Scarlet. They must be hardened to herbal drugs. Or maybe they woke up half an hour ago and have gone out to score some more. I can hear Jack outside though. He is on the phone and is shouty. Do not want to see him as he is obviously in mood and bound to say 'I told you so' but have to pee. Will just do it in Pringles tube and empty it outside later. Will be like Bear Grylls or Ray Mears.

9.15 p.m.

Have peed in Pringles tube but cardboard is leaking slightly so have wrapped it in a plastic bag and put it at bottom of rucksack. Oh God, Jack is coming in.

11 p.m.

Jack did not say, 'I told you so.' He said, 'Did you know your retarded boyfriend is round Sophie's house?' I said, 'No, and he is not retarded he just looks like that when he is thinking hard but anyway it is obviously not Justin's fault it is because your idiotic girlfriend has lured him there with her big breasts and uncomplicatedness.'

Jack said, 'She's not my girlfriend any more.' So I said,

'Oh.' And then Jack just said, 'I'm going out.' Which he did. And now am all riled up and angry and not sure who at. It is probably Jack. He is a liar. Justin is not interested in Sophie. He is probably just there to commiserate with her that me and Jack are away. And Jack has jumped to conclusions. That is it. Will just text Justin to check though.

11.30 p.m.
No answer. And Jack is back. He says he has secured agreement from Suzy that we are leaving at 6 a.m. He has erected a rucksack barrier in the pod and has gone to bed. Am not tired though so will sit up and gaze at stars through tent flap. And text Justin again.

11.45 p.m.
No answer. And Jack has told me to stop beeping because he cannot sleep. Although oddly the sound of Coke bottle and pasta maracas from two tents down does not appear to be disturbing him at all. Justin is obviously asleep. Will just wait until we are reunited tomorrow. Am still not tired though. Will go for walk to observe the dying hours of my first Glastonbury.

12.15 a.m.
Am back from walk due to too many bodies strewn over the paths. It is like scene from Hogarth's 'Gin Lane'. Also Tweenies torch ran out of batteries and tripped over a tent

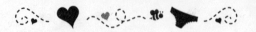

peg and skewered myself on wind chime so now probably have black eye to add to mud-drenched wild-haired look. Trevor and Scarlet are still not back. They are probably doing something with the druids.

4 a.m.
Still awake. As are several tents around me from which I can distinctly hear someone playing the theme to *Ground Force*. At least Scarlet and Trevor are back safely. They were not with the druids. They were helping Bob find Suzy who went missing in the Field of Lost Vagueness two days ago.

5 a.m.
Am asleep now. Will lie down next to Jack and the impenetrable rucksack barrier. Although sleeping bag feels a bit soggy. Maybe it is Jack's tears.

. . . .

Monday 25
9 a.m.
Was not Jack's tears. Was Pringles wee. The tube had disintegrated and contents leaked out of anti-suicide airhole in Waitrose carrier bag. Plus had put it in Jack's rucksack by mistake and now his clothes are all wet. Told him it was apple juice. Think he believed me although he did question why I was storing apple juice in a Pringles tube. Am happy none the less. It is because he is wearing

a wee-stained jumper. Whereas I am wee-free. It is retribution for lying about Justin. We are leaving as soon as Suzy wakes up. Which may be hours as it turns out she bought a herbal pill off the eel-helmet man last night.

11 p.m.
Am home. Bob got bored waiting for Suzy so he and Trevor just carried her to the sick-smelling Volvo. She is still asleep now. I envy her. She did not have to suffer a seven-hour wait on the M25 or Jack's silence treatment. Or his pervading smell of my wee (detectable even above lingering scent of vomit). I said they could drop me at Justin's so we could be reunited in our love. Jack snorted. He is horrible and I hate him. Anyway Justin was in and not with Sophie so he is definitely a liar. I threw my arms around him in full view of the reversing Volvo and said did you miss me? He said, 'You kind of smell.' And shrank away. Checked when got home. He is right. I do smell. Plus am channelling Mrs Simpson look.

Mum was shocked by appearance. I said Jersey was tougher than I expected. With less soap. James said I should sue *Bergerac* for false advertising.

11.15 p.m.
Mum has just stuck head round door to say she is looking forward to viewing digital photos. Oh God. Will check them in morning. And have bath. Am too tired now from seminal Glastonbury experience. It is not exactly how I

imagined. But on plus side have taken herbal drugs. And drunk cider. And weed in a Pringles tube. So am practically Amy Winehouse.

11.45 p.m.
Maybe could sell Pringles tube wee invention on *Dragon's Den*. Though plastic not cardboard. I bet Theo Paphitis would go for it.

12 midnight
Maybe should go to bed now and stop googling portable wee equipment.

. . . .

Tuesday 26

A terrible thing has happened. The North of England and several bits near Wales have been flooded. Sheffield, Hull, and Gloucester are almost entirely submerged according to prone-to-exaggeration GMTV. James says they are like Nineveh city and is God's way of punishing the wicked. Mum agrees and has cited mass murderer Fred West from Gloucester and John Prescott from Hull. I said what about Sheffield? Mum said Michael Palin. She does not trust him. He is too jovial. She may be right though. Not about Michael Palin. But Arctic Monkeys are from Sheffield and God would not like them if he was on earth. Or real. Which I am not sure about. Oh God, am now having existential thoughts when should be just enjoying Rice

Krispies in newly washed and infestation free hair and clothes.

At least the floods have temporarily distracted everyone from lack of digital evidence of the so-called Jersey holiday. Thank God. I have checked the camera and have only got three photos. One of Jack grinning in front of a naked man on stilts (not very Jersey). One of Trevor and Scarlet eating Vegeburgers in the Green field (not very Jersey unless it has an indigenous midget-dressed-as-drag-queen population). And one of me in eel-helmet man herbal sleeping tablet coma. Am going to have to mock up shots. Or claim camera does not work.

. . . .

Wednesday 27

11 a.m.

It is the end of an era. Warmongering Tony Blair has stepped down and Britain now has a new Prime Minister. It is no-necked greasy-hair-compromised Gordon Brown (Granny Clegg's words, not mine. I think he is rather nice. Although his head is unfeasibly big.) The Stones are having a Labour Party party to celebrate. I am not going because *a*) Jack will be there and *b*) I can't think of another reason but *a*) is good enough. Am going round Sad Ed's to get him to take photos of me looking rosy-cheeked and Enid Blytonesque. Have put on extra blusher to compensate for current post-Glastonbury pasty look.

235

3 p.m.
Sad Ed has taken four photos. They are all close-ups of
me in his back garden. He said Mum would be able to
forensically identify all other Saffron Walden landmarks if
we did them in town. As it is he is worried she will be able
to pinpoint the rhododendron to 24 Loompits Avenue.

. . . .

Thursday 28

Showed Mum holiday photos at breakfast. She seemed
satisfied. James asked why they were all taken yesterday
at 2.45 p.m., according to the timer. But luckily Mum
does not understand gadgetry (it is men's work) and told
him to be quiet and eat his muesli. It is because he is in
trouble at school again. Keanu is demanding that he takes
the dog in so he can be their wolf protector in the
playground. Mum says there is no way the dog is going
near St Regina's, or Keanu for that matter, as it is a recipe
for disaster, and ASBOs. She is right. The dog makes
Keanu look conscientious.

. . . .

Friday 29

Hurrah. Am going round Justin's tonight for a snog. It
will be our first since before Glastonbury due to me
smelling too much on Monday night and him doing
overtime mincing meat for Mr Goddard all week. Am
going to refresh all orifices. Actually just one, i.e. clean

teeth. And wear Lenor-scented clothes so do not risk rejection on odour grounds again. It will be an utterly earth-shattering moment.

9 p.m.
Was not earth-shattering. Was mediocre. And brief. In fact less than ten seconds. I was counting in head again (why do I do that?), using the infallible one elephant, two elephant method. He is still oddly distant despite me smelling lemon fresh. It is probably the Head Boy Battle. Apparently he is lagging in the Maths Club polls.

10 p.m.
Or maybe he has found out about me kissing Jack in the Truth or Dare game at Glastonbury. Oh God. That may be it. Will interrogate Jack behind the lentil bins tomorrow.

Saturday 30

Jack claims he has said nothing about the snog. He said, 'Why in God's name would I want people to know I had kissed you, Riley? I'm not mental.' Which is possibly true. It does not explain Justin's behaviour though. And he has a gig tonight. The Back Doors are playing a rugby club disco at Henham Village Hall to which I am not invited as there is not enough room in the Transit van. I said I could get a lift in the Passat so I could do groupie duties but Justin said not to bother as he will be mobbed anyway. I

pointed out that it is, in fact, our six month anniversary at about 11.59 tonight. He said we should wait and see if we have been going out a year and then celebrate. He is right. Six months is nothing when we have a lifetime ahead of us. And am probably worrying over nothing. This is just normal rock star behaviour. Gwyneth does not go to all the Coldplay gigs. She is far too busy being ethereal and doing yoga. May well try it. Though will watch *Casualty* first as trailer showed excellent helicopter crash.

july

CONDOM

VOTING
SLIP
X

Sunday 1

Mum is jubilant. Smoking has been banned in all public places. She says it is a victory for common sense. Grandpa Riley says it is a victory for killjoys and do-gooders. He says the Twilight Years' patio is too small to cope with all the Rothman's addicts who could happily puff away over their Scrabble and Parcheesi before. I said what about Mrs Munt who has emphysema and has to be in smoke-free atmosphere at all times and has been stuck on the patio for four years due to the fog-filled games room. Grandpa says he is not anti-non-smoker, it is just a matter of maths. There is one of her and twenty-three of them so it stands to reason she should be the one to go outside.

School starts again tomorrow. It is Sixth Form induction i.e. hanging around looking louche and drinking black Nescafé.

Monday 2

I was right. Spent entire day drinking Nescafé and listening to crap mix CDs on ancient common room stereo. Am now feeling all shaky due to excess caffeine and Arctic Monkeys. May have to lie down. Sad Ed says it is the pinnacle of one's Sixth Form career to get control of the 'decks' for the day. He is delighted as he now has something to aim for in life. Thought Justin might grasp opportunity that am now officially allowed to sit on saggy sofa to try to snog me vigorously on it. But he is still

241

distant. It is because he is struggling to win over the Marxist vote. They are favouring Jack who has a Lenin T-shirt. The head girl fight is already over. It will be Sophie Microwave Muffins. She has got the sympathy vote because Jack has chucked her. Also her only rival is Oona Rickets and she is bisexual and smelly. Not that they are related. It is just an observation. It is perfectly possibly to be gay and pleasant-scented.

. . . .

Tuesday 3

Sixth Form induction is utterly pointless. Mr Wilmott tried to make us do getting-to-know-each-other games where we all confess something secret about ourselves and abandon our old cliques and embrace difference. The silence was deafening until he left to sort out a locust escape in the mobile science labs and everyone got out their *Grazias* and iPods and carried on hanging out with the same people they have always hung out with.

On the plus side, the riddle of Lola Lambert Reeve's father has been solved. It is not Danny 'Duracell' Carrick or Ginger Rogers but someone called Brian from Didsbury. According to Thin Kylie who heard it off Fat Kylie who heard it off Emily's new best friend and baby guru Mark Lambert, they met on a scout and guide jamboree in the Lake District, which is proof that even the dullest of resorts are a risk to teenage pregnancy statistics. Mum will be annoyed. She has always

242

pinpointed Butlins and Magalluf as chief culprits. In contrast, the Maths Club are jubilant as no one guessed right. They have made a record £87 from all the betting. Emily should have put some money on herself. Nappies are very expensive. I once caught Treena trying to dry one with her Remington volumizer so she could re-use it.

Wednesday 4
James has begun a campaign to have a sleepover party on Saturday. He wants to invite Mad Harry, Keanu, and Maggot. I said there is no chance. He said he does not expect to get all of them past Mum's stringent checks. He is aiming high and hoping for just Mad Harry. It is a brilliant plan.

Thursday 5
Mum still not agreeing to sleepover. James offered to drop Maggot from the guest list but she is still unmoved. He said he is not giving in as he still has his trump card to play. It is dropping Keanu.

Also Granny Clegg's hip has moved to the top of the waiting list. It is because someone called Mrs Bean has electrocuted herself on a can opener. Granny is scheduled for the chop at the end of July. Mum says she will go down to help out but Granny Clegg says there is no need because Grandpa Clegg is quite capable of heating up Fray

Bentos. Mum says she is definitely going down then if Grandpa Clegg is in charge. He is notoriously crap at all things household.

. . . .

Friday 6

Mum has agreed to James's sleepover with Mad Harry following his cunning plan of dropping Keanu from the guest list. She was worried he might infect the bedding with his ringworm. As it is she made him sit on a rubber sheet at James's birthday party. James is jubilant. They are going to have Ninja rituals. Am going to absent self from house and watch environmental rock concert Live Earth at Sad Ed's. Would go to Justin's but he is still too focused on his campaign to do any snogging. I pointed out that it is weeks since he has put his tongue in my mouth with any kind of conviction. He said it will all be different once the head boy results are in. I hope so.

. . . .

Saturday 7

Sophie Microwave Muffins went into Goddard's three times today. What can she possibly want with all that meat? Unless she is planning a head girl celebratory barbecue party. Which is possible. Had to pretend was not interested though as Jack was watching me from behind the till of death. Mr Goldstein has posted him on it permanently as he has manly fingers, which do not bruise so easily.

244

Watched Live Earth with Sad Ed, Tuesday, and Scarlet. Scarlet was supposed to be watching it from the bat cave (i.e. Trevor's goth shrine bedroom) but they have had a row. It is over the O'Grady liaison. She confessed to it during a heated sexual moment (Trevor was wafting his black hair over her legs at the time). Scarlet argued that they were 'on a break' but Trevor is not cross because of the infidelity as much as who it was with. It is because the O'Gradys are at the forefront of local anti-goth feeling i.e. they are constantly calling him Dracula.

Scarlet says we should make the prom an anti-prom and go together, but not as lezzers. Pointed out that I still had a date i.e. prospective head boy and rock god Justin Statham. But Tuesday said he will go with Sophie as it is ancient American prom custom. Sad Ed said this is Saffron Walden, not South Central. How right he is. On a more environmental note, Live Earth was excellent and am definitely going to buy the new Razorlight album when am out of debt. Oh, and reduce carbon footprint, obviously. Although they should get someone other than Al Gore to be in charge. He looks like a fat woodwork teacher.

. . . .

Sunday 8

8 a.m.

Have been rudely awakened, literally, by naked James and Mad Harry in Hallowe'en masks. It was terrifying.

245

Thought was being attacked by murderous pygmy people and a wolf. They had persuaded the dog to take part in their nude antics. But more importantly, am having prom dress panic. It is less than a week to go to the most important night of my life and my only options are my fairy outfit from Grandpa Riley's wedding or the one from Uncle Jim's wedding with compost stains on it from where I tried to be Ophelia floating in the muddy river. Ooh. Maybe Mum will have a dress stashed in attic from the 1950s. Will be utter vintage prom queen. Hurrah!

9 a.m.
Mum got all thin-lipped and said she was not born in the 1950s and all she has in the attic are some baby clothes, her wedding dress, and the mint-green jumpsuit with criminally tapered legs (she did not say that bit, she actually used the word 'nice'). She is not happy about the prom because it is American and she says the only good things to come out of America are potatoes and Ford cars. Asked to see the wedding dress. It is an Eighties nightmare of nylon and lace. But it is at least knee length. Mum does not believe in long wedding dresses due to staining of hemline issues and wasting of material.

11 a.m.
Have had genius idea. Am going to butcher wedding

246

dress, fairy outfit, and compost dress and create amazing new prom-style outfit. Will be totally like that bit in *Pretty in Pink*. Will even put bit of lace on dog to recreate the moment.

12 noon
Now have bedroom strewn with bits of bodice and the dog has eaten some of the pink fur off the fairy outfit. Will put bits in bag and take it all round to Sad Ed's. He did needlework in Year Eight and knows how to do backstitch. Plus his mum has sewing machine as she used to make all of Ed's clothes. Have witnessed him in brown corduroy dungarees before. Which is bordering on child abuse.

4 p.m.
Have got new and fabulousish dress. It is quite vintage with a modern twist i.e. fairy wings and a tail. Sad Ed says it is very Alison Goldfrapp. Have tried it on at home. James (now fully clothed) said I looked like something from Middle Earth. This is a compliment in his book. Mum says it is a shame I will never get to wear her wedding dress when I walk down the aisle. I said am not getting married as it is bourgeois convention and is only a bit of paper. Dad said, 'I wish someone had told me that,' but he said it too loud and Mum heard him and sent him to declog the gutters.

Monday 9
9 a.m.
Scarlet and Trevor are back together.

10 a.m.
Scarlet and Trevor have broken up again. They are like Pamela Anderson and Tommy Lee with their on again/off again antics. But without the silicone implants and sex tapes. Scarlet says this time it is for good though. She is sick of his controlling ways. And he has possible erectile issues. Which is too much information. They will be back together within days, if not minutes, anyway. She cannot resist his pale weedy charms.

12 noon
Oh God. Evil and unsubstantiated rumours are circulating John Major High about Justin's potential gayness. Ali Hassan (aka head mathlete) asked me if it is true he wears women's underwear. Think have quashed them though by explaining mitigating circumstances i.e. his were all filthy at time.

Tuesday 10
Rumour situation worse. There are now rumours that the original rumours have been substantiated by an unnamed source close to Justin. Will deny everything. That is what Suzy does and she is an esteemed Labour councillor.

3 p.m.

Justin has hauled me into his campaign headquarters (aka the Sixth Form kitchen aka leaky microwave corner) to grill me about the pants rumour. I said it wasn't me it was Jack. Then he said how did Jack know and I said I may have let it out by mistake at Glastonbury but was under influence of cider at the time so was mentally diminished (the O'Gradys are always using this excuse in court) and was only telling him anyway as example of how much we trust each other etc. He said, 'You have broken that trust irredeemably.' Was momentarily shocked by his use of five syllable word during which time he stalked off. Possibly to repair damage done by Jack's evil rumour. It will all be OK though. He will forgive me when he realizes I did it out of love. And when I let him do 'It' on Friday. Suzy says sex is the best way to heal an argument.

4 p.m.

Have texted Jack. THANKS FOR RUINING MY LIFE. It is almost true.

4.15 p.m.

Jack has texted back. NOT ME. WOULD NEVER HURT YOU.

Am ignoring it. He is a compulsive liar.

Wednesday 11

Justin is still not speaking to me. He is too busy trying to salvage his campaign in the dying hours (voting is tomorrow morning). He is wearing visible boxer shorts (Marks & Spencer) to confirm his masculinity. Just the sight of them makes me want him more. Or maybe it is because he is playing it cool. It is the oldest trick in the book, according to Scarlet. I asked her if Trevor is still playing it cool. She said arctic, but she is not falling for it again.

Also, disaster has struck Sad Ed. Mike Wandering Hands's wandering hands have wandered again. Edie caught him in a passionate clinch with his latest victim in a layby near Newport. I asked how. He said she still has stalking issues. Anyway, Edie is leaving after all and taking Tuesday with her. They are flying out on Sunday. On the plus side it means she will still be able to be Sad Ed's date for the prom. Though he is going to have to spend most of his time scanning the upper school canteen for potential replacements.

. . . .

Thursday 12

It is election day. Have texted Justin good luck but no reply as yet. He is probably using phone to talk last minute tactics with his team. Just had thought. Why am I not on team? Am excellent political co-ordinator, as proven by my role in Jack's successful election as Prime Minister of John Major High (role abandoned due to lack

of any discernible powers). Maybe that is why. He thinks I am secretly loyal to Jack. He is wrong. I do not care about Jack at all. He is nothing to me.

11 a.m.
Have voted. For Justin, obviously. And for Oona Rickets, despite her smell and lesbian manifesto. At least she has average sized breasts. Scarlet is an utter traitor and has voted for Jack. It is because he has promised to instigate a goth tolerance day. Sad Ed says he is reserving the right not to reveal his political colours. He will have voted for Jack as well. He is hoping to take Tuesday's place as lead singer in the Jack Stone Five. He has no chance. He cannot even hold 'Frère Jacques' without going flat. Exit polls are putting Jack and Justin neck and neck. It may come down to Mr Wilmott's deciding vote. He has Simon Cowell-like jurisdiction in these matters.

3 p.m.
Jack has won the election by three votes. But it is a hollow victory. It is because Laurie Walsh (who once had a trial for Tottenham youth) dropped out of the race with suspected groin strain and all his supporters (ten of them) voted for Jack because he once went to White Hart Lane when he was eight. On the plus side, Sophie Microwave Muffins Jacobs is NOT head girl. It is smelly Oona. Voting was neck and neck so Mr Wilmott got the deciding vote and went for the underdog. It is not because he thinks she

is better. It is to avoid accusations of anti-lesbianism and possible protest action.

Also, it turns out Oona encouraged her gay and lesbian alliance voters to support knicker-wearing Justin. So my pants rumour may actually have helped him in the end despite ultimate failure. Tried to tell him this and give him a commiseratory hug but he was too busy trying to revive Sophie Microwave Muffins who was sobbing all over the saggy sofa. Oh God. This is all wrong. I should be ensconced in a position of power, not watching my boyfriend whispering stuff to someone with discernible breasts and who does 'It', i.e. not me.

There is no other way forward. Cannot compete on breast front so will have to outdo Sophie on doing 'It' grounds. Am going round to seek advice from Suzy immediately and will astound him with my sexual prowess at the prom.

7 p.m.
Am now sex genius. There is nothing I do not know. Except things that are illegal or hurt, which I said I did not want to learn about as may have bad dreams. Also have assorted pack of condoms as do not want to end up like Emily Reeve, who I saw on way home with her mum and Lola Lambert. She has bleeding nipples. (Emily. Not her mum. Or Lola Lambert.) Scarlet says I should not do anything unless I am absolutely sure he is the ONE and she is glad she fended off Trevor now that he is not hers;

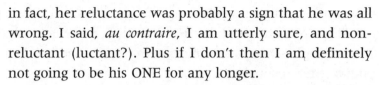
in fact, her reluctance was probably a sign that he was all wrong. I said, *au contraire*, I am utterly sure, and non-reluctant (luctant?). Plus if I don't then I am definitely not going to be his ONE for any longer.

When I left Jack ran down the block paving and cornered me behind the sick-smelling Volvo. He said, 'Don't do it. He's not worth it.' I said, 'He's worth a million of you.' Which is actually off *Our Mutual Friend* but sounded excellently dramatic and made Jack go very quiet. Then he said, 'Just so you know, it wasn't me who spread the pants rumours, it was Sophie.' I said, 'Why would she do that if she likes Justin so much?' He said, 'To get you in trouble.' And then I couldn't think of anything clever to say so I just said, 'Bog off, Jack,' and left before he could have the last word.

He is wrong about me and Justin. And will show him tomorrow when we are totally the King and Queen of the John Major High prom.

. . . .

Friday 13

11 a.m.
Am above worrying about Friday 13th Twilight Zone issues. Nothing can go wrong. Tonight is the most important night of life so far as in approximately twelve hours will be losing virginity. Not sure exactly where yet but as long as it is not round the back of Goddard's or in the lower school toilets does not matter as will be swept

away on emotion, not admiring surroundings.

Also it is Mum's birthday. Have given her an electric fly swat. She has been coveting one for ages to add to her anti-vermin arsenal.

3 p.m.
Electric fly swat declared a success. Has already despatched three bluebottles and stunned the dog into silence when it got caught in crossfire.

5 p.m.
Am getting dressed then can practise looking confident in haute couture prom dress. Scarlet has texted to see if I want to meet round hers then Bob can take us all in the Volvo. She says there is no shame in going to the prom alone. On the contrary it is utterly feminist and modern. I said I was old-fashioned and would be waiting for my date to pick me up in a limousine, or at least a pine-scented Viceroy taxi.

6 p.m.
Grandpa has been round to see me in prom dress. Actually he brought Jesus round for tea as their microwave is on the blink but he was very excited about it all none the less. He said I reminded him of a young Grandma Riley. James said she had varicose veins and kept bees. He said, 'Yes, that's it, the bees.' It must be my ironic veil. Or maybe the wings.

7 p.m.

Can see Thin Kylie out of the window in her 'prom dress' i.e. a tube of gold lycra with bits cut out in the middle. She is getting a lift on Mr Hosepipe's fire engine. It is very romantic. But not as romantic as my carriage will be when it gets here. Oooh. Maybe it is an actual carriage with horses.

7.10 p.m.

No sign of Justin. Mum has stuck her head round door to ask what time he is coming exactly as she and Dad want to pop over to Marjory's and could I watch James for half an hour. Realized I hadn't checked. In fact, realized he has never officially asked me to prom at all. But he does not need to. He is my boyfriend so it is unwritten. Said he will be here by 7.30. Am sure of it.

7.45 p.m.

Still no sign of Justin. Dad has offered to run me to the school in the Passat. Have declined. It would be too humiliating. He might try to dance.

7.45 p.m.

Oooh. Doorbell. This must be him. Hurrah. Have condom (pineapple flavour, on loan from Sad Ed) stashed in special hidden pocket (fashioned by Sad Ed for this purpose exactly) and orifices are all clean (and not just teeth this time—have borrowed Suzy's 'feminine deodorant').

255

8 p.m.

It wasn't Justin. It was Jack. I said, 'What are you doing here?' He said, 'I've come to take you to the prom. I'm your emergency back-up man. Like Ross, when Rachel is stood up. Or Duckie in *Pretty in Pink*.' And I must admit, in his tuxedo and Converse he did look kind of cool, and Duckie-like. But that is not the point so I said, 'Duh, Ross never took Rachel to the prom. I don't need an emergency back-up man because I have a first-choice one and he will be here any minute to explore the meaning of life with me so I would go if I were you.' He said, 'He's not coming. He's gone with Sophie. They've been seeing each other for months. That's why we broke up.'

And then I felt a bit sick, like when Dad drives over humpback bridges too quickly just to make James scream, and had to sit down. And Jack said, 'Come on, Riley. That dress deserves to be seen. So you can either stay at home and kid yourself, or you can show the world, or at least John Major High, that he didn't break you.' Which was possibly the nicest thing anyone has ever said to me. Except then I remembered that it is from *Pretty in Pink* as well and was probably just another one of his lies to get at Justin and that I hate him. So I said, 'Just bugger off, will you. Don't you have head boy duties to do?'

And then he stood up and sighed in the way that James does when he knows I have got the answer wrong on *Eggheads* and said, 'Fine. But, Riley, sex isn't the meaning of life.' So I said, 'Really, so what is then,

256

Einstein?' He said 'Love.' And then he went because Bob was beeping the Volvo horn madly.

Anyway, he is wrong. About the meaning of life. And about Justin. He will show up. Any minute. I just know it.

Won't he?

my (not so) simple life

Rachel Riley goes back to basics

Saturday 14

8 a.m.

Today is utterly the worst day of my life, and I should be jubilant because I have been waiting for tragedy to strike my boring existence for several years but, instead, am racked by torture and loss. It is because Justin Statham, Year Twelve rock god and part-time meat mincer, stood me up on prom night for Sophie Jacobs (dad invented Microwave Muffins, was once in a Fairy Liquid advert, 34C breasts). She finally overcame her obsession with possible pervert-in-school Mr Vaughan and his oversized nipples and has returned to the hairless, small-nippled chest of her first love. It is like in *The OC* when Ryan leaves beautiful and brainy Marissa to go back out with low-rent Theresa from Chino. (Although, unlike Marissa, I am not a drug addict or lesbian. And Justin does not wear wife-beaters or play pool).

Plus Mum would not let me stay in my room all evening in case I tried to self-harm with my ironic fairy wings, so I had to watch *Poirot* with her, Dad, a ten year old in a Ninja Turtle outfit and the dog (also in Ninja Turtle outfit). James did offer to be my date but the shell was off-putting. Not to mention the potential incest issues. Am too distraught to even eat Shreddies. Will possibly pine myself to death. Even Mum feels sorry for me. She has phoned in sick to my Saturday job, i.e. hunchback Mr Goldstein and his lentil-smelling health food outlet Nuts In May, with an alleged dose of unseasonal

winter vomiting bug. Although she is probably secretly celebrating, as Justin was not high on her list of potential suitors due to his *a*) long hair; *b*) decision to pursue career as rock guitarist; and *c*) mum who wears Lycra. Oh God, he is even gorgeous on paper. I miss him even more. Will sob on bed for a bit.

9.15 a.m.
Have just had excellent thought. Maybe Justin did not stand me up, but is, in fact, dead. Hurrah. Will text best friend Scarlet in hope he was killed in tragic road accident on notorious mini roundabout system.

9.20 a.m.
He is not dead but is very much alive and back with Sophie Microwave Muffins. Apparently they were all over each other behind the C Corridor fruit and nut dispensing machine last night. Scarlet says she is coming round immediately for a full report and to offer sister-hood support in my time of crisis. Plus her mum Suzy is having one of her tantric sex classes in the den and she says she cannot bear all the old people groaning. It is like an X-rated version of *Cocoon*. Am still too distressed to eat. Am an accidental anorexic.

1.00 p.m.
Scarlet has just left. I asked if she wanted to stay all day. And preferably night, lest I perish in my solitude. But

apparently the tantric sex finished at twelve so it is safe to enter the den without fear of naked geriatrics. Plus she has E4 at home whereas our Freeview is limited to BBC4, ITV3, and BBC Parliament. It is not the signal. It is Mum's ferocious parental controls. Anyway, am too depressed to watch television due to Scarlet's over-graphic description of Justin and Sophie's love-in last night (Goth Corner Mark II, Mrs Leech's biscuit cupboard, and the upper school toilets). She knows too many technical terms for genitals.

Scarlet says I should look on the plus side, i.e. that I did not actually do 'It' with Justin, now that he is not my ONE after all. But I pointed out that, maybe if I had done 'It', then he would still be my ONE and that now am going to die a virgin like Miss Crawley with the moustache and too many cats. But then Scarlet went into one of her lectures on wearing your virginity with pride. It is because she is still not back with weedy bat boy Trevor Pledger. Apparently he snogged Daisy Devlin who has a fake Marilyn Manson tattoo behind the wheelie bins. (The snogging I mean. The tattoo is on her buttock.) Prom night was clearly a hotbed of adolescent groping. Thin Kylie and Fat Kylie and their respective boyfriends Mark Lambert and Mr Whippy did some swinging behind the fire curtain. Thank God they will all be leaving school in a few days. John Major High will be almost Eton-like without their idiotic antics tainting the corridors of intellect. Though there are still several

O'Gradys too many on the register. And one Justin Statham. Oh God, please let him fail his resits so he has to go and make sausages full time. I cannot bear to look upon his poetic beauty every day, when it will never again be mine to touch. Or snog. Am going to sob a bit more.

1.15 p.m.
James and dog have been in to announce that there is soup on the table. I said I was too weak to make it downstairs. He is going to bring me some in a non-spill flask.

1.20 p.m.
Oh God. Soup is oxtail. Which reminds me of butchering Justin. Am going to have to sob again.

1.25 p.m.
Sobbing has spilt soup out of non-spill flask on M&S duvet. May well have to write to Thermos to complain. Have texted Dad to send dog up to keep me company in my hour of need. Dog will lick up soup and I will be shout-free from Mum. In my weakened state, one telling off could send me over the edge.

1.30 p.m.
Dog does not like oxtail. Has eaten flask cup instead. Have sent it back down before it tries to hawk it up on already vile polycotton bedlinen.

5 p.m.
Oh God. Must have fallen asleep in post-oxtail grief. Bizarrely, duvet is now soup-free and smelling of Lenor. Maybe God has taken pity on me and performed a modern miracle. Am like that girl in Portugal who found God in an aubergine. Or Granny Clegg when she saw Jesus's face in a slice of Nimble toast (the real one, not my one-year-old uncle).

5.15 p.m.
Am not like Portuguese girl or Granny Clegg. It was James. He washed sheets while Mum was at Marjory's next door admiring her new binoculars (she has been investing heavily in surveillance equipment ever since she caught photographic evidence of me and Justin snogging on her digital camera). He is being extra specially helpful. He says it is his new Ninja way, to protect the weak and stupid. He has brought me stain-free Marmite sandwiches for supper.

6 p.m.
Have just had a phone call from Jack, (brother of Scarlet, newly appointed Head Boy, and former best friend of two-timing Justin). But have no idea what he said because before he opened his mouth, just shouted, 'Do not say, "I told you so". I hate you, Jack Stone.' Which is almost true. I hate him for being right about Justin anyway. Why did I not listen to him? It is because I was

blinded by love. And by good hair. Oh God. Need to sob. And then eat a sandwich as am quite faint now.

7 p.m.
Have eaten several sandwiches and feel slightly less suicidal. May just manage to drag self downstairs to watch some escapist TV and take mind off real-life tragedy (TVs in bedrooms are on par with heroin and murder in Mum's eyes).

9 p.m.
Am back in bed. Entire BBC schedule reminds me of Justin e.g. car crash victim in *Casualty* had Doors poster on bedroom wall, i.e. like Justin. Man from Birmingham on crap lottery show said his favourite one out of Girls Aloud was Nicola i.e. like Justin. Am going to go to sleep instead. Will probably feel better in morning.

. . . .

Sunday 15
8 a.m.
Do not feel better. Am still in pit of despair. But think smell a bit so will have shower as do not want to end up malodorous as well as single, like Year Twelve bisexual Oona Rickets.

11 a.m.
Or Sad Ed. He has just been round to offer condolences

and reviving mini Mars bars. He is utterly depressed too. Though is also unwashed and quite ripe. It is because his girlfriend Tuesday has been repatriated to America. He says I should be happy I am not him. That is true. He has fat upper arms and his mum is in the Aled Jones Fan Club. No wonder he exists in a perpetual state of gloom. He says I should not be afraid of facing Justin at school, as he and Scarlet will be my henchmen. They do not stand a chance against Sophie Jacobs though. She has Pippa Newbold and Fi Cunningham, who can send Year Sevens into paroxysms with one flick of their highlighted Pantene hair.

1 p.m.
Thin Kylie has just been round to offer condolences and to set me up with Mark Lambert's friend 'Donkey' Dawson who works in Halfords and is renowned for having a weird helmet head and big thing. Have said no. Kylie says I am making a mistake and that I need to get back in the saddle immediately to make Justin jealous. I said I had never been in saddle and do not think that former Criminal and Retard with oversized head and penis will make rock god Justin weep with remorse. She said, 'Whatever. But Donkey is, like, a legend in Bishop's Stortford. It is like a saveloy.' Luckily at that point Mum came in and despatched Kylie before I had to listen to any more sausage/penis comparisons. Am going for lunch now. Still feeling weak with depression but Mum

is paranoid about me becoming anorexic so she wants to monitor every mouthful.

3 p.m.
Have not eaten lunch. It was bangers and mash. Mum is now convinced I have eating disorder. I do not. It is just that the sausages (Duchy Originals Pork and Herb) reminded me of 'Donkey' Dawson. Although I suspect his is of inferior quality and does not come with Prince Charles's seal of approval. On plus side, did not think about Justin for several minutes. Maybe I am in recovery.

3.15 p.m.
Am thinking about Justin again. Maybe I should call him. Maybe it has all been a terrible misunderstanding and there is a rational explanation for him groping Sophie's 34Cs behind the yoghurt-covered raisin display. Will ask James. He is full of Ninja insight and is well versed in conspiracy theories, thanks to his trusty companion Google.

3.30 p.m.
It is not good news, odds-wise. James says, statistically, seventy-five per cent of sexually active eighteen year olds have cheated at least once by the time they leave school. Plus my hair is mental and I have no breasts.

Also, spookily, just got a text from Jack. It says DON'T CALL HIM OR LURK OUTSIDE HOUSE LIKE STALKER X

270

Which is exactly what I was thinking of doing next. Although not so much like stalker, more lovelorn tragic heroine type. Maybe he has supernatural powers. That would come in useful when he is being Foreign Secretary, which is his ultimate goal, alongside winning the Mercury Music Prize for his band the Jack Stone Five. He could predict what despots and dictators are thinking and outwit them. Have texted back. Y NOT?

4.15 p.m.
Jack has replied. It says U 2 GD 4 VACANT PRETTY BOY (he means Justin).

Have texted back. NOT VACANT. BUT IS PRETTY. It is hard to believe they were ever best friends. They are so different. Justin would never accuse Jack of being vacant. Or pretty. But then Jack would never dump me on prom night for someone who was once in a Fairy Liquid advert.

4.30 p.m.
Jack has texted back. JUST DON'T DO IT RILEY. WILL EAT FONE IF HAVE TO X Which is quite funny. Although James claims Mad Harry has eaten a phone. He is hoping to become a phenomenon like fat Frenchman Monsieur Mangetout. He should take some tips from the dog. It can seemingly consume any household appliance without suffering ill effects. I caught it chewing Mum's Wisdom Spinbrush in the bathroom this morning. (Gave it a quick rinse. Mum will never know.)

4.45 p.m.
Jack has just texted again. It says. SERIOUSLY. DON'T. He is very commanding when he wants to be. Have said OK. He is right. As always. I will only be prolonging my agony. Do not want to speak to or see Justin again.

5.00 p.m.
And could not call even if wanted to now. James has been in to confiscate phone. He said his Ninja powers detected that I was about to make contact with the enemy. He means he heard beeping and got suspicious. He is like Mum when it comes to suspecting the worst. Am going for tea. Which will hopefully not be penis-shaped in any way.

6 p.m.
Was quiche. So genital-free. Ate with gusto to prove Mum wrong about anorexia. But she thinks quiche bingeing could be sign of bulimia and has taken to hovering at toilet door when I go for a wee. Also, James is still refusing to give back phone. He says I should be preparing myself mentally for school tomorrow as it could be traumatic. Oh God, he is right. I cannot go. Justin and Sophie will be all over each other on the saggy sofa and I will be nothing more than an object of pity and derision. It is utterly tragic. Hopefully will die in night from sadness. If not, will have to think of cunning plan to evade Mum's anti-truancy divining skills. She does not

allow days off unless she has forensic evidence of vomit or runny poo.

. . . .

Monday 16

Am not dead. But have cunning plan. Am going to pretend to walk to school but will actually detour to Grandpa Riley's house. He is bound to be in now that Baby Jesus is banned from Treena's place of work (The Twilight Years Day Centre) in case he is stolen by old ladies again. Plus Grandpa is notoriously lax about attending school. He says he only went when it was raining and that he left at fourteen to join the Navy anyway. This is not strictly true, i.e. Grandpa has never been in the Navy. He left to work in a shuttlecock factory. But that is not the point. Will not be missing anything at school anyway as it is Sixth Form induction, i.e. wearing black, moaning about troops in Iraq, and listening to crap mix CDs.

4 p.m.

Hurrah. Plan has been utterly successful. Have spent day watching Jeremy Kyle and CBeebies with Baby Jesus and Grandpa (am not sure which is more disturbing— enraged women in lilac velour or *The Tweenies*). Plus have eaten proscribed Wagon Wheels, Monster Munch, and Bachelor's Supernoodles (Jesus's lunch of choice), which is excellent depression food. In fact, feel quite happy and energetic. It is all the sugar and Tartrazine. Grandpa says

the whole Justin/Sophie thing was inevitable and that all men are bastards who think with their willies. (Except for Dad. Who seemingly married Mum for her freakish ability to do logarithms in her head and get red wine stains out of cream shagpile.) Asked Grandpa if he had ever cheated on Grandma Riley. He said no. But not through choice. It is because Grandma Riley had arms the size of hams and a hive of killer bees. He does not need to cheat on Treena. Her demands for sex are insatiable. Grandpa says she will wear it out at this rate. At which point had to stop eating proscribed Peperami due to sausage/penis thing again.

Mum is not suspicious at all. She asked how school was and I just shrugged, i.e. not even a lie. She rolled her eyes and started on about teenagers being uncommunicative and that mobile phones and email are to blame and in her day she had to give a full account of the school day to Granny and Grandpa Clegg, including whether or not she had been to the loo and for what purpose. Luckily James stepped in to give his full account of school: fell off top of Keanu and Mad Harry in attempt to recreate pyramid of death, looked at some newts, learned theme from *Pet Rescue* on chime bars, went to loo twice—one poo, one wee. Primary school is a cinch. He will be in for a shock when he gets to John Major High. Although he will probably relish the challenge. Plus it is not at all certain he will go to John Major. He is still angling for boarding school. He says he is concerned state secondary

274

may not offer him the wide-ranging education he requires. It is because he wants to wear a cape and learn about Death Eaters. Have told him Hogwart's does not exist but he just smiled a knowing smile. He is an idiot.

Although it is possibly true about John Major High not being up to scratch. According to Scarlet, Sixth Form induction consisted of watching *Bowling for Columbine* in the audio-visual suite (i.e. hairy librarian Mr Knox's crap video machine). Mr Wilmott is trying to counteract any possible gun-toting activity. It is wishful thinking. The only gun-toting John Major High has ever witnessed is Mr Vaughan's crap splurge guns in *Bugsy Malone*. Although they did cause irreparable damage to the B Corridor ventilation shaft. Scarlet says I might as well not bother coming in all week as the anti-vice film theme is continuing tomorrow with some anti-drug vintage *Grange Hill*. Asked her if Justin mentioned me at all. She said he only managed to wrest his tongue out of Sophie's mouth long enough to eat a KitKat. It is gross. Public snogging is utterly undignified. Although was quite nice when he used to fling me against the lockers in fit of passion.

. . . .

Tuesday 17

It is nice at Grandpa's. There is no regime of fear regarding spillage, and the TV is on all day. So is kind of like the common room, but without the snogging, black clothing, and constant demands to sign petitions against whaling

or war. Have got to give up the junk food though. Mum asked me if I had been sniffing glue when I got home. I pointed out that sniffing glue would make me spotty and lethargic, not buzzy and wild-eyed, but this did not seem to allay her fears. So admitted to eating a Wagon Wheel (to avoid menacing phone calls to Mr Wilmott) but cunningly said it was Sad Ed's. He is always eating so she will not suspect anything.

. . . .

Wednesday 18

Grandpa's is becoming a hotbed of truancy. I was not the only one watching *In The Night Garden* (drug-induced toddler programme involving weird maggot and some talking clothes pegs) and eating crisps on the faux leather sofa today. Unbelievably, Dad was also in attendance. I thought he was there to frogmarch me through the school gates, but it turns out that his boss Mr Wainwright had booked him on an Outward Bound team bonding course and Mum would not let him stay at home either. He says there is no way he is yomping around on the notoriously boggy fens with only Malcolm from IT to protect him. I do not blame him. Also he says CBeebies is possibly more educational than school. He is right. Today I learned how toothpaste is made, from a dog and a woman called Auntie Mabel who flies everywhere in a spotty plane. (Although may well write in to point out the carbon footprint implications.) Anyway, we have

276

agreed not to grass each other up to Mum. Helped Dad smear some convincing mud on his Hush Puppies. Though he does not need my assistance. He has over twenty years' experience of avoiding Mum's Paxman-like questioning.

Thursday 19

8 a.m.

Dad is going to work today. I could see him struggling internally over his Oatibix between a day of crisps on the sofa or a day of arguing about the price of photocopier fluid, but he knows better than to push his truancy too far.

3 p.m.

Unlike me. The game is up. Mum knows everything. Her face (with menacingly thin lips) loomed at the window this afternoon just as Grandpa and I were settling down to *Diagnosis Murder*. Even Jesus screamed. I said it was utterly unfair and that Dad is a complete traitor as he had promised not to say anything. Which was my first, or possibly third or fourth, mistake, as it wasn't Dad who told her. Nor was it amateur private eye Marjory from next door with her binoculars and digital camera. Devastatingly, it was Sad Ed. (It turns out there was no Sixth Form at all today due to Criminal and Retard-related damage to the 'audio-visual suite' so he had come over to listen to

Morrissey CDs and moan about Tuesday.) Apparently he tried to run away, but his size is an impediment to speed, and Mum blocked him at the hydrangeas. Inevitably, he buckled under her interrogation. Which is crap, because I have taught him the rules several times, i.e. DO NOT look into her eyes. DO NOT admit to anything. If in doubt, have coughing fit or feign idiocy or death.

Mum is using her 'It is not me you are letting down, it is yourself' method of punishment. It is a lie. She thinks I am letting her down and will end up semi-literate like Granny and Grandpa Clegg. Have promised to go to school tomorrow, even though it is last day and will consist of idiotic Year Elevens spraying silly string over the mobile science labs and saying it is the end of an era etc., etc.

It is Dad I feel sorry for. There is no way he will be let off so easily. Mum is lying in wait for his return like the beast of Bodmin Moor. I did try to backtrack and claim that he was never actually at Grandpa's and that he had just rung and I answered the phone, but she said, 'Even you are not that stupid, Rachel.' Plus apparently Marjory has camera footage of him driving in the opposite direction to Wainwright and Hogg yesterday morning. She rang earlier to offer her services to track down the 'other woman'.

7 p.m.
Dad has confessed all. He tried to plead innocence with

the same 'I only rang' trick that I used but Mum said she was not an idiot (true) and showed him Marjory's incriminating footage. James says he is disappointed in both of us and that we have insulted his Ninja ways. He and Mum are watching Channel 4 news together on the sofa with an air of annoying self-satisfaction. Even the dog has a smirk on its hairy face. It is being allowed to sit in Dad's place. Its holier-than-thou attitude will not last. It is bound to have eaten, broken, or vomited up something by tomorrow.

8 p.m.
Or earlier. Dog banished to shed for barking frenzy at Jon Snow (who has replaced Natasha Kaplinsky as its most hated newsreader). Dad is back in his rightful place on sofa.

* *

Friday 20
8 a.m.
Today is the last day of school. Hurrah. Am not filled with nostalgia at all. In fact, like Gordon Brown, am looking firmly to future. From next term, will be actual Sixth Former and will no longer have to wear idiotic kilt and cardigan. Plus school will be free of morons like Mark Lambert, who is bound to let the sheep out, set off the fire alarms, and drink too much Tizer.

On down side, am going to have to face two-timing

rock legend Justin Statham and nipple pervert Sophie Microwave Muffins. Have texted Scarlet for reinforcements. She and Sad Ed are going to call for me on the way. I said Sad Ed has already proved his incompetence in these matters but she says he is reeling with remorse and has promised to shape up for future getaways.

4 p.m.
Am reprieved. Justin was not at school. Nor was Sophie Microwave Muffins. They were at Stansted airport with Mr and Mrs Microwave Muffins, waiting to fly to a villa in the Algarve. They are going for the whole summer. He has even quit his meat mincing for her. I hope they are going on easyJet. It is notoriously unreliable and the toilets are too small to do it in (according to Thin Kylie, who has tried several times). Was nice to have henchmen though. Jack came too to ensure I did not try to detour to Stansted to fling myself at Justin's mercy. I said hardly, as, in the absence of any of us owning a car, it involved getting on a smelly bus driven by Len Viceroy, followed by two separate and overpriced trains. (Although a teary airport reunion is utterly romantic. Will try to engineer one into my life at some point. If ever find love again.)

Last day of school entirely as predicted. C Corridor was strewn with funny (in no sense) foam, and the bodies of inconsolable Sixth Formers who think they will never see each other again. As if. They will all be back in Saffron

280

Walden in three years, living at home and having tedious conversations about how brilliant school was. Unlike me, Scarlet, and Sad Ed. As soon as we have got our degrees, we are moving to a bohemian squat in Camden and will return only to consume Christmas lunch.

On the plus side, Emily Reeve brought baby Lola Lambert in. She is coming back to school in September after all. Mrs Reeve is going to look after the baby. It is an excellent multi-generational solution. There is no way Mum would look after my baby if I got pregnant. She has enough trouble with Baby Jesus as it is. Mr Wilmott was visibly relieved. Not that he wants a teen-age mum in the Lower Sixth, not even one who wears knee-length socks and pinafores. But it means his grade point average is safe again, following the announcement that one of the maths geeks is moving to Ipswich.

Plus Mark Lambert proved again that, contrary to expectations, he would make an excellent father. He selflessly dived across the foamy parquet to protect Lola from an oncoming sheep. Although apparently he was the one who let them all out in the first place. And set off the fire alarms and did Tizer sick in the language lab. I will miss him, despite his shaven head and moronic deeds. And the Kylies too. It will not be the same in registration without their endless supplies of *Heat* magazine, self-tan, and graphic details about Mr Whippy's 99. Oh, it is utterly the end of an era.

Saturday 21

7 a.m.

Ugh. Have got to haul self out of bed for day of toil at lentil bins. Mum is refusing to phone in sick for me again. Plus, have remembered that am still in debt to the tune of several hundred pounds (Glastonbury, Dad's phone bill, destruction of fake baby, etc.) so need all the money I can get, even hunchback Mr Goldstein's paltry less-than-minimum wages. On plus side Justin is no longer at Goddard's, so will not be tempted to stare mournfully across King Street at his bloodstained apron.

6 p.m.

Nuts In May particularly annoying. Sad Ed's mum, Mrs Thomas, who works there in the week, had rearranged the entire shop according to size and colour of packet (going against Mum's preferred alphabetical system, and against Mr Goldstein's preferred 'keep the tofu in the fridge and the vitamins in one place' system) while Mr Goldstein was at a yoghurt convention. He made me and Jack spend all day putting things back where they belong. Mrs Thomas will not last long if she keeps this behaviour up. Mr Goldstein is very much not open to new ideas. I bet he is rueing the day his last assistant, ailment-ridden Rosamund, decided to run off with Guru Derek to his yogic retreat in Steeple Bumpstead. At least she did what she was told. Although she did have nits and eczema.

Jack was very understanding about me not wanting to

discuss Justin lest I wept too heavily over the linseed and made it germinate. He says the sooner I move on the better and asked if I wanted to go and see Rabid Hamsters play the ATC Hut tonight. Said no. The ATC Hut is too full of memories of Justin. Oh God. Have just realized that am never going to escape my tortured past. There is no other solution. Will ask Mum if we can move away. Preferably to London, where I can bond with fellow vintage-wearing and boy-hating prodigy Kate Nash.

8 p.m.
Mum says we are not moving away from Saffron Walden because, according to *The Times*, it is officially the best place to live in England. James backed her up with education, crime, and refuse collection statistics. His Google habit is getting out of control.

* *

Sunday 22
Granny Clegg has rung to remind us that she is having her hip of doom replaced by a nice, non-death-predicting metal one at the end of the week. I said she sounded remarkably happy, considering she was about to lose her special powers. She said, on the contrary, her bladder is playing up and she is hoping it is also blessed with the gift of second sight. Then she asked how I was and I told her about me and Justin. But instead of being sympathetic she got all excited as now she thinks the bladder can

283

divine relationship problems and she can make a fortune in matchmaking skills. That is the trouble with Cornwall. Unless you want to surf or eat Rick Stein pasties, there is precious little to do except imagine your body parts are psychic. Or marry a cousin. Oooh. Perhaps Granny and Grandpa Clegg are actually related. Have always had my suspicions. They do share the same swarthy looks and borderline racist tendencies. Will ask Mum.

4 p.m.
They are not related. Mum has already obtained authenticated birth certificate proof going back three generations.

. . . .

Monday 23
Hurrah, it is the school holidays and have no homework or revision for once. Although do have lengthy booklist from Mr Knox for his AS level philosophy course. And several Shakespeares to plough through for English. In fact think have more work than ever before. At least am not James though. St Regina's does not break up until tomorrow for some reason, possibly to do with religion. Or INSET days. Or bloody-mindedness.

Normally at this point would be contemplating be-friending Thin Kylie to gain access to her kidney-shaped swimming pool, but it is unseasonally pouring with rain. Will go round Sad Ed's instead for some indoor moaning.

3 p.m.

Sad Ed is still utterly depressed about Tuesday. He says she is already sounding distant on their nightly phone calls. I said she was distant, i.e. 5,504 miles according to James. Sad Ed said it is not that. He thinks she is going to dump him for a tanned lifeguard with a six-pack called Chip or Brad, and he is contemplating moving his untimely death forward. I said how far forward. He said Thursday. I asked him what method he was thinking about and he said he is, as yet, undecided. So we went through the potential candidates. So far we have ruled out poison (impossible to procure without arousing suspicions of meddling shopkeepers); shooting (impossible to procure gun without becoming member of clay pigeon shooting club, which is beyond social acceptability); stabbing (too messy); drowning (Lord Butler pool lifeguards too enthusiastic, and shopping-trolley-clogged river Slade only two centimetres deep); and hanging (too clichéd). Pointed out that there are no methods actually left but Sad Ed is undeterred. He says he will find a way to join James Dean and Elvis as lost geniuses. He is deluded. Sad Ed will mostly be remembered for the time he fell off the climbing frame on the common and broke Emily Reeve's left leg. On plus side, endless discussion of death did not make me feel like joining Sad Ed in his quest, despite my current status as spurned lover. Scarlet says it is because I am out of Phase One post-break-up symptoms. Asked her what Phase Two is. She said

inexplicable anger and man-hating. Am waiting its arrival
eagerly.

. . . .

Tuesday 24

It is James's last day of school. He is delighted as it means he
does not have to wear uniform. He has gone as a Ninja
Turtle, predictably. Although it makes a change from his
traditional outfits of choice—Virgin Mary or Smarties packet.
Although the latter has been quarantined as Mum made it
out of a giant cardboard tube from Carpet King and it turned
out James couldn't actually walk in it and had to be rolled
around the school. Besides, it would go soggy before he even
got halfway down the road today, as it is still pouring with
rain. What is point of summer holidays if not to lounge
about garden reading *Vogue* and getting a tan (safely, of
course, with factor fifty and a giant vintage sunhat)?

4 p.m.

James has come home from school with shocking St
Regina's-related news. It is not anything to do with
Keanu. (Although apparently he got sent home for dressing
as a menacing hoodie. It was not fancy dress. It was
daywear of choice.) It is that ancient and ineffectual
headmaster Reverend Begley is retiring. Mum is delighted.
She says things have gone downhill under his woeful
lack of authority, and that now they might get a dynamic, go-getting superhead who will instigate a hothouse

atmosphere replete with banks of computers and language labs, and exclude persistent bad influences like Keanu and possibly Mad Harry. She is going to be disappointed. It will probably be current Deputy Head Mrs Barrow who can barely control her Year Threes, let alone hardened Year Five criminals.

7 p.m.

Mum has sent Grandpa Riley into a panic with her St Regina's superhead predictions. It is because she told him it will put an end to the current 'take anyone gratefully' admissions policy and that Jesus will not get a place as he is officially in the catchment for R. A. Butler (aka Rag and Bone). Grandpa is booking Jesus in for a christening asap. I said I wasn't sure that it was legal to christen someone Jesus Harvey Nichols Riley but Dad pointed out that Auntie Joyless (severe Methodist relative in Cornwall) called her offspring Boaz Jehosephat and Mary Hepzibah, which is equally ludicrous. Then Grandpa got cross and said that there was nothing wrong with Jesus's name and if that was the way we felt then only the dog was invited. He is making a mistake. The dog is bound to jump in the font or eat the kneelers.

Wednesday 25

Mum is in a Noah's Ark style panic. It is because flood waters have reached bastion of architectural and educational

supremity: Oxford. Previously she had been under impression that only Northern and unsavoury locations were in peril. She has gone to Homebase to buy sandbags. Have pointed out that we live on top of hill and that Slade is only body of water for several miles, unless you count Marjory's ornamental pond, but Mum is undeterred.

4 p.m.
Mum could be right about floods. According to James, Slade is now several inches under water, threatening to burst its banks and put the roundabout and 'slide of death' out of bounds. On plus side, it could be the answer to Sad Ed's suicide problems. Maybe God is listening after all. Will text him. Sad Ed, not God. Don't think God has a Nokia.

4.15 p.m.
Sad Ed has gone to inspect Slade to check its potential as scene of legendary untimely death.

7 p.m.
Sad Ed has confirmed that Slade is now four and a half inches deep and currently relatively shopping trolley free. He has asked me and Scarlet to meet him there tomorrow night at seven, i.e. before the Kylies arrive to do groping on the swings, and after tea. He does not want to drown on an empty stomach apparently.

Thursday 26

Today is a potentially momentous occasion, i.e. Sad Ed's untimely death. Obviously do not want him to die, but it has been his ambition since Year Seven so do not want him to be eternally disappointed in himself for not giving it a go. Besides, he is bound to fail, he is a notorious underachiever.

9 p.m.

Sad Ed still very much alive. But soggy and in bad mood. It is because he panicked when he put his head under water and saw several used condoms and a dead squirrel and changed his mind about the chosen location. But then he realized he was wedged in (Slade not being actual 'river' but more stagnant ditch) and had to be rescued by Mark Lambert's dad Mr Hosepipe (fireman, stripper, illegal mini-bike rider). It is his fault. I told him he should not have worn swimming goggles. If he had listened to me he would be dead by now. Instead he is facing potential harassment from Mark Lambert. And Mrs Thomas, when she sees what is stuck to his combat trousers. We are going to say he just overshot on the slide of death and fell in. That's what we told Mr Hosepipe. He says it happens all the time.

Friday 27

Granny Clegg goes into hospital today. She rang at 7.30 to say her last goodbyes. It is because she is convinced

289

she is going to contract MRSA. She says Hester Trelowarren saw one when she was having her hysterectomy and it was green and the size of a Rolo. She is taking a multi-pack of wet wipes to combat them. Pointed out that if they are that big she will need more than a Johnson's wipe and that possibly a can of Raid would be in order. It was a joke but she has sent Grandpa Clegg to Spar to stock up.

Also Sad Ed is ill. It is because he swallowed some Slade water. He thinks it might be rabies. Asked what his symptoms were. He feels sick and has been to the toilet five times during *Hollyoaks*. Said he will live but if he starts foaming at mouth then to call NHS Direct. Oooh. Maybe would make excellent doctor. I could be like Dr Chris and diagnose menopausal things on daytime TV.

Saturday 28

Work was uneventful. There is nothing to do now that I cannot ogle Justin through the glucosamine window display. Even Jack was miserable. It is because he was on till duty, which is fraught with potential finger-trapping injuries. Went to commiserate with Sad Ed at lunchtime but he was not in his usual place, herding Waitrose trolleys round the multi-storey car park. Asked Mrs Noakes (no chin; bad perm; calls trousers 'slacks', formerly of WHSmith, now of Waitrose deli counter) where he might be located but she says he phoned in

sick. She asked if I knew what exactly was wrong as he had been mysterious on phone and they are clamping down on sick leave ever since Gary Fletcher (former Criminal and Retard, sacked from pet food aisle for eating Bonio) phoned in with myxomatosis. I said it was not a fake sickness but was a very real failed suicide attempt. That shut her up.

Also Granny Clegg's hip replacement has been successful, i.e. hip of doom is out, new hip is in and there are no signs of marauding MRSAs on Sebastian Coe Ward as yet. She says she asked the surgeon if the hip had any mysterious markings on it. He has booked her an appointment with the psychiatric assessment unit. They must be busy in Cornwall. Half the population think they are druids.

- -

Sunday 29

Went round to see Sad Ed this morning with Scarlet. He is still bed-ridden with Slade-induced stomach issues. Though it did not stop him consuming several bowls of Coco Pops during our visit. He says he needs the energy. What for? Reading *NME*? It is certainly not for pan-Atlantic phone sex as apparently Tuesday has not answered his last seven calls. He is preparing himself for the inevitable i.e. that he will be joining me and Scarlet in the ranks of singletons shortly. Am even more depressed as remembered it is my birthday in three days. Scarlet

suggested we have a party to perk ourselves up. She means play dirgy music and drink fake blood i.e. cider and blackcurrant. I said I am too depressed to dance, even to goth stuff. Plus there is no way Mum will let me have a party after last year's fiasco when Fat Kylie shaved the dog and the maths geeks did Bacardi-related vomit in the dining room. We are going to get drunk on a punt instead (if Sad Ed can raise himself from his sick bed). It is far more vintage and dignified.

7 p.m.
Oh God. Mum has just reminded me I have a dentist appointment tomorrow with sadistic Mrs Wong. I am having braces fitted, at the age of nearly sixteen. Is there no end to my woes?

* *

Monday 30
Apparently not. Am utterly hideous. Have mouth full of metal and plastic. Am like Jaws in Dad's favourite crap James Bond film. Cannot speak without spitting at anyone within metre radius or sounding like have several speech impediments. Begged Mrs Wong to change her mind as tooth is only slightly wonky but she will not be moved. Plus she was armed with dangerous implements, and has a history of causing excess bleeding, so was too scared to argue. James has pointed out that I should be thankful I do not have to wear it at night. What is point

of that? Night is exactly when it is fine to wear it, i.e. when rest of world, and Justin Statham in particular, cannot see me. Am going to be laughing stock of common room. Will be forced to sit in 'Spaz' corner with the mathletes and Steve 'the scab' Britten, who has eczema.

Interestingly, though, Sad Ed's suicide bid was the hot topic in Mrs Wong's waiting room. Although the details appear to be a bit on the sketchy side. I overheard Mrs Dyer (unconvincing dye job, fat feet, smells of Yardley) telling Ying Brewster (child bride of Les, owner of Siam Smile Thai restaurant, formerly Dog and Bucket pub) that he swallowed five bottles of Calpol and tried to hang himself with his school tie in some sort of statement against conformity. Mrs Dyer said it is always the fat loners who go bonkers.

. . . .

Tuesday 31

The Sad Ed suicide rumours have reached new heights. Thin Kylie came over to ask if it was true he had tried to shoot himself with an assault rifle. She says it is all over the Whiteshot Estate (home of Grandpa Riley and several thousand O'Gradys). I said he was indeed recovering from suicide, but that no firearms were involved. She begged me to tell her the details but I said I am not a blabbermouth. Though someone is or these rumours would never have reached epic proportions. Then she demanded to know why I was 'talking like a mentalist'?

I showed her my brace. She said, 'You are, like, never going to pull with that. It could get caught on someone's knob.' Apparently Stacey O'Grady is still scarred from such an encounter.

Went round Sad Ed's to tell him the bad news about the suicide rumours but he says, *au contraire*, it is excellent as people think he is edgy and dangerous i.e. almost legendary. Although it will make his actual untimely death trickier as everyone will be watching him like a hawk now. I said I didn't think he should hold his breath. Anyway, he has made a Lazarus-like recovery and is definitely coming punting tomorrow, status of poos pending.

Also Granny Clegg has been given the all-clear by the hospital Psychiatric Assessment Unit, despite revealing all about the hip of doom, the bladder of love, and Jesus in the Nimble toast. Clearly she is just mildly mad compared to most of their cases.

Wednesday 1

Am sixteen. Which is, according to James, a milestone in my formative years as can now do several important things like have sex, buy cigarettes, and be gay without asking permission from Mum (in theory anyway, in reality will still be asking her permission to do 'It' when am thirty-six). And, according to MTV, should be getting ready for gigantic party complete with haute couture gown, hundreds of friends, semi-famous band, and fabulous boyfriend to snog. But, instead, am single, broke, and wearing speech-compromising braces. Not even birthday presents have cheered me up as did not get first edition Jane Austen or vintage Dior clutch bag asked for. Instead got National Trust membership (Mum and Dad); *Philosophy Made Easy* (James, in AS Level/Ninja anticipation); a giant tube of Fruit Pastilles (Granny and Grandpa Clegg, out of date); a Jordan's Porridge T-shirt, which I know for a fact came free with three coupons and a first class stamp (the dog, i.e. Mum); and *The Joy of Sex* (Baby Jesus, though assume purchased by Treena). It is my most disappointing haul yet. Mum has already quarantined the sex book to check it for age appropriateness. She is welcome to it. There is nothing joyful about excessively hairy people in compromising positions.

Plus it is raining so getting drunk in a punt has been ruled out in favour of sitting in Scarlet's den with some nibbles and Suzy's vast Eighties film collection. Scarlet was right. Am definitely in Phase Two of post-break-up

trauma. No one could be angrier or more self-loathing than I am right now.

11 a.m.
Except Sad Ed. As predicted, Tuesday has dumped him. It is not for a tanned lifeguard called Brad or Chip, but for a cheerleader called Courtney. Apparently lesbianism is very in vogue in LA at the moment. Sad Ed is beside himself. He has bypassed Phase One self-pity and is already fully in Phase Two. We are going round Scarlet's immediately to find out what Phase Three is and when it will kick in.

11 p.m.
Scarlet says we should not even be thinking about Phase Three yet, as Phase Two could last for anything up to a year. But she has had an excellent idea. We are going to channel our anger into something positive and have made a mission statement for our plans. Our inaugural annual Rachel Riley birthday resolutions are as follows:
1. Not to moon about over exes but to embrace single life.
2. To stay away from all men. (Sad Ed excepted as he is not actual man. He tried to disagree on this but was outnumbered.)
3. To remain true to our friends, forsaking all others.
4. To remember that we alone are responsible for our own happiness.

298

Scarlet is right. Life will be so much easier without the complications of love. It will be utter Simple Life (in original meaning, not version involving anorexic American lay-abouts and rednecks) and am completely committed. Am starting tomorrow. Am going to do single-type activity, i.e. staying in bed late, eating copious chocolate, and reading self-help manuals.

* * *

Thursday 2
8 a.m.

Plan slightly thwarted as got woken up at seven by dog falling down the stairs. And then Granny Clegg rang while I was trying to read *Philosophy Made Easy* (which is utterly self-improving as philosophers are too busy expanding their minds to think about sex) to tell us that there has been an emergency in St Slaughter—unpredicted by any of Granny Clegg's foretelling body parts. Grandpa Clegg's appendix has burst and he is two beds down from Granny on Sebastian Coe ward. Apparently he thought he had just eaten too much Fray Bentos so drank a glass of salt water (ridiculous ancient non-remedy) and instead ended up having emergency surgery. It is the nurses I feel sorry for. They are going to have a nightmare dealing with two Cleggs in one go. Mum has announced she is driving down tomorrow, as Granny Clegg is due out of hospital on Saturday and cannot be trusted to look after herself (Auntie Joyless

and religious cousins are at Bible Camp in Minehead willing stigmata on themselves or something). Granny Clegg said not to worry as her home help Hilary comes twice a week to do the heavy shopping and clean the loo and she can get Maureen from Spar to take Bruce (demonic offspring of dog) for a poo. But Mum says there is no way she is entrusting her own mother to a woman who thinks pasta is a vegetable (she means Maureen. Hilary is an unknown quantity, although, if past home helps are anything to go by, she has greasy hair, smokes, and drinks too much tea). She is leaving at dawn with James.

11 a.m.

Have had a genius idea. Where better to begin my new Simple Life than in Cornwall—county of nothing to do and where all men either chew straw or play the banjo. There will be utterly no temptation at all. Plus it will take my mind off GCSE results (due in three weeks and ringed in red on Mum's *Good Housekeeping* calendar in doom-laden way). I will be excellent home help to Granny Clegg and we can all bond across the generation gap. It will be like *Steel Magnolias* with me as brave and wise Julia Roberts, Mum as manic and paranoid Sally Field, and Granny Clegg as the mad one in dungarees. (Not sure who will be Dolly Parton though. Maureen wears overalls and has hair that defies any definition of style.) Am going to beg Mum to let me go.

300

1 p.m.

Hurrah. It is agreed. Am going to Cornwall tomorrow. Asked Sad Ed if he wanted to come to take his mind off the ghosts in Saffron Walden (metaphorical, not real. Although Grandpa Riley claims he once saw a headless horseman behind the Co-Op) and also his absence might possibly fuel the suicide stories, but he has extra trolley herding duty. Scarlet can't come either as she has to visit her Aunt Sadie in Somerset who is a witch. (The Stones are not having a summer holiday this year due to Suzy's sex programme filming schedule. Apparently she is up to her eyeballs in celebrity penises until September.) It is utterly unfair. Scarlet has more than her fair quota of interesting relatives i.e. sex guru mum, abortionist dad etc., etc. All I have is accountants and a naval fantasist. Anyway, it is a good thing, as she is going to do my Saturday job for me. She is more acclimatized to all those lentils, being a committed vegetarian.

* * *

Friday 3

8 a.m.

Am wedged into Fiesta with four boxes of emergency food (Mum does not trust Spar to stock wholewheat anything) and several sleeping bags (Granny Clegg's bedding dates from 1950s and is perpetually damp). Am also in priority position, i.e. front seat. Dad is not coming as Mr Wainwright is on a cruise around the Baltics with

Mrs Wainwright Mark II and has left him in charge for two weeks. He is mad with power and has gone in already to impose his authority. The dog is not coming either. It is going into kennels. Mum says Dad cannot be trusted not to let it eat the furniture or otherwise maim or destroy the house. The journey is planned with military precision. We are due to arrive in St Slaughter at 2.20 exactly, with no stops whatsoever, not even for wees (it has been nil by mouth since 7 a.m.). There is also an absolutely no talking to the driver rule to avoid distraction and possible pile-up on the A303. I am listening to Sad Ed's iPod instead. He has lent it to me, to counteract endemic lack of edgy entertainment in the west country.

12 noon

iPod battery has run out. Thank God. No wonder Sad Ed is suicidal. Barely any of his music has a tune. Though did discover he has a Britney album. It must be some ironic thing.

2.20 p.m.

Mum is freakishly good at travel timings. She should be employed by Network Rail to redo their notoriously inaccurate timetable. Though her knuckles are white and hands bent into claw shape from gripping steering wheel so hard. We are going to unpack and then reconvene at 2.25 for a light lunch and chore allocation. (Belleview has deteriorated under Grandpa Clegg's management and

302

there is a layer of mould on all the windows. Possibly due to inclement weather. Or Bruce licking them.)

2.25 p.m.
James is late for Marmite sandwiches and chores, which is unlike him. He is like Mum when it comes to punctuality, and cleaning. Come to think of it, he has been strangely quiet all journey.

2.30 p.m.
James still absent. And have had worrying thought. Do not remember him actually being in car, i.e. there was complete lack of annoying singing or fact quoting or 'are we there yetting' from back seat.

2.35 p.m.
It has finally happened. James has triumphed and is 'Home Alone'! He must have taken advantage of Mum's panic at long-distance Fiesta driving to fulfil his Macaulay Culkin ambition. Mum is going mental with worry. She has rung the house several times but there is no answer. He is probably busy rigging a complicated trap involving pulleys, hammers, and buckets of paint across the hall-way. Mum is going home immediately. I pointed out that Dad would be back in three hours to provide adult supervision but she says she might as well leave James in the care of the dog, if he is not dead already, or worse (what would this be?). She says she will be back tomorrow

303

with the escapee. Until then, I am under instructions to throw out all Fray Bentos, Viennetta, and tinned mandarins and fill fridge with health-giving food for Granny Clegg's recovery. She will go mental. She thinks hummus is the 'spit of the devil'.

10 p.m.
Mum has rung. James is safe after all. He had not rigged the house with man traps but instead had cleaned it thoroughly, including descaling the toilet, and was watching the History Channel with a bowl of Shreddies when Mum got in. There is something wrong with that boy. Although the dog had eaten two Bic biros (James had taken him out of kennels to act as his Ninja protector) and Dad had spilled an entire bottle of Jacob's Creek on the lino. On plus side, she has decided to leave me in charge of Granny Clegg, on grounds that her services are required more urgently in Saffron Walden (what with Dad being possible closet alcoholic). She has told me the secret location of Granny Clegg's savings jar (in the freezer, under the Aunt Bessie's Yorkshire puddings) for use in emergencies but in return I have had to agree to a long list of conditions, i.e:

- Do not let Bruce get in the bath with Granny Clegg;
- Do not let Bruce lick Granny Clegg's wounds;
- Do not let Granny Clegg persuade you to buy anything manufactured by Findus;
- Do not let Granny Clegg persuade you to buy

scratchcards, lottery tickets, or betting slips from 'Mad' Charley who races dogs illegally;
* Do not let Granny Clegg let Charley put Bruce into an illegal dog race or it will turn into an illegal dog fight.

11 p.m.
Granny Clegg is rich. She has amassed £273.57 in a Nescafé jar. Admittedly some of it is 'old' money (still currency in Cornwall probably), and I also noticed several chocolate coins, but none the less, it means we will be in practical lap of luxury. Am going to bed now. Though apparently Granny Clegg has been using spare room as general storage cupboard. Am wedged in between three ironing boards and an abdominiser.

1 a.m.
Cannot sleep. Leonard Cohen on iPod is tormenting me. Have realized it is first time have been in a house on own all night. What if burglars try to break in to steal the Cleggs' life savings? Am going to call Mum.

1.15 a.m.
James answered. He was up having a Ninja vigil with the dog. He told me to get a grip and that I am sixteen and need to demonstrate responsible adultness. Also, he pointed out that no one is going to break into a 1950s semi with filthy net curtains in search of treasure. This is true. Asked

about beast of Bodmin. He said to take garlic to bed as beasts of all kinds are notoriously afraid of garlic. Have got tub of hummus and wedged door shut with one of ironing boards as extra precaution.

. . . .

Saturday 4

8 a.m.
Have cleared out spare room in spring clean frenzy after ironing board fell on head in night and thought it was marauding burglar. Have thrown out boards, abdominizer, and ten hamster cages. Since when has Granny Clegg ever had a hamster? Let alone ten? On plus side, have found two utterly vintage dresses in a Spar bag. Have put them in wash and will wear them in manner of Fifties starlet on healthy Riviera holiday. Though is still raining outside so will have to wear wellies instead of peep-toe kitten heels.

Also have just spoken to Granny Clegg. They are bringing her home at two o'clock in an ambulance. She is very excited as she thinks it is going to be like on *Holby City* with sirens going and pedestrians flinging themselves to the pavement to get out of the way. She is going to be disappointed. Have also spoken to Maureen Penrice who is currently in charge of canine menace Bruce. She is bringing him back at two as well and says it cannot come soon enough. He has terrorized her Alsatian Arnie ceaselessly, as well as eaten a signed photo of Phillip Schofield.

306

3 p.m.

Granny Clegg is home. She got carried over the threshold by a beardy paramedic called Dave. She says she can die happy now. In contrast Bruce got thrown over threshold by Maureen who claimed Granny owed her £10 for dry cleaning after Bruce ate an entire jar of pickled cabbage and threw it up on her best skirt. Paid her out of the emergency jar, even though I know for a fact all her clothes are machine washable polyester and she will just spend the money on astrology magazines. Anyway, Granny and Bruce are both recovering on the flock-patterned sofa, eating barley sugar and watching the snooker. Told Granny I did not think boiled sweets were good for Bruce's teeth. She says he swallows them whole so it doesn't matter. I did not like the look Bruce gave me at that point. He is plotting against me. I can tell.

5 p.m.

Granny Clegg's occupational therapist Karl (long hair, earring, smell of patchouli) has been to check that conditions at 'Belleview' are suitable for convalescing ancient person. Conclusion—no, but he'll bring a special loo seat along in a few days when Mr Patterson on Petroc Street has finished with it. Am under strict instructions not to let Granny do any lifting/carrying or unwarranted walking at all. This is not difficult as she avoids all three as matter of course anyway.

7 p.m.
Have made honey-cured organic Wiltshire ham sand-wiches for tea (told Granny Clegg it was limited edition Spam). She has gone to bed already. She says all the painkilling drugs she is on make her sleepy. She does not mind; apparently they give her 'unmentionable dreams'. It does not bear thinking about. I, on other hand, am going for a reviving country walk with Bruce. Scarlet was right. The simple life is utterly rewarding and do not need boyfriend at all when have literary ponderings and faithful companion.

9 p.m.
Country walk not quite as reviving as hoped as actual 'country' is impenetrable moorland, rife with giant black cats and potential murderous ex-tin miners, so wandered aimlessly around only Rec, avoiding stares from bog-eyed youths.

. . . .

Sunday 5
Granny Clegg is demanding to be taken to church. I pointed out she had not been since 1994, due to installation of 'new-fangled' woman vicar but she says her new hip is making her do strange things. She thinks it may be infested with the soul of whomever it came out of. I said it was not a transplant hip but a man-made metal one but she is not convinced and has told me to put my Sunday

best on. Am wearing vintage Fifties thing with giant hole in seam but have safety-pinned it up so knickers do not show. On plus side, maybe will have revelation, i.e. God will appear to me above the font and I will repent all my sins and become a nun. It would help with the swearing off boys thing and is the ultimate Simple Life.

10 a.m.

Granny Clegg says her sister Carol died wearing safety-pinned Fifties dress. She got run over by a meat lorry. The hole is where they cut her out of it.

1 p.m.

Granny Clegg has decided she does not like church after all as it smells funny. Which is rich coming from someone whose entire house is impregnated with odour of processed meat and foot powder. I on other hand have had total church-based revelation! Have not become nun *but* during sermon (something to do with pillars of salt—possibly anti-heart disease theme) spotted utterly gorgeous boy three pews in front, i.e. was not wearing Kappa tracksuit, chewing straw, or in possession of extra limbs. He was tall, with normal complement of arms and legs, and wearing vintage Levi's. And he is black. Am going to track him down and befriend him. Ooh. We could get married and incur wrath of middle-class anti-mixed race marriage masses. Hurrah. Mum will go bonkers.

2 p.m.
Though obviously am totally off men so will just be platonic exotic friend. Though have removed brace and stored in Players tobacco tin on windowsill. Do not want to spit on anyone. Platonic or otherwise.

5 p.m.
Have lurked around all usual 'youth' spots (cigarette counter at Spar, fruit machines in Bubbles Launderette, disused playground) but to no avail. He is nowhere to be found. Maybe he was apparition. Or, more probably, does not actually live in St Slaughter as it is utterly backward.

. . . .

Monday 6
Granny Clegg says she is going on hunger strike if she has to eat any more of Mum's multigrain wholemeal batch. She says in her condition being bunged up would be a blessing as negotiating the loo is particularly tricky (I can bear witness to this after she made me 'ease' her on to the seat five times yesterday). She sent me to Spar for a loaf of Nimble and a tin of Pedigree Chum (Bruce is also on strike and will not eat Mum's health-giving vegetable-based dried dog biscuits). Went to disused playground to call Sad Ed (Granny has banned me from using her phone in case I call a sex line or America) and tell him about church boy. He said I should not be thinking about men at this crucial point in Phase Two and reminded me of our pact. I said,

310

au contraire, I was hoping to secure him as my new best male friend i.e. utterly platonic and with no sex thoughts of any kind. Sad Ed said what about him but I said I don't fancy him, so there is no challenge. Then the line got crackly and I got cut off. The signal in Cornwall is hopeless. How anyone gets anything done is beyond me. Anyway have still not located church boy so plight is pointless.

5 p.m.
Grandpa Clegg has rung to demand to be discharged. He says the nurses are possibly in league with giant pharmaceutical companies (he actually said farmacuticle) and are plotting to use him for human vivisection experiments. Plus they keep trying to look at his 'widgie'. He is worse fantasist than Grandpa Riley. Pretended line was bad, then hung up. Mum would be proud.

. . . .

Tuesday 7
10 a.m.
Oh my God. An unbelievable thing has happened. Utterly gorgeous boy from church is home help Hilary! In fact, is at this very moment making Ovaltine to Granny's secret recipe (i.e. double the Ovaltine and evaporated milk). Am in shock as cannot believe Grandpa Clegg would allow anyone black over threshold. Particularly with a girl's name. Am going to investigate immediately. Once have put on vintage Fifties dress, which says 'am interesting

311

worldly-wise Kate Nash-type', as opposed to Jordan's Porridge T-shirt, which says 'I eat cereal and am type of nerd who sends away for freebie T-shirts'.

11 a.m.
Have secured following information from Granny Clegg re 'Hilary':

- He comes twice a week, on Tuesdays and Fridays;
- He is son of Granny's favourite Welsh dentist Mr Nuamah.
- He is named after someone in the Labour Party (a man), which bodes well as parents are obviously progressive, as opposed to inbred jingoists like most of St Slaughter.
- This is a holiday job. Normally he is doing A levels and is going to be a doctor 'when he grows up', i.e. he is both clever and selfless.
- Grandpa Clegg tried to object to his presence but council said it was that or he could do his own shopping (Grandpa Clegg does not do shopping as it is woman's work). He is now of opinion that it is like being rich plantation owner and having servant.
- They refer to him as 'Chalky'. (Or at least Grandpa Clegg does. Granny Clegg uses her favoured method of silently mouthing words she is embarrassed by, with the helpful addition of sign language. Like 'gay' (limp wrist). Or 'black' (point at face). Or 'Ann Robinson' (wink menacingly).)

312

This is outrageous. Am going to offer to join him in protest against racist employers. Even if they are relatives.

12 noon

Have had groundbreaking conversation with Hilary along following lines:

Me: I'm utterly sorry that my non-multicultural grandparents call you 'Chalky'. They are a bit, um, backward.

Hilary: It's not their fault. They are of a generation that was brought up under the malign Conservative influences of Enoch Powell. Their ignorance will die with them.

Me: Totally. They are institutionally racist. It's embarrassing. Do you want a can of Lilt?

Hilary: No thanks. I am allergic to pineapples.

Me: How ironic.

Hilary: Why?

Me: Um. I just . . .

Hilary: Yeah. Whatever. And in case you were wondering, I can't dance and my penis is of average size.

Me: Right. Uh. Do want a cup of tea?

Hilary: One sugar, please.

As if I was wondering about his penis. Am still scarred by the whole 'Donkey' Dawson/Duchy Originals pork sausage thing. Plus am utterly progressive and know it is outdated

media stereotype. Anyway, Hilary is utterly modern and I think love him (platonically) even more. Cannot believe have to wait three days until I see him again.

. . . .

Wednesday 8

Interrogated Granny Clegg for more information about the Nuamahs so that I can bond with Hilary on several levels. Results as follows:

- Mr Nuamah does not eat garlic (this is plus point for the Cleggs, who are also garlic-fearers, though in their case it is because it is 'foreign muck' and, in Mr Nuamah's case, it is because he does not want toxic breath on his patients).
- They live in St Enodoc's (aka the 'big house' off the B3298).
- Mrs Nuamah does not shop in Spar, much to Maureen Penrice's relief, who thinks they will have trouble understanding her, being 'of foreign extraction'. (It is possibly true, though more to do with Maureen's unfathomable accent and use of word 'hooge'.)
- Mrs Nuamah does shop in M&S in Truro, according to Hester Trelowarren, who spotted her with a basket full of mini Jaffa Cake bites.

There is not much to go on. Though at least I know where he lives. And his preferences, snack-wise.

11 a.m.
Not that am going to stalk him.

1 p.m.
Have eaten lunch (Waitrose lemon sole goujons, aka 'Spar scampi'). May just go for bracing country walk with Bruce.

3 p.m.
Have abandoned country walk as traffic on B3298 is absurd. Have been honked at by 4x4s almost perpetually. Bruce is traumatized. Plus rain showing no signs of abating and vintage dress is too leaky due to car crash holes. Will just have to wait until Friday to see Hilary.

3.30 p.m.
Not that that was why was walking. Obviously. Was just exercising body and mind. In region of St Enodoc's.

- -

Thursday 9
Still raining.

Mum has rung to check that Granny Clegg is recovering nicely i.e. am I managing to slip health-giving foods into her somehow. I said I had got her to eat blueberries (American, and, therefore, untrustworthy) and fromage frais (French, see above) by calling it trifle, and frozen soya beans (too many issues to list), by claiming

they were giant magic peas. She said it all tasted funny but I said it was the after effects of general anaesthetic making everything a bit sour. Asked how things were at home. She said James is trying to invent powerless flight, Dad sacked Malcolm for challenging his new filing system (but reinstated him when computers crashed and no one else knew what to do), and Marjory thinks the Britchers might be aliens (strobing lights, strange noises). I said they are not aliens, it is Terry testing out his new mobile disco. Or possibly Cherie's sunbed is on the blink. Asked if anyone had rung for me. She said if by anyone I meant Justin then no. I said no, by anyone, I mean anyone. She said no. Although she did bump into Mr Goldstein renewing his car tax (Fiat Multipla) at the post office and he asked when I was coming back as apparently Scarlet is not as au fait with the whole lentil thing as I thought and has demanded that he ban several non-vegetarian-friendly gelatine-based vitamin supplements. Plus she does not abide by the 'hour' bit of lunch hour.

Also, the hospital rang to remind us to fetch Grandpa from Sebastian Coe ward tomorrow as he is being discharged, ready or not. I said it was shocking that old people have to leave hospital when they are still incapacitated, just to free up beds. The nurse said Grandpa Clegg is not incapacitated. *Au contraire*, they are sick and tired of him ranting that Gordon Brown is plotting to wipe out law-abiding *Daily Mail* readers with his chemical weapon of choice, MRSA. Apparently he has been whipping all the old people up into an anti-NHS frenzy. As the ringleader, he is out first.

But it is good news because Hilary is going to drive us there to collect him in his environmentally friendly Nissan Micra. Will barely sleep with excitement. (And also because Granny Clegg sleepwalks. Last night she came in at two to tell me to 'put the bins out, Norman'.)

Friday 10
Still raining.

9 a.m.
Am ready to collect Grandpa and feeling utterly Florence Nightingaleish. Am going to impress caring Hilary with my progressive ability to also overlook racism and rantings of all sorts. Plus am wearing swirly vintage Monsoon dress, as borrowed off sex guru Suzy. It is almost ethnic.

5 p.m.
Grandpa Clegg is home and restored to his seat of power, i.e. the broken Parker Knoll. He says he is never going back into hospital, not even if he gets smallpox or TB (the Cleggs are not immunized, in case it was a plot by Harold Macmillan to wipe out the working classes). According to Grandpa, even the food is dangerous and left-wing. He cited Moroccan chicken, Russian salad, and lentil soup

as among the chief offenders. He got a cheer from all the other old people when he left. He is their anti-establishment hero. It is a sad day. He is about as far from Martin Luther King as you can get.

But am choosing to follow Hilary's lead and be zen-like in face of ignorance. He is studying Buddhism as part of his A Level religious studies. Was worried he might be planning on being priest i.e. utterly non-sexual and possibly gay, but it turns out he took it to feed his metaphysical side. I said that was exactly why I was doing AS philosophy. He said, 'Right. You're doing Chem, Physics, Bio, and maths too, huh.' Luckily at that point a sheep wandered into the road and he had to swerve the Nissan Micra so got away with a sort of mumble. Anyway, he is applying to Cambridge to study medicine next year. Hurrah. So I will be able to take tea with him in his Quad (no idea what this is but it sounds exciting) and show him ancient East Anglian traditions like pargetting and minibike racing.

6 p.m.

Hurrah. Grandpa Clegg has burst his stitches from getting shouty about some Polish plasterers on page four of the *Mail*. Hilary is taking him back to A&E. I begged to go too, but Granny Clegg said I had better watch Bruce as he is prone to self-harming if he is left alone for too long. Apparently he chews his legs. Which, in my opinion, is better than chewing everyone else's legs, which is his

318

activity of choice at the moment. At least I got to watch Hilary manhandle Grandpa into the back seat. He has very defined biceps.

8 p.m.
Grandpa Clegg is back amongst his minions on Sebastian Coe ward. Apparently the nurses are not happy, but A&E said his ranting was disturbing the trauma victims and he was better off with his own. He has begged Granny Clegg to bring him in a week's supply of Spar pink wafers to keep his strength up. Hilary is taking him a batch tomorrow, along with a three-pack of anti-MRSA babywipes. Granny says she definitely saw one scuttle under the communal commode.

- -

Saturday 11
Raining. When will this inclement weather cease? It is playing havoc with my wardrobe. Plus hair is back in giant puffball mode.

Rang Scarlet to check how she was progressing at Nuts In May but Jack answered. He said wholefood retailing is not the same without me. Apparently Scarlet is refusing to do till duty on grounds of Health and Safety and has threatened to call inspectors in. Mr Goldstein is thinking of sacking her.

Also, iPod has gone suspiciously missing (bad) along with my brace (good). Granny says it might be the Bermuda

Triangle in the scullery, as she is always leaving sliced meats in there and they disappear within minutes. She is deluded. It is not a Bermuda Triangle. It is Bruce. He is eyeing me with a look of smug self-satisfaction. So am now forced to listen to Granny's Burl Ives records plus owe Sad Ed £129. Am like impoverished third world country, i.e. destined to be for ever in debt. Though at least am not facially disfigured any more.

. . . .

Sunday 12

8 a.m.
Not raining. Hurrah. Am going to seize moment to go to Spar on Sunday papers errand as paper 'boy' Reggie Shovel (73, anorak, trousers too short) is off sick with shingles. I said I may well write to Gordon Brown to complain about pitiful state of pensions and old people being forced into menial and undignified labour but Granny Clegg says he does it for the exercise and free *Sun*.

9 a.m.
Raining. Sun was brief blip in otherwise continuous drizzle. Granny Clegg is annoyed because the paper is soggy (used it to protect inflating hair) and she is being forced to read my *Vogue* (shiny, so water-resistant), until the *News of the World* dries out on the bar heater. Am also

320

hovering near bar heater as need to be dry for church at eleven. Granny Clegg says I am wasting my time as God only likes puritanical mentalists like Auntie Joyless (she actually said mentalist). I said I was just going out of philosophical interest. That shut her up. She thinks philosophy is bordering on witchcraft. Have also rung James to get loads of Kofi Annan facts to impress Mr Nuamah (they are from same village in Ghana). For example, he is married to a Swedish lawyer and his name means a boy born on a Friday.

9.15 a.m.
Have had genius idea. Am going to dreadlock hair. It will prevent any more moisture-based issues and is utterly non-racist!

10.15 a.m.
Am dreadlocked. Ish. Is a bit messy and dreads are inch-thick in places, but is excellent none the less. Granny Clegg says I look like I have not washed in weeks. Hurrah.

12 noon
Mr and Mrs Nuamah were not in church. Nor was Hilary. Thought they might have been called out on a dental emergency. But apparently (according to Maureen's sister Barbara, who sits two pews down to the left) they have gone shopping in Plymouth. So my

Kofi Annan facts have been utterly wasted. Tried to creep out during 'For Those in Peril on the Sea' but the lady vicar thought I was offering myself up for communion. So now am awaiting wrath of Lord for eating wafery thing and drinking vile wine (Co-Op own brand, I saw a case under the altar) when am not actually even baptized.

2 p.m.
Mobile phone has gone missing. Granny is blaming scullery Bermuda Triangle. Normally I would blame Bruce but think it might be God.

4 p.m.
No, was Bruce. Have found it buried with iPod, brace, and a pair of aertex pants in his lair (i.e. the cupboard under the stairs). The number nine key is missing so will not be able to do any emergency calling, or texting involving the letters WXY and Z. On plus side iPod looks relatively unscathed so do not owe Sad Ed anything. Will say chew marks are acceptable wear and tear and he should have insurance for such eventualities. Also brace is beyond use. Hurrah.

5 p.m.
iPod worse than I thought. Memory has wiped all but two songs. 'Hit Me Baby One More Time' (Britney) and 'I'd Do Anything' (West End cast recording of *Oliver*).

9 p.m.

Have given iPod back to Bruce. Cannot listen to stage school brats offering to lace my shoe again or may well have to join Sad Ed in his quest for untimely death.

* *

Monday 13

Raining.

Am bored. And I know I should be bonding with Granny Clegg across the generations and listening to her tales of Cornish yesteryear, but her memory is cloudy and she just keeps going on about Eamonn Holmes, who is neither Cornish nor historic. Thank God Hilary is coming tomorrow. We have so many things in common, i.e. we are both outcasts in Cornish society, and we both like philosophical things. Plus my hair is bordering on the Afro. Although may have to undread it soon as it is getting a bit itchy.

* *

Tuesday 14

Oh my God. Granny Clegg is a pawn in a giant Cornish drug ring! Hilary and I were clearing the vegetable patch at the back and have discovered marijuana plants! Actually I thought it was smelly sycamore shoots but Hilary is more worldly wise in these matters. He says we should call the police immediately, as someone is obviously infiltrating her runner bean frames and using it as an illegal narcotics

factory. We are awaiting arrival of PC Penrice (brother of Maureen and Barbara). Once he has moved Hester's chickens out of Smeg Launderette. That is the downside of free-range poultry. They have no sense of territory.

Also have undreaded hair. Hilary says it makes me look like a trustafarian. Which is not at all progressive or left-wing. I think.

2 p.m.
Oh my God. Granny is not a pawn. She is the drug baron! She cracked under interrogation by PC Penrice and confessed that she got it off 'Crazy' McCaffety's pot plant (how ironic) stall at the Illogan fete and has since been handing it out to several youths in the area. She insisted that it is just some sort of herb and they are using it in casseroles but PC Penrice was not fooled and asked her to 'accompany him to the station for further questioning'. Hilary was brilliant and demanded her right to legal representation but Granny Clegg says she doesn't trust lawyers (she has been watching too much *Judge John Deed*) and could she take Hester from over the road instead. Hilary has called his mum anyway. She is a solicitor in Truro and is bound to be used to police brutality/accused stupidity etc. Hilary and I are going to wait it out at Belleview. Mainly because other-wise half the house will disappear into Bruce's Bermuda Triangle. May do some worried sobbing. Then Hilary will take pity on me and comfort me in his manly arms.

324

7 p.m.
Granny Clegg has been released without charge. She is disappointed as she was hoping for a night in the cells. She says it is very nice in there and people brought her PG Tips every half hour and a Bird's Eye Steak Grill for tea. Felt a bit guilty and put kettle on immediately. Anyway, apparently Mrs Nuamah befuddled the police with technicalities like the fact that Granny wasn't actually selling it and thought it was some sort of oregano. Asked what Hester's contribution was. Granny said she was in charge of doling out Fox's Glacier Mints.

Anyway, the drugs have gone. Two men in suits came and dug them up during *Blue Peter*. Hilary says they are Narcs i.e. plain clothes anti-drugs policemen. It is a shame really as it would have been edgy to have a dope-smoking granny. But something good has come out of it all i.e. Hilary gave my arm a squeeze when I got a bit tearful (actual genuine tears, though caused by Bruce biting my foot, not incarcerated Granny) so he definitely likes me.

7.15 p.m.
In a platonic way, of course.

7.30 p.m.
Although it would be nice if it was in an 'I fancy you and quite want to fiddle with your admittedly only 32A bra' kind of way.

Wednesday 15

Mum rang to check up again. Have not told her about the drugs shame. She would panic and despatch Dad to remove me from Granny's den of vice. Just told her that Hilary and I were managing to cope with every eventuality. Mum said Hilary sounds like a real find. I said 'mmm' in non-committal manner. Do not want to arouse suspicion. Luckily she changed subject to James and Mad Harry who have taken to dressing in leotards and tights. I said it is excellent that they are expressing their feminine sides. She said it is not feminine sides. It is some sort of Ninja wear and they have been terrorizing Marjory with their mysterious dancing in the garden.

Have made Granny twenty-two cups of tea to make up for previous lax attitude. She has begged me to stop as her bladder is 'like Niagara falls'. There is no pleasing some people.

Thursday 16

Took Bruce to disused playground on pretext of a poo trip but actually to ring Sad Ed. He is depressed again. I said is it the metaphorical ghosts but he said no it is the extra trolley duty and it is causing him to lose will to live. I said I thought he had lost it years ago i.e. his untimely death ambitions. He says that was motivated by a desire to be legendary, his current suicidal tendencies are motivated by a desire not to have to listen to Gary Fletcher talk

about remote-controlled cars for eight hours a day. I said at least it is keeping his mind off women but he said Gary Fletcher keeps talking breasts as well. Then he asked how I was holding up with my platonic pact. I said that at no point had I tried to snog or otherwise manhandle Hilary (which is utterly true), and that I am more committed than ever to the Simple Life. (Which is sort of true.)

8 p.m.
But what if it turns out that, in fact, Hilary is my ONE? It is possible. There is a definite frisson in the air when we are in the room together.

8.30 p.m.
No. Am not going to break my pact on the grounds of a frisson. Anyway, it is probably just the static off Granny's nylon carpet.

9 p.m.
But on other hand, one cannot mess with fate. Will lure him into potential snog situation and leave the gods to do their work.

* *

Friday 17
2 p.m.
I have a date with Hilary! Well, not a date exactly, but an assignation none the less. He is taking me to his Labour

Party constituency meeting tonight. I said I was a seasoned party campaigner (vaguely true, e.g. Jack's mock election campaign. Plus am always opposing social injustices, e.g. Mrs Brain's povvy table etc.) and would love to see how the grassroots supporters were holding up in the LibDem heartlands (I heard this on Radio 4 once). He said good, as they were debating the reinstatement of Clause 4 and would value my opinion. Am going to call Jack to find out what this means immediately.

7 p.m.
Aaagh. Jack's number has been deleted off my contacts by malign forces, i.e. Bruce, and I can't call it in normal way as it involves a nine. Am going to have to improvise. Have told Granny Clegg I am going to hang out at the bus shelter. She will panic if she thinks I am 'in cahoots with commies'.

10 p.m.
Nothing happened. The back room of the Farmer's Arms was obviously not sexually charged enough. It was all the sensible footwear. Plus I think I may have got Clause 4 confused with Section something else as I said it was outrageous they were even thinking about reinstating blatant anti-homosexual laws and I would voice my opposition all the way to Number 10. Why am I not doing A Level politics? In fact, may drop French and swap. It is a dead language after all and politics is international in its

influence. On plus side, we are meeting tomorrow. He is going to show me his signed photo of someone called Barack Obama.

* *

Saturday 18

2 p.m.

Fate was conspicuous by her absence from St Enodoc's this afternoon i.e. nothing happened again. Maybe it is like Phil and Kirstie say, i.e. location, location, location. The pictures of Tony Blair looming down at us from his bedroom walls did not help. Nor did Mr Nuamah who offered to fix my 'dental misalignment'. Did not mention the missing brace. He will be wiring me up with 24-hour metalwork within minutes.

Am definitely taking up A Level politics though. Hilary showed me his photo and I said it was nice to see basketball players in suits for once instead of all that Lycra. It turns out Barack Obama is running for President in America. How was I to know that? He is way too good-looking for a politician. Where is the helmet hairdo? Where are the bad teeth?

And got devastating news when I got back to Belleview. Dad is coming on Monday to repatriate me to North Essex. It is because Mr Wainwright is back from his cruise and is reasserting his authority, much to Dad's disappointment. Also Auntie Joyless is back from Bible camp today and will no doubt reinstate herself as chief Clegg tea maker. So am now in last-chance saloon as far

as the gods and Hilary go. And that saloon is St Slaughter Church. So gods will be in abundance at least.

5 p.m.
Rang Scarlet to tell her about my new uber-left-wing friend. She is very keen to meet him. Platonically, obviously. I said I would invite him to Saffron Walden as soon as possible. Then she said that she had news too. Apparently it is ultra secret and mindblowing and she will tell me about it when I get home. I said tell me now but she said it was possibly illegal and Suzy thinks the phones have been bugged by rival TV networks so it is face-to-face information only. (Wish I had not blabbed on about Granny being drugs baron now. ITV will be ringing her up to be on *Jeremy Kyle* any minute.) Oh God. Hope Suzy has not been giving her valium again.

Also she has been sacked. It is for 'persistent contrariness'. And lateness. Apparently she did not go in until half eleven today. I said was it because her biorhythms were wrong but she said no it was because *Friends* was on T4 and it was the one where Joey gets his eyebrows plucked. Anyway Scarlet says she does not care because money is not important in the grand scheme of things. This is easy to say when your mother is a primetime TV star and does not believe in withholding hereditary wealth and ferociously instilling work ethic. In other words Scarlet does not have to clean up cat poo to earn her pocket money.

330

Sunday 19

9 a.m.

This is it. It is D-Day for establishing whether Hilary and I are meant to be platonic or underwear-touching friends. Hopefully he will be fired up by the presence of higher beings and fling me romantically across the vestry. Am wearing miniskirt and ironic Mickey Mouse T-shirt (age 8). Which is not very religious but makes bust look bigger and gives air of potential availability.

2 p.m.

Aaagh. Have been thwarted by gods. Or rather by Auntie Joyless. Who has a power beyond any divine being. She and my god-bothering cousins got back from Bible camp last night and Granny Clegg happily informed them I had 'seen the light' and had 'gone all Gloria Hunniford'. So at ten o'clock she packed me in the back of her Mini Metro with Boaz and Mary and took me to get baptized at her evangelical Methodist Mission at the back of Somerfield in Redruth. So am now soaked to skin having been dipped in underfloor paddling pool by someone called Father Abraham (incomprehensible accent, gigantic side-burns, haunted look of *Crimewatch* photofit). Plus am probably harbouring legionnaires' disease. That pool was on the utterly murky side. And had to listen to drippy Mary going on about how Jesus was her best friend. Cannot believe am related to these morons. If Jesus wants any of them as a sunbeam he is mad.

Am going round Hilary's immediately. Once have taken off wet smock. (Auntie Joyless would not let me get baptized looking like the 'whore of Babylon'.)

7 p.m.
The gods have made their intentions known. Hilary and I are destined to be no more than friends. It turns out that he has a girlfriend. She is called Paloma and is half Spanish, i.e. also an ethnic minority. He was round her house in Truro when I called for him. According to Mrs Nuamah, who answered the door, they have been together ever since they met in chess club in Year Eight.

It is inevitable. I am not multicultural enough for him. Why oh why am I not browner? It is utterly unfair and potentially racist. It is not my fault I was born so pale. I blame Mum. The Cleggs have definite ginger tendencies.

It is probably for the best though. As Scarlet pointed out, it is important that we learn to love ourselves before we can expect anyone else to love us. Sad Ed will be waiting for ever. He is filled with self-loathing.

* * *

Monday 20
The hospital has rung. Grandpa Clegg is being discharged again. Asked Granny if Hilary was going to get him but she said Dad will be here by two and he can get him in the Passat. Then she asked why I was so miserable. I said it was

potential legionnaires' disease from the religious paddling pool. She said I am lucky, apparently Auntie Joyless's friend Vivian was in hospital for months after being submerged last year, as predicted by the hip of doom. (Although on further interrogation it turns out she fell down a manhole and hospitalization was not exactly pool-related.)

3 p.m.
Dad has arrived. Asked him where James was, as I assumed he would have come along for the ride, but apparently he is too busy with his Ninja dancing. Plus Dad says he cannot endure twelve hours of him singing the Turtles theme tune. He has taken Granny Clegg to fetch Grandpa. I am watching Bruce to ensure Dad's wallet does not disappear into the Bermuda Triangle. Ooh. Knock at door. Is probably local type trying to procure oregano. Four have called already. Have sent them to see Crazy McCafferty, i.e. the evil overlord.

4 p.m.
Was not mental Cornish drug fiend. It was Hilary. He came to say goodbye! He has promised to visit me in Saffron Walden when he comes up for his Cambridge interview and I have promised to keep the red flag flying. We have swapped phone numbers and are now utterly best friends. He left just as Grandpa and his entourage got back from the hospital. Dad asked who the 'young negro' was (he is trying to be non-racist but, as usual, it backfires

333

horribly). Grandpa (who is trying to be racist) said, 'That's the houseboy, Chalky.'

- -

Tuesday 21

Am home. In non-multicultural Saffron Walden. Predictably Mum is in spasms about Hilary. She says it is not that he is black, it is that he is a man, and may try to take advantage of Granny Clegg. It is that he is black. There is no way anyone would try to take advantage of Granny Clegg. Not even Grandpa Clegg. I warned Dad this would happen, but he said if he didn't tell her she would wheedle it out of him, and then make him pay for not coming clean in the first place. He is right. She is merciless.

On plus side, James has offered to restore my mobile phone to working capacity. He claims his Ninja powers have given him healing hands. Plus he has a vast collection of electrical things and probably has a spare nine key somewhere.

4 p.m.

Phone is restored. Though nine key is pink and gigantic. Have texted Scarlet to say I am coming over tomorrow morning to hear about her potentially illegal news. She says to bring Sad Ed as she needs three of us for it to work. Oh God, hope it is not some three-way 'friends with benefits' sex orgy. Suzy is always trying to promote them.

- -

Wednesday 22

It is not a three-way sex orgy. It is Wicca! Scarlet had a revelation at her Auntie Sadie's and has decided to form a coven, as it is the ultimate in pro-women, pseudo-goth activity. Me and Sad Ed are going to be in it too as three is some sort of mystical number. I did point out that Sad Ed is not strictly female, but Scarlet says she thinks he has excess oestrogen (hence the bingo wings and manbreasts) and anyway, he can be our Spike. So I bagged to be Buffy but Scarlet says she is Buffy and I am Willow, which is not fair as I am utterly Buffy-like, but then we remembered that we are our own people and do not need to be fictional vampire-fighters so we agreed to drop the whole Buffy thing and stick with our real names (although Rachel is not at all Wicca. May change it to Hemlock or something). Scarlet's cats Gordon and Tony are going to be our familiars. I did offer the dog but she says dogs are utterly non-Wicca, plus he is bound to eat our sacred implements, when we get them. (This is true, although Gordon and Tony did not show any potential familiar activity, i.e. they spent all morning licking their genitals.) I said it was utterly brilliant as will be able to cast love spells and hook Justin into my Wicca web and possibly give Sophie warts or something. But Scarlet said we will be using our powers to do good in the world, not meddle in the affairs of ex-lovers. She is right. Although I bet she is plotting something for bat boy Trevor.

We are starting on Friday, once GCSE results are out of

the way. Apparently the worry will be sapping our Wicca Power at the moment so it is best to wait. Then we all started worrying about GCSEs and had to eat an entire packet of Waitrose chocolate florentines and watch classic *Deal or No Deal* to calm down.

- -

Thursday 23
8.30 a.m.

There is an air of general GCSE-related doom hanging over Summerdale Road. Mum is trying to pretend that she is not concerned. She actually said she will love me whatever my grades. This is not true. Her love is entirely correlated to academic prowess. This is why James is her favourite as he is naturally boffin-like. Then she offered to drive me to school in the Fiesta so that we can be first in the queue. I said not to bother as Mrs Leech (school secretary—bad hair, too much face powder, biscuit habit) is bound to have lost them under a packet of bourbons and we will be lucky to get any information before lunch-time. This is partially true. Although mostly I do not want Mum stalking round John Major playground like some Marks and Spencer-clad madwoman. I will never live it down. Me, Scarlet, and Sad Ed are going together. Bob is picking me up at ten in the smelly Volvo. I said it wasn't very witchlike, but Scarlet claims she is going to hang sacred herbs from the rear-view mirror to empower it. And cover up the lingering odour of sick.

9.45 a.m.
Oh God. This is it. Am utterly traumatized. My entire literary and generally brilliant future depends on whether or not I remembered the valency of boron etc. If only Hilary were here with his calming arm-squeezing ways.

9.55 a.m.
Sick smelling Volvo has arrived. In less than an hour will know my fate.

12 noon
Fate still unclear. GCSE results locked in school office and Mrs Leech has lost key. School caretaker Lou (former Criminal and Retard, once ate school rabbit) is looking for his spares. On plus side, Thin Kylie has brought several bottles of Strongbow in anticipation of being the first Britcher to get a qualification. Mum clearly has less faith in me than Cherie as she is ringing every five minutes to check progress. Have turned phone off as pressure may send me over edge. Will just have sip of cider to calm nerves. It is mostly apples anyway so is almost health-giving.

4 p.m.
Am bit drunk. It is because did not get results until three when Mark Lambert gave Mrs Leech a leggy into the office window (it is lucky she was wearing trousers or the view could have been potentially scarring) and in

meantime have consumed half a litre of Strongbow. But do not care. As am utter genius. Have passed all GCSEs— two As, six Bs and only one C grade, i.e. maths, which is pointless subject anyway and will never need it again. Scarlet got five As and four Bs and Sad Ed got nine Bs. He said that is his destiny in life, to be second best. He is secretly happy though. I saw him smile when Thin Kylie fell off the sheep fence. She got three Ds and is ecstatic. Even Mark Lambert got one (French, unbelievably). Mrs Duddy says it is her best Retards and Criminals cohort ever i.e. twenty-seven GCSEs at E grade or above (among thirty-one pupils). Even Mr Wilmott seemed satisfied. Although, according to Mrs Leech (wild with abandon after eight gypsy creams and a Hooch) he was on the phone to Burger King Sports Academy all morning trying to wheedle their grade point average out of Mr Medwell.

5 p.m.
James says I may have frittered my life away by only securing a C in maths. He says I will regret my casual attitude when I am struggling to secure employment now that an economic downturn is on the horizon. He is an idiot. At least Mum is more philosophical. She says I can use my A Levels to make up for my disappointment. Although she is not so philosophical about me tripping over the dog and spilling an illicit carton of Ribena on the hall carpet. Am in room now with a packet of Jacob's Cream Crackers, a bottle of Volvic, and instructions to

sober up before *Neighbours*. May just close eyes though. It is all the overexcitement. Mum is wrong about disappointment. Today has been a milestone in my formative years and will look back on it with pride (except bit where mistook sheep poo for Malteser).

· ·

Friday 24

9 a.m.

Have headache. Wish was witch already so could cast spell to despatch nausea and pain. Instead will have to drag self to bathroom for Anadin. Yesterday was colossal mistake. Am not genius. Am average. As usual. And am never drinking Strongbow again. It is stealth alcohol, i.e. makes you think it is lovely vitamin-filled appley stuff but is evil deathly poison. Plus am due at Scarlet's at eleven for our inaugural coven meeting. Hope do not have to do any actual witchery as think powers may have been depleted by cider.

5 p.m.

Did not have to do any casting of spells yet. Scarlet says we are only novices and must do some background reading first. And buy some essential witch gadgets, i.e. pentacles and wands. We are going to Cambridge next week, as Saffron Walden is understocked when it comes to occult accoutrements. Suzy is very excited by it all. She says paganism is the true religion and that we will

be at one with Mother Nature, Gaia, and various other feminine deities. Jack says we are fooling ourselves. He is against all things paranormal. It is his communist tendencies. Edna the non-Filipina Labour-friendly cleaner did not seem too happy either. Scarlet says it is only because she thinks she will be mopping bat blood off the Habitat rugs. I asked if that was at all likely. Scarlet said no. Although there might be some goat bits. I don't know why Edna is so touchy anyway, mostly she spends her time hoovering up the trail of Benson and Hedges ash that she leaves behind when she is dusting.

. . . .

Saturday 25

Have had some excellent news at work. Am getting a pay rise, i.e. £2.85 an hour, a 15p cash terms increase! It is not much, but it is the principle. It is because me and Jack did some severe lobbying, i.e. I pointed out I had several GCSEs now, including chemistry and maths, so was more qualified to sell vitamins and add up lentil bills. Then Jack baffled him with a speech about trade union rights and spinning Jennys. It is excellent as debt mountain has notched up several inches due to Bruce killing Sad Ed's iPod plus Mum is making me pay Granny Clegg back £50 out of her emergency Nescafé jar. (I said *Vogue*, *Elle*, *Cosmo*, etc. were emergencies, given the lack of intellectual stimulation in St Slaughter,

but she is not convinced.) I think Mr Goldstein was glad to have me back. Scarlet is clearly not cut out for menial labour. Apparently she got all faint after Mr Goldstein made her restock the notoriously high-up yeast extract shelf. It is her previous hardline goth tendencies. All the black clothes and staying in the dark have depleted her Vitamin D.

Also, apparently Saffron Walden has been a hotbed of employment-related shake-ups in my absence. Trainee butcher Justin has been replaced by Dean 'the dwarf' Denley. I know it is a good thing, i.e. because I am utterly not supposed to be mooning about after Justin. But Dean has weedy arms and crap hair. Plus he has to stand on a box to do any mincing. It is not at all inspiring.

Sunday 26

Was going to do witch revision today but Mum said we are all going to church as Baby Jesus is getting christened in anticipation of appointment of St Regina's go-getting Superhead. I said I couldn't go as *a*) am baptized into mental Cornish church and do not want to enrage Methodist God by crossing threshold of run-of-mill Church of England and *b*) Grandpa Riley only invited the dog due to the ridiculous names hoo-ha. But Mum said he has relented during my exile and James and I are godparents. So Baby Jesus will have a deluded Ninja and a witch as his spiritual guides.

3 p.m.

Baby Jesus Harvey Nichols Riley is now an official member of St Regina's Parish Church, as witnessed by Rachel and James Riley, godparents and general lifestyle advisers. It was not an entirely hoo-ha-free ceremony, i.e. Treena managed to blaspheme several times during the proceedings due to presence of 'knickers up the chuff' and the dog drank the holy water. Grandpa got it in on the pretence of it being a guide dog for the blind (he put on his Reactolite glasses and tripped a bit). Reverend Begley (still fit enough for vicar duties, but not for managing 270 unruly children) said it was unusual-looking for a guide dog but Grandpa pointed out that in America they have seeing eye monkeys who can make scrambled eggs and all sorts so I think Reverend Begley thought he was getting off lightly compared to a troop of gibbons in the vestry. He is mistaken. Gibbons would be a breeze compared to the dog.

5 p.m.

Mum has asked why I am not wearing my brace. Said I was wearing it at night instead. Think she believed me.

Monday 27

Bank Holiday

6 a.m.

Mum is booking me an emergency appointment with Mrs Wong for brace replacement. She swooped in a surprise fact-checking dawn raid. She is like Special Branch. When I am actual witch I will be able to befuddle her with my mystical aura though. She will be powerless in my presence. Possibly. Am going back to sleep now. Is bank holiday so no point even getting dressed. Scarlet is researching potential celebrity sex guests for Suzy, Sad Ed is at his cousins' in Leighton Buzzard, and the only shops open are Mr Patel's sticky lino emporium and BJ Video.

Tuesday 28

Thank God Bank Holiday is over. It is complete waste of a day, when I could have been usefully doing Wicca-related things. If I knew the first thing about witchcraft, obviously. Am going to library later to investigate its 'supernatural' section. And possibly write to Gordon Brown to suggest a reduction in national holidays. Mum is in agreement. She says they just clog up the roads with freedom-crazed office workers.

3 p.m.

Oh God. Something terrible and potentially Simple-Life threatening has occurred. It is nothing to do with library (supernatural section only useful if you want the *Usborne Guide to Ghost Hunting*). It is Justin. He is back. I know this because I managed to walk into him outside Gayhomes while I was being distracted by a display of wallpaper. It

was awful. (Justin, I mean. The display was the usual precarious and uninspiring tableau.) We just stared at each other for what seemed like eternity, but was probably only five seconds. Then he said, 'All right?' and went into Eaden Lilley's. He was not buying anything. It was an escape route. He hates me so much he cannot bear to be within same road as me. Plus the impact made him spill Coke Zero all down his favourite Nirvana T-shirt. He rubs Kurt Cobain's face when he needs inspiration. It is like Samson's hair. He is powerless without it. So now have soiled his musical genius, to top all my other faults. He will never want me again. Which I know I am not supposed to care about as am utter Shania Twain-style powerful woman. But the thing is, I do. It is the dirty blond hair. And the dirty T-shirt. Oh God. The Simple Life just got complicated all over again. Am totally back in Phase One.

On plus side, Mrs Wong cannot fit me in until October so am disfigurement free for over a month. Though it is wasted as Justin cannot even bear to look at me.

. . . .

Wednesday 29

This is typical. You get chucked because you have min-uscule breasts and your dad did not invent Microwave Muffins and then, once you are depressingly single, your bust finally decides to make an appearance. Mum pointed out that I was developing a cup overhang (common, and

344

on par with tattoos or fake tan in her book), and that I should go to Booths and get measured immediately (declined as do not want Mrs Dyer (unconvincing dye job, fat feet, smells of Yardley, propagator of Sad Ed suicide rumours) manhandling breasts, so measured self instead using method recommended in 2002 *Just Seventeen* annual (previous owner Thin Kylie)). Am now 34B i.e. entire size bigger. But do not care any more. My breasts are nothing but empty vessels now.

5 p.m.
Ugh. Just reread that bit about empty vessels. That sounds vile. Especially having had to sit through Cherie's drunken 'why I had breast implant' rant, i.e. 'they were like two shrivelled socks'. Mine are not at all sock-like. But no one is going to want to touch them anyway. Am going to bed to mope and listen to 'our song' some more.

Thursday 30
9 a.m.
James has confiscated my Arctic Monkeys CD. He says the perpetual Northern shouting is interfering with his Ninja calm. Also, he says he has sent for Scarlet and Sad Ed to liberate me from my wallowing. I said, on the contrary, it was more meditating on my fate. But am secretly glad. Need friends to listen to my torment. The dog is useless at this. It got bored after five minutes and

345

wandered off to lick the stair carpet. (James dropped a Mini Milk there last week and did his own mess removal. He has failed. The stain has gone but the taste lingers. Mum would be ashamed.)

5 p.m.
Am utterly back on track and in Phase Two again. It is because Jack says Justin is not coming back to Sixth Form. Rock Foundation at Braintree has been reprieved at the last minute after they promised to teach people to actually read music as well as nod and strum along to Pink Floyd. So he is going to pursue his career as a rock god. Am glad. Hopefully the twenty-mile commute will tear him and Sophie Microwave Muffins apart and then I will laugh at him when he comes crawling back to me. Gosh. Sound almost goddess-like. It is because am now in possession of genuine crystal necklace plus *Everything You Need to Know About Wicca* manual by Celestine Norton (long grey hair, mystical necklace, slightly mad look in eye). Scarlet has a sacred pentacle bowl and Sad Ed has a broom. It is not for flying (disappointingly) but is for sweeping away astral build-up. We couldn't find a cauldron so Scarlet is going to borrow Suzy's Nigella soup pot and draw some runes on it. We are going to do some revision and meet in a week to test our powers. And our wands. Apparently we have to choose our own, according to our Wiccan characters. Will get something literary-based, obviously. Maybe a replica of Harry Potter's one with the phoenix feather in it.

346

Also have three new bras (Mum-approved Marks and Spencer with no lace, no push-up padding, no Playboy symbols and an ample backstrap i.e. totally boy-repelling but at least are 34B and not 32A as previously). Sad Ed said he will be getting measured up if his current man breast weight gain continues. It is the depression. It is causing him to binge on Caramac.

Friday 31

10 a.m.

James has begged to be allowed to join the coven. It is because he read chapter one of my Wicca book while he was on the toilet this morning (he is either very fast reader or freakishly slow pooer). He is very excited by the prospect of supreme divine power and has promised to renounce the way of the Ninjas. He is going to burn his leotard later in a ritual sacrifice. I said that *a*) I did not think that Scarlet would be too happy with him joining and *b*) Mum has hidden the firelighters after the dog became inflammable with creosote last year. He is undeterred and says he and Mad Harry will form their own rival coven. Keanu is going to be their familiar. He is goblin-like and potentially evil.

2 p.m.

Summerdale Road is positively alive with people seizing the day and doing groundbreaking things. Mum has

joined a book group. It is excellent and practically like a coven, i.e. it is women only (Mum asked Dad if he wanted to join but he said he would rather chew tinfoil). Although do not think Marjory, Mrs Thomas, Mrs Noakes, and Cherie have any mystical powers. Mum was against Cherie joining but she got wind of it over the deli counter at Waitrose and demanded entry. Mum says there is no arguing with her once she has decided she wants something. It is Terry I feel sorry for. He is utterly wife-beaten. Anyway, they are taking it in turns to choose the book. It is Mum first. They are doing *The Last Family in England* in a fortnight. It is about modern family breakdown and has a Labrador as the narrator. It sounds utterly far-fetched to me. If our dog were narrating a book it would revolve entirely around furniture consumption. Although it might be enlightening as to why he is so anti Jon Snow. Mum cannot put Channel 4 on any more for fear of sending it into a panic. At least I could understand the Natasha Kaplinsky thing. Her lips are huge and her hair doesn't move. Thank God she has gone to Channel 5, which is forbidden in our house.

Am slightly concerned at potential Wicca powers. Did as book instructed and tried to manifest my goddess energy by rubbing my hands together and visualizing lightning but just got friction burn. Although it is early days yet. Will probably be breathing fire by end of the week. Still not chosen a wand yet either and James says it is sacrilege to try to recreate the phoenix-feather one

and he will be hexing me if I even try. Have checked with Scarlet and she says any straight object is fine. So have narrowed choice down to extra-long novelty Fitzwilliam Museum pencil, Mum's electric fly swat, and a cheerleader baton left over from my and Sad Ed's brief majorette phase in Year Five.

ELECTRIC FLY SWAT

KALIB

RACHEL RILEY IS UPDATING HER PROFILE

september

Saturday 1

Nuts In May is in turmoil again. Sad Ed's mum Mrs Thomas has quit. She says the 9 to 5 is interfering with her many and varied Aled Jones commitments. Mr Goldstein is back to the drawing board. He has even asked Jack if he might consider leaving school for a future in wholefood outlet assisting. Jack said no, as he is still hellbent on being an anti-war Foreign Secretary. I do not blame him. Lentils are not a career for any self respecting literary type. Besides, the till is demonic.

On plus side, have procured essential Wiccan herbs cinnamon and sage at ten per cent staff discount. Did not tell Mr Goldstein what they were for. He is Jewish and witchcraft of any kind is bound to compromise his Kosher ways. Said Mum was making Delia's shepherd's pie.

7 p.m.

Sad Ed just came round. He is having Wicca trouble. It is Mrs Thomas. She has been using the astral build-up broom to unclog the drains. He is worried it may have its energies tainted. I said Scarlet will be able to cleanse it for him with an incantation. Which is possibly true. On plus side, he says he is glad his mum is out of a job. It is not the Aled Jones stuff, it is his diet. He said the stress (and availability of discount Tofu etc.) was having an effect on his tea menu and staples like sausages and mash were being replaced by quinoa bake. Asked him how trolley herding is going. He says it is marginally better as Gary Fletcher is

353

at his nan's caravan in Hunstanton for two weeks so he has been promoted. Asked what his extra responsibility involved. He said he has to oil the brakes and check for discarded plastic bags. It is hardly mettle-building stuff.

. . . .

Sunday 2

Have put down my Wiccan devices and am devoting entire day to preparation for school. It is serious business, i.e. no longer a matter of digging old kilt and blazer out of back of wardrobe and buying an array of Biros. Instead need entire weekly wardrobe plan, customized Converse, and literaryish fountain pen. Want to look edgy and utterly vintage, but not so much that outdo superior Upper Sixth and am not welcome on the saggy sofa. It is a fine balance. Trinity Braithwaite went too far last year when she came to school in a tutu. No one spoke to her for weeks.

James does not have to worry about these matters. It is because he is not back to school until Thursday. He says it is swings and roundabouts as far as INSET days are concerned. Mum is not so happy-go-lucky. Not only has she got him under her feet for three more days, it delays the grand revealing of the new Superhead.

7 p.m.

Think am finally ready. Wardrobe planned with military precision (with aid of James, an A3 sheet of graph paper, five highlighter pens, and some Teletubbies stickers). Am

354

going for big first day impression i.e. Fifties dead lady dress. Then will introduce more vintage wear throughout week. Am saving ironic Brownie T-shirt until Friday, traditional 'go mad' day. Have customized bargain Army Surplus bag with Kooks badges (de rigueur in Sixth Form last year) and am going to take Arctic Monkeys CD in order to instil self with instant radical edge. Will be excellent and cannot wait to absorb heady atmosphere of academic prowess and youthful exuberance.

Monday 3

8 a.m.
Wardrobe chart undergone slight rejig. Mum had fit about the gaping hole, dead lady Fifties dress and sent me back upstairs to change so am now wearing denim mini with stripy 'French chic' top, which was Tuesday's outfit, meaning have had to move one-armed hairy jumper forward an entire week from next Wednesday. James is feverishly restickering the chart to reflect the rethink. But am now ready for Sixth Form appropriate breakfast of black coffee. It is compulsory not to eat until you get to Mr Patel's at first break.

8.15 a.m.
Although do not want to faint in hothouse atmosphere. Will just have bowl of Shreddies. Will tell Scarlet it was croissant. French patisserie is allowed as it is utterly cosmopolitan.

8.30 a.m.

Why is Thin Kylie leaving the house so early? *Jeremy Kyle* hasn't even started yet. She cannot be going to school. There is no way Mr Wilmott would let her stay on for A Levels. She only got three GCSEs and one of them was in Food Science.

4 p.m.

Thin Kylie *was* going to school. As was almost the entire cohort of Criminals and Retards. It is because Mr Wilmott has implemented an emergency go-getting measure, i.e. an entire vocational programme including BTEC Hair and Beauty, Bricklaying for Beginners, and Essential Car Mechanics. Scarlet says it is an excellent Labour party policy to put manual labour on a par with academic study. She is wrong. There is no way tinkering with a Datsun is the same as A Level Drama. And Mr Wilmott is not doing it to be left-wing. He is doing it because Burger King Sports Academy have got a new plumbing wing and he is worried we are losing out in the forward-thinking school stakes. He will regret it later when Mark Lambert has terrorized the sheep for another two years and half the Sixth Form are pregnant or on probation.

Also Goth Corners Mark II and III are in chaos. It is Scarlet and Trevor's on-again off-again love life. None of the trainee goths know who to sit with any more. Scarlet has been forced to take drastic measures and has

instigated a new Coven Table in between the maths geeks and the hardcore drama freaks. Some of the smaller goths are already eyeing us with jealousy. It is because we are real witches, as opposed to pretend vampires. Even Sophie Jacobs looked a bit nervous. It is because Scarlet threatened to hex her in the upper school toilets. She is powerless without Justin to protect her. I predict Scarlet will soon be Queen of A and B Corridors, and Miss Microwave Muffins will be exiled to substandard D Corridor (i.e. the 'gym', Rural Studies, and Criminals and Retards).

Common room was excellent. Even got to sit on saggy sofa for five minutes (me and Scarlet ran from double English) before Pippa Newbold sauntered in from double geography and ousted us. Am going to ditch Army Surplus bag though. It is utterly last season, according to Scarlet. Everyone is using Waitrose reusable carrier bags to lug textbooks around this term.

* *

Tuesday 4

Had first Philosophy lesson today. It was utterly mind-expanding. We had to discuss whether right and wrong actually exist or are constructs of culture. Mum would be proud—I came down firmly on the 'of course they bloody do' side. Scarlet was more for the construct argument on the grounds that it is not wrong to murder a rapist.

Plus Mr Wilmott has agreed to swap French for Politics. As long as I get a letter off Mum. Hurrah.

5 p.m.
Mum has refused to let me swap French for Politics. She says there is no way she is letting me fritter my future away on a subject that is the province of self-promoters and notorious philanderers. She has offered Physics as a halfway measure. Have declined. The only people doing Physics are the mathletes. Plus it is taught by Mr Potter who smells worse than Oona.

7 p.m.
Am doing Politics after all. It is not because Mum has relented. It is because James has forged me a freakishly authentic letter. Not only is the handwriting almost identical, but the tone is both pedantic and menacing. By the time she finds out, I will be baffling her with my knowledge of Keynesian economics. And I can always watch *Chocolat* if I need to speak any French.

. . . .

Wednesday 5
8 a.m.
Summerdale Road is awash with St Regina's Superhead anticipation. James has had hair slicked down with industrial strength Brylcreem and Mum is wearing a skirt. Even the dog is strangely neat-looking, though there is no

358

way Mum would let him near school. The potential for devastation is enormous.

4 p.m.
The new Superhead is not so super after all. He is not from tough inner-city comp or fast-tracked from a high-flying job in the city. He is from round the corner, i.e. it is sandal-wearing Nigel Pendleton, next-door neighbour of Scarlet, and fellow left-wingish and vegetarian friend of Suzy and Bob. Worse, he has asked everyone, including pupils, to call him 'Nige' as it imbues a more age-appropriate casual, friendly air. Mum is not in agreement. She says St Regina's will be in special measures by half term if he persists with this lack of footwear and lackadaisical names strategy. She could be right. I do not fancy his chances in the face of Keanu and Maggot. James is happy though. He says he is going to tell Nige about his coven idea tomorrow. I reminded him that paganism does not usually go down well at Church of England establishments. But, according to James, Nige has encouraged everyone to expand their horizons, and he says his door and mind are always open to new ideas.

Thursday 6
James has abandoned his coven. Not because Nige shut his door, or his mind. It is more Mad Harry's mind. He says it is too girly. (But wearing a leotard and tights and

doing expressive dance is fuelled with testosterone?) Anyway, they have decided to become ghost hunters instead. James says they have unearthed an ancient and prophetic manual at the library.

6 p.m.
It is not ancient and prophetic manual. It is the *Usborne Guide to Ghost Hunting*. Have just seen James reading it in bath.

. . . .

Friday 7
School has gone Facebook mad. Which is quite progressive for Saffron Walden, i.e. only several years after the rest of the country instead of an entire decade (we are still waiting for Boyzone to go out of fashion from the first time around). Me, Scarlet, and Sad Ed are going to do our profiles at the weekend. Jack says it is a false sense of community and utterly sad. He is wrong. It is brilliant. Sad Ed says we should go with MySpace as it is more band-orientated. But Scarlet says Facebook has Zombie fights and 'name that sweet' quizzes so we are definitely going down that route.

5 p.m.
James is investigating green ectoplasm in the downstairs toilet. Have pointed out that it is far more likely to be dog-related vomit, but James is not convinced. He thinks we could be under siege from creatures of the night.

360

6 p.m.

Is not ectoplasm. Is dog vomit, induced by it eating two cartons of Covent Garden pea and ham soup. James is visibly disappointed and has persuaded Dad to let him into the attic to look for unexplained presences. He is a moron. The only unexplained presences up there are Mum's 1980s jumpsuits.

7 p.m.

James says there is definite paranormal activity in the attic. He has heard scratching and, at several points, a cold shiver ran down his spine. Mum has sent Dad up to check for mice and missing roof tiles.

. . . .

Saturday 8

There has been more devastating news at Nuts In May. Ailment-ridden Rosamund is coming back! It is not that I don't like her (although the nits and flaky hands are a bit off-putting), it is that she works Saturdays so it means either Jack or I are going to be sacked, and join the ranks of idle unemployed. I said it should be Jack as he was last in and therefore first out, plus I am up to eyeballs in debt. But Jack said it should be a meritocracy, which is ultra left-wing and means who is best for the job. So then we had to be uber-efficient all day, i.e. no stealing Carob muffins, no organic tampon throwing fights, and no moaning when our fingers get stuck in the till of death. Mr Goldstein

has promised to reveal his decision next week. I have no chance. Jack is far better at the till. And knew what homeopathic remedy to prescribe Marjory for her oral thrush. I tried to give her merc. sol. but apparently that is for mouth ulcers and could have set her recovery back weeks.

On plus side, James has done my Facebook profile for me. He is more technologically advanced than me, plus he has already done ones for him and Mad Harry. They are using them to promote their ghost hunting business 'Ghost Hustlers'. Which sounds like a gay goth band. Have pointed out that they are contravening several rules pertaining to age limits and commercial use (both Facebook's and Mum's) but James says he has the brain of a thirty year old. Which is possibly true. Plus no one will ever employ them anyway.

Mine is excellent. Although photo is one Sad Ed took for Glastonbury application, i.e. I look like a man, but crucially is not in any way pornographic (Mum has set rigorous parental controls already after she saw Thin Kylie's profile which is an underwear shot and also features Mark Lambert's right buttock). Have listed interests as literature, world events, and vintage clothing. Thin Kylie lists hers as puppies, 50 Cent, and arse (no idea). Have only got three friends so far (James, Scarlet, and Sad Ed). But am waiting to hear back from Sad Ed's ex Tuesday. Anyway, am not going for quantity, it is quality that counts. Am going to be discerning and only friend kindred spirit types, or celebrities. Unlike Thin Kylie who has seven O'Gradys and all

362

of the Year Nine football team. Although they probably are kindred spirits to her. Plus have joined a group. It is 'Jane Austen is my Homegirl'. Am also looking into 'Jane Austen gave me unrealistic expectations of love', 'I love Mr Darcy', and 'I am totally a character in a Jane Austen novel'.

. . . .

Sunday 9

Rachel Riley and **Dog Riley** are now friends.

The dog is more advanced than me. Apparently it has had a profile for a month now (as designed by James). It has sixty-two friends and is in three groups: 'Dogs are better than cats', 'Dogs in clothes', and 'Pies are spanking gorgeous'.

Am going over to Scarlet's after lunch to test my Wiccan powers. Have decided to go with fly swat as wand. It makes spooky buzzing noise when it touches anything and has definite electrical energy. Have been practising with it since eight this morning. In between checking Facebook, obviously. (Still no reply from Tuesday in America. It must be the time difference. Or maybe she is scared that Sad Ed will track her down through me and cyberstalk her. It is highly possible. He has that look about him.)

5 p.m.
Am back from Scarlet's. Wiccan invocations not entirely successful. It may have been to do with the wands, i.e. an electric fly swat (me), bit of Habitat decorative willow

(Scarlet), and a plastic light sabre with missing batteries (Sad Ed). We were supposed to be doing visualization, i.e. thinking so hard about something that it actually appears. I went for a rabbit (I have always wanted one but Mum banned them on the grounds that their lifespan is woefully short and they eat their own poo and babies), Sad Ed tried for a Snickers (as he was missing vital afternoon snack for practice), and Scarlet did Jack Straw. But all that happened is that Sad Ed got dizzy from all the concentration and low blood sugar and had to have emergency hummus. So we got a bit bored and went on Facebook instead. Scarlet already has 187 friends including Gordon Brown, someone out of *Skins*, and three David Milibands. She was not sure which one was the real one (there were twenty-seven) so she has gone for the most boring profiles. Sad Ed has two: me and Scarlet, so at least am beating him. He is in five groups though: 'Jews who like Quavers' (he is not Jewish but does like Quavers and there was no 'depressive former choir boys who like Quavers'); 'If this group reaches 100,000 I will name my son Batman'; 'Put raisins back in Double Deckers'; 'Morrissey's invisible hand touches me when I sleep'; and 'What is with Lilo Lil's trousers?'

I pointed out that Barry the Blade (local madman, big beard, currently going out with Lilo Lil Simpson of wee-smelling white flares fame) might take exception and formulate some kind of hitlist but he said Barry sleeps in an Austin Allegro and is unlikely, therefore, to have internet access.

7 p.m.

Have now got thirty-five friends including Jack (who has joined Facebook on the grounds he can funnel serious friends to his MySpace page, which he has only joined as it is useful bandwise. He is still resolved not to regard it as real in any sense), Suzy (who has had a profile for a year and is friends with porn stars), several O'Gradys, and smelly lesbian Head Girl Oona Rickets. Plus have joined 'Retro is *not* the same as vintage', and the 'Back Doors Appreciation Society' (i.e. Justin's band. And I do appreciate his music. Just not his wayward groping), and have installed Superpoke.

9 p.m.
Scarlet has walled me to tell me to stop thinking about the Butcher's Boy.

10 p.m.
Dean 'the dwarf' Denley has friended me. That is nice.

. . . .

Monday 10

Rachel Riley has thrown a sheep at Dog Riley.

Facebook mania has overtaken the Sixth Form. The common room computer (no Pentium inside, teastained, actually chugs when switched on) has mysteriously disappeared and the IT room has a queue stretching down past the B Corridor fire exit. The maths geeks, who all

own their own MacBooks, and are wise to the potential money-making situation, are renting them out at £10 an hour in the upper school canteen.

5 p.m.
Have been poked by Dean 'the dwarf' Denley. Am messaging Scarlet immediately to find out the significance of this event.

6 p.m.
Oh God. It means he likes me. And not in a platonic Simple Life way but in a complicated erogenous way. It is Scarlet's ill-thought-out Butcher's Boy comment on wall. She did not make it clear enough which butcher's boy she meant. Have ignored poke. He will get hint and go away.

. . . .

Tuesday 11

Rachel Riley has been high-fiiived by Ed Thomas.

Scarlet has two new Facebook friends. They are Tamsin Watts and Tamsin Bacon (pseudo-identical twin Year Ten EMOs who obviously ring each other at 7 a.m. to co-ordinate hair accessories and stripy tights). But they are not limiting their friendship to cyberspace. They have taken to following Scarlet round corridors between lessons like Tim Burtonesque corpse bridesmaids. Scarlet says it is all part of being a Sixth Form icon, and a witch. Sad Ed agrees—Fat

Kylie followed him all the way from the toilet to Mr Patel's at break. Though it was possibly to scrounge his Nice 'n' Spicy Nik Naks. Did not mention that Dean the Dwarf had poked me twice during *Look East*. Am still ignoring him. He will go away eventually and find someone his own size.

. . . .

Wednesday 12

Dean Denley has caressed Rachel Riley.

Rachel Riley has karate chopped Dean Denley.

Ignoring not working. Instead am following James's method of engaging in Superpoke warfare. He is hoping it will catch on at St Regina's and he will be crowned first toughest in cyberspace, beating Keanu who is not allowed on the computers at school after he removed all the keys and rearranged them, thus turning 'DOG' into 'GAY' and 'CATS' into 'SHIT'.

Also Mum is beside herself with newly invigorated Superhead fervour. It is not not-so-super Nige. It is notoriously ineffectual Mr Wilmott. He has sent a letter home telling parents that John Major High is going to implement the Government's trailblazing Talented and Gifted Pupil Programme. He says it will counterbalance the special attention given to the Criminals and Retards (he did not say this, he said 'slow') by giving brainy people an extra boost. Mum is determined I am going to

be picked and has written to Mr Wilmott suggesting me.
She is wasting her time. It will be the mathletes and teen
mum Emily Reeve, who is still ahead of the pack, brainwise, despite having no sleep and stitches in her hoo-ha.

7 p.m.
Although I am quite talented and gifted in the dramatic
and literary areas, i.e. I know all of Ophelia's lines in
Hamlet off by heart, plus have watched *Pride and Prejudice*
thirty-four times. It could mean I get days off to visit
Stratford-on-Avon and have one-to-one voice coaching
lessons with Trevor Nunn. Hurrah.

Thursday 13
Jewish New Year/Ramadan

Dean Denley has given chocolate to Rachel Riley.

Rachel Riley has thrown Tiramisu at Dean Denley.

9 a.m.
Have delivered letter personally to Mrs Leech, gatekeeper
to Superhead Mr Wilmott, in anticipation of Trevor Nunn
lessons.

10 a.m.
Am going to ask Mrs Leech to intercept Mum's letter and
redirect it to the bin before Mr Wilmott sees it and

bestows me with honours. Being talented and gifted does not mean one-to-one lessons with Trevor Nunn at the RSC. It means quizzes printed off BBC Bitesize in the mobile block with pervert-in-school Mr Vaughan.

11 a.m.
Mrs Leech cannot find letter due to non-existence of filing system and vast quantity of Peak Freans on desk. She says not to worry as there are only five places and they are bound to go to the 'Asians'. She means Ali Hassan and the maths geeks, and sadistic Mrs Wong's son Alan who was *a*) once on *Junior Mastermind* (specialist subject: the life-cycle of the medusa jellyfish) and *b*) rumoured to be earmarked for the higher echelons of the triads, a rumour possibly perpetuated by himself.

5 p.m.
It is Mum's inaugural Ladies' Book Group tonight. She has printed out a list of questions and a multiple-choice quiz (with the aid of James who is already compiling the Queen Elizabeth pub quiz on a weekly basis for Grandpa Riley). It is utterly exciting and totally like *The Jane Austen Book Club*, but without that one from *Devil Wears Prada* and with more Kathy Bates types.

9 p.m.
Mum is back from Book Club. It was not at all like the Jane Austen one in the film. Apparently Mrs Noakes

objected to the book on moral grounds, Cherie had only got to page seven, and Marjory had read *White Fang* by mistake. Only Mrs Thomas had actually got to the end of the right novel. But on the plus side she loved it as she once had a Labrador too. It didn't talk though. And was called Aled, predictably. They are doing *Lace* by Shirley Conran next. It is Cherie's choice. Mrs Noakes will go mental. I know for a fact there is some vile activity with a goldfish in there (Thin Kylie read it aloud on the sheep field in Year Eight as part of her unofficial sex education programme).

. . . .

Friday 14

Scarlet Stone has used the force with David Miliband.

Saffron Walden music scene is in mourning. Rock legends the Back Doors have disbanded. Sad Ed got the call last night. It is because Justin says he will be working with real musicians from now on and cannot afford to have his technique tainted by amateurs. At least the Jack Stone Five are still going. Albeit there are now only three of them. I did offer to replace Tuesday as lead vocalist but Jack says it is more ironic with three. He is going to drum and sing from now on. They are playing Jack's eighteenth party tomorrow night at the Bernard Evans Youth Centre. We (i.e. the coven) are all going. Scarlet says we can channel our energies to illuminate Jack in a pool of

370

spiritual light (the lighting 'rig' in there is restricted to on or off). It is lucky there is a free bar, as will be penniless and jobless by this time tomorrow. There is no way Mr Goldstein is going to choose me over Jack.

. . . .

Saturday 15

Scarlet Stone has drunk dialled Trevor Pledger.

Oh my God. Jack got a car for his birthday. It is a purple vintage Beetle with ironic furry dice and a door that is held on with gaffer tape. He picked me up in it on the way to work. I said it was excellent. Though I was surprised he had gone for a polluting type and he should have asked for a Nissan Micra like Hilary, which is more environmentally-friendly, i.e. left wing. But Jack got huffy and said that Beetles are the original left-wing cars of the common people and that if I didn't like it I could walk so said I loved it as he is the only person I know with a car, bar the Passat, Fiesta, and sick-smelling Volvo. Although we had to park over a mile away from work anyway due to ferocious parking restrictions and Nuts In May's lack of staff car park.

Jack said it was right that we should travel in style anyway as it is a solemn occasion, i.e. our last day working together. He is right, it is sad. Jack is fun to work with, plus he has no ailments. And his legs are supposed to be hairy. Then we wished each other good luck and said may the best man/woman win. We are finding out at closing

371

time. Mr Goldstein is refusing to tell us before in case whoever loses gets minty and refuses to do till duty for the rest of the day.

6 p.m.
Oh my God. Am still in work. Mr Goldstein picked me after all. It is utterly amazing. But tragic for Jack, obviously, as now he will not be able to fund his gaz-guzzling but left-wing car. I said sorry to him, but Jack said it was the right decision and the best woman won. And he'll still get to do holidays and sick cover (which in case of Rosamund could be frequent). I hope it does not ruin the party later. It is very exciting as it is our first ever Sixth Form party. Am utterly not going to get drunk on Pernod and Black and snog an O'Grady.

12 midnight
Am utterly not drunk. Do not understand it at all as drunk seven bottles of something called Kaliber. Maybe it is because am sixteen and have built up liver stamina, like Fat Kylie who can do twelve Bacardis and still walk the line. Anyway, virtue is intact and have not snogged an O'Grady, or Dean Denley who hung around all evening laughing at jokes that I was unaware I was even making. Unlike Scarlet, who drank too much Carlsberg and flashed her black bra at Trevor. Luckily he was wearing dark glasses to protect his vampiric batlike eyes from the stage lights and did not see her.

Interestingly, drunk Scarlet blurted out that Jack didn't lose his job at all. Apparently he quit this morning in order to concentrate on his A Levels. Maybe Suzy is going to fund his petrol after all. But it is still odd though as Jack said it was important for future antiwar Foreign Secretaries to work as well as study in order to keep in touch with the real world. Anyway, I gave him a hug after his set with the band and said thanks. He said, 'What, for the music?' I said, 'Something like that.' Do not want him to know that I know that it is not that I am best employee after all.

⋆ ⋆

Sunday 16

Dean Denley has hugged Rachel Riley.

Rachel Riley has hadoukened Dean Denley.

The coven has expanded. Apparently drunk Scarlet decided to let the Tamsins join last night and they were installed in the den in their identical witch costumes when me and Sad Ed showed up. Sad Ed said that, as a pro-feminist coven, we should all decide together who joins. But Scarlet said that, as founder, she is head witch and gets two votes. Jack (not in coven, but watching *Popworld* in hanging seventies love-swing thing) pointed out that that was very un-Labour and it should be one member, one vote, but Scarlet turned the TV off and told him to take his unspiritual earth-bound body into the kitchen. Anyway,

we have agreed to admit them, as five is still quite a magical number, according to Celestine Norton. But they are only our apprentices and we still hold higher status. Although Tamsin Bacon claims she has already managed to make the devil appear before her. She is lying. Or on drugs.

Anyway, it is all systems go as far as the coven is concerned. It is because the Autumn Equinox is next Friday, and it is a special Wicca festival, i.e. our powers will be especially potent. We are having a sacred ritual ceremony to celebrate. Sad Ed suggested the den, as *Friday 13th Part something or other* is on TV, but according to Scarlet, Wicca is all about nature and so it has to be outdoors. We are going to use their anti-nuclear war Peace Garden instead. Then Sad Ed asked if we were going down the ritual nudity route so we had a vote. Scarlet (pro) lost four votes to two. There is no way I am running around naked in the Stones' back garden with Gordon and Tony and potentially non-go-getting Headmaster Nige ogling my nether regions from the sliding patio doors.

Monday 17

Rachel Riley is friends with Alan Fletcher.

The Riley household has been thrown into moral panic. It is because a form has arrived asking for confirmation that Mr Ernest Riley (i.e. Grandpa) still lives here. If we say yes, it means we get a £200 winter fuel payment. Mum,

who is normally ultra law-abiding, says she is tempted to say yes as he spends half the day round here with Baby Jesus watching telly with the central heating on full. James says Mum's reaction is common and is known as fake pensioner syndrome. He says he is extremely disappointed in her and has taken custody of the letter to deliver it by hand to Treena later.

But more excitingly, am now friends with Karl Kennedy off *Neighbours*, real name Alan Fletcher. Admittedly he has 10,654 friends, but am hoping for an invitation to the set, none the less. Plus got lift to school in Jack's Beetle. Was slightly squashed, what with presence of Scarlet, Sad Ed, and smelly Oona. And gaffer-taped door fell off outside Mr Patel's. But was still utterly vintage and cool. Having motorized transport is instant kudos in Sixth Form. Unless it is Mr Whippy's ice cream and shag van.

* *

Tuesday 18

Dean Denley has married Rachel Riley.

Rachel Riley has divorced Dean Denley.

Mum has asked if I want to go to France at Easter as practice for my A Level. Remembered I have yet to confess to my politics switch, due to not actually knowing anything yet as have just been watching *Yes, Minister* videos. So said no on grounds of last year's Ninja frog-eating chicken fiasco.

James has also declined but not on death chicken grounds. It is business-related. He says he is booked up until next June with ghost hunting investigations. Apparently Saffron Walden is being stalked by no less than three werewolves. He is deluded. At least one of them is freakishly hairy librarian Mr Knox.

Am going to have to improve political abilities fast. Was hoping to be fluent in polling and filibustering by now but am still struggling to remember when the NHS was invented. Will ask to borrow Jack's *West Wing* boxed set. It is much more modern and basic principles are bound to be the same as ours.

. . . .

Wednesday 19

Rachel Riley has joined 'Bartlett fans on Facebook unite!'

James is jubilant. It is because 'Nige' has implemented a new system for choosing teams in games. Everyone just decides which colour tabard they like best. I pointed out that this meant he could end up with twenty-eight on one team and two on the other but James says that is a fair consequence of forward-thinking. It is because Nige says getting picked last for games can be potentially scarring for a child. He is right. I am covered in wounds from netball, hockey, and rounders. It is not so much that am crap at sport (although am crap at sport). It is more that Miss Beadle (overweight; bulgy eyes like Joey in

376

Friends or rabbits with myxomatosis) and Miss Vicar (stick-thin; no breasts; facial hair) went through a phase of letting the Kylies be captains which meant me and Scarlet got left out due to 'lezzer legs' and 'shit hair'.

Mum was not so sympathetic. She said it was the beginning of a slippery slope and the 'Brains Badge' (sheriff-style giant star for cleverest in class—worn by James on no less than 137 occasions) will be the next thing to go. James said that it has already been binned, along with milk monitors and 'keeper of the playtime bell'. Mum is writing to the council. I left them to their philosophical PE arguments to go and watch *West Wing* with the dog. It is excellent and am definitely going to be political as well as a literary genius after university (and after have lived in bohemian squat in Camden). I would be ideal as press secretary CJ. Am going to practise talking and walking fast at same time.

7 p.m.
Have bruise on forehead and several on elbows due to talking and walking incidents. It is not that am not cut out to be political type, it is due to excessive furniture and dog in way.

. . . .

Thursday 20

Rachel Riley is not talented or gifted.

It is utterly predictable. Mr Wilmott has named his chosen few. They are Emily Reeve, Ali and Amir Hassan,

377

Alan Wong, and someone in Year Seven who can do quadratic equations. I know it is a plus thing, i.e. will not have to sit in draughty mobiles after school with Mr Big Nipples Vaughan, but it would be nice to be officially talented and gifted. Although am possibly neither as head of politics Mr Slatter (beard, Fairisle jumper, history of failing miserably in council elections) highlighted when he pointed out that England does not have a House of Representatives. It is not my fault that we are still stuck in the nineteenth century, parliament-wise.

Am depressed. Will go on Facebook for a bit and do some Zombie fighting.

1 a.m.
Mr Wilmott is wrong. Am utterly talented and gifted as have just scored 100 per cent on Name That Thundercat! Facebook quiz. Plus have poked someone. It is equally talented and gifted Hilary. Hurrah. Hopefully he will poke me back and we can do cyber snogging.

1.15 a.m.
In a platonic way.

* *

Friday 21
Autumn Equinox (i.e. important Wicca calendar date)

Kylie Britcher has poked Mark Lambert.

9 a.m.

Hilary has not poked me back yet. Maybe he is too busy with his five A Levels. Or cleaning Granny Clegg's outside privy. Anyway, have other things to think about as have remembered that am taking part in (non-naked) Wiccan ritual in Scarlet's garden later and am supposed to have honed my witching skills to perfection. Will have to do it in double Philosophy this afternoon. Wicca is utterly mind-expanding. Plus we are doing the existence of God, which is bound to end in tears.

7 p.m.

Am fully prepared for Wiccan ritual and potential spirit apparitions of all varieties. James has begged to be a witness in case he can do immediate ghost hunting, but have declined in case Suzy decides to join in, as she will definitely go naked. In fact it is unusual to see her in clothes these days. Hurrah, it is totally going to be like that bit in *The Craft* where the earth opens up and divine beings seep out into middle earth i.e. Scarlet's anti-nuclear-weapon Peace Garden.

11 p.m.

Divine beings did not seep out into Scarlet's back garden. In fact Wiccan ritual disappointing on several levels. Firstly, the Tamsins spent at least an hour arguing with Sad Ed as to where magnetic North was. Then Scarlet tripped over her cloak and dispersed the cinnamon over Sad Ed's

379

Reeboks. Then we discovered that Gordon had pooed in the pentacle in an utterly unWiccanlike fashion. Luckily Suzy had made lavender anti-breast-cancer Nigella cupcakes so we ate those and watched *Friday the 13ᵗʰ Part 27* (possibly) in the den after all. Scarlet says we need to wait for Hallowe'en, as it is higher up the calendar in importance stakes, plus the pentacle will not be smelling of cat faeces. She has given it to me to look after. Will guard it with my life.

. . . .

Saturday 22

Scarlet Stone has worshipped Gordon Brown.

Ailment-ridden Rosamund is back at Nuts In May. It turns out that Guru Derek was 'realigning' quite a few other chakras as well as hers. She says she is done with men and is devoting the rest of her life (she is twenty-eight) to finding a cure for impetigo. I told her about our Wiccan coven and she is very excited. She says it is very in touch with nature and all things homeopathic. She is going to act as our external herbal adviser. Asked her what herbs would get rid of idiot Dean 'the dwarf' Denley, who spent most of morning waving sausages suggestively through the window. She said, on the contrary, his shortness could be a magical sign and I should be embracing him. She is wrong. He is not magic. He is just an oversexed midget.

Was going to do some Wicca when I got home but James has borrowed the pentacle to test it for ghosts. I have no idea what his methods are but they seem to involve Mum's microwave Geiger counter and plaque revealing dental tablets.

Sunday 23

Rachel Riley has thrown a goblin at Dog Riley.

The dog has eaten the pentacle. James is livid as he says it was definitely supernatural, according to his ghostometer (i.e. microwave leak detector). I am livid as now have to purchase new pentacle before Scarlet finds out. Unless dog manages to poo it out whole. Which do not think will be physically possible.

Also why has Hilary not poked back yet? Maybe it is because it is Sunday and thus a holy non-poking sort of a day. Yes that will be it.

Monday 24

Rachel Riley and **Hilary Aneurin Bevan Nuamah** are friends.

There is trouble afoot on the saggy sofa. It is because Sophie Microwave Muffins has demanded that the Sixth Form Criminals and Retards (aka BTECers) are banned from the common room and use one of the mobiles or

381

Rat Corner as their HQ instead (she did not say 'HQ' she said 'youth club'). She says it is nothing to do with their intelligence, it is simply a question of overcrowding. It is a question of intelligence. Fat Kylie tried to climb on the microwave to retrieve a flump that Mark Lambert had successfully stuck to an *American Pie* poster and the door no longer shuts. Anyway, it is not happening as Jack and Oona overruled it for being non-Marxist and possibly weightist. So that shut her up. Hah. Plus had more excellent news when I got home. Hilary has finally poked me back. It was not the religious thing after all. It is because he has been on a Biology field trip to Wales for five days to look at seaweed. Am jubilant as now have access to his profile and can see everything he is up to.

5 p.m.

Am less jubilant. According to Hilary's profile his status is 'in a relationship with Paloma Jones'. So checked out her profile and she utterly looks Penelope Cruz, i.e. who used to go out with Tom Cruise before he brain washed Joey off *Dawson's Creek*. Plus she has Martin Sheen as a friend i.e. the President of the United States (*West Wing* version), which beats Karl Kennedy hands down. It is utterly depressing. Am going to have to befriend someone equally serious. I wonder if Nelson Mandela is on Facebook.

Tuesday 25

Rachel Riley has chest bumped Hilary Nuamah.

Scarlet Stone has tripped Rachel Riley.

Scarlet says my interest in Hilary is threatening my Simple Life pact, not to mention my position in the coven. She says all the Superpoking will sap my Wiccan potency and has told me to limit it to platonic activity. Although she does agree he looks utterly gorgeous in his photograph and his socialist credentials are impeccable.

Also, the coven has added political campaigning to its many services and spells. It is because Emily Reeve is sad at being separated from Lola Lambert Reeve all day and might leave school unless emergency childcare measures are implemented immediately. Scarlet is starting a campaign for a Sixth Form crèche. She says it is totally sexist not to have one and is going to cast a spell on Mr Wilmott to make him see the light. Jack has suggested a petition as well in case her magic is not strong enough yet. Mark Lambert has already signed up. Plus he has had a surprisingly good suggestion of having a fully fledged nursery so that the Criminals and Retards can learn to be childminders. He says he would definitely transfer off Bricklaying if BTEC Nursery Nursing was on offer as it is too cold outdoors and the bricks keep falling on his feet.

Wednesday 26

Scarlet Stone's stripper name is Gordon Braithwaite.

The crèche petition now has 358 signatures. Admittedly some of them might be fake, e.g. Obi Wan Kenobi. But, still, it is an excellent achievement. Not everyone is pro though. Sophie Microwave Muffins has started an anti-crèche campaign. She says it will just encourage the BTECers to get pregnant and it is bad enough they get paid to be at school as it is. What does she mean? Anyway, Scarlet says Sophie has no hope as she cast her spell on Mr Wilmott during *Gavin and Stacey* last night using her Habitat wand. She says she can feel his resolve melting under her goddess-like energy.

Thursday 27

James Riley has scored 100 per cent in *Name That TV Detective*.

Have found out what Sophie Microwave Muffins meant about the BTECers getting paid to be at school. Scarlet says it is the Education Maintenance Allowance. They get £30 a week to study instead of hang around Barry Island smoking. She says it is an excellent New Labour policy aimed at getting more poor people into university. Which is utterly not fair. The government should be paying me to be philosophizing political

384

novelist type. There are not enough of us in the world. May well take it up with Mr Wilmott later as he is clearly in a forward-thinking mood. He has ruled out a crèche but amazingly has ruled in Mark Lambert's BTEC Nursery Nursing. He says it will put us strides ahead of Burger King Sports Academy, but will have to wait until next year as it will take a while to convert the old pig shed. Emily Reeve has had good news too though. Mr Wilmott is so terrified of her leaving and bringing down his grade point average, he has agreed that she can bring Lola Lambert in on Wednesday afternoons while the rest of us do electives (aka 'swimming', aka hanging out at the Mocha). Scarlet is jubilant. She says her Wicca potential has been proven. Jack has said nothing. But I can tell his feet are firmly in the 'power of petitions' camp. Have not told Mum. She is already despairing of the education system what with Nige's new regime at St Regina's. This could send her over the edge and decide to home school. Which would be potentially appalling.

. . . .

Friday 28

James is up to something. He and Harry have shut themselves in his bedroom in the dark with the Hoover and the ghostometer. God knows what they are doing but Mum will go mental when she finds out. The Hoover has only just recovered from the time Dad used

it to clean the dog. The dog has only just recovered as well.

. . . .

Saturday 29

Scarlet Stone is all woman.

There has been a love showdown in Nuts In May. Guru Derek came in after our herbal tea break to beg ailment-ridden Rosamund to return to his retreat. He says his aura has gone green and his chi has been depleted since she left (though I suspect he is enjoying a nit-free period). He is not at all what I expected from a sex cult leader i.e. he was not beardy or wearing orange robes. He was balding and wearing an M&S V-neck. Anyway Rosamund told him to go back to Steeple Bumpstead. It is because she has been empowered by our feminist stance. Plus Mr Goldstein offered her an extra twenty-five per cent staff discount if she stayed.

I asked her if she wanted to come to tonight's coven meeting but she said she has possible ringworm and it might be contagious. Am quite glad as it is a first in the history of the coven. We are meeting in non-magical, but sibling- and parent-free Summerdale Road. James is having a sleepover at Mad Harry's and Mum and Dad are going to dinner with Mr Wainwright and Mrs Wainwright Mark II.

8.30 p.m.
Oh my God. James is not sleeping at Mad Harry's after

386

all. The phone rang in the middle of *Casualty* (decreed essential viewing as some goths were getting burned in a nightclub fire) and it was Mrs Mad Harry ringing to say 'night night'. They have done the textbook fake sleepover trick, but failed to plan for the over-protective parent situation. They are amateurs. Anyway told Mrs Mad Harry they were already asleep as did not want to worry her. Instead we are going to use our coven visualization techniques to locate them. Psychics do it all the time with missing children and paedophiles, according to Scarlet. Have borrowed some Sharwood's spices and am going to sprinkle them on our makeshift altar (aka the John Lewis nest of side tables).

9 p.m.
Oooh. Spooky. It works. Kind of. We were just doing visualizing when the phone rang again. This time it was Marjory P.I. ringing to ask why James, Mad Harry, and the dog were sitting on the grave of George H. Huggins in the grounds of St Regina's with a flask of Bovril, a microwave radiation tester, and Mum's Hoover. (Had not even noticed dog was missing, despite freakish lack of vomit, noise, or chewed furniture.) I tried to divert the issue and demanded to know what Marjory was doing in the graveyard, but she says she is using her digital spyware trying to catch so-called graffiti 'artists' in the act. Said James and Mad Harry were on a school project as do not want her alerting Mum and Dad. We are going

to collect them immediately before all supernatural activity gets banned.

10 p.m.
James and Mad Harry now safely back in their polar explorer sleeping bags and dog safely back on sofa watching *Sweet Home Alabama*. It turns out that they had been on an overnight ghost stakeout and were lying in wait ready to hoover up the spirits when they emerged from the graves. I said the Hoover was not battery-operated but they said they had plugged it in to the Sunday School kitchen. (Apparently Reverend Begley leaves the door open in case wandering tinkers need shelter and food for the night. Or idiotic ten year olds.)

11 p.m.
Coven meetings have been banned. Mum says I cannot be trusted. It is because the lounge smells of cinnamon and the nest of tables is over waxy. She says it is a shame I am not more like James. Oh the irony.

. . . .

Sunday 30

Ed Thomas is half man, half biscuit.

Mum is in a foul mood. It is because the Hoover is refusing to work. She says she is minded to add it to my debt. James stayed silent throughout the argument. He feels no guilt. He says he is quite content to watch an innocent man go to the gallows if it protects his business interests.

To add to my debt woes, it is Sad Ed's birthday tomorrow and I have no money to buy him a present. Have rung Scarlet for advice. She says to bring the fly swat over after *Popworld* and we can do a special Wiccan money spell. I said I thought Wicca was more about doing righteous deeds, not amassing wealth, but she says her Aunt Sadie is always doing it for the lottery numbers and has won £10 at least seven times.

5 p.m.

Hurrah. Have done excellent spell. We rubbed the fly swat with patchouli oil and called upon the forces of the earth to find me the money to buy Sad Ed a new iPod and pay off Suzy (Glastonbury ticket), Dad (phone bill), and Ms Hopwood-White (savaged fake baby). So by this time tomorrow I may well be a millionaire!

NICOTINE PATCH →

October

Monday 1

Kylie Britcher is, like, gasping.

The common room is in chaos. It is because the legal smoking age has been raised to eighteen and now half the Sixth Form is suffering severe nicotine withdrawal. They are all exceptionally minty and there have been three fights over custody of the CD player remote and it is only half past nine.

Also, the spell did not work. At least, no money had appeared by breakfast so gave Sad Ed my old recorder for his birthday. Said it was a special mystical Wiccan instrument. He did not mind, as he was too busy being excited about his present from his mum and dad. It is not Aled Jones-related but is driving lessons! I said what was the point, considering he is still planning on an untimely death. But he said, *au contraire*, he is now hoping to follow in Marc Bolan's footsteps and crash his car headfirst into a tree.

2 p.m.
Mr Wilmott has been called to a riot in Mrs Duddy's room aka Criminals and Retards. It is the smoking ban. I do not think Gordon Brown has thought through the consequences fully. Even Mr Patel is up in arms. His entire empire is founded on underage smoking. He says the repayments on his Touareg are in jeopardy with the loss of income.

Tuesday 2

Ed Thomas loves you, Flash, but we only have fourteen hours to save the earth.

The common room is awash with UCAS madness. You cannot see the saggy sofa for media studies prospectuses. The maths geeks are in charge of the *Guardian Guide to University* and are doling out information on male:female ratios, average beer prices, and distance in miles to nearest IKEA. What happened to choosing an establishment for its academic record? At least Jack is following tradition. He is applying to Cambridge to do Social and Political Science. I told him Hilary was going to do medicine there, as he is utterly brainy and may even run the Union. Jack said, 'Yeah? Well, he's not in yet, is he.' Why is he so narky? You would think he would be delighted to have a fellow left-wing applicant. Unless it is jealousy! Maybe he is actually still in love with me and my pro-Hilary/ anti-men stance is fanning his flames of passion. Excellent. Although obviously do not fancy Jack. Or any man for that matter. As am devoted to self-discovery (philosophical kind, not the sort Suzy promotes) and witchcraft.

Also, Mr Patel has discovered a new way to extract money from the hordes of cigarette-dependent children at John Major High. It is nicotine patches and gum on a buy-one-get-one-free deal. Thin Kylie has got five on one arm and is chewing as well.

4 p.m.

Our kitchen has been taken over by application madness as well. It is because James has to apply for secondary by the end of the month. He and Mum are going through SAT test results and value-added measures with a calculator and a pie chart system. I said I did not remember Mum being so rigorous when it came to choosing a school for me. Mum said my needs were not so complex. Plus I refused to go to Herts and Essex on grounds of brown uniform and Scarlet was boycotting Newport Grammar because Hugo Thorndyke (evil MP for Saffron Walden and environs) was on the board of governors.

- -

Wednesday 3

Kylie O'Grady believes she can fly, she believes she can touch the sky.

Mr Wilmott has banned nicotine patches from school. It is because five people collapsed in the common room from overdoses. Fat Kylie was wearing twenty-four at the time and had to be brought down with two of Miss Leech's emergency Valium.

Also, Scarlet is right. With every yin comes a yang. Hilary is definitely applying to Cambridge, which means he will be only thirteen miles up the A11 from next September. But it turns out that Paloma is already at Oxford 'reading' maths. So not only is she brainy and

beautiful, it means she is an older woman i.e. utterly exotic. May cast spell on her.

4 p.m.
Unless she is one of those freakish people who go to university at the age of fifteen and have no social skills and end up with mental issues.

4.15 p.m.
No, have checked on Facebook. She is definitely nineteen. Curse her.

. . . .

Thursday 4

Rachel Riley is away from her desk.

A terrible thing has happened. Mum watched *Watchdog* last night (her favourite paranoia-inducing programme) and is in a Facebook identity theft panic. She says evil criminals prey on idiots like me who post all their personal information on the interwebnet, and then they raid their bank accounts and steal their houses or else groom them for abuse. I said that as my Post Office account had a grand total of £1.04 in it, and my picture looks like someone out of Led Zeppelin, I hardly think they will be cyberstalking me, but she is unconvinced. She has banned all use of Facebook, MySpace, and Bebo pending further investigation. As if I would use Bebo. It is inferior in every way.

James is livid as well. He says it could seriously compromise Ghost Hustlers. He is going to use his special skills (i.e. Google, endless statistics, and air of cleverness) to persuade Mum to change her mind. I said I would try too but he said it is better if I stay clear of all discussions.

8 p.m.
God, there is nothing to do at home without Facebook. Have tried reading some philosophy but keep getting distracted by thoughts of who is Superpoking whom. It is worse than being grounded.

1 a.m.
Cannot sleep. What if Hilary has written on my wall and I miss it? Plus Scarlet's Zombies will have moved up another level and I will have no one left to bite. There is nothing else for it. Am going to have to pay Ali Hassan to use his MacBook at break tomorrow.

. . . .

Friday 5
8 a.m.
James and Mum have narrowed down their search for a secondary school. It is between John Major High, Newport Grammar, and St Gregory's Catholic Girls (now admitting boys and non-Catholics due to forward-thinking/desperate governors). Burger King Sports Academy has already been ruled out on the grounds that James's sporting

triumphs are limited to third place in last year's umbrella and yoghurt pot race. They are going to visit all three next week for their live final.

Asked James how his 'bring back Facebook' campaign was going. He said, 'Softly, softly, catchee monkey.' Have no idea what that means but he had better hurry up. Have had to use last of small change in my Postman Pat moneybox to fund my lunchtime computer session.

4 p.m.
Mum has banned use of Facebook on all computers, whether they are within her jurisdiction of 24 Summer-dale Road or not. It is because she got James to do a spot check on my profile and saw that I had used the force with Hilary less than two hours ago.

. . . .

Saturday 6
8 a.m.
Have got to go to work. But am worried that absence of abusing Dean Denley on Superpoke may give him wrong impression that actually like him and he may cross King Street in his meaty apron and try to snog me. James says I am not to worry as it is D-Day in his campaign and he is going to work his magic on Mum while I am safely out of the house. I do not hold out much hope. Mum is not easily swayed. Not even by a force as persuasive and pedantic as James.

6 p.m.
Oh my God. James is miracle worker. Mum has agreed to reinstate Facebook, with the following caveats:

- no posting date of birth;
- no posting photographs of relations in bath naked, not even when they are two;
- no pretending to be the dog online, it is a menace in real life enough as it is;
- no friending people you don't actually know;
- no friending people you think you 'know' but who are actually fictional characters or potential rapists pretending to be David Miliband.

I asked James how he had done it but he said it is down to his secret powers of mind over matter. Anyway, do not care. Have already trodden on Dean Denley, had four Zombie fights, and raked my green patch. Hurrah! James is banned completely for being underage but he says Ghost Hustlers get enough business via word of mouth. Clearly there are way too many mad people in Saffron Walden.

. . . .

Sunday 7

Dean Denley has served soup to Rachel Riley.

Rachel Riley has served Dean Denley as soup.

It was coven this afternoon but when me and Sad Ed

got there (admittedly via Mr Patel's for stocks of energy-giving, yet surprisingly low in calories, Maltesers) the Tamsins were already in the den with Scarlet trying to visualize their auras. Apparently they had been there all morning. Weirdly, they were dressed like her too i.e. channelling Helena Bonham Carter, i.e. black lace petticoat, stripy tights, and mental hair. I said to Scarlet it was a bit stalkerish and had they rung her up to check what she was wearing but she said no it is because they are natural witches and have immense psychic powers. She is fully expecting their periods to align soon. Sad Ed said what about his period. She said he can just have a giant mood swing instead of actual bleeding. Then she declared there was too much negative energy in the den for any spells so we made crisp sandwiches and watched *T4*. She is wrong about the Tamsins having natural powers though. Saw Jack in the kitchen when I went to get water to wash down claggy crisp bits and he said he saw one of them lurking behind the sick-smelling Volvo during *Popworld* trying to peer in the house for a glimpse of Scarlet.

When I got home James was testing Baby Jesus with his ghostometer in case he is the reincarnation of a historical king or scientific genius. There is no chance. Unless Einstein spent a large part of his formative years watching *Trisha* and eating Wotsits. The dog is in heaven though. It is because Jesus leaves an endless trail of orange crumbs in his wake and the dog is acting as a Hoover. Which is useful as the actual Hoover still hasn't

recovered from its night as a ghost sucker in St Regina's graveyard. Mum is still baffled as to how ten crab apples and a shrew got inside the bag.

. . . .

Monday 8

Rachel Riley has added the Entourage application. She rolls fifty-three deep.

It is the first stage in Mum and James's secondary school elimination test. They are off to Newport Grammar this morning with a checklist, cunning questions, and a bacterial swab for the toilets. James is very excited as it is Jamie Oliver's old school and he is hoping to acquire some cooking genius skills through the corridor walls by power of osmosis. Mum is less excited as their SATs are several points below the expected level for a semi-rural South of England constituency with 75 per cent owner occupation.

4 p.m.
Newport Grammar has been ruled out on grounds of toilet hygiene. Also Mad Harry was there and Mrs Mad Harry says it is top of her list. Mum is hoping they will part ways next year and James will befriend someone more intellectually equal. And who doesn't encourage his idiotic Ninja/Ghost Hustling ways. I pointed out that Mum had said the same about Scarlet, but five years later

she is utterly brilliant and we are still best friends. Mum did not say anything.

Although am wondering about best friends bit. It is not Scarlet so much as the Tamsins. I know I should be embracing them in a sisterlike fashion as we are all one against men etc., etc. But they are hogging Scarlet at the Coven Table. Also, due to Mr Wilmott's 'no more than three abreast' in the corridors rule (following several crashing incidents in wake of *Mean Girls* phase), they are flanking Scarlet like limpet henchmen and I am forced to trail behind in coach class with Sad Ed.

. . . .

Tuesday 9

Ed Thomas has opened a can of Whoop Ass.

The Tamsins are utterly getting on my nerves with their so-called psychic dressing and their hogging of Scarlet. I asked her if she wanted to come over after school to honour the Goddess Diana (the Wiccan one, not the real dead one) but Tamsin Bacon said she was too exhausted from double Economics. I said, 'What, too exhausted to even speak for herself?' And Tamsin Watts said they are not speaking for her—they are her. They are channelling her telepathically and can totally tell what she is thinking. Said, 'Is this true,' to Scarlet. Tamsin Bacon said yes. It is impossible to have a sane conversation while they are around so waited until they wafted off to GCSE science in

402

their identical ironic bunches. Then asked Scarlet if she wanted to come over. She said she was too exhausted from double Economics.

Sad Ed came over instead. Not to honour Diana. To mope. As usual. He agrees they are abusing their coven status as novices and that we should alert Scarlet to a possible takeover bid.

On plus side, I have a new friend on Facebook. It is someone called Robbie Lewis, who says he knows Jack through his band and recognized me from Velvet Elvis's first (and only) gig last term. Admittedly, I don't actually 'know' him (under Mum's strict criteria, this involves at least two years' acquaintance including several face-to-face meetings and preferably at least three friends in common), but he is eighteen and his photo looks like Johnny Borrell.

· ·

Wednesday 10

Rachel Riley has used the force with Ed Thomas.

8 a.m.

It is day two of James's secondary school search. He and Mum have already set off on the arduous journey to Bishop's Stortford to assess the suitability of St Gregory's Catholic Girls. I fear it may fall at the first hurdle, i.e. the travel arrangements involve Len Viceroy and a bus full

of unsupervised adolescents. Am also leaving early to intercept Scarlet before Tamsins get to her and warn her of their evil plans for coven domination.

4 p.m.
Scarlet is totally unsympathetic to my theory on the Tamsins. She says their telepathic powers are just evidence that they are taking witchcraft seriously, unlike me and Sad Ed. I demanded proof but she said e.g. their wands are actual wands, not a fly swat and a light sabre. Talked to Sad Ed in free period (i.e. reading *Mojo* on the saggy sofa). He says we will just have to keep an eye on them for unsisterly activity. Scarlet is clearly blinded by their devotion and matching outfits. Their wands are not real, they are from Claire's Accessories. Mad Harry has one the same.

On different note, James and Mum are very excited by prospect of St Gregory's Girls. Apparently they have excellent IT facilities and the toilets are spotless. James says he is not put off by the journey, he will just wear headphones and listen to tapes of mathematical equations. Or Will Young. They are at John Major High tomorrow. I do not hold out hope for our less than adequate language 'labs', our mobile science room, and our questionable toilet facilities. Although we do have goats and multicoloured hoops in the gym cupboard. (The goats are not in the cupboard. They are on the field. Except that time Stacey O'Grady shut them in with the basketballs and Miss Vicar.)

Thursday 11

Robbie Lewis has high fiiived Rachel Riley.

It has been an utterly pants day.

1. AS Philosophy ended with a near riot during discussion on the equal distribution of money (Scarlet, me, and povvy people for, people from mock tudor mansions against).

2. The Tamsins are still speaking for Scarlet. Today Mrs Brain told Scarlet she had sold out of cheese baps and Tamsin Bacon said, in fake Scarlet voice, 'You shrivel-minded crone.' Tamsin got sent to Mr Wilmott. How long is she going to keep up this farce? Although it is true that Scarlet thinks Mrs Brain is a shrivel-minded crone. But then so does everyone.

3. Mum and James are putting John Major High at the bottom of their school list. Mum says the science labs are positively perilous. It is because the demonstration lesson was Mr Vaughan (pervert-in-school, supersized nipples, supposed French teacher but also Head of Drama and occasional chemistry due to woeful staff shortages) showing Seven Cheesmond how to make a baking soda volcano (elementary according to James). Apparently he got his chemicals mixed up and caused a minor explosion which broke the locust dome, and they escaped and caused a biblical style plague on C Corridor. Mum says it will be a wonder if

I pass my A Levels and that she will be signing me up for crammer in Cambridge next year if things do not improve.

8 p.m.
But have had yang to my crap day yin. Just got a message from Robbie Lewis on Facebook. He says he 'likes my style'. It is because I listed Young Knives and The Dead Kennedys as my favourite bands. They are not. Young Knives look like the Maths Club and have never even heard The Dead Kennedys, but Jack says they are seminal. Robbie says he is working on some music himself and would like to play it to me some time! It is amazing. I am an utter magnet to rock stars. First Jack, then Justin, and now Robbie. Although admittedly Justin dumped me. And Robbie may turn out to be mentalist with fake photo.

8.30 p.m.
No. He is definitely not mentalist. Have checked his friends and he knows Sad Ed, Fat Kylie, and James. Plus he lists *Pretty in Pink* as his favourite ever film. We are total soul mates. Even more than Hilary. Because even though he is not necessarily left-wing, he is single.

8.45 p.m.
Although he is possibly gay.

Friday 12

Ed Thomas has added the Petrolhead application.

Sad Ed has got his first driving lesson today. It is with Mike 'Wandering Hands' Majors (41, highlights, general causer of marital break-up, object of Dad's hatred) in one of his Ford Fiestas. Sad Ed is worried Mike might take a shine to him. He is deluded. Even if Mike was gay, there is no way he would go for Ed. He is not neat or nice-smelling enough. Gay men (unlike lesbian Oona) always smell nice. It is like a rule. Ed asked Mum if he could practise on our Fiesta in the driveway to acclimatize to its layout. He says he won't actually go anywhere, just fiddle with the knobs and levers. Mum has said no. She does not trust him not to accidentally snap the gear stick with his fat fingers. Sad Ed did not mind. He says he has natural driving talent and he will be steaming down the M11 at seventy within a week. He is deluded. Mike will make him do circles round Shire Hill for at least a month.

5 p.m.
It was worse than I thought. Mike did not even let Ed leave Loompits Avenue. He is operating a stationary lesson policy until pupils can prove they have mastered their right from their left and know which pedal is go and which is stop.

Saturday 13

Rachel Riley has challenged Jack Stone to a game of Scrabulous.

Work was unusually fraught today. It is because Thin Kylie came in with Mark Lambert to try to buy drugs i.e. Guarana gum. I think Mr Goldstein's hump and Rosamund's flaky eczema sent Thin Kylie over the edge because she refused to be served on the till by anyone except me in case she caught 'leprosy or mentalism'. So ended up with fingers trapped in till again for meagre 97 pence and burst into tears. Mr Goldstein has finally relented and is going to get someone to look at it. The till. Not my finger. That is wrapped in additive- (and glue-) free plaster.

Sunday 14

Jack Stone has beaten Rachel Riley at Scrabulous by 278 to 57.

Coven is off today. It is because Scarlet is going to see her mentor—Aunt Sadie. It is in preparation for Hallowe'en in a fortnight. Scarlet does not want a repeat of the Autumn Equinox pentacle poo fiasco. Which reminds me, need to get a pentacle as dog ate last one. Not sure if it is in or out as have not seen it since. But would not want to use it anyway. Mum is less squeamish. She just disinfects things once they have made their passage through the intestines. She says she is just being economical. She is being weird.

408

Anyway, am going to spend day doing useful and self-improving things instead, i.e. reading *White Teeth*, i.e. Zadie Smith's seminal novel about living in multicultural and gritty London. Will be like fantasy fiction for A Level students in Saffron Walden. The only grit we have is Barry the Blade and his ongoing habit of fishing in the bins for kebab bits. Will just check Facebook though in case have message from Robbie.

11 a.m.
Nothing as yet. Although my Zombie lieutenant has eaten several of Dean Denley's foot soldiers. Will start reading once have had brain-stimulating elevenses (rich teas and lemon barley. Mum is cutting back on Duchy Originals chocolate gingers. She says we are getting too much of a taste for the high life.)

3 p.m.
Got distracted by James and Mad Harry ghostbusting in the garage. They are convinced there is ghost residue behind the creosote. Still no message from Robbie. Will just do a bit more Zombie fighting.

4 p.m.
And maybe clean out my virtual aquarium.

5.30 p.m.
And eat dinner.

6.30 p.m.

Oh my God. It has happened. I got a message from Robbie during what would normally have been *Eggheads* but is now designated computer time (James and I have stopped watching this due to probability of Challengers winning dropping to 14,000 to one, according to James's calculations). He wants to meet me after school tomorrow down the Battleditches (aka Dogshit Alley, aka snoggers' paradise!). Have said yes. Mum would go bonkers if she knew, but am going to make Sad Ed come with me as protection. I would ask Scarlet but in current mode, i.e. ventriloquist act with the Tamsins, she might put him off. Oh hurrah. Am going to meet Razorlightesque soul mate at last and bond over seminal films and music. Will just phone Jack and get him to play Dead Kennedys down the phone to me so do not sound like complete idiot.

. . . .

Monday 15

Rachel Riley is away from her desk again.

8 a.m.

Have texted Sad Ed to check he is still on for tonight. He has agreed, but is not entirely happy with proceedings due to it possibly breaching Simple Life pact etc., etc., but have pointed out that it is entirely non-sexual (at the moment) and anyway I saw him ogling Tamsin Bacon's

410

black lace goth bra last week and I did not tell Scarlet so he owes me.

5 p.m.

Meeting did not go entirely as planned. Mainly because I have been the victim of a cunning online identity theft honeytrap thingy, i.e. it was not an actual real meeting. It was an evil trap, laid by Mum and her demonic assistant James. It turns out Robbie Lewis is not a real person at all. He is James, in one of his many internet guises, using a name stolen from a detective TV series and a picture of Johnny Borrell pasted from the MTV website. Mum made him lure me into his clutches to prove that I am incapable of using Facebook responsibly. It was utterly humiliating. James walked up with the dog and said, 'Waiting for anyone?' I said no, we were trying to commune with dead Saxons in a witchlike manner. James said, 'Oh really. And I suppose the name Robbie Lewis means nothing to you, then.' Then Mum leapt out from behind a conker tree and immediately imposed an internet ban. She says James could easily have been a paedophile or a murderer and I am lucky that it is her hiding in the bushes. She is wrong. A murderer would be easier to outwit. Sad Ed caved under pressure immediately. He told Mum he had begged me not to go and was only there to protect my innocence. He has no stamina.

Begged Mum to change her mind but she says until I can prove I am a responsible adult, there is to be no social

networking of any kind. James is utter stooge. Am going to plot his downfall immediately, as have nothing to do now that Facebook is out of bounds. Will pretend to be a vampire and lure him to possible drowning on the slide of death.

5.30 p.m.
Mum has just told me not to even think of plotting revenge against James or she will come down on me like a tonne of bricks. She is like Mel Gibson in that crap film where he can tell what women are thinking all the time. Except without the bouffant hair and alcohol issues.

Tuesday 16
8 a.m.
What is the point of doing anything if you can't tell your 126 closest Facebook friends what you are up to? Am itching to Superpoke somebody. Even Dean Denley. But Mum is watching the computer like a hawk. Plus she has got James to block my Facebook account and set up several complicated passwords and a firewall. Not even Dad can get through them to check the golf results. He has gone round to Clive's instead, who has no security. And Nutella.

4 p.m.
It is worse than I thought. Not having access to Facebook is moving me rapidly down the coven hierarchy. Scarlet

and the Tamsins were Superpoking until midnight last night. Plus the entire common room has formed a new group. It is 'Who tipped Nutriment on the saggy sofa?' Begged Sad Ed to try to work out what James has changed my password to (it is not Shredder, Aragorn, or Einstein—checked on Ali Hassan's MacBook at a cost of £2.45 in first break (he has started a credit book for me due to hopeless state of finances)) but Ed says it is more than his life is worth. This is possibly true. James is unmovable as well. He says I am lucky to be alive and should be thanking him, not moaning and trying to get the dog to eat his ghostometer.

Wednesday 17

Still no Facebook access. Mum says I have yet to convince her I am not going to do anything stupid. (This is because I let the dog in the shower this morning and it ate the soap and started foaming at the mouth and James thought it had rabies and called 999.) Thank God it is half term next week and I will not have to suffer the endless in-jokes or cheering from the saggy sofa when anyone friends a celebrity. Fat Kylie has got the one with bad skin out of Take That and Kerry Katona now. And Sophie Nipples Pervert has got half of *Hollyoaks*. I am an utter outcast. It is like at primary when everyone was playing *Grange Hill* and I had to do hopscotch on my own. Tried to do some Wicca and channel positive energy with my

wand and my goddess altar (one of James's old Barbies and a Denby plate) but all the hoo-ha has sapped my skills. Am going to be ejected from coven if this carries on. Although at least am marginally more magical than Sad Ed. He broke his wand fighting Gary Fletcher in the Waitrose car park after work. They were trying to re-enact Anakin Skywalker versus Obi Wan Kenobi in *Revenge of the Sith*. It is sellotaped up now. Scarlet will go mental.

. . . .

Thursday 18

Cannot even speak to Mum to beg her for mercy this morning. She is locked in the bathroom with Shirley Conran's *Lace*. It is because it is book group tonight and she wants it fresh in her memory so she can out-opinion everybody. She is going to regret it. She will want to be cleansing her memory immediately if the bits Thin Kylie read out are anything to go by. James is in agreement. He says he read several chapters while he was waiting for a poltergeist to make an appearance in the dining room last night and it is shocking stuff. Although he says at least it has neo-feminist overtones and some excellent equestrianism. Have no idea what he is talking about. But it sounds sisterhoody. Maybe Mum and everyone will swap sexual secrets and release the bonds of conformity.

9 p.m.

There was no sexual secret swapping. And no releasing

414

of bonds. Instead there was an almighty argument about porn (Cherie—for, everyone else—against, Marjory—does fancying Trevor McDonald count?) and Mrs Noakes has formed a puritanical splinter book group, which is only going to do Catherine Cookson. Cherie is not invited. Mum is not joining either. She says there is only so much Northern suffering she can take. She is going to stick to arguing about Jeffrey Archer with Dad. He has no strong opinions and bows to her greater knowledge at all times.

I noticed James 'borrowed' *Lace* while she was busy inspecting some dog-related damage on the sideboard. Will note information in brain for potential revenge.

. . . .

Friday 19

Hurrah, it is half term. James is jubilant. It is because environment-mad Nige has set Year Six a holiday project. They have to work out the size of their family's carbon footprint and find ways to reduce it. James is taking it very seriously. He is hoping to harness paranormal energy, or the dog, and power the toaster with it.

. . . .

Saturday 20

James has already started his environmental carbon footprint crackdown. He has imposed a strict 'no hot breakfast' rule, including toast. So had to have Marmite

on bread. Even the kettle is out of bounds so there is no tea. Dad told Mum to tell James to stop beggaring about, but Mum is backing him all the way. Not so much on green grounds but more because she does not want to be named and shamed in show and tell assembly. It is outrageous. How am I supposed to prepare for eight gruelling hours at the coalface, or lentilface, when have only had cold bread for breakfast?

. . . .

Sunday 21

8 a.m.
The carbon footprint thing is having an utterly detrimental effect on family relations chez Riley. It is only 8 a.m. and Mum has already shouted at Dad for leaving the telly and DVD player on standby after *Match of the Day* last night. He said he was sick of having to reset the clock every morning and, anyway, claims on standby consumption have been completely exaggerated. James has now shut himself in the meter cupboard with a torch to test the theory.

11 a.m.
Tests inconclusive. It appears leaving telly on standby may actually use up more energy than watching it. So Mum is thinking of banning TV altogether. But Dad pointed out that the results could have been skewed by Grandpa showing up halfway through and letting Baby Jesus blow-dry the dog. James says it is not that, it is the poltergeist

416

causing paranormal magnetism and making the dial whizz round. Have left them to their idiotic discussions. At least I still have a CD player in room and can listen to inspiring girl music, i.e. the Kates (Nash and Bush, the latter borrowed from Suzy who claims Kate based her 'hot hippy' look entirely on her) until it is time for coven.

11.15 a.m.
This carbon footprint thing is getting out of hand. James has now turned the electricity off completely. He says we should try to get by for at least a day without it. I said what about lunch? He said we can eat salad and nuts like our ancestors. He is mistaken. If the Cleggs are anything to go by our ancestors ate Fray Bentos and Viennetta.

12 midday
Electricity back on. It is because Baby Jesus goes berserk if he doesn't get to watch preschool kitchen menaces *Big Cook Little Cook*. Mum says no carbon footprint is worth putting up with that racket. Plus the freezer was starting to defrost and she had only just stocked up on organic pork loin.

7 p.m.
Am back from coven. Which was less than satisfying. Me and Sad Ed had to watch while Scarlet and the Tamsins performed their Hallowe'en salutation, complete with matching headwear. Tamsin Bacon actually said, 'Look and learn, amateurs.' It is outrageous. Wicca is not a

spectator sport. It is a divine expression of the power of nature and sisterhood, according to Celestine Norton. Sad Ed did not mind though. He just ate chocolate digestives in the loveswing. He says all the standing up and gesticulating plays havoc with his back.

To make matters worse, got home to find entire house in darkness. James has imposed a candles only rule. It is like being in a medieval castle (but with carpets and HobNobs). Though suppose atmosphere of gloom is quite literary and inspiring. Maybe will have genius novel idea and make fortune and buy coven and refuse to let Tamsins take part.

8 p.m.
Lights back on. The dog caught fire on one of the candles and tipped over the dining table in its frenzy to put out the flames.

· ·

Monday 22
Half term

10 a.m.
There has been a horrific carbon footprint related incident. Am in shock and will have to lie down for a bit.

11 a.m.
Am slightly recovered now. Though still marginally

nauseous. It is because in his zeal for saving electricity James burst into the bathroom fully naked and climbed into my bath. He says sharing bath water is quite normal and that I have nothing to hide. He is wrong. It is not normal, except possibly in the Stones' house where wandering around naked is almost obligatory. Plus I have everything to hide. It was gross. Had to shriek for Mum to remove him immediately. But dog got excited by racket and tried to join in and now Mum is in mood because floor is soggy and is blaming me for overreacting. Am going round Scarlet's now for emergency counselling. Plus they are fully electricitied up and will be able to use appliances without fear of retribution.

2 p.m.
Scarlet was not in. According to Jack she is trying to summon the Goddess of the Waxing Light round at Tamsin's. I said which one. He said, 'Does it matter?' This is true. They are equally annoying. He let me in anyway to enjoy some energy wasting TV and use Suzy's diffuser as hair is in severe danger of looking like Fi Cunningham's Labradoodle if it does not get severe product and implement attention.

. . . .

Tuesday 23
Mum is tiring of the carbon footprint economy drive. James had her using sticky labels to remove crumbs from

the carpet this morning now that the Hoover is out of bounds. Although I noticed he was happy to use it yesterday when he thought there was an apparition in the toilet. There was not. It was Mum's Glade Wisp room deodorizer on overdrive. Also the dog keeps crashing into things in the darkness.

Still no sign of Scarlet. I rang earlier and Suzy said she was out with the Tamsins buying sacred purple cord at Booths but had left Hallowe'en homework instructions for me and Sad Ed. We have to practise weaving corn to make ritual fertility symbols. Will do it extra specially well, and also purchase superpowered pentacle so can win Scarlet back.

5 p.m.
Could not find corn so have woven moist wholemeal spaghetti. It is made of wheat so is utterly crop-based.

. . . .

Wednesday 24.
Yet again my plans have been thwarted by James's ridiculous homework. Mum is refusing to drive me to occult-friendly Cambridge for emergency pentacle purchasing as it will clog the atmosphere with carbon emissions. She says there is nothing wrong with the shops in Saffron Walden and I will just have to improvise. She is lying. There is everything wrong with the shops in Saffron Walden. Am going into town though. Beggars

can't be choosers. As James points out on an almost daily basis.

4 p.m.
Am back from town and have witnessed something entirely suspicious. I saw one of the Tamsins (not sure which, but possibly Bacon as her hair is marginally higher) drinking Fanta with head goth and Scarlet's ex Trevor Pledger in the Mocha, despite him being declared an official enemy of the coven and therefore utterly out of bounds. She is plotting something. I can tell. Or maybe Scarlet is getting her to be a messenger and is actually planning to throw herself at his batlike mercy. If I had Facebook I could check for signs of illicit wall activity. It is entirely compromising, gossip-wise. On plus side, have bought pentacle. It is sort of circular china dish with interesting markings on it. Found it in Oxfam. It is bound to be some sort of Wicca relic.

* *

Thursday 25
Pentacle is not Wicca relic. Is James's ashtray (aka olive dish) from pottery last year. Mum had a clearout in the attic when James was doing his ghost hunting up there. Interesting markings are old Smartie lid imprints. I said she should be ashamed of herself, giving away the art-works of her precious children. What if one of us turns out to be Damian Hirst? She said if she kept all the tat we

421

brought home from school we would be knee deep in macramé owls and fingerpainted loo rolls by now. Plus there is no way James is going to be a painter. He does not like getting mess on his fingers. This is true. Anyway, will not let on provenance of pentacle to Scarlet. Will say it is genuine ancient artefact.

· ·

Friday 26

Something terrible and O'Grady related has happened. It is overwaxed eyebrows, i.e. mine. Fat Kylie did it round at Thin Kylies. They came over this morning begging for me to be a 'model' for beauty practice. They said they needed a total 'before case' so they could do one of those *Swan* makeovers. For some reason, possibly boredom due to internet and electricity ban, I said yes. So had to endure several minutes of pain and now have insane surprised expression. Plus I let them give me semi-permanent false eyelashes so resemble crap transvestite. Mum is livid. I pointed out that if we had Facebook I would be too busy to do idiotic things like this. She is weakening, I can tell.

· ·

Saturday 27

New transvestite look did not go down well at work. Mr Goldstein made me stay in the stockroom in case I put the hippies off their tofu. Rosamund says I am messing with my natural femininity. But she uses crystal deodorant and

422

doesn't shave her legs so she is hardly a trustworthy source of beauty tips. Dean Denley did not seem put off. He offered me a battered sausage roll at lunchbreak. This was not a euphemism. Thank God. Declined though. Damaged meat products are just not as enticing from a midget.

On plus side, James's carbon footprint economy drive ends at seven tonight. James has begged to have it made permanent but Dad says it is cunning twist night in *Casualty* and he does not want to miss it. Plus Grandpa and Treena are coming over for Sunday lunch and they will not eat salad, not even in an emergency.

7.30 p.m.
Thank God. Have gone appliance mad and dried hair, epilated legs, whisked smoothies, and toasted four slices of granary. Dad has put the central heating on full and the TV, DVD, CD player, and SatNav on standby. James says we will regret it when we are all knee deep in polar ice cap meltwater, but Dad says he does not pay tax to live in third world conditions.

Sunday 28
End of British Summertime (i.e. clocks go back)
11 a.m.
There has been a royal scandal, according to Grandpa and Treena, purveyors of crap Sunday tabloids into the broadsheet environs of Summerdale Road. An unnamed

HRH has been caught on camera in a drugs and sex scandal. James says it is bound to be Harry as he is ginger and common. This secured him his second warning of the day. (He earned his first for trying to suck a shapeshifter out of the tumble dryer.) I do not rate his chances much. Mad Harry (not ginger, but common) is coming over later and they are bound to do something mental and dangerous.

5 p.m.
It is three strikes and out as far as James is concerned. He has been caught with his pants down. (Not literally, that would have been potentially horrendous—am still recovering from bath sharing trauma.) Mum found him and Mad Harry reading *Lace* in the shed. They had claimed they were whittling anti-vampire stakes. Mum is livid and has banned sex books permanently and any ghost-related activity for a week. James says she will regret it when Saffron Walden is overrun with creatures of the night. She says she will take her chances. Also Dad is in trouble. He pointed out that it was her book and therefore partially her fault. He is now weeding the runner bean patch.

I on other hand have played blinding hand by backing Mum all the way and an utter miracle has happened. She has relented over the Facebook ban (I pointed out that I had endured thirteen days of abstinence, whereas James only gets seven). Am now back online in the virtual arms of my cyberfriends. Hurrah. Have missed it so much. Pippa Newbold has been poking Stan Barret (once saw Paul

Weller in John Lewis), which is interesting, as two weeks ago she was poking Duncan Evans (resident common room 'DJ', i.e. has portable CD player and Pete Tong T-shirt). Also, more worryingly, Trevor Pledger is now friends with Tamsin Bacon. Have checked for poke activity, however there is no clear evidence on this. But interestingly this happened at 2 p.m. this afternoon, after she had phoned in sick to coven with depleted chi (coven subsequently cancelled as Tamsin Watts won't come without Tamsin Bacon, and Sad Ed was still in his pyjamas eating Minstrels and watching *Vanity Fair*). But am not dwelling on this because most importantly Hilary Nuamah has changed his status from 'in a relationship' to 'it's complicated'. What can this mean? Am going to message him immediately. Once have checked Paloma's status.

6 p.m.
Hurrah! Spanish beauty Paloma is 'complicated' too. So now coast is possibly clear for me to battle my urges and potentially resist Hilary's charms. Or not. Hurrah!

. . . .

Monday 29

Rachel Riley is saving the cheerleader to save the world.

Something is definitely afoot in Goth Corner Mark II. Trevor spent the entire lunch break staring at the Coven Table from over the top of his congealed blood (aka

Bonne Maman cherry jam) sandwiches. I pointed this out to Scarlet but she says he is obviously just still hung up on her, and that it is all quite pathetic. I hope she is right. Although I wish he would stop as his new contact lenses (all black) are entirely off-putting.

Cheered up when got home though. Hilary has confirmed my suspicions. He broke up with Paloma this morning. It is because she thinks she is in love with her long division tutor, Dr (not a real one, a made-up one) Whitaker. So clearly perverts are not limited to secondary schools but are happily embedded in universities as well. Anyway, Hilary says he is holding up OK but that it's good to 'see a friendly face', i.e. me. Have said he can use my virtual shoulder to cry on anytime. Oooh. Or maybe he will want real one and will hitch through the night to Saffron Walden and throw himself at my mercy as I am the only person to understand his alienation and sorrow.

. . . .

Tuesday 30

Rachel Riley is Claire Bennet—angsty, paranoid, but kind of hot.

Ed Thomas is Hiro Nakamura—short, overweight, but with a sacred sword.

Hilary is still in Cornwall. According to Granny Clegg he dropped off two steak and kidney pies and a Sara Lee cheesecake (out of quarantine now that Grandpa Clegg has been assured it does not contain actual cheddar) on his way to school this morning. I said I was surprised the council were still paying for his services, considering her hip of doom was completely recovered, but she says Grandpa Clegg is enjoying having a 'servant' and takes to his bed every time the health visitor lady comes round to check on his progress.

Wednesday 31

Hallowe'en

Rachel Riley has thrown a pumpkin at Dean Denley.

Hurrah, it is Hallowe'en, ancient pagan festival and key date in my new Wicca-based calendar. Am utterly ready, i.e. have pentacle, black cloak (James's recycled Ninja cape) and have been practising my thirteen witch goals. Which is kind of like the Ten Commandments, but less about coveting oxen. I have completed five so far, i.e.

1. know yourself (duh);
2. know your craft (can remember at least one chant);
3. learn (am always learning, it is impossible not to under Mum's regime);
4. keep your words in good order (not sure if this is about reciting poetry or not swearing but am excellent at Kipling and have not said the B word for a day);

5. breathe and eat correctly (am always breathing and have eaten health-giving wholemeal toast and Manuka honey for breakfast, which is totally Wicca as bees are magical anti-bacterial ones).

Have still got several to go, including 'apply knowledge with wisdom' (no idea what this means), meditate (dog does not like humming noise), and achieve balance (fell off front wall trying to stand on one leg). But on plus side, am definitely going to out-Wicca Sad Ed. He has only done two. And his cape has a floral flock design as it is the bedspread from the Aled shrine room. We are meeting at Scarlet's after school and then we are going to have a solemn parade to the maze. (Labyrinths of all kinds are ancient mystical symbols with power seeping out of their pathways, according to Scarlet. Although we are waiting until trick or treating is over, as do not want ceremony disturbed by nine year olds in Batman outfits high on Swizzels and Um Bongo.) It is going to be excellent. James is also excited. He is foregoing trick or treating as he says he will be too busy hustling the souls of the dead as they all emerge from their burial grounds to wreak havoc on the living. He and Mad Harry are offering a mobile exorcism service. They have persuaded Dad to drive them around in the Passat (Mum has got Conversational French for the Over-40s). He has agreed on the grounds they are delusional and no one will ring them and he will be able to watch *Morse* repeats in peace.

428

They are mental. The financial rewards in trick or treating far outweigh exorcism. Mark Lambert made £56.70 one year and he didn't even have a costume. Although it may have involved menaces.

11 p.m.
Hallowe'en has been cancelled. It is because Scarlet is in a complete strop. Not only did neither of the Tamsins turn up, but, according to Scarlet, I am utterly unWiccalike and have compromised her channels of communication with middle earth. (It is because Barry the Blade appeared from behind the climbing frame (in his costume of choice—i.e. hairy tramp) and made me scream in terror.) I pointed out it wasn't entirely my fault as Scarlet was supposed to have brought frankincense or dragon's blood to purify the ground but Suzy didn't have either so she used half a bottle of Suzy's Merlot instead, which is not at all sacred. Sad Ed is in trouble as well. He was in charge of Wicca catering, i.e. mead and marigold custard (as recommended by Celestine Norton) as offerings to the Goddess. But he brought Shloer and butterscotch Angel Delight. Scarlet says she is thinking of ditching the coven and going back to normal gothness, as it is less fraught with potential failure. She called Bob and got him to pick her up in the Volvo and take her home so she can ask the runes what to do. He was dressed as Superman, with a Gordon Brown mask on top of his head. I asked him where the party was. He said, 'What party?'

429

Dad and James are still missing in action. Clearly Dad underestimated the number of potential paranormal emergencies in Saffron Walden and has been ferrying James and Mad Harry and their tools (ghostometer, Hoover, dog (who, they claim, can sniff weird things) around town all night). I wonder if they saw the Tamsins. Maybe something paranormal happened to them, i.e. they were sucked into a vortex and are now hovering above my head as I write.

6 Eggs

november

Thursday 1

Scarlet Stone has slapped Tamsin Bacon.

The Tamsins were not sucked into a vortex. They were busy being beguiled by Trevor Pledger's batlike charms on the bench outside Gayhomes. (Or rather Tamsin Bacon was. Tamsin Watts just watched and sucked a Chupa Chup.) It is all over school. According to one of the minigoths, Trevor has had his eye on Tamsin Bacon for weeks and gave her a Hallowe'en ultimatum to choose between him and the coven. Scarlet is mental with anti-sisterhood anger. She says it is a double betrayal as she taught Tamsin Bacon everything she knows about being a Goddess and now she is breaking vows with the bat boy, who is obviously only doing it to make her jealous and beg him to take her back. I am not so sure about this but Scarlet has declared open warfare with Trevor none the less. It is ultimatums all round as she has given Tamsin Watts until midday to decide who to sit with at lunch. She is going to try to lure some of the more impressionable minigoths as well with promises of Wiccan implements and communication with middle earth. I said that she said Wicca was not a weapon with which to meddle in the affairs of ex-lovers, but then she hit me with a Frube so I shut up.

12.30 p.m.
Scarlet is jubilant. It is not that she has been chosen by Tamsin (clearly she would rather eat yoghurt-covered

raisins while her best friend gropes bat boy). It is because she has acquired three apprentice goths, including Melody Bean who has a tarantula. Scarlet has made them sign up to our sisterhood Simple Life/witchcraft pact and given them instructions to get wands by next Monday. She made me and Ed renew our vows too. Have not told her about Hilary. Do not want to push her back over edge of post-Hallowe'en torture. A syndrome also being experienced by James. And Dad. It is not due to their failure to cleanse Saffron Walden of evil spirits. It is because Mum found out what they were up to and has quarantined the Hoover and banned Dad from going out for a fortnight. Only the dog is happy. It got five Crème Eggs and a Curly Wurly on its rounds last night despite failing to sniff anything weird.

Friday 2

Scarlet Stone has jabbed Trevor Pledger in the eye. (This is not a Superpoke. This is actual.)

Scarlet is livid. Trevor has won back two of the minigoths. It is because he promised them they could play with his rats at the weekend. Plus Gemma Ellington said her boyfriend was worried the Simple Life vows would interfere with their sex life. (They are in Year 7. They do not have a sex life.) Also Trevor and Tamsin were all over each other in the custard queue at lunch. Even Sad Ed

said it was putting him off his food. A feat that has not happened since he got gastroenteritis, and even then he managed a packet of Hula Hoops. I pointed out that at least we still had Melody Bean. This seemed to cheer Scarlet up a bit, as it means we have custody of the tarantula (Arthur). She has told Melody to bring it to coven on Sunday so we can absorb its supernatural powers. I hope she does not mean literally. I do not want to be consuming tarantula. Anyway she is a vegetarian so it would be illegal. She won't even eat barbecue beef Pringles.

Saturday 3

Ed Thomas is temporarily closed for refurbishment.

Am utterly disillusioned with the whole work ethic thing, i.e. I spend literally eight hours (minus lunch break minus two Fruesli and herbal tea breaks) slaving away every Saturday in the lentil-scented sweatshop yet my debt is still epic in proportion. According to Mum (who has subsumed all smaller debts, loan shark style, and is charging me interest at two per cent as a lesson in money management) I will not be debt-free until at least February next year. I said what about overtime in the holidays, but she says she has already taken that into account, as well as Christmas present money and WHSmith tokens, which she will exchange on a face value basis.

435

I pointed out that it is Christmas party season coming up and I have not had any new clothes since Granny Clegg let me keep the dead lady dresses. Plus Scarlet gets a clothing allowance of £200 a term to spend wherever she likes. Mum said she wore the same shoes for four years as a child. Granny Clegg just snipped the ends off so her toes could hang out. But then she relented and offered to take me to Gray Palmer and get me something sensible, and of her choice. Declined as will end up in knee length skirt and roomy cardigan. Not even Kate Moss could get away with that. At least Hilary understands me. It is because his parents are also strict and make him work for a living. Although admittedly Mrs Nuamah is not limited in her wardrobe choices to beige Marks and Spencer.

On plus side, Scarlet came into work today to hang out, i.e. hide behind the Frugrains to spy on Trevor and Tamsin Bacon who were picketing Goddard's for selling non-Hugh Fearnley-Whittingstall chickens. I said she should be pleased as she is utterly anti-chicken suffering but she says it is a hollow protest as Tamsin is only doing it to steal her vegetarianism as well as her boyfriend. It is a bit rich that Trevor is joining in anyway, considering his ambition is to drink human blood. Scarlet is jubilant despite having to watch Trevor fanging Tamsin's neck in front of the chops. It is because *a*) Tamsin Watts was not spectating—Scarlet says she will be at coven tomorrow for sure and will prove essential in our battle to hex Tamsin Bacon as she has inside info; *b*) Dean Denley

swilled the protestors away with a bucket of Domestos and it has bleached their black karate slippers irreparably; and *c*) Rosamund made her a herbal poultice to banish negative energy.

. . . .

Sunday 4

Ed Thomas has left 'The invisible hand of Morrissey touches me when I sleep'.

Ed Thomas has joined 'Morrissey lives in my wardrobe'.

Trevor has won the battle of the minions by three goths to one. Tamsin Watts failed to show up to coven today. Scarlet rang her but she says the pressure from Tamsin Bacon is too much, plus they have just bought matching ra-ra skirts and it would be a waste not to wear them to the lower school disco. Scarlet pointed out she was turning her back on the one true religion (i.e. Wicca) and that all her mystical powers will dissipate into the ether but Tamsin Watts says Tamsin Bacon is going to form a rival coven with bigger and better hexing powers. Then, to top everything, Jack came in eating peanuts out of the pentacle, which pushed Scarlet over the edge and she had to go and lie down in her bedroom with the lights out for two hours. Me and Sad Ed commandeered the pentacle and went back to his to practise throwing Mojos into it.

. . . .

Monday 5

Scarlet was off school today sick. She says she has potential black death and has been hexed by the Tamsins in their rival coven. It is not black death, it is flu. But I am going round after school for an emergency Wicca ritual. Scarlet says it will reverse the hex and despatch it back whence it came. She has also instructed me to scout out potential coven members in the common room to boost our ranks and out-coven the other coven.

6 p.m.

Have not acquired any new coven members. Oona Rickets said no on the grounds that Sad Ed is involved and thus it is not a female caucus. I pointed out his utter lack of masculinity but she says a penis is a penis, whatever it's attached to. Then Fat Kylie disagreed and demanded to see aforementioned penis to compare it to 'Donkey' Dawson's to prove her point. At which point Sad Ed remembered he had double music and left very rapidly. Fat Kylie and Thin Kylie have also refused on the grounds they 'ain't no lezzers', and Emily Reeve declined on the grounds she had to feed Lola Lambert. There is no way I am asking Sophie Microwave Muffins. There is nothing mystical about her. Except her liking for supersized nipples. Scarlet said it did not matter anyway as she was feeling particularly potent thanks to Rosamund's herbal poultice so we burned a black candle in the Nigella soup pot and thought evil thoughts about

the Tamsins. Although I have to say some of thoughts were a bit distracted due to presence of Edna cleaning burnt cheese off the Smeg oven with a cake slice.

Tuesday 6
Scarlet is still off school with black death. She has texted me with strict instructions to check the Tamsins at hourly intervals for signs of the reverse hex working. I said what sort of signs? She said hair loss or giant boils.

3 p.m.
Do not think the hex has worked. The Tamsins were both looking utterly normal (i.e. corpse-like) with no visible abcesses or loss of hair. Will tell her it is taking time to manifest itself. Will not tell her I saw Trevor draw a skull on Tamsin Bacon's left thigh during lunch. Do not want to upset her in her fragile state.

Wednesday 7
Scarlet is back. She says she is hex-free and full of divine power (and Lemsip Max). Also she claims my reports on the rival coven are less than illuminating and she is clearly the only one with Wicca insight.

1 p.m.
Scarlet has been given an official warning by Mr Wilmott.

It is for stalking. She spent all first break following Tamsin Bacon around school in the hope of seeing her hair fall out. She would have got away with it if she hadn't tried to get into the same toilet cubicle. Mr Wilmott said under normal circumstances he would refer Scarlet to the school psychiatrist (aka Mental Morris) but that she is an exception to all rules (i.e. he is scared Suzy will steam into his office with her vast bosom and even vaster knowledge of education policy). Instead he has imposed a restraining order. She is not allowed within two metres of Tamsin Bacon until the end of term.

Anyway, I am too busy to be concerned with Scarlet's hexing. It is because Mr Slatter has announced an A Level Politics visit to the Houses of Parliament at the end of the month. Hugo Thorndyke (Con), evil MP for Saffron Walden and environs, is going to show us the corridors of power and infamous tea-room, where all the back-handers and sneaky deals are done. So am now in utter moral dilemma due to having still not told Mum about dropping French for made-up Mickey Mouse subject. Will ask James for advice. He is like Mum's mini-me and will be able to gauge her potential reaction.

7 p.m.
James says I have two options. I can either come clean and hope that my honesty will temper her anger and she will limit my punishment to being grounded for a month and paying for extracurricular French lessons on top of

440

my mounting debt. Or I can lie and pretend it is a visit to the French Institute. Have gone for option two. Will just bring back a postcard of Edith Piaf and some Orangina and she will be none the wiser.

. . . .

Thursday 8

Rachel Riley is Lisa Simpson.

Ed Thomas is Lilo Lil Simpson.

Scarlet is depressed. It is because her restraining order is causing issues at lunch. Tamsin Bacon measured the distance between Goth Corner Mark II and the Coven Table and it is only 187 cm. So Scarlet made us shunt the table thirteen centimetres to the right but then the maths geeks complained that we were 'cramping their style' (as if this is possible). So then we shunted forward instead but we accidentally crashed into the Criminals and Retards table and spilt Primark Donna's Yazoo all over Davey MacDonald's Hi-Tecs. And then all hell broke loose with the Dairylea Dunkables and Mrs Brain had to take cover behind the wholemeal pitta bread (tough and cheese-resistant). She is not blaming Scarlet though. She is blaming Jamie Oliver. She says he is the root cause of all school food problems. Mr Wilmott *is* blaming Scarlet however. She has got detention and is banned from the canteen for two days. She has to eat lunch in Mrs Leech's

441

office. This is not a punishment. Mrs Leech is an endless source of gossip and Peak Frean biscuits. She will never want to be rehabilitated.

. . . .

Friday 9

Dean Denley has joined 'Midget cowboy wrestling'.

Mr Wilmott is going to regret his restraining order. Scarlet is already party to several snippets of staffroom gossip, thanks to Mrs Leech and her inability to guard secrets for longer than an hour. According to Scarlet:

- Miss Vicar is actually a man (although Mrs Leech got this off Mark Lambert so it is utterly unreliable);
- Cowpat Cheesmond is on Prozac (reliable, she has seen the bottle in among the chicken wormer);
- Mr Vaughan has done it in the stationery cupboard with Miss Mustard, which sounds like Cluedo, but is not. Miss Mustard is Bridget Mustard, aka the lab assistant aka locust monitor.

Also, James has got a spelling bee next week. Everyone had to pick a letter out of the hat and learn as many words from the dictionary as possible. It is so 'everyone has a chance to shine'. James has got T. Mad Harry has got Q. Which, frankly, seems unfair as there are only about ten Q words and there are billions of Ts. James says he does not mind. He is relishing the challenge. Also Nige says he is not

concerned so much with results as with taking part. Mum is not in agreement. She says results are everything and correct spelling is the lynchpin of civilized society, along with punctuation and antibacterial cleansers. James said it is because she is a Tyrant. And Theoretically Teratoid.

* *

Saturday 10

Rachel Riley is Tantalized by Tetrahedrons.

Oh God. It is Scarlet's birthday on Monday and have nothing to give her, plus no money to buy anything. Am going to have to beg Mr Goldstein for credit and give her some incense sticks or something. Or maybe he has some out-of-date carob muffins. Will throw myself at his hunchlike mercy.

1 p.m.
Mr Goldstein is entirely unsympathetic. He says he does not give credit, not even to trusted staff members, (he did not say trusted, but I am sure he meant it) and that Rosamund had the last of their out-of-date mushroom pâté for her cat, Marjoram. There is nothing for it. Am going to have to search attic for more childish pottery that I can pass off as Wiccawear.

6 p.m.
The dog is getting confused with James's spelling bee

practice. It has just been told to Transmigrate to the Transmission Territory (i.e. go and watch telly on the sofa). I think it preferred it when James spoke Elvish. It was marginally more understandable. Even I am having trouble. Asked him if he wanted to come and scour the attic for priceless collectables but he said he was Too Tetchy to Tolerate Trangams. Told him he was a Tenuous Twit.

7 p.m.
Have found a jewel-encrusted eggcup (me), five collages of goat pictures (me), and a portrait of the queen (James). Will give Scarlet the eggcup and say it is a chalice.

7.15 p.m.
James says it is not the queen, it is Des Lynam. Mum was right. He has no artistic potential at all.

. . . .

Sunday 11
Remembrance Sunday

Rachel Riley is Transacting.

A terrible thing has happened. The coven has disbanded! It is because Scarlet says seventeen is too old for childish activity like witchcraft. Also her hex has not worked and Tamsin has not lost any hair or got boils. She has a new plan. She is going to flirt outrageously with Trevor and win him back, thus utterly destroying Tamsin Bacon. I said this was totally anti-Simple Life and broke all the rules of our platonic relationship pact. But Scarlet says she is not actually going to do 'It' with Trevor, she is just going to pretend she will, then kick him where it hurts (probably literally knowing her), and it is utterly feminist and strong woman. I am not at all sure this is true, but there is no arguing with Scarlet once she has set her mind on something. She is going to invite him to her party next Friday and wear outrageously revealing clothes. This is Suzy's preferred method of getting what she wants. It is almost 100 per cent reliable.

Am sad about the coven disbanding though. Not only is my eggcup/Wicca chalice birthday present now utterly irrelevant, but will have nothing to do on Sundays. James took pity on me and asked if I wanted to join Ghost Hustlers. I said I thought they had also disbanded (though not voluntarily but under Mum's instructions). James says it is now a covert operation. Anyway, I declined due to ghosts being made up. And then he started in on the T words again and called me Tiresome and Tacky so I left.

. . . .

Monday 12

Rachel Riley is Transpiring.

Got a lift to school with Jack again today. It is in honour of Scarlet's birthday. Asked Scarlet when she was starting

445

her driving lessons but she says she has refused Bob and Suzy's offer on the grounds that cars are evil and polluting and utterly non-Labour friendly. I notice she is happy to swan around town in Jack's Beetle and the vomit Volvo though.

Gave her the chalice anyway. Said it was an ironic eggcup. She said no it isn't. You made it in Mrs Barrow's class in Year Three. Luckily she was too busy with her campaign to win back Trevor to complain officially. She Superpoked him three times last night and 'accidentally' raked his green patch. It is lucky the coven has disbanded and we are back on the Alternative Music Club Table otherwise Trevor would have witnessed her doing unmentionable things with a Fruesli bar. As it is Dean Denley had to leave the table clutching his Incredibles lunchbox. (Not a euphemism. It is red plastic with a picture of Elastigirl on it.)

Tuesday 13

Scarlet Stone has sat courtside with Trevor Pledger.

It is James's spelling bee today. Thank God. So far this morning he has managed to get Tincture, Transgender, and Tickety-boo into conversation. Even Mum is finding it all a bit wearing. Also his mania for T words has revealed a few shortcomings in her own lexicon. I saw her having to look Totipalmate up in the OED after

Shreddies. (It means web-footed. She has claimed victory on the grounds it was used totally out of context.)

5 p.m.
Mum is writing to the council. It is because James came second in the spelling bee, even with ten out of ten. The victor was Maggot Mason, who won despite spelling 'calamity' with a k. It is because he has shown the greatest value-added improvement on last term (true, as he used to spell most words with a k). Mum says St Regina's is going the way of notorious anti-establishment establishment Summerhill, where pupils can choose not to attend lessons and are all too busy engaging in underage sex and binge drinking. I said this was taking it a bit far as, to my knowledge, there is no groping or alcoholism among the Year Sixes yet, but she says unmonitored spelling bees are the tip of the iceberg.

. . . .

Wednesday 14
Scarlet's win back/harassment campaign of head bat boy Trevor is reaching new peaks. Today she wore her full length vegetarian leather coat over a corset and knee-high boots. I said I was amazed Suzy had let her leave the house like that. Jack said, *au contraire*, the corset is Suzy's, as is the whip.

In stark contrast, mother-daughter activity at Summerdale Road consisted of cleaning out the mung bean cultivator.

The dog had accidentally dropped a chipolata in it during one of its illegal forays onto the Formica worktop, and it was cultivating things besides healthy-giving beanshoots, i.e. health-compromising mould and some sort of jelly-like glue that James claimed was ectoplasm and demanded to save in a marmalade jar. He is wrong. Although it might be worth saving and sending to GCHQ as potential chemical weapon.

Also, Mum reminded me I am having a new brace fitted by sadistic Mrs Wong tomorrow. Admittedly, as am only having platonic relationships from now on, it is non-love life compromising. But will still be hideous again. Well, more hideous. Hair is always this mental. It is lucky am not doing French as all the cedillas would result in excess spitting and would fail any potential oral tests. In fact, she should be grateful am doing politics. Bad teeth are essential political wear.

. . . .

Thursday 15

Rachel Riley is speechless.

A miracle has occurred. Mrs Wong has refused to give me a brace. It is not because she has had sudden moment of clarity and given up sadism. It is because of NHS cutbacks. She says my problem is not severe enough to warrant free treatment and it will cost £350 if I want it done privately. Mum has refused on the grounds I am never going to be

model material. Hurrah. Although am bit sad about the model thing. Said she should be blinded to the negative in her children. She said chance would be a fine thing. Thank God for New Labour's criminal underfunding of dentistry. Will text Scarlet to show support for this progressive policy.

. . . .

Friday 16

Rachel Riley is Kate Nash.

Ed Thomas is Nashville, Tennessee.

Hurrah, it is Scarlet's party tonight. Though, obviously, it is purely going to be a celebration of music and laughter, now that sex and snogging are off the agenda. Me and Sad Ed have got our sleepover stuff ready (Morrissey T-shirt, toothbrush, copy of *Mojo*—Sad Ed; vintage silk pyjamas, entire make-up hoard, copy of *To Kill A Mockingbird*—me) and the common room is awash with anticipation. There are already rumours that she has secured the White Stripes as entertainment. This is not true. It is Duncan Evans and his CD player, as usual. Plus Jack is going to do an acoustic set. Although quite how you do an acoustic set on drums I am not sure. But there is only one invitee that Scarlet cares about, and that is infidel bat boy Trevor Pledger. Will he betray Tamsin Bacon and make an appearance, or is he ensnared in Tamsin's evil web of hexes?

3 a.m.

Apparently he is ensnared in Tamsin's web of hexes. Although Scarlet says it is not too late. She is waiting up until at least four in case he has got lost on the way or something. She is mental. Am going to bed as have to be fresh as a daisy for the lentil bins in less than six hours. There is no sign of Sad Ed. He was last seen at eleven when someone tried to shut him in the fridge. Jack offered to sweep the house but I do not think someone as gargantuan as Sad Ed requires forensic checking. He is either visible, or he is not in the house. But party has been success on Simple Life terms. Have snogged no one. And got complimented on silk (actually viscose and possibly not vintage as have 'do not tumble dry' label on them) pyjamas by Jack. He said I look like 1920s Evelyn Waugh heroine, i.e. out of *Brideshead Revisited*. See—it is utterly possible to be platonic with boys. Even ones you used to fancy.

3.15 a.m.

Unless he means *Vile Bodies*. Which does not sound very nice.

. . . .

Saturday 17

Jack Stone is.

Rachel Riley is not.

450

8 a.m.
Oh God. Have had two hours' sleep. It is due to Scarlet waking me up at five to ask whether I thought she should go round to Trevor's house and have it out with him. Answer—no, you mentalist, it is five in the morning, go to bed and channel some positive energy. Cannot believe have to be at work in an hour. Will beg Suzy to phone in sick for me. She is excellent liar.

8.10 a.m.
Suzy says she learnt her lesson the last time and is not double-crossing my mother again. Also to please not burst into the bedroom as Bob is always fruity in the morning. Left rapidly with eyes shielded from potential genital exposure. Will shower and eat Waitrose pain au chocolats. Am totally bound to feel better after that.

8.30 a.m.
Still feel horrible. Plus ate five pain au chocolats to combat low blood sugar and am now buzzing mentally. Cannot possibly walk five hundred yards into town. Am going to throw self at Jack's mercy and beg for lift in left-wing Beetle.

9 a.m.
Hurrah. Am back in bed with strong tea and T4. Jack utterly took pity on me and offered to do my shift. He is such good friend. Maybe he will even offer to give me his

451

pay packet in order to alleviate third world debt. Possibly not. Anyway, can catch up on sleep, and *One Tree Hill*, and go home at 5.30 and Mum will be none the wiser.

9.15 a.m.
Unless she goes shopping for sesame snaps or other wholefood type fayre. Will call James and get him to divert her with suggested spring clean. That is like red rag to bull and she will be up to her elbows in Cillit Bang for hours.

6 p.m.
Hurrah. Am revived. It is not entirely due to day in bed watching *Veronica Mars* on Sky Plus with Scarlet, but is more in shock at James's terrifying new haircut, i.e. utterly bald. How can this have happened? Am going to interrogate Mum immediately.

7 p.m.
As always, it is O'Grady related. Apparently the Kylies came over and begged Mum to lend them James as a model for their hairdressing practice—they have a wet cut practical on Thursday. Mum agreed, on the grounds that they cannot do a worse job than Big Tony at Hair 2000, plus he was hindering her spring cleaning with his insistence at being in charge of hoovering (it is his new covert ghost detecting method). This was her crucial mistake. The Kylies can always do a worse job, no matter

452

how bad the alternative is. Anyway, James and the dog came back from the Britchers' two hours later, with an ASBO haircut, i.e. Mohican and a lightning flash shaved into one side. (James, not the dog. Apparently it spent two hours trying to mate Fiddy, despite having no testicles.) Mum had complete panic and shaved him completely with Dad's Gillette Mach 3 (the best a man can get). So now he looks like nit-riddled Irish orphan from *Angela's Ashes*. Mum says it is better than looking like an O'Grady.

Sunday 18

Have had thought. What has happened to Sad Ed? According to Jack, who heard it off Dean Denley, who heard it off Tracey Hughes (Waitrose tampon and deodorant aisle, Mum answers phones at police station), he did not show up for trolley herding duty yesterday. What if he had sudden untimely death urges at Scarlet's party and drove off in the sick-smelling Volvo and crashed it into one of the many and perilous mini roundabouts? Will pop over after Shreddies to check he is alive.

11 a.m.

He is alive. But shamefaced. It is because he got off with Melody Bean at Scarlet's party on Saturday night. I reminded him of our pact but he said the mind was willing, but the flesh was weak. Also he had two bottles of

453

cider and his vision was impaired. On the plus side, he claims it was a sex thing (or snogging, as he says he passed out before they got to the pants bit) and he will not be pursuing a meaningful relationship with her on any level.

It is still an outrage though. What with Sad Ed's antics, and Scarlet's hot pursuit of Trevor, I am clearly the only one able to ignore my lustful urges and retain any sense of dignity or integrity.

4 p.m.
Oh my God. Hilary has got an interview for Cambridge in two weeks. Granny Clegg rang to ask Mum if he could stay with us for the weekend to acclimatize himself to upcountry ways! Hurrah.

5 p.m.
Except I do not fancy him. Am strong woman. With no urges whatsoever. Men are not responsible for my happiness. I am responsible for my happiness.

6 p.m.
Am still totally excited though.

* *

Monday 19

Melody Bean has stroked Ed Thomas.

Jack picked me up for school again this morning. He said

he had excellent news to tell me. It is that he has got an interview for Cambridge in two weeks. I said it was indeed excellent, as he can take Hilary with him so he doesn't get lost. Then Jack remembered he had to collect Oona and made me get out at Mr Patel's.

School was good though. It is because Mr Wilmott has announced that, in lieu of a school play (all theatrical performances suspended after the lower school did *Jesus Christ Superstar* and Herod (Kyle O'Grady) had an impromptu bareknuckle fight with the apostles), we are going to have a charities week, utterly run by the Sixth Form. And Mr Vaughan. I said I was going to sign up for the slave auction but Scarlet has forbidden it on grounds of it being racist, sexist, and anti-workplace rights. She has banned the Kylies' charity *Swan* makeovers on the same grounds. Sad Ed is not signing up. It is in case Melody Bean tries to buy him. She is clearly not of the opinion that it was a sex thing and is aiming for a meaningful relationship. Sad Ed had to miss double English to avoid bumping into her on B Corridor. So it proves that not only does snogging compromise your happiness, but also your academic potential.

Tuesday 20

Ed Thomas has joined 'Leona Lewis is not the future of music'.

Have signed up to be a slave. So has Scarlet. It is not because she has declared them racism- and sexism-free. It is because Tamsin Bacon has signed up and she is refusing to be outcharitied by her former protégée. Plus she will get to wear a revealing outfit on stage and potentially lure Trevor back into her clutches. Before she chucks him again. Even Sad Ed has relented. It is because Scarlet told him to. And he is more scared of her than Melody and her tarantula.

* * *

Wednesday 21

Rachel Riley is small, but imperfectly formed.

Mum is making us change all our bank accounts. It is yet another identity theft panic. This time it is not Facebook that is the culprit but mad-eyebrowed Chancellor Alistair Darling. He gave the entire country's child benefit records to a motorbike courier who has´ now lost them. I am unsurprised. Stacey O'Grady was a motorbike courier for a bit and he was always 'losing' stuff. Though it was usually DVDs, not tedious government documents. Mum now thinks rogue couriers will be hacking into Barclays and money laundering her millions. I said I only had £1.04 in my Post Office account so I do not think I am potentially at risk but·she is not taking any chances. Dad is livid. He says he has only just sorted out the BT direct debit after three hours on the phone to some foreign call centre (it is in Cardiff).

* * *

456

Thursday 22

Sad Ed has been thrown back into the pit of despair. It is his driving lessons. Mike Wandering Hands says at this rate Sad Ed will be twenty-one before he is legally in charge of a vehicle. I said it was just psychological trick to make him work harder. But Sad Ed says he does not think so. It is more to do with the fact that he broke the faux walnut knob off the gearstick.

Friday 23

Ed Thomas is young, gifted, and fat.

Hurrah. Have got new moneymaking scheme. It is not illegal drugs or prostitution. It is babysitting for my godson and uncle Baby Jesus. Grandpa and Treena are taking positive steps to improve their relationship, i.e. Treena is going to let Grandpa go with her down the Queen Elizabeth instead of making him stay at home while she mainlines Vodka Reef. I am going round this evening to enjoy free biscuits and Sky. In a responsible, child-friendly manner of course.

1 a.m.
Grandpa pays worse than Mr Goldstein. I have amassed a mere £10 for five hours of pure hell. Admittedly, I should have known better than to take the dog with me. But it eating the doormat is nothing compared to

Baby Jesus's unsociable habits. Treena is operating a free and easy bed routine, i.e. letting Jesus fall asleep in front of telly, whatever time that might be. (This is not down to baby whispering or any other Suzy-style weirdy stuff but is because otherwise he wails ceaselessly and bangs his head against his cot in a disturbing manner.) So had to put up with him until ten o'clock. He ate all the biscuits and refused to let me watch E4. Tried to instil some spiritual guidance in him, i.e. explain several deadly sins, including gluttony and not-sharing (not sure if this is one, but couldn't remember them all and there is no Bible at Harvey Road to check these matters) but his response was to stick a Cheerio up his nose and I had to get Mrs O'Grady from next door to suck it out with a curly-wurly straw (did not want to call Mum as she would ban me from baby-sitting for sure). Anyway, Mrs O'Grady is experienced in these things—she has raised at least nine children and most of them are alive. Then, it turns out there is a lock-in at the Queen Lizzie and so Grandpa and Treena did not get in until quarter to one and had spent all my pay on the fruit machine and Frazzles. Have got an IOU slip written on a barmat instead. Which is hardly legal currency. Will put it in Mum's debt collection box (a WHSmith petty-cash tin, locked, with keys stashed in unknown hidey hole). She is good at extorting payment out of Grandpa.

Saturday 24

Dean Denley has thrown confetti at Rachel Riley.

Oh my God. A groundbreaking and non-lentil based event has occurred at health food outlet Nuts In May. It is the presence of rock god and former meat mincer Justin within the taupe-stained walls. He came in just after Rosamund had finished showing me her new rash, to buy kelp tablets (to make his hair grow extra rock star long). But then he asked me if I wanted to go to his gig at the Bernard Evans Youth Centre next Saturday. I said yes. Well, actually, I said 'gghhhmmpph' as was eating one of Mr Goldstein's patented oatmeal and raisin bars at the time, but it's almost the same thing. Although I think he may have taken my red face and enthusiasm the wrong way because he said, 'Just as a friend. Sophie will be there. Bring Scarlet too if you want. And Jack.'

Hurrah, it is obvious he shares my platonic desires. Or else he is lacking friends. Or else he is utterly brilliant and wants to show off to his enemies. Whichever, I do not care. I am totally going. Though will not tell Scarlet yet. She is bound to take it the wrong way. Even though fact that I did not fall into heap under dried chick pea bins and weep inconsolably proves I am totally over him.

Unlike Dean 'the dwarf' Denley. The presence of his predecessor over the road sent him into a mincing frenzy. I think he is worried Mr Goddard may sack him and beg

Justin to come back. It is the height disadvantage. He has to stand on a chair to do any hacking.

. . . .

Sunday 25

Rachel Riley has tripped up Dean Denley.

Hurrah! Another brilliant Justin-related thing has happened. He has Facebook-friended me! Am overjoyed with Superpoke potential. Cannot decide whether to throw a sheep at him or challenge him to 'name that *Baywatch* babe'. Which one says 'I platonically like you and am utterly not going to try to get anywhere near your undersized nipples despite fact that you are rock genius with good hair'?

4 p.m.
James has issued a Justin-related Facebook warning. He says he will be monitoring exchanges on an hourly basis and there will be penalties for breaches. Pointed out that he is banned from Facebook entirely. He said under Mum's terms he is banned from actually partaking of Facebook but she made no mention of not watching other people do it. He is a pest.

8 p.m.
Oh God. Just got a Facebook event invitation from Scarlet. It is an emergency meeting to discuss 'pact slippage', i.e.

she knows about Justin. Curse Facebook status updates. Cannot even keep my platonic relationships private any more.

9 p.m.

Jack has just hit me over the head with a diseased frog. (In the virtual sense, of course. The house is thankfully frog-free following the demise of Donatello, Michaelangelo, and Raphaelo at the hands, or claws, of the death chicken.) What is everyone's problem? I lit a menorah with Justin. Which is entirely non-sexual.

. . . .

Monday 26

Rachel Riley is blaming the dog.

Scarlet is going bonkers about the Justin thing. She says I am going to end up in Phase One again if I am not careful or, worse, in Phase Nought, i.e. back within his evil (but manly) arms. I said, *au contraire*, it is utterly Simple Life as it will prove once and for all that I am totally capable of platonic relationships, and is actually a forward-thinking step. Plus he is not evil. She said, yeah right. Then she pointed out that I can't go to the gig anyway as Hilary will be in residence and I will be too busy showing him cultural things. I said what could be more cultural than a guitar solo from a potential rock god. She said, 'What isn't?' Sad Ed is not so judgmental. Partly

because there would be all sorts of pot calling kettle black issues due to his liaison with tarantula-loving poetess Melody Bean, plus he wants to go to the gig to see 'whether Justin's sound has evolved', i.e. he wants to beg to be in the band again.

Scarlet is mistaken anyway. I am utterly not interested in Justin in the non-platonic sense.

5 p.m.
Am I?

6 p.m.
No am not. As have Hilary as top platonic friend to resist and he is a trainee doctor which trumps being able to play 'Stairway to Heaven' any day. Have checked with James. It is official. Plus Jack is second in line to the non-platonic throne. Admittedly am not entirely sure he fancies me still, or that I fancy him, but he is still an excellent reserve as his car is left-wing and he can do a Johnny Cash impression.

. . . .

Tuesday 27

Scarlet Stone has joined 'I don't think the David Miliband on Facebook is the real David Miliband'.

Hurrah, it is the Politics A Level trip to the Houses of Parliament tomorrow. Scarlet has already drawn up a

list of complaints to raise with Hugo Thorndyke, evil MP for Saffron Walden and environs. It is lucky Mr Slatter has not given Hugo a list of attendees or he would be changing his mind about educating the next generation in the ways of democracy immediately. He is a sworn enemy of the Stones ever since Suzy tried to smear him in his election campaign. Sad Ed is disappointed about not coming. Not because he wants to absorb the ancient atmosphere of the corridors of power. It is that he has double Art and is struggling with his gouache. Also it means he will utterly be at the mercy of Melody without me and Scarlet to protect him. I said it was all mind over matter. He said it is not his mind he is worried about. It is his penis. At which point I ended the discussion. James is also sad he is not coming. It is because the Houses of Parliament are allegedly stalked by no less than forty-three apparitions. He says Ghost Hustlers over the centuries have made pilgrimages to try to capture the fearsome 'bleeding Speaker' on camera. He has begged me to take pictures instead. Have agreed. Although will tell Mum they are French ghosts. She still thinks I am going to see *La Vie en Rose* sans subtitles.

. . . .

Wednesday 28

David Miliband is no longer friends with Scarlet Stone.

9 a.m.
Am utterly filled with potential political excitement. Have gone for an outfit that says 'I am quirky yet utterly democratic and will not start shouting about troops in Iraq at any point.' Scarlet has gone for militant EMO. A look that only says 'I will harass you about the war endlessly and possibly throw fetid fruit.' We are just waiting for Len Viceroy to show up in his new super-coach (the old one was too riddled with vomit smell and only had two gears). According to Mr Slatter it has an onboard toilet and drinks dispenser. Which will alleviate the usual hazard of losing several people at Junction 8 services when we stop for a wee and a can of Tango.

9.25 a.m.
Supercoach is not so super. Toilet is blocked after yesterday's Over-70s Horticultural Club outing to Peterborough and the drinks dispenser is a coolbox of Pepsi. Still, it does not matter as am too excited about seeing Gordon Brown shouting at some Tories to think about refreshments. Scarlet is already in trouble though. Mr Slatter did a bag check and made her remove half a dozen organic eggs and a flour-filled condom. It is for the best. Do not want anything else going wrong. Although, judging by previous school trips to the Paris Travotel and Davey MacDonald's swan-helmet ballet performance, the odds are not in our favour.

464

10 p.m.

As predicted, all did not go quite as smoothly as it might. It is Scarlet's fault. She has been banned for ever from the Houses of Parliament, and school outings, on the following grounds:

- trying to engage man-voiced Ruth Kelly in a discussion about VAT on tampons;
- trying to infiltrate the debate floor during a row about pineapple imports;
- trying to perform a citizen's arrest on Hugo Thorndyke for crimes against the working poor.

I have also been banned. It is not for political agitation. It is for spilling Monster Munch all over the political carpet. Plus my camera got confiscated by a man in tights. I pointed out I was in no way an evil Al Qaeda spy plotting to blow up the seat of government but he said 'rules is rules'. It is going to be sent back once they have checked it for incriminating evidence. Politicians are so out of date. It is lucky I had Scarlet's mobile phone with me.

. . . .

Thursday 29

James has uploaded Scarlet's mobile phone photos onto his computer and is going through them with a fine-toothed comb (actually a magnifying glass and his ghosto-meter). So far he has found no evidence of bleeding

465

apparitions. Although there is excellent evidence of Scarlet getting thwacked by Hugo Thorndyke's *Telegraph*.

. . . .

Friday 30
St Andrew's Day (Scotland)

Ed Thomas is wondering if spicy tomato crisps count towards his five a day.

Hurrah, Hilary arrives in less than twenty-four hours. It is utterly significant and groundbreaking for the Riley household. Even Mum thinks so. She is going on a special shopping trip for Hilary-friendly products. I have warned her not to fall prey to outdated media stereotypes, or indeed Grandpa Clegg stereotypes, but I fear this may have fallen on deaf ears. I definitely saw desiccated coconut on her shopping list. It is also just twenty-four hours until Justin's gig. Though am not getting hopes up. It is merely an observation. Am utterly resolved on Simple Life pact. Although the presence of both political and rock geniuses may send me over edge. It will be true test of mettle.

december

TURKEY

Saturday 1

Dean Denley has thrown Santa at Rachel Riley.

Rachel Riley has sent the Grinch after Dean Denley.

Cannot believe I have to go to work on such a momentous day. Have begged Jack to do my shift so that I can pace up and down the stairs in anticipation but he says he did not give up his job so that he can play bloody Buttons whenever I have random Prince Charmings to moon over. He is wrong. Hilary is totally not Prince Charming. He is far too intellectual for that. Anyway it is probably not jealousy but is just worry about Justin's gig tonight. Scarlet says he is coming to watch, though it is totally for business, not pleasure. He wants to make sure rock foundation does not upstage Music A Level. Scarlet is also coming on business reasons, i.e. to ensure I stay within pact confines. Plus I told her Trevor is going to be there. She is struggling in her bid to win him back. According to Melody Bean he has given Tamsin Bacon one of his pet rats. Scarlet said he is only doing it to make her jealous, as evidenced by the fact that the rat in question is 'Benson', who has one foot missing, and not king rat 'Hedges'. I agreed. Do not want to get her all riled up again.

6 p.m.
Oh hurrah! Hilary is here. He is actually right now on my sofa watching *News 24* with James and the dog. Mum is in

catering overdrive. As suspected, she offered him coconut macaroons. Thank God I warned her that he didn't like pineapples or our fridge would be full of Del Monte by now. As it is the tinned tomatoes have had to move to the cupboard under the stairs to make way for rice and kidney beans. James is also in overdrive. It is because Hilary knows more cunning facts than James. Apparently James tested him on heraldry for over an hour this afternoon and he only failed on one count (King Ethelred the Unready). The dog is not so happy. It is no longer the centre of any sort of attention. It tried to make up for it by singeing itself on the gas fire but only got a rolling of the eyes and a firm tutting. Mum does not shout in front of guests, unless they are related.

6.30 p.m.
Cherie and Thin Kylie have just been over on pretext of borrowing a cup of flour. This is utter lie. It is to ogle Hilary and his potential 'Donkey' Dawson area. Mum saw through their plan anyway and sent them packing. They should have asked to borrow some Kraft cheese slices. Everyone knows Cherie does not cook.

6.45 p.m.
Marjory has just been over. It was not on pretext of borrowing flour. Or Kraft cheese slices. It was in digital spyware panic that a dangerous youth was holding us hostage. She means Hilary. She spied him with her

470

binoculars from the landing window and assumed he was a cat burglar. Is it any wonder I am desperate to move to bohemian Camden with such provincial neighbours? Oh, how I long to dwell amongst the drug dealers and gangsters that Amy Winehouse gets to enjoy. It is so unfair. Thank God we are going out before Terry gets back from five-a-side and comes over to entertain us with his comedy Nigerian accent. I cannot wait until the gig. Nor can Hilary. It is because live music in Redruth is generally limited to Steeleye Span and someone called Bobby Helmet. Am wearing my ironic tiara so that I stand out in crowd. Do not want Justin to miss me. It is not that I want him to see Hilary and be utterly jealous. It is more so that he knows I am supporting him in our new platonic relationship. I hope Scarlet is not wearing her goth corset thingy. Do not want Hilary to get wrong impression and think that I consort with loose women. I really hope they get on. It is utterly important that my best friend is friends with my best platonic potential boyfriend type person.

1 a.m.
Hurrah, it has been a successful gig all round. Justin winked at me from the stage (so I am happy), but forgot several chords in his guitar solo and the words to 'Ruby' (so Jack is happy). Sad Ed has persuaded Justin to let him be their emergency roadie and third emergency keyboard player (so he is happy). And, even though Scarlet was wearing her corset, Hilary said it was the sign of someone confident in

her own skin and with her own political and religious ideals (so she is happy). In fact they hit it off brilliantly and Hilary is staying the night at hers so that they can continue their discussion on renationalizing the railways. Jack said I should come back too but Scarlet said I would just get bored. She is right. Plus Sad Ed got minty about having to walk home on his own and being potentially raped by Melody Bean (who spent entire evening flashing false purple eyelashes at him over a carton of Strawberry Ribena—doubly banned in our house as, even though it is stain-making, Ribena should be purple and blackcurrant flavour). Said he was idiot as girls cannot rape men. He said Tuesday managed it. Anyway, agreed in end on grounds it is totally a sisterhood thing to do as Hilary's theory on fiscal rules took Scarlet's mind off Trevor and Tamsin who were groping in the VIP area (the toddler room). Plus Bob and Suzy are far more multicultural and will not try to give him fried plantains (i.e. bananas as Waitrose is sorely lacking in exotica) for breakfast.

. . . .

Sunday 2

Dean Denley has thrown an elf at Rachel Riley.

Mum is not at all happy about Hilary defecting to the Stones. Nor is Granny Clegg who rang at half seven this morning to check that he is not homesick. As if. She is worried that Suzy may corrupt him with her lack of morals and abundance of sexual implements. She and

Suzy have never seen eye to eye. It is because Suzy thinks sex is as important as breathing and Granny Clegg has not done it since England won the world cup.

Anyway, I have been despatched to rescue Hilary and repatriate him to 24 Summerdale Road in time for lunch (non-racist lasagne, but with questionable tropical fruit yoghurt for pudding). Hurrah, we will be able to spend entire afternoon together listening to my vast (thirty-nine CDs) music collection and discussing Zadie Smith (have not actually read it yet but have Googled plot and know the key bits).

2 p.m.

Hilary is back but is having a post-lunch power nap. It is because he and Scarlet did not go to bed until four this morning. I said was it Suzy and one of her all-night cheese and yoga parties but Hilary said no, he and Scarlet had been talking about Tibet and completely lost track of time. Then I remembered that I need to prove my political credentials so showed him the photo I took of Scarlet getting thwacked by Hugo Thorndyke (Con), evil MP for Saffron Walden and environs. He said it was brilliant and totally subversive and that we should send it to the *Spectator* as further evidence of Tory suppression. Have posted it on Facebook instead. It has a far bigger and more influential audience than the *Spectator*. Hope he finishes nap soon as want to show him round important cultural sights in Saffron Walden, e.g. Barry Island and Mr Patel's.

4 p.m.

Hilary is up but is shut in the spare room for pre-interview revision. James and the dog are both under strict instructions not to pester him under any circumstances. James argued that his in-depth questioning could prove the difference between success and failure for Hilary but Mum says she didn't think the medicine professors would be asking him 'True or False—horses can't be sick'. May just knock on door and see if he needs any brain-stimulating digestive biscuits though.

4.15 p.m.

Answer no. It is clear that he is single-minded in his efforts to join the ranks of geniuses that have thronged the refectory tables at Magdalene (not Maudlin as had previously thought) College and that nothing will distract him from his task.

4.30 p.m.

Hilary has gone round to Scarlet's house. She rang to say they were having Suzy's Labour Party activist friends round to dinner and the conversation might prove stimulating. I said I might find it stimulating too (i.e. I might find Hilary stimulating) but she said, 'No you won't, you will try to change the topic to Hilary Duff's hairdo and eat all the Kettle Chips as usual.' Which is possibly true. Anyway, he is going to stay the night and get a lift to Cambridge in the morning. Bob is going to take him and

Jack in the sick-smelling Volvo on his way to Addenbrookes. I suppose it makes utter sense, like Scarlet says. Mum is annoyed again though. She had made prawn jambalaya for tea.

10 p.m.
Although what if Hilary is not just stimulating Scarlet's mind but also her pant-covered areas?

10.15 p.m.
No, am being paranoid. Scarlet is paragon of virtue as far as pact goes. Even Trevor stuff was only ploy to get back at Tamsins, not actually man-based activity. How could I be so doubting? I am like that apostle whose name I can't remember.

10.30 p.m.
Doubting Thomas. That's it.

. . . .

Monday 3
8 a.m.
Am utterly on tenterhooks. It is in sympathy with Hilary and his efforts to overcome his lowly birth (i.e. Cardiff) and join the university elite. Have texted Scarlet to check how he is holding up. She says he is doing well under Suzy's calming influence. Hope she has not given him any of her home remedies (i.e. Valium). Texted again to say to

give him kiss and good luck from me. She said, 'With pleasure.' Am not concerned. Will not be Doubting Riley. Am strong non-jealous woman.

8.15 a.m.
Jack texted to say 'THANKS 4 THINKING ABOUT ME. NOT.' He has definite overuse of sarcasm. It will curry no favour with the interviewers at Cambridge if he continues in that vein all day. Anyway have texted back to say, *au contraire*, was thinking of him, but assumed he could tell that, telepathically. It is not strictly true but Jack is easily placated.

8.17 a.m.
Got another text from Jack. WHATEVER. That boy is heading for failure. He is obviously too het up to concentrate. Unlike calm Hilary. Texted Scarlet to say maybe I should drop round before school to offer words of advice to both candidates but she says they are in capable hands and not to bother until after school. Said I would see her in double philosophy. She said 'Not likely.' She is going with Bob in the Volvo to be official bag carrier. Am still not Doubting though. Scarlet is my sister. Not actual, as there is no way Mum would have let abortionist Bob near her high-waisters, but in mind, and endeavour.

3.15 p.m.
Thank God school is over. Could not concentrate at all in philosophy, i.e. if you were stuck in a drifting hot air

476

balloon with a lawyer, a doctor, and a pilot etc., who would you chuck out first? Said would chuck out fireman on grounds there is a height requirement so he is bound to be biggest, but not sure there was one in there in first place. Anyway am going over immediately for full debriefing. And also to collect Hilary as Mum says Granny Clegg is going bonkers over the treachery and is threatening to come up to Saffron Walden herself to oversee matters. Also because she is worried as he told her it was an Oxbridge interview and she can't find Oxbridge on a map and thinks he may have been tricked by people traffickers or aliens.

6 p.m.

It is good news. Hilary says his opinions on the Hippocratic oath and euthanasia went down well with the forward-thinking faculty and that he is pretty sure of a place. Jack is also jubilant. It is because the woman who interviewed him had a poster of Billy Bragg on her wall so he says they spent the entire interview discussing the 'demise of agitpop'. I said it was clear why Magdalene beat Selwyn in *University Challenge*. Jack said, 'Whatever'. Anyway, Hilary is back in Summerdale Road for his final night. We are having risk-free fish and chips and Dad has set up his *Lovejoy* video collection. He says it will provide a unique insight into East Anglian life. He is mistaken. The only thing it will provide insight into is Ian McShane's criminal hairdo. It is like claiming *Doc Martin* is accurate portrayal

477

of Cornwall. Although Granny Clegg is under mistaken belief that it is fly-on-the-wall documentary. She actually wants to move to non-existent Port Wenn so that Martin Clunes can attend to her many and varied ailments instead of Australian lady Dr Kimber. Have bagged place on sofa next to Hilary none the less. Will be able to point out places we can visit together once he is installed in hallowed halls of learning next year. Hurrah!

Tuesday 4

Hilary Aneurin Bevan Nuamah has left the building.

9 a.m.
Hilary has gone. He left at half past eight with a tear in his eye and a Tupperware box of Marmite sandwiches. We all lined up outside the house to wave him on his way. Scarlet came over especially. As did Thin Kylie, Cherie, Marjory, and Mrs Hooton from number 21. He has totally won over the neighbourhood. Except Sad Ed who is annoyed because he said Morrissey was the acceptable face of bigotry. And the dog, who is annoyed because it has had no attention for several days now, despite destroying several Constable placemats and an entire McVities Jamaican Ginger Cake. It got shouted at as soon as Hilary's eco- and Labour-friendly Nissan Micra pulled away and is jubilant at being restored to its rightful place as resident menace.

478

Oh, I will miss Hilary. It is totally like Cherie says, he is a breath of fresh air in these parts (except without the panting and possible innuendo). Am going to beg to go to Cornwall for Christmas. Scarlet is in agreement. She says she will happily accompany us. She is such good friend.

4 p.m.

Mum says there is no way we are going to Granny Clegg's for Christmas. She is still recovering from 2002, the year of the partially frozen turkey drumsticks. Am undeterred though. Will have to think of cunning plan. Oooh, maybe Grandpa Clegg will herniate himself due to over-stimulation from the *Daily Mail* and need round-the-clock care. Hurrah. Will pray for illness and misfortune to befall Belleview. It is utterly in a good cause, after all.

Wednesday 5

Rachel Riley is behind you! Oh no she isn't. Oh yes she is!

There is good news, Simple Life-wise. Scarlet is totally over Trevor and Tamsin. They were groping on the sheep field at lunch, which normally would have been a cue for Scarlet to discard some of her clothing and wander provocatively through the sheep poo, but instead she declared that she is not interested any more and Tamsin can have him. She says his arms are weedy and he is too obsessed with bats. Which I did point out to her a year ago, but love is blind. I

479

said it was good news that she is so committed to our pact of platonic love. But she got a text at that point and disappeared behind the bike sheds (formerly smokers' corner, now nicotine patch corner) to reply. It is probably from Edna the non-Filipina cleaner. Suzy gave her a mobile for her birthday and she has taken to texting people randomly to update them on domestic issues and her 'thought for the day'. Scarlet once got a text saying, 'GORDON KILLED BILL FOSSET'S RABBIT. WE SHOULD EAT MORE RABBITS. THEY IS BLOODY VERMINOUS.'

Thursday 6

Ed Thomas joined the group 'Left-handed people are up themselves'.

Oh my God. The picture of Hugo Thorndyke, evil MP for Saffron Walden and environs, thwacking Scarlet over the head with a *Telegraph*, is on the front page of the *Herts and Essex Reporter*. The common room is mad with potential political agitation. Scarlet is being hailed as uber-left heroine of Twelve Hopwood-White. So am I. It is because the article credits me as the photographer. Whatever happened to journalistic integrity? I blame Alastair Campbell and his insistence on naming and shaming sources. Thank God Mum does not get the paper (on the grounds it concentrates far too much on Sawbridgeworth and the 'footballer belt'). She would be going mental with potential

punishment as it breaks a legion of rules, not least doing politics A Level. Scarlet said she did offer the story to the *Walden Chronicle* but they turned it down. It is because the editor Deirdre Roberts's cousin is married to Hugo Thorndyke's sister. Or vice versa.

5 p.m.

It is all over. Mum has clawed her way through my web of deceit with her forensic abilities and proved that I lied about French. It is all Marjory's fault. She does not get the *Reporter* either but Dr Braithwaite (huge hands, lazy eye, bottle of whisky in desk drawer) does, and she was browsing through it while she was waiting to get her verruca frozen. I tried to deny any involvement but then Mum produced her trump card. Which was not actually a card but was my confiscated camera. It arrived home in this morning's post in a Houses of Parliament jiffy bag. Mum does not believe in privacy law and opens anything, regardless of whom it is addressed to, including next door's post, which arrives through our door with alarming regularity due to postman Beefy Clarke being dyslexic. And lazy.

Have been sent to room whilst Mum and James devise suitable punishment. I did point out that whole deception had been James's idea but he said he did it to test my resolve. He is sneak.

8 p.m.

Punishment has been decreed. It is one to one conversational

French lessons with Mum on Sunday mornings. It is potentially torturous. She speaks as slowly as she drives and her favoured topics are *'Je voudrais le potage, s'il vous plaît'* and *'Ma voiture est cassée'*.

. . . .

Friday 7

9 a.m.

Something terrible has occurred. Again. My Facebook account has mysteriously disappeared. And this time it cannot possibly be Bruce and his canine Bermuda Triangle. Scarlet has already texted to ask why I have not responded to her throwing a turkey at me at seven this morning. Told her that mysterious forces had swallowed my profile into the internet ether. She got all overexcited and said it was an evil Tory plot to censor free speech due to my candid Hugo Thorndyke shot. She is going to alert Hilary so they can mount a counter publicity campaign. I said she had done enough damage already, thank you. Anyway, she is wasting her time. Think it is just Mum and her faithful anti-free speech sidekick James.

4 p.m.

Was right. It is Mum and James. Tried to set up a pseudonym account, i.e. reviving my underused self-appointed nickname Ray Riley, but immediately door burst open and James came in accusing me of playing with fire and that if Mum catches me it will be curtains.

482

On-fire ones I presume. I said I was at risk of becoming a social pariah due to my inability to hurl random objects at my 'friends'. He said, *au contraire*, everyone will be bored with it in two months and will be using YouTube instead. He has already put video camera on his Christmas list. He is wrong anyway. Facebook will never fade away. I will just have to go quiet for a while then re-emerge, like metaphorical butterfly, beautiful and with extra Superpoke power. Plus can check what is happening online anyway as have worked out Sad Ed's password. It is Frobisher (i.e. his toy rabbit).

Saturday 8

It is bad enough only earning £19.95 a day without then having to post every last penny into Mum's Fort-Knox-style money collecting tin. Mum has offered to top it up with £5 a week if I take on more dog-related responsibilities but have declined. The dog only responds well to James. It is their shared love of all things hobbit. Have also declined suggestions of extra babysitting for Baby Jesus on the grounds that it is mentally depleting. James has begged to do it instead. He says he will happily drum some spiritual sense into him. He has more chance. He is morally superior in every way and can sing the books of the Bible off by heart. Mum has said no, on legal grounds, although I can tell she thinks it would be better. Even my own mother has no faith in me. Plus there was no sign of

Justin on the iron supplement aisle today. He is clearly being non-platonic somewhere with Sophie Microwave Muffins. According to Scarlet, who overheard Pippa Newbold telling Duncan Evans on the saggy sofa two days ago, they are going to get engaged as soon as they leave school. They are such a cliché. Thank God it is Sunday tomorrow. Traditional day of lounging around in bed until eleven then watching *T4* round Scarlet's whilst consuming vast quantities of Nigella recipe cakes.

. . . .

Sunday 9

8 a.m.
Or not. Have just been rudely awakened by Mum and her Conversational French toolkit, i.e. a set of Linguaphone tapes and a menu from La Poule au Pot in Sawston. She is making us start as soon as have consumed Shreddies (i.e. le cereal).

9 a.m.
Mum has confiscated Shreddies due to my new method of chewing each individual Shreddie twenty times. Pointed out it was for digestive purposes and had read about it in her hypochondriac's bible (aka Dr Le Fanu's *Book of Family Health*) but she was having none of it. James is joining us in readiness for fast-track French at St Gregory's Girls' next year. He is confidently expecting to be put straight into GCSE.

484

11.30 a.m.

Thank God that is over. Mum is far stricter than Mr Vaughan when it comes to conjugating verbs. And not making up words. James excelled though. He successfully used '*zut alors*' in a sentence and knew the French for carburettor. As a reward Mum is letting him have Mad Harry over for the afternoon. She will regret it. They are bound to try some illicit ghost hunting. James is convinced that Marjory is actually a bride of Dracula (she is not, she has slightly elongated canine teeth). He has been staking her out since last Monday.

5 p.m.

James and Mad Harry are in serious trouble. It is for throwing holy water at Marjory over the fence to 'see if she melted'. Also they were catapulting garlic cloves through the conservatory doors. Mum says enough is enough. The ghostometer has been confiscated and the *Usborne Guide to Ghost Hunting* is being returned to the library tomorrow. James says he does not mind. He has a new purpose in life. It is to become the owner of a circus of midget animals. He is of mistaken belief that he can make fortune from strapping monkeys in cowboy hats to the backs of Falabella ponies and getting them to jump over a string of obstacles. He is going to be in charge of finance and costumes while Mad Harry is going to be ringmaster. They are idiots.

Monday 10

Granny Clegg rang this morning. It was not to inform me she had developed a new fortune-telling body part or that Grandpa Clegg had burst his colon or anything else useful. It was to ask whether chickens are mammals (she and Grandpa Clegg have been rowing about this for two days apparently). But it is excellent anyway as have solved the absence of Hilary/ban on Cornwall conundrum and without the need to resort to ill/dying relatives. I have seized the day and invited the Cleggs to come here for Christmas instead. That way, Hilary can drive them in his Nissan Micra and stay the night so as to minimize motorway madness and crash potential. Granny Clegg thinks it is a brilliant idea. So does Grandpa Clegg. It is not so much at coming to visit his eldest (and cleanest) daughter and delightful grandchildren, more at being chauffered by Hilary. He thinks it is ultimate in his admission to the upper middle classes. He is fooling himself. He will never be granted admission. Not when he thinks vests are acceptable outer wear. Have not told Mum yet. Will be surprise Clegg reunion. She will be utterly over the moon.

. . . .

Tuesday 11

Scarlet thinks the Hilary plan is excellent. She has even offered to put him up for the night if things are too overcrowded at Summerdale Road. I said that was very

kind but that as we are just platonic friends, he can sleep in my bed with me. Scarlet says she will join us under the covers as it will totally be like Brownie camp. Or squatting. Agreed as it is totally sister-like/left-wing activity. Sad Ed wanted to come too but we said no. There is no way my John Lewis junior bed can take the weight. Plus Mum has banned him from sleepovers after his midnight feast in Year Eight in which he consumed the entire contents of her superior biscuit box. (Only brought out for guests. The rest of us are limited to digestives, HobNobs, and rich teas.)

Wednesday 12

School is awash with slave madness. Forty-three people have now signed up to be sold by Mr Wilmott and his charity gavel (i.e. a broken woodwork hammer) and he has had to close the list a week early for fear that there will be no one left to actually do the buying bit. Scarlet is boy-cotting it again now that she is no longer interested in bat boy. But she says she will still support me and Sad Ed in our quest for total submission. I said it was not total, i.e. there was no sex involved, but she says that is not what the Kylies say. They are under distinct impression that it is tantamount to minor prostitution. It is not a deterrent. It is the lure that has made them both sign up. Am having slight second thoughts though. Not about sex. As am totally committed to platonic pact and will explain that to whoever buys me. It is

worry that no one will actually buy me. Or will go for 10p while Sophie Microwave Muffins secures £100 in a bidding war between Mr Vaughan and several of the PE staff (male and female). Although suppose at least will get more than Sad Ed. His general air of moroseness is not conducive to being useful manservant.

- -

Thursday 13

Granny Clegg rang again this morning to check whether or not she could bring Bruce. Have said yes on the more the merrier grounds. James is getting suspicious though. It is because I dived over the breakfast table to grab phone before he could answer (luckily Mum was cleaning up dog-related mess on the downstairs loo door at the time). He says he hopes I am not plotting anything. I said people in glass houses should not throw stones. It is because I have seen his plans for the midget circus and they include harvesting fleas from the dog.

- -

Friday 14

Cherie has just been over offering Mum the 'night of her life'. It was a spare ticket to see the Spice Girls reunion concert. Clearly Cherie does not know Mum very well. The night of Mum's life would involve Jeremy Paxman and some Dettol. Cherie is going to ask Suzy instead. She is totally pro Spice Girls due to their girl power message.

Plus she is hoping to get Victoria Beckham on her celebrity sex sofa soon. She is desperate to gauge the actual proportions of David's willy.

· ·

Saturday 15

Oh joy. Another day with Rosamund and her many complaints. The only positive thing I can say about the world of lentil retailing is that at least I am not stuck outside in the harsh elements like Sad Ed who spent the day herding trolleys in a criminally thin polyester overall. He claims he now has frostbite and trolley foot (invented workplace injury caused by moronic dog-food eating supervisor repeatedly running over one's feet with a train of trolleys to see how many it is possible to endure without bones actually breaking). He actually asked if there were any vacancies at Nuts In May. He must be desperate. Sad Ed does not engage with wholefood unless it is emergency.

· ·

Sunday 16

Oh God. Cannot do any more conversational French with Mum. She is punishing me for failing at my punishment now. It is because she made me book a single hotel room with an en suite shower and I apparently asked for a wet double. Plus I forgot to demand a cursory check of the toilet facilities. James said he is stunned that I managed a

489

B at GCSE and it is just further proof that exams are not worth the paper they are printed on these days. James is in trouble too though. It is not his French (which is freakishly advanced). It is because he and Mad Harry 'borrowed' one of Marjory's guinea pigs for the midget circus and it is now lodged under the fridge with the dog going bonkers around the kitchen. She is regretting confiscating the ghostometer, I can tell.

. . . .

Monday 17

Hurrah, it is Charities week. Activities today are:

- Year Seven toasted sandwich lunch stall. (Brevilles encrusted with the remains of last year's Sports Day groundbreaking charity marshmallow and banana combo. So Mrs Brain not too in danger of being put out of business.)
- Throw wet sponges at a teacher (Miss Vicar and Miss Beadle). All sponges have been quality checked for hidden weapons after Darryl Stamp concealed pointy Yu-Gi-Oh toys inside them at the summer fete three years ago.
- Criminals and Retards sponsored silence. This is doomed to failure. But they have been banned from sponsored walks, sponsored swims, and sponsored transferring Rice Krispies from one bowl to another using only a straw and the power of suction, so this is the last resort.

Plus Mr Wilmott has announced that the end of term disco on Friday will continue in the slave vein and be a toga party. He is making a colossal mistake. Togas have too many access points. The Kylies will be pregnant by 9 p.m.

Tuesday 18

Mum is agitated. At first thought she may have guessed secret Clegg Christmas plans but it turns out that it is just James's non-nativity at St Regina's. Nige has instigated a no-faith embracing celebratory talent show concert, complete with an opt-out policy for anyone who would rather string coloured pasta together instead. He says it will be less stressful for parents and pupils. Mum is not in agreement. The veins on her forehead are particularly bulgy. It is fear at James's role. He has refused to divulge the nature of his performance but he has gone to school in his leotard.

There is trouble at John Major High as well. It is not nativities. (They got banned several years ago after Suzy's temporarily successful campaign to portray the realities of childbirth complete with screaming and fake blood.) It is the BTEC hair and beauty *Swan* makeovers tomorrow. Only three people have signed up: underage O'Grady menace Kyle, his chavette-in-training girlfriend Primark Donna, and Mark Lambert. (On the grounds there is not much you can do with a skinhead. He is wrong. They will

491

wax him within an inch of his life.) Mr Wilmott has now changed the rules so that you can pay £10 and nominate someone for it instead. It is a stroke of genius. There has been a flurry of enemy-nominating activity at the upper school notice board and rumours abound (via the Maths Club gambling ring) that they have already raised £170. They are taking bets on who will look the worst. Odds are on Cowpat Cheesmond (gigantic beard with concealed food, lingering smell of manure, nominated by the Year Nine Criminals and Retards for not letting them kill chickens last Tuesday). I hope Sophie Microwave Muffins does not nominate me. I have already suffered at the hands of their grooming incompetence. My eyebrows are only just back to their unkempt selves. Oooh. Maybe I could nominate her though. Will ask Mum if I can borrow £10 for a good cause when I get home.

5 p.m.
Mum is not in a mood for handing out money to any causes. It is the no-faith celebration at St Regina's. It did not go entirely to plan and James and Mad Harry managed to lose all the school gerbils. Their act involved making the gerbils run around James's leotard while he did his scary dancing.

. . . .

Wednesday 19
Oh my God. There has been an incredible *Swan*

492

makeover-related event. It is malodorous bisexual Head Girl Oona with the hairy armpits (nominated by the entire common room on smell grounds). She has been Kylied and is fully waxed (including a particularly tricky bikini line, according to the Maths Club), deodorized and has had her hair dyed brunette (it was supposed to be burgundy but Fat Kylie used the wrong packets, as usual). But Fat Kylie's mistake is Oona's gain as she looks utterly stunning. Ooh, maybe am lesbian after all. It would be ultimate in Simple Life anti-men activity. And last efforts were somewhat half-hearted, i.e. only tried for two hours and was distracted by visions of Fat Kylie's minky. Yes. That is it! Am going to be lesbian. Possibly. Will not tell Scarlet and Sad Ed yet though. Saw Sad Ed looking somewhat non-platonically at Oona Mark 2 and do not want him as love rival. Although I would totally win on thin upper arms and breast grounds. Scarlet is a different matter though. She has excellent lesbian credentials including a KD Lang CD and access to vibrators.

Thursday 20

Hurrah, it is the John Major High first inaugural Charity Slave Auction. Am wearing Brownies T-shirt and miniskirt, an outfit that says I am willing and able to do my best, but not as willing as either of the Kylies. Plus Brownies T-shirt shows an interest in all-girl activity i.e. Oona will purchase me for potential lesbian discussions.

Sad Ed is wearing a waffle jumper and beanie hat. He will be lucky to get any bids at all.

5 p.m.
Have not been bought by Oona. In fact, she did not bid for me at all. Instead have been bought for a meagre £4.50 by Jack. And was not exactly frenzied bidding war. In end only he and Dean 'the dwarf' Denley stuck their hands up. Thank God Jack took pity on me to save me from the idiotic mincing midget. Although am disappointed at the Dwarf putting such a low price on love. £4.40 is hardly inspiring. He could get Leanne Jones to do him in a phone box for less.

In contrast, Sad Ed went for £28 after a three-way fight between Oona, poetess stalker Melody Bean, and Mark Lambert. Oona won. Obviously she wants him for some heavy duty carrying work. Sad Ed is delighted. And relieved. Mark Lambert was going to make him dance naked in the long jump pit (aka cat toilet). Slavery takes place tomorrow. We are at the mercy of our masters for a full six and a half hours, plus after-school activity by prior arrangement and an extra cost of £2.50 an hour. Maybe could charge Jack privately to alleviate my debt. Would be excellent PA type person, i.e. I look excellent in pencil skirts. Plus could be like Alastair Campbell and advise him on which outfit to go for to impress his electorate. Will ask him tomorrow.

Friday 21

4 p.m.

Have surprisingly excellent day as Jack's 'slave'. He and
Oona were doing a common room Christmas makeover
(which explains the purchase of Sad Ed for saggy sofa
moving services). So just had to help him scrape all the
Blu-tack (aka chewing gum) stuck to the walls and paint
out the mural of dying Iraqis in front of Tony Blair in a
devil suit left by last year's A Level Art group. It is in
preparation for the next cohort of wannabe Tracey
Emins. Do not know why we are bothering though. It is
bound to be something equally clichéd. Jack turned down
my offer of extra-curricular slavery though. He says it is
bad enough having Edna trying to make him wear weird
clothing combinations without me doing it too. He is so
ungrateful. Edna is only doing it because she forgets
where she has put half the washing, or else dyes it all
yellow. He did offer to escort me to tonight's toga party
instead. I said no, as I will be too busy being a lesbian with
glamorous Oona. He said, 'There is no way you are gay,
Riley. And I should know.' Which is possibly true as he
has 'tested the goods' so to speak, and they did respond.
But am not going to let him out-left-wing me. I can be
gay if I want. And will show him tonight. Though will
have to contend with Sad Ed. He is jubilant after a day
spent cleaning the sofa with Oona (findings £3.80, four
condoms, and a packet of custard creams). I reminded
him of his no-sex with the opposite sex pact but he said

Oona doesn't count as she is a lesbian. He has no chance anyway. He has had to borrow one of his mum's superking pink polyester Argos sheets for his toga and it is still quite gapey around the manboob area. Whereas I am in John Lewis 200-thread-count Egyptian cotton (queen size), which is far more lesbian-friendly. Scarlet is wearing black satin. So will have to keep close eye on her.

12 midnight

Am not lesbian. At least not yet. It is because Oona did not come to the toga party due to having a prior anti-Taliban clothes swap in Harlow. Why did I not think to check these things? So had to slow dance to whingeing James Blunt with Jack. He said it was part of my duties as a slave. I pointed out that he hadn't paid his extra £2.50 but he said, *au contraire*, he had slipped Mr Wilmott a fiver behind Goth Corner Mark I. Think this is a lie. Agreed as it is Christmas after all. And is good that he would pay so much for a dance with me. Plus it was actually quite pleasant. He smells nice and his arms are deceptively strong. Ooh, maybe do still fancy him after all. Even though he has a penis and is not gay.

12.15 a.m.

No. That is not Simple Life at all. Especially as Scarlet is my sister which makes Jack my brother which makes it practically incest. Am definitely committed potential lesbian.

496

Saturday 22

Oh God. Have just realized that have not done any shopping and have only got three days to go until Christmas, one of which will be spent hawking lentils, one of which the shops do not open (except for Mr Patel's porn, junk food, and nicotine patch emporium), and one of which will be spent making merriment at the giant Clegg reunion so will too busy heating Fray Bentos and pouring Stones Ginger Wine to leave the house. Plus, have no idea what to get anyone and utterly no money with which to do it. In contrast, James has saved £56 and has drawn up a shopping schedule and options for every recipient in case WHSmith has sold out of his favoured items. Begged him to lend me some money and do the choosing and buying (which is the sort of responsibility he would have leapt at under normal circumstances) but he said he needs every last penny for the circus. On plus side he had an alternative suggestion. It is to do my shopping at Nuts In May using today's wages, before Mum commandeers them for the petty cash debt tin. It is genius.

6 p.m.

Not a brilliantly successful day on several counts. Firstly, had underanticipated wealth of Christmas-type goods on offer at Nuts In May so gift list is now as follows:

- Mum—additive-free sanitary towels (to show I do not think she is anywhere near being menopausal, she will be thrilled);

- Dad—CD of calming pan pipes (to play in car as radio is still stuck on Kiss FM after Bruce ate the tuning knob);
- James—sesame snaps (his snack of choice);
- Scarlet—Vitamin D capsules (to combat hours spent in darkened bedroom during goth phase);
- Sad Ed—box of creatine (so he can convert manboobs into muscle);
- Baby Jesus—beetroot crisps (will say they are 'special purple Skips');
- Grandpa—giant jar of omega 3 fish oil for brain power and joint lubrication;
- Treena—giant tube of organic KY jelly for actual lubrication;
- Dog—four packets of Linda McCartney sausages (it will eat real cardboard so these will be breeze);
- Cleggs—nothing. (They do not believe in wholefood, vitamins, vegetarian products, or anything wheat-free. Christmas with me will be present enough.)

Secondly, Justin came in. It was not for more kelp tablets (hair now approaching undersized nipple line). It was to 'collect his Christmas kiss'. I said I thought he was getting engaged to Sophie Microwave Muffins. He said, 'Not any more, she came on yesterday.' So I said I couldn't do it then and there due to a no fraternizing at work rule but that I'd think about it. He said, 'Cool, well, pop over on New Year's Eve and I'll give you one while Sophie's in the

498

bog.' So am now in platonic Simple Life quandary. On the one hand, he is my two-timing ex, and is going out with someone else, so it would be utterly unsisterly and evil. On the other, he is gorgeous, she is a cow, and I am an utter lesbian in training, so where's the problem?

Thirdly, Rosamund is on a root vegetable diet and it is having a bad effect on her digestion. Mr Goldstein had to put her on stockroom duty as the smell was putting customers off their purchases. He is obviously immune to the usual odour of decaying vegetation that pervades his store.

But am festive none the less as tomorrow Granny and Grandpa Clegg will be here for the secret reunion. Which means Hilary will be here. Hurrah! Am going to spend entire morning making sure Mum is in excellent mood as do not want to spoil events for her.

. . . .

Sunday 23

11 a.m.

Plan already foiled. It is entirely James and Mad Harry's fault. Mum found them making the dog jump over a series of obstacles in the back garden (i.e. her Vileda supermop collection, suspended on the patio chairs). Which would not have been so bad except that they had strapped Baby Jesus to his back. Mum has gone mad and has banned any midget circus activity. She has also banned Grandpa from the house for the rest of the day. He was encouraging the

whole proceedings. At least his presence will not incense the Cleggs. They have still not resolved the Terry Wogan greatest living presenter/annoying twat row.

4 p.m.
Where is Hilary? He left at least six hours ago, according to Scarlet who ate virtual figgy pudding with him at half seven. She is already here with her overnight bag for our three-in-a-bed platonic sleepover.

5 p.m.
Still no sign. And Mum has demanded to know why we are watching the driveway with James's binoculars. She says it is bad enough having one amateur private eye on the road without us jumping on Marjory's idiotic bandwagon. Said we were observing festive robins at play.

6 p.m.
The Cleggs and their plethora of Spar bags are here! And with them is their chauffeur Hilary. Hurrah! The delay was caused by an overturned Bernard Matthews lorry on the M11, complicated by both carriageways stopping to do some seasonal looting. They are settled on the sofa with two bottles of Mackesons and *You've Been Framed*. On the down side, Hilary has gone home as he has a crucial Christingle service tomorrow. Scarlet said he could go with her to the one at St Regina's. So I pointed out that she is anti all

500

religion on the grounds that it is the opium of the masses but she said she has had a rethink and it is utterly New Labour to be religious fanatic and uber left-wing, look at mad Catholic Ruth Kelly. Hilary said no anyway, as he is in charge of handing out oranges. But he is going to stay the night when he picks the Cleggs up instead. Mum asked when that might be. Granny said next Monday. Hurrah, so Hilary will be here for New Year. Plus we can enjoy a multigenerational family Christmas for a whole week. Mum is now having a lie down in her bedroom. I think she is overcome with joy at their surprise festive arrival. She has barely been able to utter a word. Except, 'Colin, fetch a J-cloth,' when Bruce weed on the lino. Dad has mopped up and is now at Waitrose with James, shopping for emergency Fray Bentos and a bulk pack of Andrex. He is dropping Scarlet off on the way. I said Hilary's absence was no reason for her not to feel at home in the arms of the Clegg reunion but she says Harry Hill brings her out in a rash.

10 p.m.
Entire house has gone to bed with festive Clegg exhaustion. In fact, Mum has not actually left hers since the lie down earlier. Dad was in charge of tea. Which was surprisingly good, i.e. proscribed steak and ale pie and Ben and Jerry's mini pots (Waitrose does not stock Viennetta). On down side, have got dog in my room. It is to prevent any Bruce versus Dog kerfuffle in the night. They have already established rival lairs. The dog has got

the kitchen and the sofa and Bruce has got Granny Clegg's chair and the downstairs loo.

. . . .

Monday 24

Christmas Eve

10 a.m.

Mum is back with a vengeance. And not to my advantage. Have been ordered to take Cleggs on pilgrimage to Cromwell Road Spar as punishment for surprise reunion. It is to give Mum time to adjust all her military style festive catering and entertainment arrangements. James is aiding her with his highlighters and Tippex. Dad is avoiding all responsibility by going to work for his office Christmas lunch. He is under strict instructions not to consume alcohol in any quantity whatsoever. Mum says she will need all the backing she can get over the next forty-eight hours. James pointed out that actually she had the Cleggs for the next 192 hours, at which point Mum decided she needed another lie down. I do not understand her concern. It is Christmas, what could possibly go wrong?

3 p.m.

Have lost Cleggs. It is utterly not my fault. It is because Bruce got shouted at in the Spar by Mrs Overton behind the till for eating two cob rolls, so Grandpa Clegg shouted at Mrs Overton because apparently Maureen in the Spar at St Slaughter lets him do it all the time. Then Granny

shouted at Grandpa for shouting and Bruce ran off in the hoo-ha with the Cleggs in hot pursuit. They were last seen heading down Peaslands Road towards the Lord Butler Leisure Centre. Mum is mental with concern. Not at their safety but at the possibility of them doing something idiotic to bring shame on the Saffron Walden wing of the family. Have been despatched with James to bring them home. Mum has ordered Dad back from lunch as well. She says she cannot cope single-handedly. This is stop press news as normally Dad does not get a look in when it comes to household management of any sort due to his habit of not sticking rigidly to Mum's many and varied systems.

5 p.m.
The Cleggs are back. James found them. They were round at the Britchers' having a Bruce and Fiddy reunion. He was alerted by the sound of 'comedy' Indian accents coming from the lounge window. Mum is livid. I said she should be happy that they are safe and have not embarrassed themselves or us, but she says they have spoiled their tea by eating two bags of frozen sausage rolls and a jar of cocktail onions. There is no pleasing some people. Also Mum is mad because there is still no sign of Dad. Hope he has not been caught in hideous pre-Christmas snarl-up on the A11 and is lying bleeding in a ditch somewhere.

6 p.m.
Dad is back. Was not bleeding in ditch. Was slumped in

back of Malcolm from IT's Honda Civic having consumed four glasses of Le Piat D'Or. (Which, allegedly, the French adore, though saw no evidence of this in St Abbatage. They were all too busy on the vile aniseed ball-flavoured pastis.) Mum has sent him to his room with a bottle of Evian and four pounds of potatoes to peel. It is a harsh punishment. Though necessary due to impending gigantic festive Clegg/Riley lunch. Mum is doing all the preparation tonight. The turkey is defrosting in the bath, James is doing the crosses in the sprouts and I am on foil cutting. Which is, according to James, statistically the hardest job to mess up. It means I am unable to attend midnight mass (actually at eleven and actually mostly involving drinking Bacardi Breezers in the back pews and singing too loudly in 'Hark the Herald') but do not mind. Tomorrow is a milestone in Anglo-Cornish relations and am eagerly anticipating Clegg and Riley barriers being broken down and everyone linking arms to sing festive favourites. (Except James who has an aversion to Band Aid. It is the line about snow in Africa. Which is apparently inaccurate as Morocco does, occasionally, enjoy icy conditions). Mum is worrying over nothing. It will be brilliant. I know it.

. . . .

Tuesday 25
Christmas Day (i.e. Jesus's birthday in all senses)
7 a.m.
A terrible thing has happened. The Clegg/Riley peacemaking

Christmas lunch has been cancelled. It is not the Wogan argument rearing its ugly head, it is Bruce and the Dog rearing theirs. They have eaten ten pounds of semi-defrosted turkey between them, and a saucepan full of sprouts. Clearly they broke into the bathroom and kitchen in the night, working as one gigantic all-consuming canine force. Mum is lying on the bed with James wafting her with a fan (actually a copy of *Good Housekeeping*, how ironic) to revive her. Dad says not to panic as we can emergency defrost some other meat for lunch instead. But James pointed out that there is no other meat in the freezer due to gargantuan size of turkey so it is potatoes and bread sauce all round unless Mr Patel has branched out into organic poultry. He has not. He does not need to with his expanding nicotine patch empire. Dad says it is partially my fault as I was on dog duty in the night. I said it is not my fault that it has developed a freakish ability to chew handles off doors silently and anyway what about Bruce, i.e. it is Granny Clegg's fault. But Granny Clegg says Bruce got thirsty in the night so she let him out to go to the toilet and it is Mum's fault for putting a turkey in the bath. Cannot believe Granny Clegg lets Bruce drink toilet water. Especially Mum's. It is blue and infused with two kinds of Harpic. No wonder Bruce is troubled. Both the dogs have been banished to the back garden. It is not so much punishment as to avoid inevitable turkey and sprout vomit on carpet incidents. I said to Mum to look on the plus side, i.e. Grandpa and Treena are taking Baby Jesus round to her

cousin Donna's instead so that is three fewer fussy eaters to cater for. She just stared glassily at the ceiling while James did extra frenetic wafting. Need to think of festive rescue plan, and fast.

11.30 a.m.
Have had genius idea. We can eat the dog's Christmas present for lunch i.e. the Linda McCartney sausages. Hurrah, have retrieved them from bottom of freezer and put the oven on. I, Rachel Riley, am single-handedly saving Christmas. Is totally like *Christmas Carol* when Scrooge shows up with a turkey for Bob Cratchit and the one with the crutches. I am metaphorical Ebenezer and my vegetarian sausages are a symbolic bond of friendship across a divide.

1 p.m.
Grandpa Clegg does not like his sausages. He says they are suspiciously gristle-free. I said they are also meat-free. He went pale and had to leave the room. It is his strict anti-vegetarian stance. Granny Clegg is more forward-thinking. She just drenched hers in Bisto. She said the claggy texture was quite pleasant. On plus side, feast has revived Mum slightly and she has agreed that present opening can go ahead at 2 p.m.

4 p.m.
Normality reigns once more, i.e. have had usual

unsatisfactory haul of Christmas gifts from relatives:

- Black baseball boots (Mum and Dad, but not Converse, actually from Clarks and, therefore, utterly unwearable);
- *Little House on the Prairie* (James, he said it is the ultimate Simple Life);
- Kendal Mint Cake (the dog, and not actually cake, as James pointed out);
- Cats of the World calendar (Granny and Grandpa Clegg, March missing);
- Brazil nut toffee (Bruce, 99p Trago Mills price sticker on bottom).

Apparently Dad wanted to write off my debt as a present but Mum pointed out that I would not have learned my lesson and would spend the rest of my life assuming I can rack up credit card bills and that they will happily sign cheques for me. I said I would utterly not assume that that is the case and had learned my debt lesson, but then James pointed out that, statistically, this is unlikely, and deprivation is really the only way forward. I said that it was their fault that their Christmas gifts from me were so ungenerous then, but it turns out that the Nuts In May presents went down quite well. James has already eaten all his sesame snaps and is now doing expressive dance to Dad's calming pan pipes CD. Mum was especially pleased with her sanitary towels, which she said were 'practical' (this is her highest form of

praise). It is shame we ate the dog's sausages though. Have given him and Bruce some of my Brazil nut toffee to make up for it. (They are back in the house, albeit within the confines of the wipe-clean kitchen lino.)

7 p.m.
Dog and Bruce are unusually quiet. Mum says their co-operation is a pleasant surprise. It is also pleasant surprise that she is utterly back to normal, i.e. Cillit Banging every available surface and swooping with coasters before any beverage hits a wooden surface. It is because Christmas and its inherent chaos is over (Boxing Day does not count in her book) and she can go back to her normal frugal and hygienic regime.

7.15 p.m.
Christmas chaos is not over. It turns out that the dog's and Bruce's silence was not by choice. It is the Cleggs' Trago Mills Brazil nut toffee. It has glued their jaws together. Mum says they can jolly well stay like that until tomorrow as they have already eaten enough for a week. But Granny Clegg is worried Bruce might suffocate as he has excess mucus, so James is trying to prise his teeth apart with a spatula. Am going to retire to my room and revive self with tales of Simple Life exploits in *Little House on the Prairie*. Modern life is far too fraught for me.

* *

Wednesday 26
Boxing Day

The dogs are still stuck. James is now trying to reheat the toffee to melting point with Mum's hairdryer. But all that is happening is that the dogs are getting voluminous hairdos. Mum has called Mr Mercer the vet for an emergency appointment. He says he will do it, but he is charging double as it is a bank holiday. Dad has agreed to foot the bill from his golf account, although there was a brief frisson when he suggested that it was Mum's inbred relatives who had caused the hoo-ha with their cut-price toffee so maybe she should pay with her Evening Classes account. That argument was shortlived and Dad is driving them to surgery after *Goldfinger*. It is a shame. The peace is rather pleasant. It is almost *House on the Prairie*-like. Except with less bear-killing and more people saying things like, 'Ooh, isn't Sean Connery hairy.'

3 p.m.
The dogs are unstuck. And slightly dazed. At a cost of £200. James asked what miracle method Mr Mercer had used (he is hoping to patent it for forthcoming dog toffee incidents). Dad said a sharp pokey thing and a chisel. It is hardly the height of medical advancement.

· ·

Thursday 27
Even I cannot take any more festive Clegg activity. Am

escaping to Scarlet's to exchange gifts. Sad Ed is collecting me in ten minutes. He is texting from behind the hedge to alert me to his arrival though. It is because last time he saw Granny Clegg she told him he looked like a young Geoff Capes and admired the 'meat' on him. He says she is detrimental to his self-esteem. Which is already dangerously low.

5 p.m.
Hurrah. Got an ironic Charlie and Lola diary from Scarlet. It is excellent thoughtful gift. Got Selection Box from Sad Ed. Which is nice, but potentially less thoughtful. Especially as he knows I do not like the Twirl or the Boost. Have given them to him already as extra gift. Although he is already pleased with his creatine. And has his eyes on Scarlet's Vitamin D as well. He says potentially he could overdose on either and achieve untimely death relatively painlessly. Watched essential Christmas film *Gremlins* (not *It's A Wonderful Life*, as I had thought) in the den with Jack, Bob, and Suzy. I said Suzy looked remarkably well, given that she must have been working tirelessly over the festive period. Suzy said it is down to a healthy diet of sex and Bellinis. And having Marks and Spencer make the nut roast, potatoes, gravy, and pudding. They are so forward-thinking. Anyway, have been invited to their annual New Year's Eve party. So has Hilary. Did not tell Scarlet about Justin thing. Think am not going to go. Cannot forsake best friend on crucial

night of year for cheap meaningless pact-breaking snog. Scarlet would never do anything like that to me.

10 p.m.
Would she?

. . . .

Friday 28

There is more Clegg-related chaos at home. This time Bruce's head is stuck behind a radiator. Which would not be so bad except the heating is on timer and due on any minute and only Mum knows how to work the controls and she is at Marjory's with strict instructions not to disturb her under any circumstances. Dad is trying to grease him out with some Swarfega. Have decided to pay emergency visit to exiled Rileys on Whiteshot Estate, i.e. Grandpa Riley, child bride Treena Riley, and Baby Jesus Harvey Nichols Riley. James is coming too. And the dog. They are all weary of the Cornish immigrants. They just do not understand our more civilized way of life. Plus the festive season is officially over at Summerdale Road. The tree is down and 'Now That's What I Call Christmas' is banned. Mum says she does not want to see another Quality Street or hear Noddy Holder shriek 'It's Christmas' for at least twelve months.

5 p.m.
Thank God for semi-chav relatives. It is still utterly festive

at 19 Harvey Road. In fact, cannot move in living room without getting partially strangled on foil paper chains. There was a minor issue when the dog panicked at Baby Jesus's outfit of choice (it is Power Ranger, he got it for his birthday off Donna). But Grandpa gave him a Baileys chocolate liqueur and he calmed down considerably. So have spent pleasant six hours eating Wagon Wheels and playing Treena's new 'Sounds of the 80s' DVD quiz. James won. There is nothing he does not know. (Except the ongoing why does Aladdin not have nipples question.)

. . . .

Saturday 29

Oh my God. Have seen a ghost. Not a real one, or would be calling James into action with his revived ghostometer, but metaphorical one, on the vitamin aisle at Nuts In May. It is Tuesday Weeks, daughter of Dad's ex-girlfriend alcoholic Weirdy Edie, niece of ineffectual headmaster Mr Wilmott, and ex-lover of second best friend with suicidal tendencies and upper arm issues Sad Ed. I demanded to know what she was doing in this hick town. She said, 'Buying drugs, there's no law against it. Or is there now in this tinpot island?' She is so American, i.e. utterly unable to understand irony. Cannot believe I ever envied her. Anyway, I said not in here, I mean in the bigger sense, i.e. in Saffron Walden, home of previous love of your life. She said, oh that. Apparently she is back at Mr Wilmott's for a few days while Edie is on a spa break in

512

Arizona. She means rehab. Again. I said I hoped she wasn't thinking of coming to Scarlet's New Year's Eve party as the stress could send Sad Ed over the edge again. She said *au contraire*, Suzy had already invited her. And besides, it has been four months and is utterly pathetic that Sad Ed is still moping around over her. I said he is not, he has embraced a Simple Life and is devoting himself to more important matters. But she was already halfway up King Street by that point. Will not tell Sad Ed. Will just keep them in separate rooms. It is a big house. He need never know.

. . . .

Sunday 30

Thank God Hilary is coming tomorrow. It is not just that I am keen to see him, what with our excellent platonic relationship. It is that the Cleggs are driving everyone mad with their discovery of QVC on our Freeview box. It is like shopping at Trago Mills from the comfort of the sofa. So far they have bought a Lean Mean Grilling Machine (though do not think you can grill fishfingers or pie in this manner) and a set of three fitballs (for Bruce).

Scarlet has rung twice to check that Hilary is coming to the party. Which is very kind. Although a bit overkeen, as I pointed out. She said she is not overkeen, and anyway, why am I bothered? I said I am not bothered. She said nor is she and put the phone down. Which is odd, as have checked diary and she should not be premenstrual for at

least three days. But am trying to banish unseasonal Doubting Riley thoughts as Christmas is time of goodwill to all men, and especially women.

. . . .

Monday 31

New Year's Eve

Hurrah. It is New Year's Eve. And am feeling utterly jubilant as have checked resolutions (i.e. from birthday, not from last New Year as am totally different person now, i.e. not in the thrall of two-timing meat-mincing small-nippled philanderer, albeit with nice hair) and have fulfilled all of them, i.e. have not mooned about over Justin, have remained true to Scarlet above all others, and have utterly remembered that I, Rachel Riley, am responsible for my own happiness.

The Simple Life has been brilliant. In fact, will get Scarlet and Sad Ed to reswear our pact tonight. May even get Hilary to join in. He is due at five. (He rang from Chieveley services to advise on arrival times. He is trying to stay in my mum's good books after I warned him she is holding him partially responsible for the week's events due to his key role as chauffeur. It is because James said he was like Charon, i.e. ferrying the evil dead across the Styx to hell.) Hilary says we can go straight to Scarlet's if I like. This is an excellent plan. Especially as need to install ourselves in Scarlet's bedroom, possibly with locked door, to avoid Sad Ed and Tuesday encounter and potential untimely death.

514

10 p.m.

Hurrah. We are in Scarlet's bedroom in an utterly Simple Life style New Year celebration. Plus we have all renewed our vows not to do any snogging. Ever. Scarlet seemed a bit hesitant. But once Hilary had led the way she agreed. Jack said we are all mental and that there is no way any of us will stick to it. He is wrong. We are utterly united in our stance. And do not care that just yards away half of Saffron Walden is snogging under Suzy's sustainable mistletoe. We are missing nothing. And anyway, Hilary can tell us what is going on when he gets back from the toilet.

10.10 p.m.

Have just reinforced my anti-men stance to Scarlet. She said, 'Do you really not fancy Hilary at all?' I said, neither his brain nor his biceps were of interest to me in anything other than a platonic way. In fact, I do not fancy any men at all. Or women for that matter (have felt no urges despite trying to fantasize about Oona in a Kurt Cobain T-shirt several times). Jack said 'Are you sure, you really don't like anybody?' I said no. And Scarlet said, 'Good for you.' Which it utterly is.

10.20 p.m.

Jack has gone back to party and Scarlet has gone for an emergency wee. I pointed out that Hilary is not back yet so there will be no room. She said she will use the ensuite

515

in Suzy's. She is mad. There is bound to be someone in there doing drugs or sex. Or both.

11.00 p.m.
Scarlet and Hilary are still not back. I fear they may have fallen foul of malign influences, i.e. Suzy. Sad Ed says we should go after them. Am in utter quandary as on one hand, do not think can cope on my own if Sad Ed bumps into Tuesday but on other, have to stop Scarlet failing in pact and trying to snog Hilary.

11.10 p.m.
Have decided to stay here. It is sisterlike thing to do. Even if Scarlet were to fall foul of her urges and try to break the pact, Hilary will be immune to her advances as it is obvious I am more his type. Plus Ed is not actually worried about Scarlet. He has run out of Pringles and wants to replenish his supply. Have texted Jack to bring some up.

11.30 p.m.
Thank God Jack is such loyal friend. The Pringles have proved essential. It is Sad Ed. He has had a turn for the worse. It is not the sensory deprivation at being shut in a black-painted goth shrine, it is evil Tuesday. She wandered into Scarlet's room on the pretext of looking for a bong. She is such a liar. She just wanted to flaunt her lipstick lesbian look in front of Sad Ed to torment him. So slammed door in her face in excellently dramatic manner.

(There are times when being sisterhoody is pointless.) But it was too late. Sad Ed had gone all white and breathless so had to sit him down and force BBQ Pringles into his mouth to revive him. He is a bit better now that his sugar and salt levels are up. But is decidedly minty about me not telling him she was back. I said he was utterly ungrateful and that he is lucky to have me, i.e. I am not keeping him here for my amusement. It is for his own good. He said, 'You're right. She is bad for me. Utterly bad.' He is resolved to stay with me until midnight. And then we will depart in a dignified manner. Out of Scarlet's window.

11.50 p.m.
Sad Ed has gone. And in a totally undignified manner, i.e. down the stairs shouting 'Tuesday!' at the top of his voice. It is flesh again. And his mind. They are both utterly weak.

11.55 p.m.
Jack has just been in to tell me to stop being an idiot and go downstairs for the midnight bongs (clock, not drugs, although with Suzy, anything is possible). Have refused. I will stay strong. I do not need the company of men. Not him, or Hilary, or Justin. I need only myself.

11.59 p.m.
Oh God. Cannot do this. Am going downstairs for reckless snogging. It is pointless to deny it any longer. I cannot live

without love. I have just been sticking my head in sand for the sake of a stupid pact. Hilary is my ONE. And if he refuses, there's always Justin. Or even Jack, as a last resort. Yes, have made mind up. The so-called Simple Life is not all it is cracked up to be after all. In fact, I quite like life being complicated. Scarlet will understand.

Anyway, it is a New Year. And new rules apply . . .

Joanna Nadin was born in Northampton and moved to Saffron Walden in Essex when she was three. She did well at school (being a terrible swot) and then went to Hull University to study Drama. Three years of pretending to be a toaster and pretending to like Fellini films put her off the theatre for life. She moved to London to study for an MA in Political Communications and after a few years as an autocue girl and a radio newsreader got a job with the Labour Party as a campaigns writer and Special Adviser. She now lives in Bath with her daughter and is a freelance government speech writer and TV script-writer. Joanna was shortlisted for the Queen of Teen crown for her fantastic books about the life of Rachel Riley.